poison study

'Yelena, I'm offering you a choice. You can either be executed, or you can be Commander Ambrose's new food taster. His last taster died recently, and we need to fill the position.'

I gaped at him, my heart dancing. He had to be joking. He was probably amusing himself. Watch hope and joy shine on the prisoner's face, then smash it by sending the accused to the noose.

I played along. 'A fool would refuse the job.' My voice rasped louder this time.

'Well, it's a lifetime position. The training can be lethal. After all, how can you identify poisons in the Commander's food if you don't know what they taste like?' He tidied the papers in the folder.

He was serious. My whole body shook. A chance to live! Service to the Commander was better than the dungeon and infinitely better than the noose. Questions raced through my mind: I'm a convicted killer, how can they trust me? What would prevent me from killing the Commander or escaping?

'What shall I tell the executioner?' Valek asked.

'I am not a fool.'

poison study

MARIA V. SNYDER

This edition published in Great Britain 2015
by Harlequin MIRA, an imprint of Harlequin (UK) Limited,
Eton House, 18-24 Paradise Road,
Richmond, Surrey, TW9 1SR

© Maria V. Snyder 2005

ISBN 978 1 848 45239 8

47-0613

MIRA Ink's policy is to use papers that are natural, renewable and recyclable products and made from wood grown in sustainable forests. The logging and manufacturing processes conform to the legal environmental regulations of the country of origin.

Printed and bound by
CPI Group (UK) Ltd, Croydon, CR0 4YY

ACKNOWLEDGEMENTS

Without the support from my husband, Rodney, this book wouldn't exist. Thanks, dear, for all the printing, the copying, the critiquing, the willingness to be a single parent from time to time, for not complaining about conference fees, for being there when the rejections came in, and the million other things that I don't have room to list! To my children, Luke and Jenna, for understanding (most of the time) that I'm not playing on the computer (really, I'm not). To my parents, James and Vincenza McGinnis, thank you for always believing in me. To my sister, Karen Phillips, for reading the book and for giving me the support that only a sister can give. To Chris Phillips for his good ideas, and for putting up with all of us. And I can't forget the babysitters: Sam and Carole Snyder, Becky and Randy Greenly, Amy Snyder, Gregory Snyder, Melissa Read and Julie Read—without you I would still be on Chapter Two.

Many thanks go to my fellow Muse and Schmooze critique group members: Shawn Downs, Laurie Edwards, Julie Good, Lisa Hess, Anne Kline, Steve Klotz, Maggie Martz, Lori Myers, Kim Stanford, Jackie Werth, Michael Wertz, Judy Wolfman and Nancy Yeager. Without your help and support this book wouldn't have made it this far.

A heartfelt thanks to Helen French. She made the call I had been dreaming of, and her enthusiasm for this project has been wonderful. Thanks to Mary-Theresa Hussey, who has been an excellent editor. Thanks to my agents, Sally Wecksler and Joann Amparan-Close, for helping with the contract.

Very special thanks go to Alis Rasmussen, who took the time to read and critique my manuscript. Your advice was truly invaluable.

To my husband, Rodney, for all the support he has given, is giving and will give. I'm spoiled rotten.

In loving memory of Frances Snyder, Jeanette and Joseph Scirrotto.

'They would talk to you and make jokes while they were feeding you poison.'
—Kathy Brandt on chemotherapy; a good friend who lost the battle.

THE TERRITORY OF IXIA

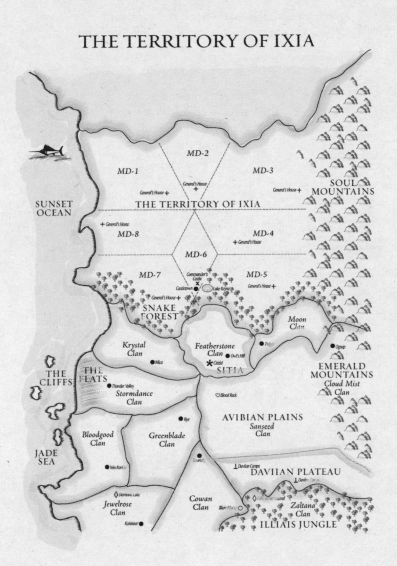

SOUL MOUNTAINS

MD-2

MD-1

MD-3

General's House

General's House

General's House

SUNSET OCEAN

THE TERRITORY OF IXIA

General's House

MD-8

MD-4

General's House

MD-6

MD-7

Commander's Castle

MD-5

General's House

Castletown

Lake Krync

General's House

SNAKE FOREST

Moon Clan

Krystal Clan

Featherstone Clan

Owl's Hill

Felwa

Mica

Citadel

SITIA

Ognap

THE CLIFFS

THE FLATS

Thunder Valley

Stormdance Clan

Blood Rock

EMERALD MOUNTAINS

Cloud Mist Clan

Bloodgood Clan

Greenblade Clan

Rye

AVIBIAN PLAINS

Sanseed Clan

JADE SEA

Vein Ravine

Booruby

Daviian Camps

DAVIIAN PLATEAU

Daviian Camp

Diamond Lake

Cowan Clan

Blain Market

Zaltana Clan

Jewelrose Clan

Kohinoor

ILLIAIS JUNGLE

I

LOCKED IN DARKNESS that surrounded me like a coffin, I had nothing to distract me from my memories. Vivid recollections waited to ambush me whenever my mind wandered.

Encompassed by the blackness, I remembered white-hot flames stabbing at my face. Though my hands had been tied to a post that dug sharply into my back, I had recoiled from the onslaught. The fire had pulled away just before blistering my skin, but my eyebrows and eyelashes had long since been singed off.

"Put the flames out!" a man's rough voice had ordered. I blew at the blaze through cracked lips. Dried by fire and fear, the moisture in my mouth had gone and my teeth radiated heat as if they had been baked in an oven.

"Idiot," he cursed. "Not with your mouth. Use your mind. Put the flames out with your mind."

Closing my eyes, I attempted to focus my thoughts on making the inferno disappear. I was willing to do anything, no matter how irrational, to persuade the man to stop.

"Try harder." Once again the heat swung near my face, the bright light blinding me in spite of my closed eyelids.

"Set her hair on fire," a different voice instructed. He sounded younger and more eager than the other man. "That should encourage her. Here, Father, let me."

My body jerked with intense fear as I recognized the voice. I twisted to loosen the bonds that held me as my thoughts scattered into a mindless buzzing. A droning noise had echoed from my throat and grew louder until it had pervaded the room and quenched the flames.

The loud metallic clank of the lock startled me from my nightmarish memory. A wedge of pale yellow light sliced the darkness, then traveled along the stone wall as the heavy cell door opened. Caught in the lantern's glow, my eyes were seared by the brightness. I squeezed them shut as I cowered in the corner.

"Move it, rat, or we'll get the whip!" Two dungeon guards attached a chain to the metal collar on my neck and hauled me to my feet. I stumbled forward, pain blazing around my throat. As I stood on trembling legs, the guards efficiently chained my hands behind me and manacled my feet.

I averted my eyes from the flickering light as they led me down the main corridor of the dungeon. Thick rancid air puffed in my face. My bare feet shuffled through puddles of unidentifiable muck.

Ignoring the calls and moans of the other prisoners, the guards never missed a step, but my heart lurched with every word.

"Ho, ho, ho…someone's gonna swing."

"Snap! Crack! Then your last meal slides down your legs!"

"One less rat to feed."

"Take me! Take me! I wanna die too!"

We stopped. Through squinted eyes I saw a staircase. In an effort to get my foot onto the first step, I tripped over the chains and fell. The guards dragged me up. The rough edges of the stone steps dug into my skin, peeling away exposed flesh on my arms and legs. After being pulled through two sets of thick metal doors, I was dumped onto the floor. Sunlight stabbed between my eyes. I shut them tight as tears spilled down my cheeks. It was the first time that I had seen daylight in seasons.

This is it, I thought, starting to panic. But the knowledge that my execution would end my miserable existence in the dungeon calmed me.

Yanked to my feet again, I followed the guards blindly. My body itched from insect bites and from sleeping on dirty straw. I stunk of rat. Given only a small ration of water, I didn't waste it on baths.

Once my eyes adjusted to the light, I looked around. The walls were bare, without the fabled gold sconces and elaborate tapestries I had been told once decorated the castle's main hallways. The cold stone floor was worn smooth in the middle. We were probably traveling along the hidden corridors used solely by the servants and guards. As we passed two open windows, I glanced out with a hunger that no food could satisfy.

The bright emerald of the grass made my eyes ache. Trees wore cloaks of leaves. Flowers laced the footpaths and over-flowed from barrels. The fresh breeze smelled like an expen-sive perfume, and I breathed deeply. After the acidic smells of excrement and body odor, the taste of the air was like drinking a fine wine. Warmth caressed my skin. A soothing touch compared to the constantly damp and chilly dungeon.

I guessed it was the beginning of the hot season, which meant that I had been locked in the cell for five seasons, one season shy of a full year. It seemed an excessively long time for someone scheduled for execution.

Winded from the effort of marching with my feet chained, I was led into a spacious office. Maps of the Territory of Ixia and the lands beyond covered the walls. Piles of books on the floor made walking a straight line difficult. Candles in various stages of use littered the room, singe marks evident on several papers that had gotten too close to the candle's flame. A large wooden table, strewn with documents and ringed by half a dozen chairs, occupied the center of the room. At the back of the office a man sat at a desk. Behind him a square window gaped open, permitting a breeze to blow through his shoulder-length hair.

I shuddered, causing the chains to clatter. From the whis-pered conversations between prison cells, I had determined that condemned prisoners were taken to an official to confess their crimes before being hanged.

Wearing black pants and a black shirt with two red diamonds stitched on the collar, the man at the desk wore the uniform of an adviser to the Commander. His pallid face held no expression. As his sapphire-blue eyes scanned me, they widened in surprise.

Suddenly conscious of my appearance, I glanced down at my tattered red prison gown and dirty bare feet roughened with yellow calluses. Dirt-streaked skin showed through the rips in the thin fabric. My long black hair hung in greasy clumps. Sweat-soaked, I swayed under the weight of the chains.

"A woman? The next prisoner to be executed is a woman?" His voice was icy. My body trembled on hearing the word *executed* aloud. The calm I'd established earlier fled me. I would have sunk sobbing to the floor if the guards weren't with me. The guards tormented anyone who showed any weakness.

The man tugged at the black ringlets of his hair. "I should have taken the time to reread your dossier." He shooed the guards away. "You're dismissed."

When they were gone, he motioned me to the chair in front of his desk. The chains clanged as I perched on the edge.

He opened a folder on his desk and scanned the pages. "Yelena, today may be your lucky day," he said.

I swallowed a sarcastic reply. An important lesson I had mastered during my dungeon stay was never to talk back. I bowed my head instead, avoiding eye contact.

The man was quiet for a while. "Well-behaved and respectful. You're starting to look like a good candidate."

Despite the clutter of the room, the desk was neat. In addition to my folder and some writing implements, the only other items on the desk were two small, black statues glittering with streaks of silver—a set of panthers carved to lifelike perfection.

"You've been tried and found guilty of murdering General Brazell's only son, Reyad." He paused, stroking his temple with his fingers. "That explains why Brazell's here this week, and why he has been unusually interested in the execution schedule." The man spoke more to himself than to me.

Upon hearing Brazell's name, fear coiled in my stomach. I steadied myself with a reminder that I was soon to be out of his reach forever.

The Territory of Ixia's military had come to power only a generation ago, but the rule had produced strict laws called the Code of Behavior. During peacetime—most of the time, strangely enough for the military—proper conduct didn't allow the taking of a human life. If someone committed murder, the punishment was execution. Self-preservation or an accidental death were not considered acceptable excuses. Once found guilty, the murderer was sent to the Commander's dungeon to await a public hanging.

"I suppose you're going to protest the conviction. Say you were framed or you killed out of self-defense." He leaned back in his chair, waiting with a weary patience.

"No, sir," I whispered, all I could manage from unused vocal cords. "I killed him."

The man in black straightened in his chair, shooting me a hard look. Then he laughed aloud. "This may work out better than I'd planned. Yelena, I'm offering you a choice. You can either be executed, or you can be Commander Ambrose's new food taster. His last taster died recently, and we need to fill the position."

I gaped at him, my heart dancing. He had to be joking. He was probably amusing himself. Great way to get a laugh. Watch hope and joy shine on the prisoner's face, then smash it by sending the accused to the noose.

I played along. "A fool would refuse the job." My voice rasped louder this time.

"Well, it's a lifetime position. The training can be lethal. After all, how can you identify poisons in the Commander's food if you don't know what they taste like?" He tidied the papers in the folder.

"You'll get a room in the castle to sleep, but most of the day you'll be with the Commander. No days off. No husband or children. Some prisoners have chosen execution instead. At least then they know exactly when they're going to die, rather than guessing if it's going to come with the next bite." He clicked his teeth together, a feral grin on his face.

He was serious. My whole body shook. A chance to live! Service to the Commander was better than the dungeon and infinitely better than the noose. Questions raced through my mind: I'm a convicted killer, how can they trust me? What would prevent me from killing the Commander or escaping?

"Who tastes the Commander's food now?" I asked instead, afraid if I asked the other questions he'd realize his mistake and send me to the gallows.

"I do. So I'm anxious to find a replacement. Also the Code of Behavior states that someone whose life is forfeit must be offered the job."

No longer able to sit still, I stood and paced around the

room, dragging my chains with me. The maps on the walls showed strategic military positions. Book titles dealt with security and spying techniques. The condition and amount of candles suggested someone who worked late into the night.

I looked back at the man in the adviser's uniform. He had to be Valek, the Commander's personal security chief and leader of the vast intelligence network for the Territory of Ixia.

"What shall I tell the executioner?" Valek asked.

"I am not a fool."

2

VALEK SNAPPED THE folder closed. He walked to the door; his stride as graceful and light as a snow cat traversing thin ice. The guards waiting in the hall snapped to attention when the door opened. Valek spoke to them, and they nodded. One guard came toward me. I stared at him, going back to the dungeon had not been part of Valek's offer. Could I escape? I scanned the room. The guard spun me around and removed the manacles and chains that had been draped around me since I'd been arrested.

Raw bands of flesh circled my bloody wrists. I touched my neck, feeling skin where there used to be metal. My fingers came away sticky with blood. I groped for the chair. Being freed of the weight of the chains caused a strange sensation to sweep over me; I felt as if I were either going to float away or pass out. I inhaled until the faintness passed.

When I regained my composure, I noticed Valek now stood

beside his desk pouring two drinks. An opened wooden cabinet revealed rows of odd-shaped bottles and multicolored jars stacked inside. Valek placed the bottle he was holding into the cabinet and locked the door.

"While we're waiting for Margg, I thought maybe you could use a drink." He handed me a tall pewter goblet filled with an amber liquid. Raising his own goblet, he made a toast. "To Yelena, our newest food taster. May you last longer than your predecessor."

My goblet stopped short of my lips.

"Relax," he said, "it's a standard toast."

I took a long swig. The smooth liquid burned slightly as it slid down my throat. For a moment, I thought my stomach was going to rebel. This was the first time I had taken something other than water. Then it settled.

Before I could question him as to what exactly had happened to the previous food taster, Valek asked me to identify the ingredients of the drink. Taking a smaller portion, I replied, "Peaches sweetened with honey."

"Good. Now take another sip. This time roll the liquid around your tongue before swallowing."

I complied and was surprised to taste a faint citrus flavor. "Orange?"

"That's right. Now gargle it."

"Gargle?" I asked. He nodded. Feeling foolish, I gargled the rest of my drink and almost spat it out. "Rotten oranges!"

The skin around Valek's eyes crinkled as he laughed. He had a strong, angular face, as if someone had stamped it from a sheet of metal, but it softened when he smiled. Handing me his drink, he asked me to repeat the experiment.

With some trepidation, I took a sip, again detecting the faint orange taste. Bracing myself for the rancid flavor, I gargled Valek's drink and was relieved that gargling only enhanced the orange essence.

"Better?" Valek asked as he took back the empty cup.

"Yes."

Valek sat down behind his desk, opening my folder once more. Picking up his quill, he talked to me while writing. "You just had your first lesson in food tasting. Your drink was laced with a poison called Butterfly's Dust. Mine wasn't. The only way to detect Butterfly's Dust in a liquid is to gargle it. That rotten-orange flavor you tasted was the poison."

I rose, my head spinning. "Is it lethal?"

"A big enough dose will kill you in two days. The symptoms don't arrive until the second day, but by then it's too late."

"Did I have a lethal dose?" I held my breath.

"Of course. Anything less and you wouldn't have tasted the poison."

My stomach rebelled and I started to gag. I forced down the bile in my throat, trying hard to avoid the indignity of vomiting all over Valek's desk.

Valek looked up from the stack of papers. He studied my face. "I warned you the training would be dangerous. But I would hardly give you a poison your body had to fight while you suffered from malnutrition. There is an antidote to Butterfly's Dust." He showed me a small vial containing a white liquid.

Collapsing back into my chair, I sighed. Valek's metal face had returned; I realized he hadn't offered the antidote to me.

"In answer to the question you didn't ask but should have, this—" Valek raised the small vial and shook it "—is how we keep the Commander's food taster from escaping."

I stared at him, trying to understand the implication.

"Yelena, you confessed to murder. We would be fools to let you serve the Commander without some guarantees. Guards watch the Commander at all times and it is doubtful you would be able to reach him with a weapon. For other forms of retaliation, we use Butterfly's Dust." Valek picked up the vial of antidote, and twirled it in the sunlight. "You need a daily dose of this to stay alive. The antidote keeps the poison from killing you. As long as you show up each morning in my office, I will give you the antidote. Miss one morning and you'll be dead by the next. Commit a crime or an act of treason and you'll be sent back to the dungeon until the poison takes you. I would avoid that fate, if I were you. The poison causes severe stomach cramps and uncontrollable vomiting."

Before full comprehension of my situation could sink in, Valek's eyes slid past my shoulder. I turned to see a stout woman in a housekeeper's uniform opening the door. Valek introduced her as Margg, the person who would take care of my basic needs. Expecting me to follow her, Margg strode out the door.

I glanced at the vial on Valek's desk.

"Come to my office tomorrow morning. Margg will direct you."

An obvious dismissal, but I paused at the door with all the questions I should have asked poised on my lips. I swallowed them. They sank like stones to my stomach, then I closed the door and hurried after Margg, who hadn't stopped to wait.

Margg never slowed her pace. I found myself panting with the effort to keep up. Trying to remember the various corridors and turns, I soon gave up as my whole world shrank to the sight of Margg's broad back and efficient stride. Her long black skirt seemed to float above the floor. The housekeeper uniform included a black shirt and white apron that hung from the neck down to the ankle and was cinched tight around the waist. The apron had two vertical rows of small red diamond-shapes connected end to end. When Margg finally stopped at the baths, I had to sit on the floor to clear my spinning head.

"You stink," Margg said, disgust creasing her wide face. She pointed to the far side of the baths in a manner that indicated she was used to being obeyed. "Wash twice, then soak. I'll bring you some uniforms." She left the room.

The overpowering desire to bathe flashed like fire on my skin. Energized, I ripped the prison robe off and raced to the washing area. Hot water poured down in a cascade when I opened the duct above my head. The Commander's castle was equipped with heated water tanks located one floor above the baths, a luxury even Brazell's extravagant manor house didn't have.

I stood for a long time, hoping the drumming on my head would erase all thoughts of poisons. Obediently I washed my hair and body twice. My neck, wrists and ankles burned from the soap, but I didn't care. I scrubbed two more times, rubbing hard at the stubborn spots of dirt on my skin, stopping only when I realized they were bruises.

I felt unconnected to the body under the waterfall. The pain and humiliation of being arrested and locked away had been inflicted on this body, but my soul had long since been driven out during the last two years I had lived in Brazell's manor house.

An image of Brazell's son suddenly flashed before me. Reyad's handsome face distorted with rage. I stepped back, reflexively jerking my hands up to block him. The image disappeared, leaving me shaking.

It was an effort to dry off and wrap a towel around me. I tried to focus on finding a comb instead of the ugly memories Reyad's image called forth.

Even clean, my snarled hair resisted the comb. As I searched for a pair of scissors, I spotted another person in the baths from the corner of my eye. I stared at the body. A corpse looked back at me. The green eyes were the only signs of life in the gaunt, oval face. Thin stick legs looked incapable of holding the rest of the body up.

Recognition shot through me like a cold splash of fear. It was *my* body. I averted my eyes from the mirror, having no desire to assess the damage. Coward, I thought, returning my gaze with a purpose. Had Reyad's death released my soul from where it had fled? In my mind I tried to reconnect my spirit to my body. Why did I think my soul would return if my body was still not mine? It belonged to Commander Ambrose to be used as a tool for filtering and testing poisons. I turned away.

Pulling clumps of knotted hair out with the comb, I arranged the rest into a single long braid down my back.

Not long ago all I had hoped for was a clean prison robe before my execution, and now here I was sinking into the Commander's famous hot baths.

"That's long enough," Margg barked, startling me out of a light doze. "Here are your uniforms. Get dressed." Her stiff face radiated disapproval.

As I dried myself, I felt Margg's impatience.

Along with some undergarments, the food taster's uniform consisted of black pants, a wide red satin belt and a red satin shirt with a line of small black diamond-shapes connected end to end down each of the sleeves. The clothes were obviously sized for a man. Malnourished and measuring only four inches past five feet, I looked like a child playing pretend with her father's clothes. I wrapped the belt three times around my waist and rolled up the sleeves and pant legs.

Margg snorted. "Valek only told me to feed you and show you to your room. But I think we'll stop by the seamstress's first." Pausing at the open door, Margg pursed her lips and added, "You'll need boots too."

Obediently, I followed Margg like a lost puppy.

The seamstress, Dilana, laughed gaily at my appearance.

Her heart-shaped face had a halo of curly blond hair. Honey-colored eyes and long eyelashes enhanced her beauty.

"The stable boys wear the same pants and the kitchen maids wear the red shirts," Dilana said when she had stifled her giggles. She admonished Margg for not spending the time to find me better-size uniforms. Margg pushed her lips together tighter.

Fussing around me like a grandmother instead of a young woman, Dilana's attentions warmed me, pulling me toward her. I envisioned us becoming friends. She probably had many acquaintances and suitors who came to bask in her attentions like cave dwellers drawn to a blazing hearth. I found myself aching to reach out to her.

After writing my measurements down, Dilana searched through the piles of red, black and white clothing stacked around the room.

Everyone who worked in Ixia wore a uniform. The Commander's castle servants and guards wore a variation of black, white and red color clothes with vertical diamond-shapes either down the sleeves of the shirts or down the sides of the pants. Advisers and higher-ranking officers usually wore all black with small red diamonds stitched on the collars to show rank. The uniform system became mandatory when the Commander gained power so everyone knew at a glance who they were dealing with.

Black and red were Commander Ambrose's colors. The Territory of Ixia had been separated into eight Military Districts each ruled by a General. The uniforms of the eight districts were identical to the Commander's except for the color. A housekeeper wearing black with small purple diamond-shapes on her apron therefore worked in Military District 3 or MD–3.

"I think these should fit better." She handed me some clothes, gesturing to the privacy screen at the far end of the room.

While I was changing, I heard Dilana say, "She'll need boots." Feeling less foolish in my new clothes, I picked up the old uniforms and gave them to Dilana.

"These must have belonged to Oscove, the old food taster," Dilana said. A sad expression gripped her face for a moment before she shook her head as if to rid herself of an unwanted thought.

All my fantasies of friendship fled me as I realized that being friends with the Commander's food taster was a big emotional risk. My stomach hollowed out while Dilana's warmth leaked from me, leaving a cold bitterness behind.

A sharp stab of loneliness struck me as an unwanted image of May and Carra, who still lived at Brazell's manor, flashed before my eyes. My fingers twitched to fix Carra's crooked braids and to straighten May's skirt.

Instead of Carra's silky ginger hair in my hands, I held a stack of clothes. Dilana guided me to a chair. Kneeling on the floor, she put socks on my feet and then a pair of boots. The boots were made of soft black leather. They came up over my ankle to midcalf, where the leather folded down. Dilana tucked my pant legs into the boots and helped me stand.

I hadn't worn shoes in seasons and I expected them to chafe. But the boots cushioned my feet and fit well. I smiled at

Dilana, thoughts of May and Carra temporarily banished. These were the finest pair of boots I'd ever worn.

She smiled back and said, "I can always pick the right-size boots without having to measure."

Margg harrumphed. "You didn't get poor Rand's boots right. He's too smitten with you to complain. Now he limps around the kitchen."

"Don't pay any attention to her," Dilana said to me. "Margg, don't you have work to do? Get going or I'll sneak into your room and shorten all your skirts." Dilana shooed us good-naturedly out the door.

Margg took me to the servants' dining room and served me small portions of soup and bread. The soup tasted divine. After devouring the food, I asked for more.

"No. Too much will make you sick," was all she said. With reluctance I left my bowl on the table to follow Margg to my room.

"At sunrise be ready to work."

Once again I watched her retreating back.

My small room contained a narrow bed with a single stained mattress on a stark metal frame, a plain wooden desk and chair, a chamber pot, an armoire, a lantern, a tiny woodstove and one window shuttered tight. The gray stone walls were unadorned. I tested the mattress; it barely yielded. A vast improvement over my dungeon cell, yet I found myself somewhat dissatisfied.

Nothing in the room suggested softness. With my mind and eyes filled with Valek's metal face and Margg's censure, and the harsh cut and colors of the uniforms, I longed for a pillow or blanket. I felt like a lost child looking for something to clutch, something supple that wouldn't end up hurting me.

After hanging my extra uniforms in the armoire, I crossed to the window. There was a sill wide enough for me to sit on. The shutters were locked, but the latches were on the inside. Hands shaking, I unlocked and pushed the shutters wide, blinking in the sudden light. Shielding my eyes, I squinted beneath my hand, and stared at the scene in front of my window in disbelief. I was on the first floor of the castle! Five feet below was the ground.

Between my room and the stables were the Commander's kennels and the exercise yard for the horses. The stable boys and dog trainers wouldn't care if I escaped. I could drop down without any effort and be gone. Tempting, except for the fact that I would be dead in two days. Maybe another time, when two days of freedom might be worth the price.

I could hope.

3

REYAD'S WHIP CUT INTO my skin, slashing my flesh with a burning pain. "Move," he ordered.

I dodged ineffectively, hampered by the rope tied to my wrist, which anchored me to a post in the center of the room.

"Move faster, keep moving!" Reyad shouted.

The whip snapped again and again. My tattered shirt gave no protection from the stinging leather. A cool, soothing voice entered my skull. "Go away," it whispered. "Send your mind to a distant place, a warm loving place. Let your body go."

The silken voice didn't belong to Reyad or Brazell. A savior, perhaps? An easy way to escape the torment, tempting but I held out for another opportunity. Determined, I stayed, focusing on avoiding the lash. When exhaustion claimed me, my body began to vibrate of its own accord. Like an out-of-control hummingbird, I darted around the room, avoiding the whip.

★ ★ ★

I woke in darkness soaked with sweat, my crumpled uniform twisted tight around my body. The vibration in my dream replaced by a pounding. Before falling asleep, I had wedged a chair under the doorknob to prevent anyone from barging in. The chair rattled with each thud.

"I'm up," I shouted. The racket stopped. When I opened the door, Margg stood frowning with a lantern. I hastened to change my uniform and joined her in the hallway. "I thought you said sunrise."

Her disapproving stare seared my lips shut. "It *is* sunrise."

I followed Margg through the labyrinth of the castle's hidden hallways as the day began to brighten. My room faced west, shielding me from the morning sun. Margg extinguished the lantern just as the scent of sweet cakes filled the air.

Inhaling, I asked her, "Breakfast?" A hopeful, almost pleading, note crept into my voice, galling me.

"No. Valek will feed you."

The image of breakfast laced with poison did wonders for suppressing my appetite. My stomach tightened as the unwanted memory of Valek's Butterfly's Dust came to mind. By the time we had reached his office, I had convinced myself that I was about to collapse, soon to be vanquished by the poison if I didn't receive the antidote.

When I entered the room, Valek was in the process of arranging plates of steaming food. He had cleared off a section of the table. The displaced papers balanced in messy piles. He gestured to a chair; I sat, searching the table for the small vial of antidote.

"I hope you're..." Valek studied my face. I stared back, trying not to flinch under his scrutiny.

"It's amazing what a difference a bath and a uniform can make," Valek said, absently chewing on a slice of bacon. "I'll have to remember that. It might be useful in the future." Placing two plates of an egg-and-ham mixture before me, he said, "Let's get started."

Feeling dizzy and flushed, I blurted out, "I'd rather start with the antidote." Another long pause from Valek caused me to fidget in my seat.

"You shouldn't be feeling any symptoms. They won't arrive until later this afternoon." He shrugged and went to his cabinet. He used a pipette to extract a measure of the white liquid from a large bottle, and then locked the antidote back inside the cabinet. My interest in the location of the key must have been obvious because Valek used some type of sleight of hand to make the key disappear. Handing me the pipette, he sat down on the opposite side of the table.

"Drink up so we can start today's lessons," he said.

I squeezed the contents into my mouth, cringing at the bitter taste. Valek took the pipette from my hands and exchanged it for a blue jar. "Take a sniff."

The jar contained a white powder, resembling sugar but smelling like rosewood. Gesturing to the two plates cooling in front of me, Valek asked me to pick the one sprinkled with the poison. I sniffed at the food like a scent hound nosing for prey. A faint odor of rosewood emanated from the left plate.

"Good. Should you pick up that aroma from any of the

Commander's food, reject it. The poison is called Tigtus and a single grain of the powder will kill within the hour." Valek removed the tainted food. "Eat your breakfast." He indicated the other plate. "You'll need your strength."

I spent the remainder of the day smelling poisons until my head ached and spun. The multitude of names and aromas began to confuse me, so I asked Valek for some paper, quill and ink. He stilled.

"I don't know why you continue to surprise me. I should have remembered that General Brazell educates his orphans." Valek flung a book of papers, a quill and ink down in front of me. "Take them back to your room. We've done enough for today."

I silently cursed myself for reminding Valek why I had been the next person to be executed as I gathered the book and writing implements. Valek's hard, unforgiving expression revealed his thoughts. Taken off the streets, fed and educated by Brazell, I had repaid Brazell's kindness by murdering his only child. I knew Valek would never believe the truth about Brazell and Reyad.

General Brazell's orphanage was a topic of ridicule from the other Generals. They thought he had gone "soft" after the takeover of Ixia fifteen years ago. This impression suited Brazell. Seen as a kindly old benefactor, Brazell could continue unchallenged in his administration of Military District 5.

I hesitated at the entrance of Valek's office, noticing for the first time the three complex locks on the thick wooden door. Absently fingering the locking mechanisms, I lingered in the doorway until Valek asked, "Now what?"

"I'm not sure where my room is."

Valek spoke as if talking to a slow-witted child. "Ask the first housekeeper or kitchen maid you find, they're always scurrying about this time of day. Tell her you're in the west servant wing, ground floor. She'll show you."

The kitchen maid I snared into helping me was more talkative than Margg and I took full advantage of her good nature. She guided me to the laundry room to obtain some linens for my bed. Then I had her show me the way to the baths and the seamstress's work area. Dilana's piles of uniforms might come in handy someday.

In my room, I opened the shutters to let in the fading light from the setting sun. Sitting down at my desk, I wrote exhaustive notes on what I had learned that day, including a rough map of the servants' corridors. I considered more exploration of the castle, but Valek had been right, I needed my strength. I hoped I would have time to explore later.

During the next two weeks, the training proceeded in a manner so similar to the first day that I lapsed into a routine, arriving at Valek's every morning to train. After fourteen days of sniffing poisons, I found that my sense of smell had heightened. But then Valek announced I was strong enough to begin tasting poisons.

"I'll start with the deadliest one," he said. "If you don't die from it, the other poisons wouldn't kill you either. I don't want to waste all my time training you only to see you die in the end." He placed a slender red bottle on his desk. "It's nasty. Affects the body immediately." Valek's eyes lit up as he admired the poison. "It's called Have a Drink, My Love, or My Love for short because the poison has a history of being used by disheartened wives." He squeezed two drops of the poison into a steaming cup. "A larger dose would definitely kill you. With a smaller dose, there is a chance you'll survive, but you'll become delusional, paranoid and completely disoriented for the next few days."

"Valek, why do I have to taste My Love if it has immediate results? Isn't that what a food taster is for? I taste the Commander's food. I keel over, dead. End of the tale." I tried pacing around the room but kept tripping over stacks of books. Frustrated, I kicked two piles into their neighbors, scattering books into a messy heap on the floor. Valek's gaze pierced me, draining the odd feeling of satisfaction I had gotten from kicking the books.

"A food taster's job is much more complex than that," Valek explained, pulling his hair back from his face. "Being able to identify which poison taints the Commander's food can lead me to the poisoner." Valek handed me the cup. "Even if you only have a split second to shout out My Love before passing out, it would narrow down the list of suspects. There are a number of assassins who are partial to My Love. The poison is grown in Sitia, the southern lands. It was easy to obtain before the takeover. With the closure of the southern border, only a handful of people have enough money to purchase it illegally."

Valek went over to the mess on the floor and started restacking the books. His movements were so graceful that I wondered if he had been a dancer, but his words betrayed to me that his fluid gestures were those of a trained killer.

"Yelena, your job is very important. That's why I spend so much time training you. A shrewd assassin can watch a taster for several days to discover a pattern." Valek continued his lecture from the floor. "For example, the taster might always cut a piece of meat from the left side, or never stir the drink. Some poisons sink to the bottom of the cup. If the taster only sips off the top, then the assassin knows exactly where to place the poison to kill his intended victim." He finished picking up the books. The new piles were neater than the rest of the stacks on the floor. It seemed an invitation to Valek to continue straightening the books. He cleared a bigger path through his office.

"Once you drink the poison, Margg will help you to your room and take care of you. I'll give her your daily dose of But-terfly's Dust antidote."

I stared at the steam drifting from the tea. I picked up the cup, the heat warming my icy hands. When Margg entered the room, it felt as if the executioner had just mounted the dais, reaching for the lever. Should I sit down or lie down? I looked around the room, seeing nothing. My arms started to tingle as I realized I had been holding my breath.

I raised the cup in a mock salute, and then drained the contents. "Sour apples," I said.

Valek nodded. I had only enough time to put the cup on the table before my world began to melt. Margg's body undulated toward me. Her large head sprouted flowers from her eye sockets. A moment later her body filled the room as her head shriveled.

I sensed movement. The gray walls grew arms and legs that reached for me, trying to use me in their fight against the floor. Gray spirits rose from under my feet. They dived, poked and cackled at me. They were freedom. I tried to push the Margg thing away, but it clung and wrapped itself around me, digging through my ears and pounding on my head.

"Murderer," it whispered. "Sneaky bitch. You probably slit his throat while he slept. Easy way to kill. Did you enjoy yourself as you watched his blood soak the sheets? You're nothing but a rat."

I grabbed at the voice, trying to make it stop, but it turned into two green-and-black toy soldiers who held me tight.

"She'll die from the poison. If not you can take her," the Margg thing said to the soldiers.

They pushed me into a dark pit. I plunged into blackness.

The stench of vomit and excrement greeted me when I regained consciousness. They were the unmistakable odors of the dungeon. Wondering how I had ended up back in my old cell, I sat up. A surge of nausea demanded my attention. I groped around for the slop pot and encountered the metal leg of a bed, which I clutched as dry heaves racked my body. When they stopped, I leaned against the wall, grateful to be on the floor of my room and not back in the dungeon. Beds were a luxury not included with the subterranean accommodations.

Summoning the strength to stand, I located and lit my lantern. Dried vomit caked my face. My shirt and pants were soaking wet and smelled foul. The liquid contents of my body had collected in a puddle on the floor.

Margg took good care of me, I thought sarcastically. At least she was practical. If she had dumped me on the bed I would have ruined the mattress.

I thanked fate that I had survived the poison and that I had awakened in the middle of the night. Unable to endure the feel of my sodden uniform any longer, I made my way to the baths.

On my return, voices stopped me before I reached the hallway leading to my room. Extinguishing my lantern in one quick motion, I peeked around the corner. Two soldiers stood in front of my door. The soft light of their lantern reflected the green-and-black colors of their uniforms—Brazell's colors.

4

"SHOULD WE CHECK IF she's dead?" asked one of Brazell's soldiers. He held the lantern up to my door, his overloaded weapon belt jingling with the motion.

"No. That housekeeper checks every morning and gives her a potion. We'll hear about it soon enough. Besides, it stinks in there." The other soldier waved his hand in front of his face.

"Yeah. If the smell don't kill the mood, taking off her vomit-soaked uniform would make any man gag. Although..." The lantern soldier's hand briefly touched the manacles hanging from his belt. "We could drag her down to the baths, clean her up, and have some fun before she dies."

"No, someone would see us. If she survives, we'll have plenty of time to peel off her uniform. It'll be just like opening a present, and definitely more entertaining when she's awake." He leered. They laughed.

They continued down the hallway and were soon out of

sight. I clung to the wall and wondered if what I had just witnessed had been real. Was I still having paranoid hallucinations? My head felt as if it had soaked too long in a pool of water. Dizziness and nausea rippled through my body.

The soldiers were long gone before I worked up the nerve to go back to my room. I pushed the door wide and thrust my lantern in front of me, shining the light into every corner and under the bed. A harsh, acrid odor was the only thing to attack me. Gagging, I unlocked the shutters and threw them open, taking deep breaths of the cool, cleansing air.

I looked at the noxious puddle on the floor. The last thing I wanted to do was clean up the mess, but I knew I would never be able to sleep while breathing in that foul smell. After raiding housekeeping's supplies, and stopping for the occasional bout of nausea, I managed to scrub the floor without fainting.

Exhausted, I stretched out on the bed. It felt lumpy. I turned in my blankets, hoping to find a comfortable position. What if Brazell's soldiers came back? Asleep in bed, I would be an easy target. I had cleaned myself up so there was no need to drag me to the baths. The room smelled like disinfectant, and I had forgotten to put the chair under the doorknob.

Imagination kicked in, a vivid scene of me manacled to the bed, helpless while the soldiers stripped me slowly to heighten their anticipation and savor my fear.

The walls of my room seemed to thicken and pulse. I bolted out into the hallway, expecting to see Brazell's soldiers lurking around my door. The corridor was dark and deserted.

When I tried to reenter my room, I felt as if someone pressed a pillow against my face. I couldn't get my feet to move past the doorway. My room was a trap. The paranoia effect of My Love or common sense? I wondered. Indecision kept me standing in the hallway until my stomach growled. Guided by my hunger, I searched for food.

Hoping to find the kitchen empty, I was dismayed to see a tall man wearing a white uniform with two black diamonds printed on the front of his shirt mumbling to himself as he lurched around the ovens. His left leg didn't bend. I tried to sneak back out but he spotted me.

"Are you looking for me?" he asked.

"No," I said. "I was…looking for something to eat." I craned my neck back to see his face.

He frowned and shifted his weight to his good leg as he studied my uniform. Too thin for a cook, I thought, but he wore the proper clothes and only a cook would be up this early. He was handsome in a subtle way, with light brown eyes and short brown hair. I wondered if this was Dilana's Rand that Margg had talked about.

"Help yourself." He gestured toward two steaming loaves of bread. "You just won me a week's wages."

"Excuse me," I said while cutting off a large piece of bread. "How could I win you money?"

"You're the new food taster. Right?"

I nodded.

"Everyone knows Valek gave you a dose of My Love. I took a chance and bet a week's wages that you would live." He stopped to take three more loaves out of the oven. "A big risk, since you're the smallest and skinniest food taster we've ever had. Most everyone else had wagered that you wouldn't pull through, including Margg."

The cook rummaged through one of the cabinets. "Here." He handed me some butter. "I'll make you some sweet cakes." Grabbing various ingredients from a shelf, he proceeded to mix up a batter.

"How many food tasters have there been?" I asked him between bites of buttered bread. Working alone didn't seem to suit him. He seemed glad to have some company.

With his hands in constant motion, he said, "Five since Commander Ambrose has been in power. Valek loves his poisons. He poisoned many of the Commander's enemies, and he likes to keep in practice. You know, testing the food tasters from time to time to make sure they haven't grown lazy."

The cook's words crawled up my spine. I felt as if my body had liquefied and pooled into a giant mixing bowl. I was just a puddle of ingredients to be beaten, stirred and used. When the cook poured the batter onto the hot griddle, my blood sizzled along with the sweet cakes.

"Poor Oscove, Valek never liked him. Testing him constantly until he couldn't handle the pressure. The 'official' cause of death was suicide, but I think Valek killed him."

Flip. I stared as the cook deftly flicked his wrist, turning the cakes over. My muscles trembled in synch with the sound of frying sweet cakes.

Here I was worried about Brazell, when one misstep with

Valek and… Flip. I would be gone. He probably held a couple of poisons in reserve just in case he decided to replace the taster. Glancing over my shoulder, I imagined Valek coming into the kitchen to poison my breakfast. I couldn't even enjoy talking with a chatty cook without being reminded that tasting potentially poisoned food wasn't the only danger of my new job.

The cook handed me a plate loaded with sweet cakes, took three more loaves of bread out of the oven and refilled his bread pans with dough. Piping-hot sweet cakes were such a rare treat that I devoured them despite my unsettled stomach.

"Oscove was my friend. He was the Commander's best food taster. He used to come to my kitchen every morning after breakfast and help me invent new recipes. I have to keep things interesting or the Commander will start looking for a new cook. Know what I mean?"

I nodded, wiping butter off my chin.

He thrust out his hand. "My name's Rand."

I shook his hand. "Yelena."

I stopped at an open window on my way to Valek's office. The rising sun was just cresting the Soul Mountains to the east of the castle. The colors in the sky resembled a ruined painting, as if a small child had spilled water on the canvas. I let my eyes feast on the vibrant display of life as I inhaled the fresh air. Everything was in full bloom, and soon the cool morning breeze would warm to a comfortable level. The hot season was in its infancy. The days of sweltering heat and limp, humid nights were still a few weeks away. I had been training with Valek for a fortnight, and I wondered how long My Love had held me unconscious.

Tearing myself away from the window, I walked toward Valek's office, arriving at his door just as he was leaving.

"Yelena! You made it." Valek smiled. "It's been three days. I was beginning to worry."

I studied his face. He seemed sincerely glad to see me.

"Where's Margg?" he asked.

"I haven't seen her." Thank fate, I thought.

"Then you'll need your antidote," Valek said while moving back to his cabinet.

Once I swallowed the liquid, Valek headed toward the door. When I didn't follow, he gestured to me.

"I have to taste the Commander's breakfast," he said, setting a quick pace.

I huffed along behind him.

"It's time you meet the Commander and watch how food tasting should be done."

We turned into the main hallway of the castle. Valek didn't miss a step, but I stumbled and stifled a gasp. The famous tapestries from the King's era were torn and soiled with black paint. In Brazell's orphanage we had been taught that each tapestry represented a province of the old kingdom. Hand-quilted with gold threads during the course of many years, the colored silk pictures told a story about the history of each province. Now in rags, they still told a very powerful tale about the Commander's rule.

The Commander's disdain for the opulence, excesses and

injustices of the former ruler and his family was well known throughout Ixia. From monarchy to military, the changes in Ixia were severe. While some citizens embraced the simple but strict rules in the Code of Behavior, others rebelled by refusing to wear their uniforms, by not requesting permission to travel, and by escaping to the south.

Based on the offense, the insurgents' punishment matched exactly what was written in the Code. No uniform meant two days chained naked in the town's square. It didn't matter if the offender had a legitimate reason; the punishment was always the same. Ixia's people discovered that there wasn't going to be any guessing about their punishment. No bribing or good-old-boy networking either; the Commander meant business. Live by the Code or face the consequences.

I pulled my eyes away from the tapestries in time to see Valek disappear through an arched doorway decorated with lavish stonework. Splintered wooden doors hung crookedly on their hinges, but the intricate carvings of trees and exotic birds were still visible. Another victim of the takeover, and another reminder of the Commander's intent.

I stopped in amazement just past the broken doors. This was the castle's throne room. Inside was a sea of desks occupied by numerous advisers and military officers from every Military District in the Territory. The room hummed with activity.

It was hard to distinguish individuals in the commotion, but I finally spotted Valek's smooth stride as he went through an open door at the back of the room. Finding a path around the maze of desks took some time. When I arrived at the door, I heard a man's voice complaining about cold sweet cakes.

Commander Ambrose sat behind a plain wooden desk. His office was stark in comparison to Valek's and lacked personal decorations. The only object in the room that did not have a specific purpose was a hand-size statue of a black snow cat. The cat's eyes glinted with silver, and bright specks of the metal peppered the beast's powerful back.

The Commander's black uniform was perfectly tailored and immaculate, indistinguishable from Valek's except that the diamonds stitched on his collar were real. They twinkled in the morning light. The Commander's black hair was sprinkled with gray and cut so short that the strands stood straight up.

In Brazell's classroom, we had learned that the Commander avoided public appearances and having his portrait painted. The fewer people who knew what he looked like, the less his chances were of being assassinated. Some thought he was paranoid, but I believed that since he had gained power by using assassins and covert warfare, he was merely being realistic.

This was not the Commander I had envisioned: burly, bearded and weighed down with medals and weapons. He was thin, clean shaven, with delicate features.

"Commander, this is Yelena, your new food taster," Valek said, pulling me into the room.

The Commander's gold almond-shaped eyes met mine. His gaze had the sharpness of a sword point. It pressed against my throat and fastened me to the floor. I felt myself being drawn out and examined. When he looked over at Valek, I swayed with relief.

"From what Brazell's been hollering about, I expected her to breathe fire," the Commander said.

I stiffened on hearing Brazell's name. If Brazell was complaining to the Commander, I could be back in line for the noose.

"Brazell's a fool," Valek said. "He wanted the drama of a public hanging for his son's killer. I personally would have taken care of her immediately. It would have been within his rights." Valek slurped the Commander's tea and sniffed the sweet cakes.

My chest was tight. I was having trouble drawing in air.

"Besides, it's clearly written in the Code of Behavior that the next to be hanged gets the job offer. And Brazell was one of the authors." Cutting a piece of one sweet cake from the center and the other from the side, Valek put both pieces in his mouth, chewing slowly. "Here." He handed the plate to the Commander.

"Brazell does have a point," the Commander said. He picked up his tea and stared at the contents. "When does she start? I'm getting tired of cold food."

"A few more days."

"Good," the Commander said to Valek, then turned to me. "You arrive with my food and taste quick. I don't want to be looking for you. Understand?"

Feeling light-headed, I answered, "Yes, Sir."

"Valek, I'm losing weight because of you. Lunch is in the war room. Don't be late."

"Yes, Sir," Valek said and headed for the door. I followed. We wound our way through the tangle of desks. When Valek stopped to consult with another adviser, I glanced around. A handful of the Commander's advisers were women, and I noticed two female Captains and one Colonel. Their new roles were one of the benefits of the takeover. The Commander assigned jobs based on skills and intelligence, not on gender.

While the monarchy preferred to see women work as maids, kitchen helpers and wives, the Commander gave them the freedom to choose what they wanted to do. Some women preferred their former occupations, while others jumped at the chance to do something else, and the younger generation had been quick to take advantage of the new opportunities.

When we finally reached Valek's office, Margg was dusting around Valek's piles of papers on the table. It looked to me as if she was spending more time reading the papers than straightening them. Didn't Valek notice? I wondered what Margg did for Valek besides cleaning.

Margg turned a pleasant face to Valek, but as soon as he walked away she glared fiercely at me. Must have lost a lot of money betting against my survival, I thought. I smiled at her. She managed to control her outraged expression before Valek glanced up at us from his desk.

"Yelena, you look exhausted. You make me tired just looking at you. Go rest. Come back after lunch and we'll continue with your training."

I didn't really feel tired, but rest sounded like an excellent idea. As I moved along the hallway, Valek's comment wormed its way through my mind. My pace slowed and I dragged my feet toward my room. I was so preoccupied with the physical effort of walking that I bumped right into two of Brazell's guards.

"Lookie, Wren, I found our rat!" one guard exclaimed, grabbing my wrist.

Alert, I gaped at the green diamonds on the guard's uniform.

"Good for you," Wren said. "Let's show your catch to General Brazell."

"The General isn't fond of live rats. Especially this one."

The guard shook me hard. Pain coursed up my arm to my shoulder and neck. In a panic, I searched the hallway for help. It was deserted.

"That's right, he prefers them skinned alive."

I'd heard enough. I did what any good rat would do. I bit down on the guard's hand until I tasted blood. Yelping and cursing in surprise, his grip lessened. I jerked my arm out of his grasp and ran.

5

I WAS ONLY A COUPLE OF STEPS away from Brazell's guards when they recovered from their surprise and began to chase me. Being terrified and unburdened of weapons, I had a slight advantage. It wouldn't last. I was already puffing with the effort.

The corridors were mysteriously empty as I ran through them. If I did find someone, I wasn't really sure they would or could help me. Like a rat, my only hope of escape was to find a hole to hide in.

I ran without a plan, caring only about keeping ahead of the guards. The corridors blurred together until I imagined I was running in place and it was the walls that were moving. I slowed for a moment to get my bearings. Where was I?

The light in the hallway was waning. My pounding steps kicked dust up from the floor. I had headed toward an isolated part of the castle, a perfect place for a quiet murder. Quiet because I wouldn't have enough air in my lungs to scream.

I made a quick right turn into a corridor that led off into darkness. Momentarily out of the guards' sight, I pushed against the first door I encountered. Groaning and creaking, it yielded slightly under my weight, and then stuck tight. A gap big enough for my body, but not my head. Hearing the guards turn down the corridor, I threw myself against the door. It moved another inch. I tumbled headfirst into a dark room, and landed on the floor.

The guards found the door. I watched in horror as they tried to muscle it open. The gap began to expand. I scanned the room. My eyes adjusted to the gloom. Empty barrels and rotten sacks of grain littered the floor. A pile of rugs was stacked against the far wall below a window.

The door surrendered a couple more inches to the guards' efforts before lodging again. I stood, and stacked the barrels on top of the rug pile. Scrambling up them, I reached the window, only to discover it was too small for me to fit through.

The door cracked ominously. I used my elbow to shatter the windowpane. Pulling the ragged glass fragments out of the frame, I tossed them to the floor. Blood ran down my arm. Heedless of the pain, I jumped down, pressed myself against the wall next to the doorway, and fought to stifle the harsh sound of my breathing.

With a loud groan, the door stopped mere inches from my face as the guards stumbled into the storeroom.

"Check the window. I'll cover the door," Wren said.

I peeked around the edge. Wren's companion walked to the pile of rugs and barrels, crushing glass beneath his boots.

My plan wasn't going to work. Wren blocked my escape route. The broken window would only delay the inevitable.

"Too small, she's still here," the guard called from above.

My rough breathing had accelerated into fast gasps. I felt light-headed. The rat trap had sprung. I was immobilized in its metal jaws.

My thoughts jumbled into a cloud of images. I clutched at the door, trying not to fall. A buzzing sound burst uncontrolled from my throat. I was unable to suppress the drone. Trying harder only caused the sound to grow louder.

I staggered out from behind the door. With all the noise I made, the guards didn't even glance in my direction. They seemed frozen in place.

My lungs strained for air. On the verge of passing out, the buzzing then released me. The sound still rang in the room, but it no longer came from me.

The guards continued to be unresponsive. After taking several deep breaths, I bolted from the room. I wasn't going to waste time trying to understand. The buzzing sound followed me as I ran back the way we had come.

The loud hum ended as soon as I started seeing other servants hurrying through the hallway. Odd looks were cast my way. I realized I must be quite a sight. I forced myself to stop running as I tried to calm my hammering heart.

My throat burned from panting, my uniform was stained, pain throbbed in my elbow, and bright red beads dripped off my fingers. Looking at my hands, I saw deep cuts from handling the glass. I gazed at the blood on the floor.

Turning around, I saw a line of crimson drops disappearing down the corridor. I clutched my arms to my chest, but it was too late. I had left a blood trail, and there were Brazell's guards, like trained dogs, following it.

They were coming around the corner at the far end of the hall. Undetected so far, I knew any sudden movement would draw their attention. I joined a group of servants, hoping to blend in. Pain pulsated in harmony with my laboring heartbeat.

When I reached a turn, I risked a glance over my shoulder. The guards stood at the spot where my blood trail had ended. Wren gestured as he argued with his partner. I slipped around the corner unnoticed, then bumped right into Valek.

"Yelena! What happened to you?" Valek grabbed my arm. I winced. He let go.

"I...fell...on some glass." It was weak. I hurried to cover it. "I'm on my way to get cleaned up." As I began to walk past Valek, he grasped my shoulder, spinning me around.

"You need to see a medic."

"Ah...okay." I tried once more to get past Valek.

"The medic is this way." Valek pulled on my shoulder, forcing me to follow him back down the corridor toward the guards. Foolishly, I hoped they wouldn't see me, but as we walked past they smiled, falling into step behind us.

I glanced at Valek. There was no expression on his face. His grip on my shoulder tightened. Was Valek leading me to some secluded spot where the three of them could kill me? Should I make a break for it? But if Valek had wanted me dead, he had only to withhold the antidote to Butterfly's Dust.

When the hallway emptied of people, Valek let go of my shoulder and swung around to face the two guards. I stayed close behind him.

"Are you lost?" Valek asked the guards.

"No, sir," said Wren. A foot taller than Valek, his hands were the size of my head. "Just want to reclaim our prisoner." Wren tried to reach around Valek to grab me.

Valek deflected his hand. "*Your* prisoner?" Valek's voice sliced through the air like steel.

The guards looked at each other in disbelief. Valek had no weapons. While the other guard was shorter than Wren, he still outweighed the other two men. Identical cocky smirks touched both guards' faces. I wondered if sneering and glaring were part of their training. Rand the cook would probably bet a month's wages on Brazell's soldiers winning this argument.

"Actually, General Brazell's prisoner, sir. Now, if you would…" Wren gestured for Valek to step aside.

"Tell your boss that *Valek* doesn't appreciate having his new food taster chased through the castle. And that I would like her to be left alone."

The guards glanced at each other again. I was beginning to suspect they had only one brain to share between them. Regarding Valek with a more focused expression, they shifted their posture into a fighting stance.

"We have been ordered to bring the *girl* to the General. Not messages," Wren said, pulling his sword from his belt.

With the sound of ringing metal, the second guard flourished his weapon as well. Wren asked Valek to move aside once more. Faced with two swords, what could Valek do? Run for my life is what I would do, so I shifted my weight to the balls of my feet, preparing to flee.

Valek's right hand blurred into motion with two quick snaps of his wrist. It looked as if he had saluted both guards. Before the men could react, he was between them, too close for swords. He crouched low, put his hands on the floor and spun. Using his legs, Valek windmilled both guards to the ground. I heard a clatter of metal, a whoosh of air from Wren and a curse from the other before they both lay motionless.

Baffled, I watched Valek gracefully move away from his fallen opponents. He counted under his breath. When he reached ten, he bent over each man and removed a tiny dart from each of their necks.

"It's a dirty way to fight, but I'm late for lunch."

6

STEPPING OVER THE PRONE forms of the sleeping soldiers, Valek took my injured arm and inspected it. "Not as bad as it looks. You'll live. We'll see the Commander first, then the medic."

Valek hurried me through the castle. My arm began to throb. I lagged behind. The thought of facing the Commander's stony gaze dragged at my feet. Finding the medic, then sinking into a hot bath was without a doubt more appealing.

We entered a spacious round chamber that served as the Commander's war room. Slender, stained-glass windows stretched from the floor to the ceiling and encircled three-quarters of the chamber. The kaleidoscope of colors made me feel as if I were inside a spinning top. Dizzy, I would have stumbled except I caught a glimpse of something that rooted me to the floor.

A long wooden table filled the center of the room. Sitting

at the head of the table with two guards standing behind him was the Commander. His thin eyebrows were pinched together in annoyance. A tray of untouched food sat by his side. Also seated around the table were three of the Commander's Generals. Two of the Generals were busy eating their lunch, while the third's fork hovered in midair. I focused on the hand; white knuckles equaled white-hot rage. With reluctance I met General Brazell's gaze.

Brazell lowered his fork, his face taut. His eyes held lightning. I was the target, and like a rabbit caught in the open, I was too frightened to move.

"Valek, you're..." Commander Ambrose began.

"Late," Valek finished for him. "I know. There was a slight altercation," he said. He pulled me closer.

Intrigued, the other two Generals stopped eating. I flushed, stifling a strong desire to bolt from the room. Having no contact with any high-ranking officers, I recognized the Generals only by the colors on their uniforms. My trip to the Commander's dungeon was the first time I had been past the borders of MD–5. Even during the first ten years I had lived in Brazell's orphanage, I had only caught brief glimpses of him and his family.

Unfortunately, after I had turned sixteen, the sight of Brazell and his son Reyad became my daily nightmare. I had been flattered by the attention of my benefactor; his gray hair and short beard framed a square-shaped, pleasant face that shouted respectability. Stout and sturdy, he was the ultimate father figure to me. Brazell told me I was the smartest of his "adopted" children and that he needed my help with some experiments. I readily agreed to participate.

The memory of how grateful and naive I had been sickened me. It was three years ago. I had been a puppy. A puppy still wagging her tail as the bag's opening was tied shut.

Two years I had suffered. My mind recoiled from the memories. I stared at Brazell in the war room. His lips were pressed tight as his jaw quivered. He fought to contain his hatred. Faint with fatigue, I saw Reyad's ghost appear behind his father. Reyad's slashed throat hung open, and blood dripped down, staining his nightshirt. A distant recollection of a tale about murder victims haunting their killers until their business was settled filtered through my mind.

I rubbed my eyes. Did anyone else see the ghost? If so, they hid it well. My gaze slid to Valek. Was he haunted by ghosts? If that old story was to be believed, he would be swamped by them.

Worry that I might not be completely rid of Reyad pulsed through me, but not a trace of remorse. The only thing I was sorry for was not having the courage to kill Brazell when I had the chance. Sorry that I was unable to save my "sisters and brothers" at Brazell's orphanage from turning sixteen. Sorry that I was unable to warn May and Carra, and help them run away.

The Commander's voice brought my attention back to the war room.

"Altercation, Valek?" He sighed like an indulgent parent. "How many dead?"

"None. I couldn't justify the disposal of soldiers merely following General Brazell's orders to hunt down and kill our new food taster. Besides, they weren't very smart. Seems she was on the verge of giving them the slip when she ran into me. Good thing though, or I might not have found out about the incident."

The Commander studied me for a while before turning to Brazell.

It was all Brazell needed. Leaping from his chair, he shouted, "She should be dead! I want her dead! She killed my son!"

Valek said, "But the Code of Behavior…"

"Damn the Code. I'm a General. She killed a *General's* son and here she is…" Emotion choked off Brazell's voice. His fingers twitched as if he wanted to wrap his hands around my throat that instant. Reyad's ghost floated behind his father, a smirk on his face.

"It's a dishonor to me that she lives," Brazell said. "An insult. Train another prisoner. I want her dead!"

Instinctively, I stepped behind Valek. The other Generals were nodding their heads in agreement. I was too terrified to look at the Commander.

"He has a sound argument," the Commander said without a trace of emotion tainting his voice.

"You have never deviated from what's written in the Code of Behavior," Valek argued. "Start now and you'll begin a trend. Besides, you'll be killing the brightest food taster we've ever had. She's almost trained." He gestured to the tray of cold food beside the Commander.

I glanced around Valek to see the Commander's expression. Thoughtful, he pursed his lips while he considered Valek's argument. I crossed my arms, digging my fingernails deep into my flesh.

Brazell, sensing a change of heart, took a step toward the Commander. "She's smart because *I* educated her. I can't believe you're going to listen to this upstart, conniving, sneaky thief—" Brazell stopped. He had said too much. He had insulted Valek, and even I knew that the Commander had a special fondness for Valek.

"Brazell, leave my food taster alone."

My breath hissed with relief.

Brazell attempted to argue, but the Commander silenced him. "It's an order. Go ahead and build your new factory. Consider your permit approved." He dangled a carrot in front of Brazell. Was a new factory worth more than my death?

Silence followed as everyone waited for Brazell to comment. He gave me a look full of venom. Reyad's ghost grinned, and I guessed from his cat-that-got-the-rat smile that the permit approval was very important to Brazell. More important than he let on to the Commander. The rage and indignation over my missing the noose was genuine, but he could build his factory now, and then kill me later. He knew where to find me.

Brazell left the room without saying another word. The amused ghost mouthed the words "See you next time," before following his father.

When the other Generals started to protest the permit approval, the Commander listened to their arguments in silence. Momentarily forgotten, I studied the two Generals. Their uniforms were similar to the Commander's except that they wore black jackets with gold buttons. Instead of real diamonds on their collars, each General had five embroidered diamonds stitched on their coats over their left breasts. No medals or ribbons decorated their uniforms. The Commander's troops wore only what was needed for recognition and for battle.

The diamonds on the General sitting close to the Commander were blue. He was General Hazal in charge of Military District 6, just west of Brazell's MD–5. General Tesso's diamonds were silver for MD–4, which bordered to the north of Brazell's. If a district planned a big project, like building a new factory or clearing land for farming, a permit approved by the Commander was required. Smaller projects, like installing a new oven at a bakery or building a house within the district, only needed approval from that district's General. Most Generals had a staff to handle the processing of new permit applications.

It was apparent from the Generals' complaints that Brazell's permit was in the initial processing stages. Discussions with the bordering districts had started, but the Commander's staff had not yet reviewed and authenticated the factory's plans. Usually once the staff recommended approval, the Commander signed off on the application. The Code of Behavior only stated that permission must be received prior to building, and if the Commander wanted to bypass his own process he could do so.

We had been taught the Code of Behavior at the orphanage. Anyone wishing the honor of running errands into town had to memorize and recite the Code perfectly prior to gaining the privilege. Besides reading and writing, the education I had received from Brazell had also included mathematics and the history of Ixia's takeover by the Commander. Since the takeover, education was available to everyone and not just a privilege for the men of the richer classes.

My education, though, took a turn for the worse when I began "helping" Brazell. Memories threatened to overwhelm me. My hot skin felt tight. I trembled, forcing my mind to the present. The Generals had finished their rebuttal of the Commander's decision. Valek tasted the Commander's cold food, and pushed it closer to him.

"Your concerns are noted. My order stands," the Commander said. He turned to Valek. "Your food taster had better live up to your endorsements. One slip and you'll be training her replacement prior to your reassignment. You're dismissed."

Valek took my arm and steered me from the chamber. We walked down the hallway until the door of the war room clicked shut. Then Valek stopped. The features on his face had hardened into a porcelain mask.

"Yelena…"

"Don't say anything. Don't threaten or bully or intimidate. I've had enough of that from Brazell. I'll make every effort to be the best taster because I'm getting used to the idea of living. And I don't want to give Brazell the satisfaction of seeing me dead." Tired of examining Valek's every facial expression and straining to hear every small nuance in his voice for clues to his mood, I moved away from him. He followed me. When we reached an intersection, Valek's hand grasped my elbow. I heard him utter the word *medic* as he guided me to the left. Without once looking at his face, I let him steer me to the infirmary.

As I was led to an empty examining table, I squinted at the medic's all-white uniform. The only color on the uniform was two small red diamonds stitched on the collar. My mind was so muddled with fatigue that it took me some time to figure out that the short-haired medic was a female. With a grunt, I stretched out on the table.

When the woman left to get her supplies, Valek said, "I'll post some guards outside the door, in case Brazell changes his mind." Before leaving the infirmary, I saw him speak with the medic. She nodded and glanced toward me.

The medic returned with a tray full of shiny medical instruments that included a jar of a substance that looked like jelly. She scrubbed my arms with alcohol, making the wounds bleed and sting. I bit my lip to keep from crying out.

"They're all superficial, except this one," the medic said as she pointed to the elbow I had used to break the glass. "This wound needs to be sealed."

"Sealed?" It sounded painful.

The medic picked up the pot of jelly. "Relax. It's a new method for treating deep lacerations. We use this glue to seal the skin. Once the wound heals, the glue is absorbed into the body." She scooped out a large amount with her fingers and applied it to the cut.

I winced at the pain. She pinched my skin together, holding it tight. Tears rolled down my cheeks.

"It was invented by the Commander's cook, of all people. There are no side effects and it tastes great in tea."

"Rand?" I asked, surprised.

She nodded. Still holding the skin together, she said, "You'll need to wear a bandage for a few days and keep the cut dry." She blew on the glue for a while before releasing her grip. She bandaged my arm. "Valek wants you to stay here tonight. I'll bring you dinner. You can get some rest."

I thought eating might require too much effort, but when she brought the hot food, I realized I was starving. A strange taste in my tea caused me to lose my appetite in an instant.

Someone had poisoned my tea.

7

I WAVED DOWN THE MEDIC.

"There is something in my tea," I cried. I began to feel light-headed. "Call Valek." Maybe he had an antidote.

She stared at me with her large brown eyes. Her face was long and thin. Longer hair would soften her features, her short style merely made her resemble a ferret.

"It's sleeping pills. Valek's orders," she said.

I let out a breath, feeling better. The medic gave me an amused look before she left. My appetite ruined, I shoved the food aside. I didn't need sleeping pills to help me give in to the exhaustion that lapped up my remaining strength.

When I woke the next morning, there was a blurry white blob standing at the end of my bed. It moved. I blinked and squinted until the image sharpened into the short-haired medic.

"Did you have a good night?"

"Yes," I said. The first night in a long time free of nightmares, although my head felt as if wool had been shoved into it, and a rank taste in my mouth didn't promise for a good morning.

The medic checked my bandages, made a noncommittal sound and told me breakfast would be a while.

As I waited, I scanned the infirmary. The rectangular room held twelve beds, six on each side, and spaced so that they formed a mirror image. The sheets on the empty beds were pulled tight as bowstrings. Orderly and precise, the room annoyed me. I felt like rumpled bedding, no longer in control of my soul, my body, or my world. Being surrounded by neatness offended me, and I had a sudden desire to jump on the empty beds, knocking them out of line.

I was farthest from the door. Two empty beds lay between the three other patients and me on my side of the room. They were sleeping. I had no one to talk to. The stone walls were bare. Hell, my prison cell had more interesting decorations. At least it smelled better in here. I took a deep breath. The clean, sharp smell of alcohol mixed with disinfectant filled my nose, so different from the dungeon's fetid air. Much better. Or was it? There was another scent intermixed with the medical aroma. Another whiff and I realized that the sour odor of old fear emanated from me.

I shouldn't have survived yesterday. Brazell's guards had me cornered. There was no escape. Yet I had been saved by a strange buzzing noise that had erupted from my throat like an unruly, uncontrollable offspring. A primal survival instinct that had echoed in my nightmares.

I avoided thoughts about that buzz because it was an old acquaintance of mine, but the memories kept invading my mind.

Examining the past three years, I forced myself to concentrate on when and where the buzzing had erupted, and to ignore the emotions.

The first couple of months of Brazell's experiments had merely tested my reflexes. How fast I could dodge a ball or duck a swinging stick, harmless enough until the ball had turned into a knife and the stick into a sword.

My heart began to pound. With sweaty palms I fingered a scar on my neck. No emotion, I told myself sternly, flicking my hands as if I could push away the fear. Pretend you're the medic, I thought, asking questions to gain information. I imagined myself dressed in white, calmly sitting next to a fevered patient while she babbled.

What came next? I asked the patient. Strength and endurance tests, she answered. Simple tasks of lifting weights had turned into holding heavy stones above her head for minutes, then hours. If she dropped the stone before the time was up, she was whipped. She was ordered to clutch chains dangling from the ceiling, holding her weight inches above the floor, until Brazell or Reyad gave permission to let go.

When was the first time you heard the buzzing? I prompted the patient. She had released the chains too early too many times and Reyad became furious. So he forced her outside a window six floors above the ground, and let her hold on to the ledge with her hands.

"Let's try it again," Reyad said. "Now that we've raised the stakes, maybe you'll last for the whole hour."

The patient stopped speaking. Go on, tell me what

happened, I prodded. Her arms had been weak from spending most of the day hanging from the chains. Her fingers were slick with sweat; her muscles trembled with fatigue. She panicked. When her hands slipped off the ledge, she howled like a newborn. The howl mutated and transformed into a substance. It expanded out, enveloped and caressed her skin on all sides. She felt as if she was nestled in a warm pool of water.

Next thing she remembered she was sitting on the ground. She glanced up at the window. Reyad watched her with his face flushed. His perfect blond hair an unusual mess. Delighted, he blew her a kiss.

The only way she could have survived the fall was by magic. No. Absolutely not, she insisted. It had to have been some strange wind currents or landing the right way. Not magic.

Magic, a forbidden word in Ixia since Commander Ambrose came to power. Magicians had been treated like disease-riddled mosquitoes. They were hunted, trapped and exterminated. Any hint or suggestion that someone had magic was a death sentence. The only chance to live was to escape to Sitia.

The patient was growing agitated, and the other occupants of the room were staring at her... Me. Small doses, I told myself. I could handle the memories in modest quantities. After all, I hadn't been hurt by the fall, and Reyad was sweet to me for a while. But his kindness only lasted until I started failing his tests again.

To distract myself from the memories, I counted the cracks in the ceiling. I was up to fifty-six when Valek arrived.

He carried a tray of food in one hand and a file folder in

the other. I eyed the steaming omelet with suspicion. "What's in it?" I demanded. "More sleeping pills? Or another new poison?" Every muscle in my body had stiffened. I tried unsuccessfully to sit up. "How about giving me something to make me feel good for a change?"

"How about something to keep you alive?" Valek asked. He pulled me to a sitting position and offered a pipette filled with my antidote. Then he placed the tray of food on my lap.

"No need for sleeping pills. The medic told me you picked up on that taste last night." Valek's voice held a note of approval. "Taste your breakfast and tell me if you would allow the Commander to eat it."

Valek hadn't been exaggerating when he said I'd have no days off. Sighing, I smelled the omelet. No unusual odors. I cut the omelet into quarters, examining each for any foreign material. Taking a small piece from each section, I put them into my mouth one at a time and chewed slowly. Swallowing, I waited to discern any aftertaste. I sniffed the tea and stirred it with a spoon before sipping. Rolling the liquid over my tongue, I detected a sweet taste before I swallowed.

"Unless the Commander doesn't like honey in his tea, I wouldn't reject this breakfast."

"Then eat it."

I hesitated. Was Valek trying to trick me? Unless he had used a poison I hadn't learned, the breakfast was clean. I ate every morsel, and then drained the tea while Valek watched.

"Not bad," he said. "No poisons...today."

One of the medics brought another tray to Valek. This tray

held four white cups of an olive-colored liquid that smelled like mint. Replacing my breakfast tray with the new one, Valek said, "I want to go over some tasting techniques. Each of these cups contains mint tea. Taste one."

Clasping the closest mug, I took a sip. An overwhelming flavor of mint pervaded my mouth. I choked.

Valek grinned. "Taste anything else?"

I attempted another mouthful. The mint dominated. "No."

"All right. Now pinch your nose tight and try again."

After some fumbling with my bandaged arm, I managed to gulp the tea while holding my nose. My ears popped. I marveled at the taste. "Sweet. No mint." My voice sounded silly so I released my grip. Immediately, the mint eclipsed the sweetness.

"Correct. Now try the others."

The next cup of mint tea hid a sour taste, the third had a bitter flavor, and the fourth was salty.

"This technique works for any drink or food. Blocking your sense of smell eliminates all flavors except sweet, sour, bitter and salt. Some poisons are recognizable by one of those four flavors." Valek paged through his folder. "Here is a complete list of human poisons and their distinct tastes for you to memorize. There are fifty-two known poisons."

I looked through the inventory of poisons. Some of them I had already smelled. My Love was at the top. The list would have saved me from the dizziness, nausea, headaches and occasional delusional effects of the poison. I brandished the paper in the air. "Why didn't you just give me this list instead of making me sample My Love?"

Valek stopped paging through his folder. "What would you learn from a list? Kattsgut tastes sweet. What does that taste like? Honey sweet? Apple sweet? There are different levels of sweetness and the only way to learn them is to taste them yourself. The *only* reason I'm giving you this list is because the Commander wants you working as soon as possible." Valek snapped his folder shut. "Just because you aren't going to taste those poisons now doesn't mean you won't in the future. Memorize that list. Once the medic releases you from the infirmary, I will test your knowledge. If you pass, then you can start work."

"And if I fail?"

"Then I'll be training a new taster."

His voice was flat, monotone, but the force behind it caused my heart to lock.

Valek continued. "Brazell will be in the castle for another two weeks. He has more business to attend to. I can't have you guarded all day, so Margg is preparing a room for you in my suite. I'll come back later to see when you'll be discharged."

I watched Valek walk to the door. He glided across the room, balanced and athletic. I shook my head. Thinking about Valek was the absolute worst thing I could be doing. Instead, I focused on the list of poisons clutched in my hand. I smoothed the paper out and hoped my sweat hadn't smeared the ink. Relieved that the writing was legible, I began to study.

I barely noticed when the medic came to check on my arm. She must have taken the tray of teacups, because it disappeared from my lap. I had blocked out all the noise and commotion of the infirmary so that I jumped when a plate containing a round pastry was thrust under my nose.

The arm that held the plate led to Rand. His grin was gleeful.

"Look what I smuggled past Medic Mommy! Go ahead. Eat it before she comes back."

The warm dessert smelled like cinnamon. Melted white icing dripped down the sides, causing the cake to stick to my fingers when I picked it up. I examined the pastry closely, inhaling the aroma in search of a foreign smell. One small bite revealed multiple layers of dough and cinnamon.

"My God, Yelena, you don't think I'd poison it?" Rand's face was pinched tight, as if he was in pain.

Exactly what I'd been thinking, but admitting it to Rand would offend him. His motives for being here were unclear. Seeming nice and friendly, he could be holding a grudge over his friend Oscove, the previous food taster. But then again, he was a potential ally. Who better to have on my side? Rand, the cook, whose food I'd be eating on a daily basis, or Valek, the assassin, who had a nasty tendency of poisoning my meals?

"Occupational hazard," I tried.

He grunted, still put out. I took a big bite of the pastry.

"Wonderful," I said, appealing to his ego to give me another chance.

Rand's face softened. "Good, isn't it? My latest recipe. I take a long strip of pastry dough, cover it with cinnamon, roll it up into a ball, bake it, and then spread the icing on while it's hot. I'm having some trouble with the name though. Cinnamon cake? Ball? Swirl?" Rand stopped his rambling to find a chair.

After quite a bit of twisting to compensate for his unbendable left leg, he finally settled into a comfortable position.

While I finished the pastry, Rand continued. "Don't tell Medic Mommy I gave you that. She doesn't like her patients eating anything but a thin gruel. She says the gruel promotes healing. Well, of course it has an effect!" He threw his arms up, exposing several burn scars around his wrists. "It tastes so terrible that anyone would get better just to get a decent meal!"

The wild gesture caused the other patients to glance our way. Rand leaned in closer to me and asked in a quiet voice, "So, Yelena, how are you feeling?" He looked at me as though he was appraising a selection of meat, determining which one would make the best roast.

I was wary. Why would he care? "Gambling again?" I asked.

He leaned back. "We're always gambling. Gambling and gossiping is all we servants do. What else is there? You should've seen the commotion and betting that went on when you were spotted being chased by Brazell's goons."

Appalled, I said, "Nobody came to help me. The hallways were deserted."

"That would be involvement in a situation that doesn't affect us directly. Servants don't ever do that. We're like cockroaches scurrying around in the dark." Rand's slender fingers waggled. "Shine a light...*poof!*" He flicked his long fingers for emphasis. "We disappear."

I felt like the unlucky cockroach that got caught by the light. Always scrambling to stay one step ahead while the shadow of a boot crept closer.

"Anyway, the odds were against you. Most lost big, while only a few—" Rand paused dramatically "—won big."

"Since you're here, I suppose you won big."

He smiled. "Yelena, I'm always going to bet on you. You're like one of the Commander's terriers. A tiny, yappy dog you wouldn't look at twice, but once it grabs your pant leg, it won't let go."

"Poison the dog's meat and it won't bother you anymore."

My sour tone deflated Rand's grin. "Trouble?"

Surprised that the castle's gossip network hadn't already started laying odds about Valek's test, I hesitated. Rand liked to talk, and he could get me in trouble. "No. It's just being the food taster and all…" I hoped that would satisfy him.

Rand nodded. He spent the rest of the afternoon alternating between reminiscing about Oscove and digressing about potential new recipes. When Valek appeared, Rand stopped talking, his face paled and he mumbled something about having to check on dinner. Lurching from his chair, he almost toppled in his haste to flee the room. Valek watched as Rand staggered out of the infirmary.

"What was he doing here?"

Valek's expression remained neutral, but the stillness of his body made me wonder if he was angry. Carefully choosing my words, I explained to him that Rand had come to visit.

"When did you meet him?"

A casual question, but again there was an undercurrent to his words. "After I recovered from My Love, I went in search of food and met Rand in the kitchen."

"Watch what you say around him. He's not to be trusted. I would have reassigned him, but the Commander insisted he stay. He *is* a genius in the kitchen. Some kind of protégé. He started cooking for the King at a very young age."

Valek stared at me with his cold blue eyes, warning me away from Rand. Maybe that's why Valek hadn't liked Oscove. Being allied with someone who had been loyal to the King could cast more suspicion on me. But letting Valek scare me off rankled. I stared back at him with, I hoped, an indifferent look.

Valek looked away. I was jubilant. In my mind, I had finally won a round.

"You leave the infirmary tomorrow morning." Valek was curt. "Get yourself cleaned up and report to my office to take the test. I won't think you're ready even if you pass, but the Commander ordered me to have you available by lunch." He shook his head in annoyance. "It's a shortcut. I hate shortcuts."

"Why? You won't have to risk yourself anymore." I regretted the words as soon as they had left my mouth.

Valek's gaze was lethal. "In my experience, shortcuts usually lead to death."

"Is that what happened to my predecessor?" I asked, unable to stifle my curiosity. Would Valek confirm or deny Rand's theories?

"Oscove?" Valek paused. "He didn't have the stomach for it."

8

WHEN I AWOKE THE NEXT morning, Valek's list of poisons was still clutched in my hand. I reviewed the poison inventory until the medic discharged me.

Bruised muscles protested every movement as I headed for the door. I should have been happy to leave the infirmary, but my nerves preoccupied me. My stomach felt as if it contained a live mouse, trying to chew its way out.

The guards stationed outside the infirmary door startled me. But they weren't wearing Brazell's colors, and I belatedly remembered that Valek had assigned them as protection until I reported to his office.

I glanced around to get my bearings, but had no idea which direction led to my room. I had been living in the castle for eighteen days, but I was still uncertain of its inner layout. The basic shape of the castle itself eluded me, having never seen it from the outside.

The prison carriage that had brought me to the castle had been a square box with airholes. I had refused to peer out like some caged animal. When I reached the castle, I squeezed my eyes shut in an attempt to block out the anguish of being chained, groped and dragged to the dungeon. I guess I could have focused on potential ways to escape, but I had accepted my punishment when I had killed Reyad.

As much as I hated to ask the guards for directions to my room, I had no choice. Wordlessly they guided me through the castle. One walked in front, the other followed. Only after the lead man inspected my room was I allowed inside.

My uniforms hung undisturbed in the armoire. But instead of being hidden inside a drawer, my journal lay open on the top of the desk. Someone had read my impressions of poisons and other information. The queasy feeling in my gut was replaced by a cold, hard sensation. The mouse had died, reflecting my sour mood perfectly.

I suspected Valek. He was bold enough to have gone through my personal papers. He had probably even reasoned that it was his duty to make sure I wasn't plotting something. After all, I was just the food taster, and not entitled to any privacy.

Grabbing the journal and uniforms, I left my room and headed for the baths. The guards waited outside while I soaked in the water. I took my sweet time. Valek and his test could wait; I wasn't going to carry out his orders like some idiotic drone.

Chased by Brazell's guards, finding poison in almost all of my meals, and being wagered on like some damn racehorse didn't cause me to be as angry as I was about Valek reading my journal.

Arriving at Valek's office, I cut off any smart remark he could make by demanding, "Where's your test?"

Amusement touched Valek's face. He rose from behind his desk. Sweeping his arm with a dramatic flourish, he indicated two rows of food and drinks on the conference table. "Only one item isn't poisoned. Find it. Then eat or drink your selection."

I tasted each item. I sniffed. I gargled. I held my nose. I took small bites. I spat. Some of the food had grown cold. Most of the meals were bland, making the poison easy to spot, while the fruit drinks masked the poison.

Finishing the last item, I turned to Valek. "You bastard. They're all poisoned." What a nasty trick; I should have suspected he would pull a stunt like that.

"Are you sure?"

"Of course. I wouldn't touch anything on that table."

Valek's gaze was stony as he walked toward me. "I'm sorry, Yelena. You've failed."

My heart plunged into my stomach. The dead mouse resuscitated and began to gnaw holes in my gut. I searched the table. What had I missed?

Nothing. I was right. I challenged Valek to prove me wrong.

Without hesitation he raised a cup. "This one is clean."

"Drink it." I remembered that cup. It was laced with a bitter poison.

Valek's hand wavered a bit. He sipped. I bit my lip. Maybe I was wrong. Maybe it was the cup next to it. Valek held my gaze as he rolled the liquid around his tongue. He spat.

I wanted to jump, to cheer, to dance little circles around him. Instead I said, "Blackberry poison."

"Yes," Valek said. He alternated between examining the cup in his hand and absentmindedly staring at the rows of cold food.

"I passed?"

He nodded, still distracted. Then he walked to his desk, and he gently placed the cup down. Shaking his head, he picked some papers up only to put them back unread.

"I should have known you would try to trick me."

My heated tone drew his eyes. I wished then that I'd remained silent.

"You're all fired up. And it isn't because of the test. Explain yourself."

"Explain? Why do *I* have to explain? Maybe *you* should explain why you read my journal." There, I'd said it.

"Journal?" Valek looked at me in amazement. "I didn't read anything of yours. But if I had, it would have been within my rights."

"Why?" I demanded.

An incredulous look settled on Valek's face. His mouth opened and closed several times before he was able to voice his thoughts. "Yelena, you confessed to murder. You were caught straddling Reyad's body with a bloody knife in your hand. I searched your file for a motive. There was none. Only a report that you refused to answer all questions."

Valek stepped closer. He lowered his voice. "Since I don't know what motivates you to kill, I can't predict if you'll do it again or what might set you off. I'm bound by the Code of Behavior, so I had to offer you the choice of becoming the new taster." He drew a deep breath and continued. "You'll be very close to the Commander on a daily basis. Until I can trust you, I'll be watching you."

My anger leaked away. Why should I expect Valek to trust me when I didn't trust him?

My composure returned. "How do I win your trust?"

"Tell me why you killed Reyad."

"You're not ready to believe me."

Valek averted his gaze to the conference table. I covered my mouth with my hand. Why had I used the word *ready?* Ready implied that he would believe me at some point. Pure wishful thinking on my part.

"You're right," he said.

We seemed to be at an impasse.

"I passed your test. I want my antidote."

Roused into action, Valek drew a dose, handing it to me.

"Now what?" I asked.

"Lunch! We're late." He hustled me out the door. I gulped the white liquid as we moved.

As we neared the throne room, the noise of many voices speaking at once echoed through the halls. Two of the Commander's advisers were arguing. Officers and soldiers clumped behind the two advisers. The Commander leaned against a nearby desk, listening intently.

The group debated the best way to locate and recapture a fugitive. The right side insisted upon using an oversupply of soldiers and tracking dogs, while the left claimed that a few clever soldiers would work. Brute force versus intelligence.

The exchange, while loud, lacked anger. The guards stationed around the room stood relaxed. Surmising that this type of debate was common, I wondered if the fugitive was a real person or just part of a hypothetical exercise.

Valek moved next to the Commander. I stood behind them. The debate made me squirm because I couldn't help imagining myself as the poor soul being hunted.

I pictured myself running through the woods, out of breath, and straining to hear the sounds of pursuit. Unable to blend into a town because a new face would alert the soldiers on patrol. Bored soldiers whose only job was to watch, who were familiar with the town's inhabitants.

Every citizen of the Territory of Ixia had a specific job. After the takeover, everyone had been appointed an occupation. A citizen was allowed to move to a different town or Military District, but proper forms were required. A completed transfer request needed approval from the supervisor, and proof that a position was being held at the new address. Without the proper documents, a civilian found in the wrong neighborhood was arrested. Visiting other districts was acceptable, but again only as long as the proper papers were obtained and shown to the soldiers on arrival.

While working in isolation with Brazell and Reyad, I had obsessively thought about escape. Thinking of freedom had been better than dwelling on my life as a laboratory rat. With no family or friends outside the manor to hide me, though, the southern lands were my best option, assuming I could penetrate the well guarded border.

I had created elaborate fantasies of stealing away to Sitia, finding an adoptive family and falling in love. Corny, sentimental rubbish, but it was my only elixir. Every day when the experiments began, my mind would focus on Sitia, finding bright colors, loving gestures and warmth. Holding those images in my mind, I endured Reyad's tests.

But even if I had been given the opportunity to escape, I don't know if I would have seized it. Although I remembered nothing of my birth family, I did have a family living within the manor house. The other lost children who had been taken in. My sisters. My brothers. My children. I learned with them, I played with them and I took care of them. How could I abandon them? To think of May or Carra taking my place was too much to bear.

I bit on my finger until I tasted blood, and dragged my thoughts back to the present. I had escaped from Brazell. He would leave the castle in two weeks and return home, probably to the next round of experiments with a different laboratory rat. My heart went out to her, whoever she was. Brazell was brutal. She was in for a rough time. But I had saved her from Reyad.

Pulling my hand away from my mouth, I inspected the bite mark. Not too deep, it wouldn't scar. I traced the network of semicircular scars that covered my fingers and knuckles. When I looked up, I caught Valek staring at my hands. I laced them behind my back.

The Commander raised his hand. Quiet descended in an instant. "Excellent points from both sides. We will put your theories to the test. Two teams." Pointing to the two main debaters, the Commander said, "You'll be the Captains. Assemble your team and organize a plan of attack. Recruit as needed. Valek will supply a fugitive from one of his men. You have a fortnight to prepare."

The noise level rose as the Commander headed toward his office with Valek and I close behind.

Valek shut the office door, muffling the commotion. "Is Marrok's escape to Sitia still bothering you?" he asked.

The Commander frowned. "Yes. Sloppy work, that pursuit. Marrok must have known you were in MD–8. You really need to train a couple of protégés."

Valek looked at him in mock horror. "But then I wouldn't be indispensable."

A quick smile graced the Commander's face, before he spotted me lingering near the corner. "Well, Valek, you were right about this one. She survived your test." Then to me, he said, "Come here."

My feet obeyed despite my hysterical heart.

"As my official food taster, you're to report to me with my breakfast. I'll give you my daily itinerary and expect you to be present at each meal. I will not accept tardiness. Understand?"

"Yes, Sir."

He glanced at Valek. "She looks fragile. Are you sure she's strong enough?"

"Yes, Sir."

The Commander appeared unconvinced. His golden eyes

tracked from me to Valek as he contemplated. I hoped with desperation that he wasn't looking for an excuse to fire me.

"All right. Since I missed lunch, Valek, you will join me for an early dinner. Yelena, you start as my food taster tomorrow morning."

"Yes, Sir," Valek and I said in unison. We were dismissed.

We returned to Valek's office to gather my extra uniforms and journal. Valek escorted me to his living quarters, located in the central part of the castle. As we traveled the main hallways, I noticed that the bright areas of stone on the wall outnumbered the darker zones. A vast array of paintings must have been taken down. We also passed several large, colorless rooms that had been redesigned as either offices or barracks.

It occurred to me that the Commander's functional style and stark standards had robbed the castle of its soul. All that remained was a dead stone building reassigned to purely utilitarian purposes.

I was too young to remember what life was like before the takeover, but I had been taught in Brazell's orphanage that the monarchy had been corrupt and its citizens unhappy. The takeover had been just that; to call it a war would be inaccurate. Most of the King's soldiers had switched loyalty to the Commander. They had been disgusted with promotions based on bribery and blood ties instead of hard work and skill. Orders to kill people for minor infractions because a member of the elite was angry caused sour feelings among the men.

Women had been recruited to the Commander's cause, and they made excellent spies. Valek assassinated the key supporters of the King. When the King tried to raise an army to fight the Commander's army, he had no defenders. The Commander captured the castle without a fight, and little blood was shed. Most of the nobility had been killed, but a few had escaped to Sitia.

Valek and I arrived at a pair of massive wooden doors, guarded by two soldiers. Valek spoke with the guards, instructing them that I was to be allowed access as needed. We entered a short hallway with two doors on opposite sides. Valek unlocked the door on the right and explained to me that the other led to the Commander's apartment.

Valek's living quarters turned out to be an expansive suite of rooms. Coming in from the gloomy hallway, I was struck by the brightness of the main, L-shaped living area. Windows as thin as a tiger's stripes allowed sunlight to pour in.

Piles of books occupied every corner and tabletop. Hand-size gray rocks, streaked with white, and multicolored crystals were scattered throughout.

Small black statues of animals and flowers glinted with silver. The statues dotted the room. Delicate and intricately detailed, they were similar to the panthers on Valek's office desk, and were the room's only decoration.

A considerable collection of weapons hung on the walls. Some of the weapons were old, dust-covered antiques that hadn't been used in years, while others shined. One long, thin knife still had fresh blood on the blade. The crimson liquid gleamed in the sunlight, causing a chill to snake through my body. I wondered who had been on the wrong end of that blade.

To the left of the entrance was a stairway, and three doors lined the right wall of the living area.

Valek pointed to the first door on the right. "That room is yours until Brazell leaves the castle. I suggest you get some rest." He picked up three books from an end table. "I'll be back later. Don't go out. I'll bring you dinner." Valek left, but then came back before the door shut. "Lock the door behind me. You should be safe here."

Safe, I thought, turning the bolt, was the last thing I could ever feel here. Anyone who knew how to pick a lock could sneak in, grab a weapon and have at me. I examined the swords on the wall, and sighed with some relief. The weapons were anchored securely. I tugged hard on a mace, just to be sure.

The clutter surrounding my door was thicker than around the other two, and I discovered why when I entered. Clean, box-shaped areas were outlined by the thick dust that still coated the floor, bed, bureau and desk. The room had been used for storage. Instead of cleaning it, Margg must have just moved the boxes out and considered her job done.

Margg's minimal work was a not so subtle hint of her vast dislike for me. Perhaps it would be best to avoid her for a while.

Inside the room, the bedding was filthy. A musty smell permeated. I sneezed. There was a small window, and after wrestling with the shutters, I managed to open it.

The furniture was made of expensive ebony. Intricate carvings of leaves and vines curled down chair legs and across drawers. When I wiped the dust off the headboard, I uncovered a delicate garden scene with butterflies and flowers.

After I stripped the bed of its dirty sheets and stretched out on the mattress, my impression of Margg as a harmless grump-with-a-grudge evaporated. At that moment I saw that a message had been written in the dust on the desk.

It read, "Murderer. The noose waits.

I VAULTED FROM THE BED. The message disappeared from view, but I didn't feel any better. Little darts of fear pulsed from my heart as my mind leaped from one horrible scenario to the next.

Was Margg warning or threatening me? Was she planning to earn the money she'd lost betting against me by turning me over to Brazell's goons for a fee?

But why warn me? I calmed myself. Once again I had overreacted. From what I'd seen and heard about Margg, her message was probably for the satisfaction of seeing me squirm. A peevish gesture because she was angry at having to do extra work for me. I decided it would be best not to give her any indication that I'd seen or had been affected by her childish note. Thinking back on it, I would bet that she had also read my journal, leaving it wide open on the desk just to annoy me.

Valek had suggested I rest, but I was on edge. I went into

Valek's living room. Margg's note had reminded me to stick to my instincts and not trust a soul. Then my worries would be minimized to tasting for poisons and avoiding Brazell.

If only it was that simple or I was that strong. Naiveté and blind trust may have been driven out of me by Brazell and Reyad, but deep down in the small corners of my heart I still clung to the hope that I might find a true friend.

Even a rat needs other rats. I could empathize with the rats. I, too, scurried around, looked over my shoulder and sniffed for poisoned traps.

Right now, I scrambled just to stay alive until the next day, but someday I would be searching for a way out. Knowledge was power, so I planned to sit tight, to listen and learn all I could. I started with Valek's living area. Lifting a rock off one of the tables, I began to pick my way through the clutter in his suite, surface snooping only because I suspected Valek would booby-trap his drawers.

I found a couple of texts on poisons that interested me, but their contents dealt mostly with assassination and intrigue. Some of the books had worn leather bindings and were written in an archaic language that I couldn't decipher. Valek was either a collector, or he had stolen the books from the dead King's library.

I was at the bottom of the stairs when I spotted a diagram of the castle's layout. It had been wedged into the corner of a picture frame hanging on the right wall of the staircase. Finally, something I could use. As I examined the map, I felt as if a translucent mask had been lifted off my face, allowing me to see the castle clearly.

Postponing my explorations of the rooms upstairs, I retrieved my journal. The map was displayed in full sight. Valek wouldn't be upset that I had seen it. He'd probably be happy that I didn't need to ask for directions every time I had to go somewhere new. I cleared a space on the couch, wormed into a comfortable position and began to copy the map.

I jerked awake. My journal slammed to the floor. Blinking in the candlelight, my eyes searched the room. I had been dreaming of rats. They had poured down from the walls, welled up from the floor and swarmed after me. A sea of biting rodents that seized clothes, skin and hair in their sharp little teeth.

A shudder shook my body. I lifted my feet off the floor as I scanned the room. No rats, unless I included Valek. He was halfway around the room, lighting the lanterns.

As I watched him finish, I thought about Valek being a fellow rat. No. Definitely not. A cat. And not just any ordinary, household cat, but a snow cat. The most efficient predator in the Territory of Ixia. Pure white, the snow cat was the size of two massive dogs fused together. Quick, agile and lethal, the snow cat killed before its prey even suspected danger. They stayed mostly in the north where the snow never melted, but had ventured south when food grew scarce.

No one in the history of Ixia had killed a snow cat. The predator either smelled, heard or saw the hunter before he could get close enough to strike with a handheld weapon. They bolted like lightning upon hearing the twang of a bowstring. The best the northern people could do was feed the cats, hoping to keep them on the snowpack and away from populated areas.

After lighting the last lantern, Valek turned toward me. "Something wrong with your room?" He picked up a tray and handed it to me.

"No. Couldn't sleep."

Valek snorted with amusement. "I see." He gestured toward the tray. "Sorry your dinner is cold. I was detained."

Automatically testing for poisons, I took a couple of small spoonfuls. I glanced at Valek to see if he was offended by the gesture. He was not. His face still held an amused expression. Between bites, I asked Valek if anyone else had a key to his suite.

"Just the Commander and Margg. Will that help you sleep better?"

Ignoring his question, I asked, "Is Margg your personal housekeeper?"

"Mine and the Commander's. We wanted someone we could trust. Someone instantly recognizable. She was with us before the takeover, so her loyalty is beyond doubt." Valek sat at his writing desk, but turned his chair to face me. "Remember when you were in the war room?"

Confused by the change in subject, I nodded.

"There were three Generals in the room. Brazell, you knew, but can you identify the other two?"

"Tesso and Hazal," I answered, proud that I had remembered.

"Can you describe them? Hair color? Eyes?"

I hesitated as I thought back. They had worn Generals' uniforms, and they had been eating lunch. I shook my head. "I think General Tesso had a beard."

"You identified them by their uniforms and didn't look at their faces. Correct?"

"Yes."

"That's what I thought. That's the problem with the uniform requirement. It makes a person lazy. A guard will see a housekeeping uniform and just assume that person belongs in the castle. It's too easy for someone to sneak about, which is why I keep the Commander surrounded at all times by loyal people. And why Margg is the only house-keeper permitted to clean the Commander's and my suites and offices."

Valek's tone made me feel as if I had been transported to a classroom. "Why not dismiss all the servants in the castle and use your own people?"

"Soldiers make up the majority of our army. Civilians who joined prior to the takeover were made advisers or given other prominent positions. Some of the King's servants were already on our payroll, and the others we paid double what they earned working for the King. Well-paid servants are happy servants."

"Does the entire castle's staff get paid?"

"Yes."

"Including the food taster?"

"No."

"Why not?" I hadn't even thought about receiving wages until Valek mentioned it.

"The food taster is paid in advance. How much is your life worth?"

10

NOT EXPECTING AN ANSWER, Valek swiveled back to his desk.

Ah, well, he had a point. I finished the cold food. When I set the tray aside to go to my room, Valek turned back to me.

"What would you buy with the money?"

A list rushed from my mouth, surprising even me. "A hair brush, nightclothes, and I'd spend some at the festival."

I wanted nightclothes because I was tired of sleeping in my uniform. I didn't dare sleep in my undergarments for fear I'd have to run for my life in the middle of the night. And the annual fire festival was approaching. It was sort of an anniversary for me. It had been during the previous fire festival that I had killed Reyad.

Although the Commander outlawed all forms of public religion, he encouraged the festivals as a form of boosting morale. Only two annual festivals were permitted.

I had been in the dungeon during the last ice festival, missing the indoor event where artists and craftsmen displayed their work. The ice festival was always held during the cold season when there was nothing to do but huddle by the fire and make crafts. It was a local event with each town hosting its own festival.

The fire festival was a massive carnival that traveled from town to town during the hot season. The festival began in the far north, where the warm weather lasted a few short weeks, and then wound its way south.

Traditionally, additional performances and contests were scheduled for the weeklong celebration at the castle in the middle of the hot season, and I was hoping I might be permitted to attend. Valek had indicated to me that he would be teaching me additional tasting techniques in the afternoons, but the rest of the time between meals had, so far, been mine.

I had always loved going to the fire festival. Brazell had given the children in his orphanage a small allowance so we could go each year. It had been the most anticipated event at Brazell's manor house. We would practice all year to qualify for the various contests, and save every penny possible for the entry fee.

Valek's practical voice interrupted my thoughts. "You can get some nightclothes from the seamstress, Dilana. She should have included them with your uniforms. As to the rest, you'll have to make do with what you can find."

Valek's words brought home the realities of my life; meaning fire festivals were not included. I might get a chance to see the festival, but I wouldn't be able to sample the spicy chicken steaks or taste the wine.

Sighing, I picked up my journal and went into my room. A dry, warm breeze caressed my face. I cleaned the rest of the dust, but I only wiped away half of Margg's message. She had been right in a way. The noose did wait for me. A normal life was not in my future. Her message would serve as a reminder to me to not get too comfortable.

I was either going to screw up and be replaced as the food taster, or I was going to foil an assassination attempt with my own death. I might not technically die from a broken neck, but the haunting image of an empty noose would always plague me.

The next morning I hovered outside Dilana's workroom. She sat in a small patch of sunlight, humming and sewing. Her golden curls gleamed. Unwilling to disturb her, I turned to go.

"Yelena?" she called.

I stepped back into view.

"My goodness, girl, just come in. You're always welcome." Dilana put her sewing down, and patted the chair next to her. When I joined her in the sunlight, she exclaimed, "You're as thin as my finest thread. Sit. Sit. Let me get you something to eat."

My protests didn't stop her from bringing me a large slice of buttered bread.

"My Rand sends me a steaming loaf of honey bread every morning." Her light brown eyes glowed with affection.

I knew she would stand over me until I took a bite. Not wanting to hurt her feelings, I suppressed my desire to taste the bread for poisons. Only when my mouth was full was she satisfied.

"How can I help you?" she asked.

Between bites, I asked about nightclothes.

"My goodness! How could I have forgotten? You poor dear." She bustled around the room, assembling quite a collection.

"Dilana," I said to stop her. "I only need a few things."

"Why didn't you come sooner? Margg should have said something to me." Dilana was genuinely upset.

"Margg," I began, then quit. I wasn't sure how Dilana felt about her.

"Margg's a mean old grump, a spiteful hag and an overgrown bully," Dilana declared.

I blinked at her in surprise.

"She instantly dislikes anyone new, and she's basically a plague on the rest of us."

"But she was nice to you."

"She hounded me for weeks after I first arrived. Then I snuck into her wardrobe and tightened all her skirts. It took her two weeks of physical discomfort to figure out what was happening." Dilana swooped down next to me, smiling. "Margg can't sew a stitch, so she had to tuck in her pride and ask for my help. Since then she's treated me with respect."

Dilana grabbed my hand in hers. "Unfortunately, you're her new target. But don't let her get to you. If Margg's nasty, be nasty right back. When she sees you're not easy prey, she'll lose interest."

I had trouble believing that this lovely woman was capable of such underhandedness, but her smile held a glimmer of mischief.

She draped a pile of nightclothes over my arms, and added an array of brightly colored ribbons.

"For the festival, my dear," she said, answering my quizzical look. "To augment your beautiful dark hair."

"Have you found a fugitive for the exercise?" the Commander asked Valek as soon as Valek arrived in his office for lunch.

I was tasting the Commander's food when Valek once again destroyed my tentative sense of well-being. Granted, I had been working as the official food taster for the last ten days, but my stomach had finally stopped its painful contractions whenever I was near the Commander.

"Yes. I know the perfect person for the job." Valek settled into the chair facing the Commander.

"Who?"

"Yelena."

"What!" Having given up all pretense of minding my own business, my exclamation echoed the Commander's.

"Explain," the Commander ordered.

Valek smiled at his reaction as though he knew all along what the Commander would say. "My people are trained to avoid capture. Assigning one of them wouldn't be fair to the search party. Therefore, we need a person not skilled in the art of evasion, but who is intelligent enough to bring some challenge to the exercise."

Valek stood to continue his lecture. "The fugitive needs an incentive for a good chase, yet must return to the castle. I can't use a real prisoner. None of the servants have any imagination. I briefly considered the medic, but she's needed here in case of emergencies. I was about to assign one of your soldiers when I thought of Yelena."

Valek gestured toward me. "She's smart." He counted with his fingers to emphasize his words. "She'll have an incentive to perform well, and an incentive to return."

"Incentives?" A frown creased the Commander's face.

"The food taster receives no wages. But for this extra job, and others like it in the future, she can be paid. The longer she evades capture, the higher the payment. As for the incentive to return, that should be obvious."

It was to me. The daily antidote to Butterfly's Dust kept me alive. If I didn't return to the castle by the next morning, they would be searching for a corpse.

"And if I refuse?" I asked Valek.

"I'll recruit one of the soldiers. But I'll be disappointed. I thought you would appreciate the challenge."

"Maybe I don't…"

"Enough." The Commander's voice was curt. "It's preposterous, Valek."

"That's the whole point. A soldier would make predictable moves. She's an unknown."

"*You* might outguess our fugitive, but the people I've assigned to the exercise aren't that quick. I'm hoping to find someone who can be trained as your assistant. I understand what you're waiting for, but I don't believe it'll happen anytime soon. We need someone now." The Commander sighed. It was the most emotion I'd witnessed from him. "Valek, why do you constantly undermine my orders to instruct an assistant?"

"Because so far I have disagreed with your choices. When the suitable candidate appears, then all efforts to train him will be fully endorsed."

The Commander glanced at the tray in my hands. Taking the food, he ordered me to fetch some hot tea. A thinly disguised ruse to be rid of me while they argued. I was more than happy to oblige.

On my way to the kitchen, I mulled over the possibility of playing fugitive for Valek. My first reaction had been negative; I didn't need any more problems. But as I contemplated the challenge of eluding searchers, combined with the chance to earn some money, the exercise started to look like an excellent opportunity. By the time I reached the kitchen, I hoped Valek would win. Especially since I would be outside the castle for a day, and any skills I learned from being a fugitive might prove useful in the future.

"Something wrong with lunch?" Rand asked, hurrying toward me, concern pulling the corners of his mouth tight.

"No. Just need some hot tea."

Relief softened his face. I wondered why he was so worried that lunch had been unsatisfactory. An image of a younger Rand rebelling against the Commander by ruining food as a form of sabotage entered my mind. I dismissed the thought. Rand wouldn't serve inferior food; his ego centered on his edible creations. There must be something else between him and the Commander. Uncertain that our new relationship would survive asking personal, perhaps sensitive, questions, I held my tongue.

I'd known Rand for almost two weeks now, but I still hadn't figured him out. His moods ran the gamut and changed without notice. Rand liked to talk. He dominated most conversations and asked only a few personal questions. I doubted he really heard my answers before he rambled on again.

"While you're here," Rand said, pulling a white cake from one of the cooling racks that hung on the wall like shelves, "can you try this? Let me know what you think."

He cut me a slice. Iced with whipped cream, the layers of vanilla cake were separated by a mixture of raspberries and cream.

I tried to mask that my first bite tasted for poison. "Good combination of flavors," I said.

"It's not perfect, but I can't pinpoint the problem."

"The cream is a little too sweet," I said, taking another bite. "And the cake is slightly dry."

"I'll try again. Will you come back tonight?"

"Why?"

"I need an expert opinion. It's my entry for the fire festival's baking contest. Are you going?"

"I'm not sure." When I had mentioned the festival the other night, Valek hadn't said that I couldn't go.

"A bunch of us from the kitchen are going. You can come with us if you want."

"Thanks. I'll let you know."

On my way back to the Commander's office, an unpleasant thought wove its way into my mind. I had been staying close to Valek because Brazell was still in the castle and wasn't slated to leave until after the festival. If I played fugitive, what would happen if Brazell found out? What if I accidentally encountered him at the festival?

Coming to the conclusion that I was safer within the castle walls until Brazell left, I decided to decline both Valek's and Rand's offers. But by the time I delivered the tea to the Commander, Valek had already won his argument. He quoted cash incentives to me before I could say a word.

The sum for remaining "free" for an entire day was a large amount.

"The exercise is scheduled to take place during the fire festival. A busy time for the soldiers. Should we postpone it until after?" Valek asked the Commander.

"No. The added commotion will increase the level of difficulty for our pursuers."

"Well, Yelena, that gives you only a few days to prepare. Fair enough, since some prisoners plan an escape route, while others see an opportunity and bolt. Are you interested in the challenge?" Valek asked.

"Yes." The word sprang from my gut before the rational

"no" in my mind could escape. "On the condition that Brazell not be informed of my participation."

"Isn't having a room in my personal suite an indication that I'm properly concerned with your well-being?" Valek's voice huffed. I realized that I had insulted him.

When I had offended Rand, I quickly tried to make amends. With Valek, I tried to think of another comment to annoy him further, but I couldn't produce one that quick.

"Speaking of Brazell," the Commander interrupted. "He gave me a gift. A new dessert that his chef invented. He thought I might like it."

Commander Ambrose showed us a wooden box full of thick, brown squares stacked on top of each other like tiles. They were smooth and shiny, but the edges looked as if they had been cut with a dull knife, ragged and shedding brown flakes.

Valek picked up a piece and sniffed it. "I hope you didn't try any."

"It's too blatant, even for Brazell, to be poisoned. But, no. I didn't."

Valek handed the container to me. "Yelena, take some pieces out at random and taste them."

I sorted through the squares and selected four. They were each about the size of my thumbnail and all four fit on the palm of my hand. If I hadn't been told they were a dessert, I probably would have guessed they were pieces of brown candle wax. My fingernail left an impression on the top, and my fingertips felt slightly greasy after handling them.

I hesitated. These were from Brazell, and I didn't remember his cook being especially inventive. I shrugged off my trepidation. I had no choice.

Thinking wax, I anticipated tasting wax. I bit into the hard cube expecting it to crumble between my teeth. It must have been the expression on my face that caused the Commander to rise, because I didn't say a word. The sensations in my mouth had me enraptured.

Instead of crumbling, the dessert melted, coating my tongue with a cascade of flavor. Sweet, bitter, nutty and fruity tastes followed one another. Just when I thought I could say it was one, I would taste them all again. This was unlike anything I had ever encountered. Before I knew it, all four cubes were gone. I longed for more.

"Unbelievable! What is it?"

Valek and the Commander exchanged puzzled looks.

The Commander said, "Brazell called it Criollo. Why? Is there poison in it?"

"No. No poisons. It's just…" The proper words to describe it failed me. "Try it," was all I could manage.

I watched the Commander's face as he bit into one of the squares. His eyes widened and his eyebrows arched in surprise. His tongue dashed along his lips and teeth as he tried to suck all the remaining flavor from them. He grabbed another piece.

"It's sweet. Different. But I don't taste anything unbelievable about it," Valek said, wiping the brown flakes from his hands.

It was my turn to exchange looks with the Commander.

Unlike Valek, he had an appetite for fine cuisine. He recognized excellence when he tasted it.

"I'll bet that little rat won't last an hour," Margg's muffled voice said through the kitchen door. I had been about to enter when I had heard her.

"I'll give fifty to one to anyone stupid enough to think the rat'll last the day. And one hundred to one to the sucker who thinks she won't be caught." After Margg called the odds, the room erupted with sounds of betting.

I listened with growing horror. Margg couldn't be talking about me. Why would Valek tell Margg about the exercise? It'd be all over the castle by tomorrow. Brazell would find out.

"I'll bet a month's wages that Yelena stays free all day," Rand's voice boomed out. The rest of the kitchen staff grew quiet.

My emotions seesawed from betrayal to pride. They were betting on me, and I couldn't believe Rand had bet a month's wages. He had more confidence in me than I did in myself. I tended to agree with Margg on this one.

Margg's laughter echoed on the tiled walls. "You've been in the kitchen too long, Rand. The heat's cooked your brain to mush. I think you're starting to like the little rat. Better lock up your knives when she's here or she may…"

"All right, that's enough," Rand said. "Dinner's over. Everyone out of my kitchen."

I moved down the hallway and out of sight. Since I had promised Rand I would taste his cake, I looped back to the kitchen after everyone had gone. Rand was sitting at one of the tables chopping nuts. There was a slice of his raspberry-and-cream cake on the table.

He pushed the plate to me. I tasted it.

"Much better. The cake is incredibly moist. What's different?" I asked.

"I added pudding to the batter."

Rand was unusually quiet. He didn't mention the betting. I wasn't going to ask.

He finished chopping the nuts. After cleaning up, he said, "I better get some sleep. We're going to the festival tomorrow night. Are you coming?"

"Who's going?" I stalled. I hated to miss out on the first night of the festival. Hated to let Brazell ruin the only fun I'd have. Although, if Margg was going as well, I'd stay with my original decision.

"Porter, Sammy, Liza and maybe Dilana." Rand's tired eyes lit up ever so slightly when he said Dilana's name. "Why?"

"When are you leaving?" Again my heart was ready to overrule the logical and safe choice.

"After dinner. It's the only time everyone is free. The Commander always orders an easy meal for the first night of festival so the kitchen staff can leave early. If you want to come, just meet us here tomorrow."

Rand headed to his rooms, which were adjacent to the kitchen, and I went back to Valek's suite.

The dark apartment was empty. Locking the door, I groped around and found some flint. As I lit the lanterns, I passed by Valek's desk and noticed a paper lying on top. Glancing around to make sure Valek wasn't hiding in the shadows, I looked at the sheet. Names had been written on it, and then scratched out. My name had been circled. Underneath was the comment that I would make a perfect fugitive for the exercise.

This was probably how Margg had known. I remembered seeing her reading papers in Valek's office before. Depending on how long these papers had been here, she could have known for a while. That woman was going to get me killed. If I survived long enough, I'd have to face her. Unfortunately, it would have to wait until after I played fugitive for Valek.

As for my escape plan, I searched through Valek's piles of books. I remembered seeing some appropriate titles, and I was rewarded by finding two on the techniques of pursuit, and one on the best ways to elude capture. Nobody said I couldn't do a little research. Borrowing Valek's texts, I took a lantern and retired to my room.

I studied the books until my vision blurred with fatigue. Changing into my new nightclothes, I extinguished the lantern and collapsed into bed.

I was jolted awake by the frightening awareness that someone was in my room. Instant, sweat-soaked fear gripped me. A black shape loomed over me. Yanked out of bed, I slammed into the wall. One, two, three gasps passed. Nothing more happened. The assault had stopped, but I remained pinned.

My eyes adjusted to the dark. I recognized my attacker's face. "Valek?

II

VALEK'S FACE, INCHES FROM mine, resembled a statue, silent, cold and devoid of emotion. My door had been left ajar, and even the faint glow of lantern light slipping through the gap at the threshold couldn't lend his blue eyes any warmth.

"Valek, what's wrong?"

Without warning, he released me. Too late I realized that he had held me suspended above the floor. I landed in a heap at his feet. Wordless, Valek left my room. I staggered upright, feeling as if I had too many arms and legs, and managed to catch up to him in the living room. He stood in front of his desk.

"If this is about the books…" I said to his back, guessing that he was angry with me for borrowing his manuals.

He turned. "Books? You think this is about books?" His voice held amazement for a brief moment before it turned sharp and cutting. "I've been a fool. All this time I admired your survival instincts and intelligence. But now…" He paused, and then looked around the room as if searching for the right words.

"I overheard some servants discussing you as the fugitive. They were placing wagers. How could you be so stupid, so indiscreet? I considered killing you now to save myself the trouble of hunting for your dead body later."

"I didn't tell a soul." I allowed anger to color my voice. "How can you think I would jeopardize my own life?"

"Why should I believe you? The only other person who knew was the Commander."

"Well, Valek, you're the spymaster. Couldn't someone have overheard the conversation? Who else has access to this room? You left your notes in full view on your desk." Before he could leap to another wrong conclusion, I hurried on. "They were conspicuous. If I noticed them with just a quick glance, then they begged for inspection to someone seeking information."

"What are you saying? Who are you accusing?"

A ridge of flesh grew above Valek's nose as his eyebrows pinched together. Alarm flashed across his face before being doused by his stone guise. His fleeting expression told me a great deal. Either Valek had been so convinced that I had gossiped to the servants that he hadn't considered other options, or he couldn't accept the possibility of a breach in his security. For once I had thrown him off balance, if only for a second. Someday I would dearly love to see him in an ungainly heap at my feet.

"I have my suspicions," I said. "But I'll accuse nobody without proof. It's unfair, and who would believe me?"

"No one." Valek snatched a gray rock from his desk and hurled it toward me.

Stunned, I froze as the stone whizzed past and exploded on the wall behind me. Gray debris pelted my shoulder and rained to the floor.

"Except me." He sank into a chair. "Either I'm addicted to risk or you're starting to make sense and we have a leak. An informer, a gossip, a mole. Whoever he is, we need to find him."

"Or her."

Valek frowned. "Do we play it safe and find another fugitive? Or cancel the exercise? Or continue as planned and make you both fugitive and bait? Enticing our spy to reveal himself." He grimaced. "Or herself."

"You don't think Brazell will come after me?"

"No. It's too soon. I don't expect Brazell to try to kill you before his factory is up and running. Once he gets what he wants, then it's going to get interesting around here."

"Oh good. I can barely stay awake now from all the boredom." My voice dripped with sarcasm. Only Valek would consider an attempt on my life a fascinating diversion.

He ignored my remark. "It's your choice, Yelena."

My choice wasn't contained in one of Valek's scenarios. My choice was to be someplace where my life wasn't in danger. My choice was to be where I didn't have an assassin for a boss, and some unknown person trying to make my already intense life even more complicated. My choice was freedom.

I sighed. The safer course of action was the most tempting, but it wouldn't solve anything. I had learned the hard way that avoiding problems didn't work. Run and hide were my trademark impulses, which only led to being trapped in a corner with no recourse other than to blindly strike out.

The results were not always favorable. The lack of control unnerving. My survival instinct seemed to have a mind of its own. Magic. The word floated at the edge of my mind. No. Someone would have noticed by now. Someone would have reported me. Or would he if that someone was Brazell? Or Reyad?

I shook my head, banishing the thoughts. It was in the past. I had more immediate concerns. "Okay. I'll dangle on the hook to see what fish swims out. But who's going to hold the net?"

"I will."

I let out a slow breath. The tight feeling around my stomach eased.

"Don't alter your plans. I'll take care of everything." Valek picked up the paper with my name on it. He dipped the corner of the page into a lantern, setting it on fire. "I should probably follow you to the fire festival tomorrow night. Unless logic has made you decide to turn down Rand's offer and stay in the castle." He let the burning paper float to the floor.

"How did you—" I stopped. I wasn't going to ask. It was well known that he didn't trust Rand, so I shouldn't be surprised that Valek had an informant in the kitchen.

Valek hadn't said I couldn't go. I made a sudden decision. "I'm going. It's a risk. So what? I take a risk every time I sip the Commander's tea. At least this time I might get a chance to enjoy myself."

"It's hard to have fun at the festival without money." Valek crushed the dying embers of the paper under his boot.

"I'll manage."

"Would you like an advance on your wage as fugitive?"

"No. I'll earn the money." I didn't want Valek to do me any favors. I was unprepared for thoughtfulness from him. For Valek to soften even a little might destroy our strange tug-of-war relationship, and I was reluctant for it to alter. Besides, thinking kind thoughts about Valek could be extremely dangerous. I could admire his skills, and be relieved when he was on my side in a fight. But for a rat to like the cat? That scenario ended only one way. With one dead rat.

"Suit yourself," Valek said. "But let me know if you change your mind. And don't concern yourself about the books. Read all the books you want."

Heading back to my room, I paused with my hand resting on the doorknob. "Thanks," I spoke to the door, unwilling to look at Valek.

"For the books?"

"No. The offer." My eyes traced the wood grain.

"You're welcome."

The castle hummed with activity. Smiling servants rushed through the corridors, laughter echoed off the stone walls. It was the first day of the fire festival, and the castle's staff hurried to complete their chores so they could attend the opening cele-

bration. Their excitement was contagious, and even after a
restless night of sleep, I was beginning to feel like a child again.
Determined to push the ugly image of someone stalking me
at the festival to a far, dark corner of my mind, I allowed
myself to savor the anticipation of the evening's events.

I fidgeted through an afternoon lesson with Valek. He was
trying to teach me how to spot a tail. It was mostly common-
sense advice, and some techniques that I had already read about
in one of his books, and my mind wandered. I wasn't planning
on looking over my shoulder all night. Sensing my mood,
Valek ended the session early.

Soon after, I grabbed a clean uniform and the colored
ribbons Dilana had given me and headed toward the baths. At
this time of day, the steaming pools were empty. I washed fast,
and sank into one of the baths. Inching my way into the hot
liquid, I let each muscle relax, oohing and aahing until the
water reached my neck.

Only when the skin on my fingers began to wrinkle did I
leave the water. I had been avoiding the mirror for a month.
Now, curious, I scanned my reflection. Not as skeletal,
although I needed to gain some more weight. My cheeks were
hollow and my ribs and hipbones poked through my flesh.
What had once been dull, uncombable black hair now shone.
The scar on my right elbow had turned from bright red to a
deep purple.

Swallowing, I looked far into the mirror. Had my soul
returned? No. Instead, I saw Reyad's smirking ghost floating
behind me, but when I turned around he was gone. I

wondered what Reyad wanted. Revenge most likely, but how would you confront a ghost? I decided not to worry about it tonight.

Changing into a clean uniform, I braided the brightly colored ribbons into my hair, I let the ends fall past my shoulders and loosely down my back.

When I reported to the Commander to taste his dinner, I expected a tart comment on my unmilitary hairstyle. All I received was one raised eyebrow.

After dinner, I raced to the kitchen. Rand greeted me with a huge smile. The staff was still cleaning, so I helped scrub the countertops and floors to avoid the awkwardness of just standing around waiting. Rand reigned over an immaculate kitchen, and only when the kitchen was spotless was the staff dismissed.

While Rand changed out of his stained uniform, I watched a small group of people talking among themselves as they waited for him. I knew them all by sight and reputation, but hadn't spoken to any of them. Occasionally, one or two glanced warily in my direction. I suppressed a sigh, trying not to let their nerves bother me. I couldn't blame them. It wasn't a secret that I had killed Reyad.

Of the group, Porter was the oldest. He was in charge of the Commander's kennels. Another holdover from the King's reign, he had been deemed too valuable to be replaced. He scowled more than he smiled, and Rand was his only friend. Rand had told me stories about Porter in an "I can't believe anyone would believe such nonsense" tone of voice, but wild rumors that Porter had mental links with the dogs made him an outcast.

The uncanny way the dogs responded and understood Porter seemed abnormal. Almost magical. The suspicion of magic was enough for everyone to treat Porter like he had a contagious disease. Still no one had proof, and his rapport with the animals was useful. Something the Commander prized.

Sammy was Rand's fetch boy. A thin child of twelve, his sole purpose was to obtain anything Rand needed. I'd seen Rand yell at Sammy then hug him in the space of a heartbeat.

Liza was a quiet woman only a few years older than me. She was the castle's pantler, in charge of the pantry's inventory. Liza plucked at her uniform sleeve like she was nervous, but I guessed talking with Porter was better than being near me.

When Rand emerged from his rooms, we left the castle. Sammy raced ahead of the group, too excited to stay with us for very long. Porter and Liza continued their discussion, while Rand and I trailed behind.

The night air was refreshing. I could smell the clean scent of damp earth tinged with the distant aroma of wood smoke. It was my first trip outside in almost a year, and before we went past the gate in the immense, stone buttress that surrounded the castle complex, I peered back. Without a moon it was too dark to see any detail besides the few lighted windows and the towering walls. The complex appeared deserted. If Valek followed, I couldn't spot him.

When we cleared the gate, a breeze greeted us as the day's hot air cooled. I walked with my arms held slightly away from my body, allowing the air to flow past me. My uniform rippled in the wind and my hair blew. I inhaled, enjoying the fresh

evening scent. We walked through the grass field that surrounded the guard walls. No buildings were permitted within
a quarter mile of the castle. The town, once named for Queen
Jewel, was renamed Castletown after the takeover. Jewelstown
had been built by the King in the valley south of the castle
complex as a gift for his wife.

The fire festival's tents had been set up in the fields just west
of Castletown.

"Isn't Dilana coming?" I asked Rand.

"She's already there. Some big emergency came up this
afternoon. When the dancers opened the costume boxes
they discovered that some animal had eaten holes in all of
the outfits. They called Dilana to help mend them before
the opening ceremony." Rand laughed. "I bet the panic
that reigned after they opened the boxes would have been
fun to watch."

"Fun for you, but not for the poor woman in charge of
costumes."

"True." Now silent, he limped beside me. Because of our
slower pace, we fell farther behind the others.

"Where's your cake?" I hoped I hadn't ruined his good mood.

"Sammy ran it down this morning. The baking contest is
judged on the first day so they can sell the entries while they're
fresh. I want to check the results. How come you're not
entering any competitions?"

A simple question. One of many about the festival that I had
been avoiding with some success since Rand and I became
friends. At first I suspected his interest to be an attempt to gain

some insider information for the next round of betting. But now that the gambling was finished, I realized his interest was genuine.

"No money for the entry fees," I said. The truth, but not the entire story. I would need to completely trust Rand before I would tell him about my history with the fire festival.

Rand clucked his tongue in disgust. "It doesn't make sense not to pay the food taster. Otherwise, what better way to obtain information about the Commander than to bribe the taster?" He paused, then turned to me, his face serious. "Would you sell information for money?"

12

I SHIVERED AT RAND'S QUESTION. Was he asking just to ask or was he offering to pay me for information? I imagined Valek's reaction if he discovered that I had taken a bribe. Having no money was better than facing his wrath.

"No. I wouldn't," I said.

Rand grunted. We walked in an unnatural silence for a while. I wondered if Oscove, the old food taster, had taken money for information. It would explain why Valek hadn't liked him and why Rand suspected Valek of killing Oscove.

"If you'd like, I'll pay the entry fee for you. Your help has been invaluable, and I've certainly won enough money on your resourcefulness," Rand said.

"Thanks, but I'm not prepared. It'd be a waste of money." Besides, I was determined to enjoy the festival without money just to prove to Valek that it could be done.

Despite promising myself I wouldn't, I glanced back over my shoulder. Nothing. I tried to convince myself that not seeing Valek was a good thing. If I could spot him, then anyone could. Still, the nagging feeling that maybe he had decided to let me take my chances wouldn't quit. Stop it, I told myself. Don't worry. Then again, I'd be an idiot to walk around the festival blind to danger.

I felt as if I balanced on a high wire, trying not to fall. Could I watch for trouble and have fun at the same time? I didn't know, but was determined to try.

"Which competition would you have entered?" Rand asked.

Before I could answer, he waved his hands in front of me. "No! Don't tell me! I want to guess."

I smiled. "Go ahead."

"Let's see. Small, thin and graceful. A dancer?"

"Try again."

"Okay. You remind me of a pretty bird, willing to sit on the windowsill as long as nobody comes too close, but prepared to fly away if somebody does. A songbird. Perhaps you're a singer?"

"You've obviously never heard me sing. Are all your guesses going to come with a lengthy discussion of my personality?" I asked.

"No. Now be quiet, I'm trying to think."

The glow from the festival was growing brighter. I heard the distant buzz of music, animals and people blended together.

"Long, thin fingers. Maybe you're a member of a spinning team?" Rand guessed.

"What's a spinning team?"

"Usually there's one shearer, one carder, one spinner and one weaver in a team. You know, sheep to shawl. The teams race to see who can shear a sheep's wool and turn it into a garment first. It's pretty amazing to watch." Rand studied me for a while. I began to wonder if he had run out of guesses.

"A jockey?"

"Do you really think I could afford to buy a racehorse?" I asked in amazement. Only the very wealthy citizens had horses to race for sport. The military used horses for the transportation of high-ranking officers and advisers only. Everyone else walked.

"People who own racehorses don't ride them. They hire jockeys. And you're the perfect size, so stop looking at me like I'm daft."

As we arrived at the first of the massive multicolored tents, our conversation ceased as we absorbed the frenzied activity and panoramic sights that assaulted us. When I was younger, I used to stand amid the chaos and feast on the energy of the fire festival. I had always thought the name of the festival was perfect, not because it occurred during the hot season, but because the sounds and smells pulsated like heat waves, making my blood sizzle and pop. Now, after spending close to a year in a dungeon, I felt the force slamming into me as though I were a brick wall. A wall whose mortar threatened to crumble from the overload of sensations.

Torches blazed and bonfires burned. We walked into a slice of captured daylight. The performance and competition tents were scattered throughout the festival, with small open stands tucked in and around them like children clinging to their mothers' skirts. From exotic gems to flyswatters, the merchants sold an array of goods. The aroma of food cooking made my stomach grumble as we passed several barbecue pits, and I regretted having skipped dinner in my haste to get here.

Entertainers, contestants, spectators and laughing children ebbed and flowed around us. Sometimes the press of people hurried us along from behind and sometimes we struggled to go forward. We had lost track of the others. If he hadn't linked his arm in mine, I probably would have been separated from Rand as well. Distractions peppered the festival. I would have followed the lively music to its source or lingered to watch a skit, but Rand was determined to see the results of the baking contest.

As we moved, I examined faces in the crowd, searching for green-and-black uniforms even though Valek had said Brazell wouldn't be a threat. I thought it prudent to avoid him and his guards altogether. Unsure of who I was looking for, I watched for unusual faces. It was the wrong way to detect a tail. Valek had taught me that the best agents were unremarkable in appearance and didn't draw attention to themselves. But I figured if a skilled spy followed me, my chances of spotting him or her was small.

We met up with Porter and Liza in a small tent filled with a sweet aroma that made my stomach ache with hunger. They were talking to a large man in a cook's uniform, but they stopped when we entered. Surrounding Rand, they congratulated him on his first-place win. The heavy man declared that Rand had broken a festival record by winning five years in a row.

While Rand examined the array of baked goods lining the

shelves, I asked the man who had won in Military District 5. I was curious if Brazell's cook had won with his Criollo recipe. The man's brow creased with concentration, causing his short, curly black hair to touch his thick eyebrows.

"Bronda won it with a heavenly lemon pie. Why?"

"I thought General Brazell's chef, Ving, might win. I used to work at the manor."

"Well, Ving won two years ago with some cream pie and now he enters the same pie each year, hoping it'll win again."

I thought it odd that he hadn't entered his Criollo, but before I could deduce a reason, Rand jubilantly swept us out of the tent. He wanted to buy everyone a glass of wine to celebrate his victory.

We sipped our wine and wandered around the festival. Sammy materialized on occasion from the crowd to report some wonder with great delight, only to rush off again.

Twice I spotted a woman with a serious expression. Her black hair was pulled into a tight bun. Wearing the uniform of a hawk mistress, she moved with the grace of someone used to physical exercise. The second time I saw her she was much closer, and I made eye contact. Her almond-shaped, emerald eyes narrowed, staring boldly back at me until I looked away. There was something familiar about her, and it was some time before I figured it out.

She reminded me of the children in Brazell's care, and was more similar to my own coloring than to the pale ivory complexion of most of the Territory's people. Her skin was bronze. Not tanned from the sun but a natural pigmentation.

Then our aimless group was snared in a flow of spectators heading into a big red-and-white-striped tent. It was the acrobatics tent, where trampolines, tightropes and floor mats were covered with brightly costumed men and women. They were all trying to pass the qualifying round. I watched as one man performed a beautiful series of flips on the tightrope, only to be disqualified when he fell during his solo tumbling run.

Out of the corner of my eye I saw Rand watching me. His expression triumphant.

"What?" I asked.

"You're an acrobat!"

"I *was* an acrobat."

Rand waved his hands. "Doesn't matter. I was right!"

It mattered to me. Reyad had tainted acrobatics. The time when I felt satisfaction and enjoyment from performing was gone, and I couldn't imagine getting any happiness from it now.

From the benches in the tent, our small kitchen group watched the contestants. Grunts of effort, sweat-soaked costumes and thumping feet made me long for the days when all that worried me was finding time to practice.

Four of us in Brazell's orphanage had taken up acrobatics. We had scavenged and begged for materials to set up a practice area behind the stables. Our mistakes sent us crashing to the grass until the stable master took pity on our bruised bodies. One day we arrived to find a thick coating of dung-scented straw carpeting our practice area.

Brazell's teachers had encouraged us to discover something we could excel in. While some found singing or dancing to be their calling, I had been fascinated by the acrobatic displays since my first fire festival.

Despite hours of practice, I failed during the qualifying round at my inaugural competition. The disappointment stabbed my heart, but I healed the ache with resolve. I spent the next year covered with black-and-blue marks, nursing sprains too numerous to count. When the festival returned, I passed the qualifiers and the initial round only to fall off the tightrope in the second. Each year I worked hard and advanced steadily. I won through to the final round the year before Brazell and Reyad claimed me as their laboratory rat.

Brazell and Reyad didn't allow me to practice acrobatics, but that didn't stop me from slipping away whenever Reyad was on some mission for his father. What did stop me was getting caught by Reyad a week before the festival, when he arrived home early from a trip. I was concentrating so hard that I failed to notice him astride his horse until I finished my tumbling routine. His expression, a mixture of anger and elation, caused the beads of sweat on my skin to turn into ice crystals.

For disobeying his orders, I was forbidden to go to the festival that year. And as an added deterrent to disobedience, I was punished for the duration of the festival. Each evening for five nights, Reyad forced me to strip. With a cruel grin on his face, he stared at me as I stood shivering despite the warmth of the night. He draped heavy chains from a metal collar around my neck to metal cuffs on my wrists and ankles. I wanted to scream, to beat him with my fists, but I was too terrified to anger him further.

Pleasure at my fear and humiliation made his face flush as he drove me with a small whip to perform acrobatics of his own devising. A lashing sting on my skin was the reprimand for moving too slow. The chains battered my body as they swung with my movements. Their weight dragged at my limbs, making each tumble an exhausting ordeal. The cuffs began to rub my wrists and ankles raw. Blood streaked down my arms and legs.

When Brazell participated in the experiments, Reyad meticulously followed his father's instructions, but when he was alone with me the indifferent exercises turned vicious. Sometimes he would invite his friend, Mogkan, to assist him, and they made my hell a contest to see who invented the best way to test my endurance.

I was in constant fear that I would madden Reyad enough to force him to cross the only line he seemed to have drawn. For all the torture and pain he inflicted, he never raped me. So I somersaulted and cartwheeled with chains just to keep him from crossing that line.

Rand's heavy arm fell across my shoulders. I flinched back into the present.

"Yelena! What's wrong?" Rand's eyes, full of concern, searched mine. "You looked like you were having a nightmare with your eyes open."

"Sorry."

"Don't apologize to me. Here…" He handed me a steaming meat pie. "Sammy brought these for us."

I thanked Sammy. When my attention focused on him, his eyes grew wide, and his young face whitened. He averted his gaze. Without thinking, I took a small bite and tasted for poison. Finding nothing, I ate and wondered what wild stories had been told about me to cause Sammy's fearful reaction. Children Sammy's age usually enjoyed scaring each other with imaginative horror tales.

We used to frighten ourselves at the orphanage after the lanterns had been blown out and we were in bed waiting for sleep. Whispered stories about monsters raging and magician's curses made us gasp and giggle. We told gruesome tales about the older "graduates" of the orphanage, who just seemed to disappear. No explanation was given to us of where they were working, and we never encountered any of them in town or in the manor house. So we created horrible scenarios about their fates.

How I missed those nights with the other children when I was finally able to rest after spending a day with Reyad. He had isolated me from the others. Taken from the girls' dorm, I had been given a small room next to Reyad's suite. At night, with my body aching and my spirits crushed, I would lie awake and recite those tales in my mind until I fell asleep.

"Yelena, we can go."

"What?" I looked at Rand.

"If this is upsetting you. We can go. There's a spectacular new fire dance."

"We can stay. I was just…reminiscing. But if you want to see the fire dance, I'll go along."

"Reminiscing? You must have hated being an acrobat."

"Oh no, I loved everything about it. Flying through the

air, the complete control over my body as I spun and twirled. The thrill of knowing I was going to land the perfect dismount before I even hit the ground." I stopped. The confusion on Rand's face made me want to laugh and cry at the same time. How could I explain to him that it wasn't the acrobatics that upset me but the events that they had triggered? Reyad's cruel punishment for practicing. Sneaking out to participate in the festival the following year, which had led to Reyad's death.

I shuddered. Those memories of Reyad were like a trap in the corner of my mind, and I wasn't ready to spring it. "Someday, Rand, I'll explain. But for now I would like to see the fire dance."

He hooked his arm around mine as our kitchen group left the tent and joined in the flow of people. Sammy raced ahead, shouting over his shoulder that he would save us some good seats. A drunken man bumped into me and I stumbled. He mumbled an apology and saluted me with his mug of ale. Trying to make a bow, he landed in a heap at my feet. I would have stopped to help him, but I was distracted by the appearance of blazing staffs of wood. I felt a pulsating rhythm vibrating through the soles of my feet as the fire dancers spun the flaming props around their heads and paraded into the tent. Amazed by the dancers' intricate movements, I stepped over the drunk.

But with the excitement and press of people through the entrance, Rand's grip was broken. I wasn't concerned until I found myself surrounded by four immense men. Two of the men wore blacksmith's uniforms, while the other two wore farmer's work uniforms. Excusing myself, I tried to slip past them, but they only pressed closer, trapping me.

13

TERROR WELLED IN MY THROAT; I was in trouble. I screamed for help. A gloved hand clamped over my mouth. Biting into the leather, I tasted ashes, but couldn't reach skin. The blacksmiths grabbed my arms and pushed me forward, while the farmers walked in front, blocking me from sight. In all the commotion around the dance tent, nobody noticed my abduction.

I struggled, dragged my feet and kicked. Their pace never slowed. I was lugged farther away from the lights and safety of the festival. Craning my neck, I looked for a way to escape. The blacksmith next to me moved closer to block my meager view. His thick beard was filled with soot and half of it had been singed off.

We stopped behind a dark tent. The farmers stepped aside and I saw a shadow pull away from the fabric.

"Did anyone notice? Did anyone follow you?" the shadow asked with a woman's voice.

"It went perfect. Everyone was focused on the dancers," the blacksmith with the leather gloves replied.

"Good. Kill her now," the woman ordered.

A knife flashed in Leather Gloves's hand. I renewed my struggle, managing to break free for an instant. But the farmers pinned my arms while Singed Beard grabbed my legs. They held me suspended above the ground. Leather Gloves raised his weapon.

"No knives, you idiot! Think of the bloody mess. Use this." She handed Leather Gloves a long thin strap. In a blink the knife disappeared. He wrapped the garrote around my neck.

"Nooo…" I screamed, but my protest was cut off along with my air supply as he tightened the strap. Intense pressure squeezed my neck. I jerked my limbs in vain. White dots swirled before my eyes. A faint buzzing sound dribbled from my lips. Too faint; the survival instinct that had saved me from Brazell's guards and Reyad's torture was too weak this time.

Over the roar of blood in my ears, I heard the woman say, "Hurry up! She's starting to project."

Ready to step off the edge of consciousness, a drunken voice said, "Excuse me, sirs, do you know where I can get a refill?"

The pressure on my neck lessened as Leather Gloves drew his knife. I let my body go limp and was rewarded by being dumped on the ground. The other three men stepped over me to face the intruder. Suppressing the urge to gasp for breath, I sucked in air with desperation. I muffled my efforts, unwilling to let anyone know I could still breathe.

From my new position, I saw Leather Gloves lunge toward the drunk. The clang of metal rang through the air as the knife stabbed into the man's pewter beer mug instead of his chest. With a hard jerk of his wrist, the mug blurred into motion. The knife flew through the air, imbedding into the fabric of the tent. Then the drunk struck Leather Gloves on the head with the mug. Leather Gloves crumpled to the ground.

The others, mere steps away when their companion went down, rushed the intruder. The farmers grabbed his upper arms and shoulders while Singed Beard punched him twice in the face. Using the farmers to support his weight, the drunk lifted both legs off the ground and wrapped them around Singed Beard's neck. With a loud snap, Singed Beard fell.

Still clutching his mug, the drunk swung it to the right into one farmer's groin. As the farmer doubled over, the drunk brought the mug up, smashing it into the farmer's face.

Then the intruder swept his beer mug to the left and slammed it into the other farmer's nose. Blood gushing, the farmer yelped in pain and released his grip on the drunk. The drunk launched a second blow to the farmer's temple. The farmer collapsed to the ground without a sound.

The fight had lasted seconds. The woman hadn't moved at all, her intent gaze had been focused on the skirmish. Recognizing her as the dark-skinned woman I had spotted twice before at the festival, I wondered what she would do now that her goons were beaten.

Regaining some strength, I contemplated my odds of reaching the knife in the tent before she did. The drunk wiped blood off his face. Bodies were littered around his feet.

I tried to stand on shaky legs. The woman's head snapped toward me as if she had forgotten I was there. Then she started to sing. Her sweet, melodious tune wound its way through my mind. Relax, it said, lie down, be still. Yes, I thought as I sank back down. My body mellowed. I felt as if she were tucking me into bed, drawing the blanket up to my chin. But then the blanket was yanked over my head, pushing against my mouth and nose, suffocating me.

I thrashed, wildly clawing my face to remove the imaginary blanket. Out of nowhere, Valek appeared before me, yelling in my ear, shaking my shoulders. Stupidly, belatedly, I realized he was the drunk. Who else but Valek could win a fight against four large men when armed only with a beer mug?

"Recite poisons in your mind!" Valek shouted.

I ignored him. Lassitude overcame me. I ceased fighting. All I wanted to do was sink into the darkness and follow the music to its depths.

"Recite! Now! That's an order!"

Habit saved me. Without thought, I obeyed Valek. Names of poisons marched through my mind. The music stopped. The pressure on my face eased, and I could breathe again. I gasped noisily.

"Keep reciting," he said.

The woman and the knife had disappeared. Valek pulled me to my feet. I swayed, but he steadied me with an arm on my shoulder. I clutched his hand for a second, suppressing the urge to throw myself sobbing into his arms. He had saved my life. When I regained my balance, Valek went back to the men. I knew Singed Beard was dead, but I was unsure of the others.

Valek turned one prone form over and cursed. "Southerners," he said with disgust. He moved around the others, feeling for pulses. "Two alive. I'll have them taken to the castle for questioning."

"What about the woman?" I croaked. Talking was painful.

"Gone."

"Will you search for her?"

Valek gave me a strange look. "Yelena, she's a southern magician. I took my eyes off her, so there's no way I can find her now."

He grabbed my arm and steered me toward the festival.

My muscles trembled as the shock of the attack worked through my body. It took a while for his words to sink in.

"Magician?" I asked. "I thought they were banished from Ixia." Killed on sight was more like it, but I couldn't bring myself to say those words aloud.

"Although very unwelcome, some visit Ixia anyway."

"But, I thought…"

"Not now. I'll explain later. Right now I want you to catch up with Rand and his friends. Pretend nothing has happened. I doubt she'll try again tonight."

The bright firelight stabbed my eyes. Valek and I stayed in the shadows until we spotted Rand near the acrobatics tent.

He was searching for me and calling my name. Valek motioned for me to join my friend.

I had taken only two steps when Valek said, "Yelena, wait."

I turned. Valek waved me closer. When I reached him, his hand reached toward my neck. I stepped back, but recovered and stood still. His hand brushed my skin as he pulled the garrote off my throat. He handed it to me as if it was a poisonous snake. Shivering in disgust, I flung it to the ground.

Rand's relief, when he saw me emerge from the crowd, rolled off him like a breaking wave. I hesitated. Why would he be so concerned? For all he knew, I had only been lost. I caught a sweet whiff of wine as Rand approached.

"Yelena, where have you been?" His words slurred.

I hadn't realized he had drunk that much wine, which would explain why he had been so desperate to find me. Alcohol poisoned the mind, exaggerated the emotions.

"The tent was too crowded. I needed some air." My voice caught on the word *air* as the horror of being strangled swept through me. I glanced back at the shadows. Was Valek still watching or had he gone to arrest those men? And where was the dark-skinned woman? Earlier, I had been so happy to get out of the castle, but now I wanted nothing more than to have strong stone walls around me, and to be safely back in Valek's suite. Now, *that* was an odd combination, the words *Valek* and *safe* in the same thought.

"I thought I'd catch up with you later," I lied to Rand as I scanned the festival crowd. I didn't enjoy deceiving him. After all, he was my friend. Maybe even a good friend who had been

concerned enough to search for me when I had been separated from him, and who probably would have been the only
person to be upset by my murder. Despite his fight on my
behalf, I was certain that Valek would have only been annoyed
at having to train a new food taster.

The fire dance had just ended and people poured from the
tent. The rest of the kitchen group waited outside. Dilana had
joined them. Rand dropped my arm like a lump of dough and
went over to her. She smiled at him, teasing him about chasing
after the food taster when he had promised to meet her.

Drunkenly, he begged for her forgiveness, explaining that
he couldn't afford to lose me since I had helped him win the
baking contest. She laughed. Throwing one of her heartwarm-
ing smiles my way, Dilana hugged Rand, and arm in arm they
headed back to the castle.

The rest of us followed. I found myself once again last in
the procession, but this time I had Liza as a companion.

She scowled at me. "I don't know what Rand sees in you,"
she said.

Not a friendly way to start a conversation. "Excuse me," I
said, keeping my tone neutral.

"He missed the fire dance looking for you. And ever since
you came around, the kitchen routine has been destroyed.
The staff's flustered."

"What are you talking about?"

"Before you showed up, Rand's mood swings were predictable. Cheerful and content when Dilana was happy and
the gambling was profitable, moody and sullen when they

weren't. Then…" Liza stressed the word. Her plain cornmeal face creased into an ugly expression, which she aimed at me. "You befriend him. He starts snarling at the kitchen staff for no reason. Even winning a big payoff, Rand's still depressed. It's frustrating. We've come to the conclusion that you must be trying to steal him away from Dilana. We want you to stop, leave him alone and stay out of the kitchen."

Liza had picked the worst time to accost me. Having just escaped a brush with death had put matters into perspective. I wasn't in the best frame of mind. Pure rage flared; I grabbed her arm and spun her around to face me. We stood nose to nose.

"*You* have concluded? The combined brainpower of the kitchen staff probably couldn't light a candle. Our *friendship* is none of your business. So I suggest you rethink your hypothesis. If there's a problem in the kitchen, then deal with it. You're wasting your time whining about it to me." I pushed her away. I could tell by her shocked expression that she hadn't expected such a fierce response.

Too bad for her, I thought as I hurried to catch up with the others, leaving her to walk alone. What did she want me to do? Had she assumed that I would meekly agree to stop talking to Rand just to smooth things in the kitchen? I wasn't going to let her unload her problems on me; I was already overloaded with my own. Like why would a magician from Sitia want to kill me?

At the castle, I said good-night to Rand and Dilana and rushed to Valek's suite. As much as I wanted to be inside, I cajoled one of the outer-door guards to check Valek's rooms for intruders before I went in. Murder attempts combined with an overactive imagination made me jumpy, fearing ambushes. Even sitting on the couch in the middle of the living room with every lantern blazing, I didn't feel safe until Valek arrived near dawn.

"Haven't you slept?" he asked. A fist-size, dark purple bruise on his jaw contrasted against his pale skin.

"No. But neither have you," I said peevishly.

"I can sleep all day. You need to taste the Commander's breakfast in an hour."

"What *I* need are answers."

"To what questions?" Valek began to extinguish the lanterns.

"Why is a southern magician trying to kill me?"

"A good question. The very same one I was going to ask you."

"How should I know?" I shrugged in frustration. "Brazell's guards I could understand. But magicians! It's not like I've been going around making southern magicians angry."

"Ahhh…that's a shame. Since you have a real talent for angering people." Valek sat at his desk and rested his head in his hands. "A southern magician, Yelena, a master-level southern *magician*. Do you know that there are only four master magicians in Sitia? Four. And since the takeover, they've stayed in Sitia. On occasion they send a minion or two with minor magical abilities into the Territory to see what we're up to. So far each spy has been intercepted and dealt with. Commander Ambrose will not tolerate magic in Ixia."

The magicians of the King's era had been considered the

elite. Treated like royalty, they had been quite influential with the King. According to the history of the takeover, Valek had assassinated every one of them. I wondered how, especially since he couldn't capture that woman tonight.

Valek stood up. He grabbed a gray rock off his desk. Tossing the stone from hand to hand, he paced around the living room.

Remembering Valek's near miss with the last rock he'd held, I pulled my feet off the floor and hugged my knees to my chest, hoping to make myself a smaller target.

"For the southerners to risk one of their master magicians, the reason has to be…" Valek shook the stone in his hand, searching for the right word. "Momentous. So why are they after you?" He sighed and sank down on the couch next to me. "Well, let's try to reason this out. You obviously have some southern blood in your heritage."

"What?" I had never thought about my heritage. I had been found on the street, homeless, and been taken in by Brazell. Speculation about my parents had only been on whether they were dead or had just abandoned me. I had no memories of my life prior to my arrival at the orphanage. Mostly, I had been thankful that Brazell gave me shelter. For Valek to make such a matter-of-fact statement stunned me.

"Your coloring is a bit darker than the typical northerner. Your features have a southern quality. Green eyes are very rare in the Territory, but are more common in Sitia." Valek misread my frozen expression. "It's nothing to be ashamed of. When the King was in power, the border to Sitia was open to commerce and trade. People moved freely between the regions, and marriages were inevitable. I would guess you were left behind right after the takeover when people panicked and fled south before we closed the border. It was complete mayhem. I don't know what they were expecting when the Commander came to power. Mass killings? All we did was give everyone a uniform and a job."

My mind reeled. Why hadn't I been more curious about my family? I didn't even know what town I had been found in. We had been told daily of our good fortune, reminded that we had food, clothes, shelter, teachers and even a small allowance. It had been repeatedly pointed out that many children with parents weren't as well off as we were. Was it a form of brainwashing?

"Well, anyway, I digress," Valek said into the silence. He stood and resumed his pacing. "I doubt it was missing family members. They wouldn't want to kill you. Is there anything else, besides murdering Reyad, that you did in the past? Witnessed a crime? Overheard plans for a rebellion? Anything at all?"

"No. Nothing."

Valek tapped the rock against his forehead. "Then let's assume this has to do with Reyad. Perhaps he was in league with some southerners and your killing him ruined their plans. Maybe they're scheming to retake Ixia. Or they think you know something about this plot. But I've heard nothing about Sitia attacking us. And why would they? Sitia knows the Commander is content to stay in the north and vice versa." Valek rubbed a hand over his face before continuing.

"Perhaps Brazell has gotten creative in his old age and hired southerners to kill you; thereby accomplishing his desire to see you dead without implicating himself. No. That doesn't make sense. Brazell would have hired thugs, no need for a magician. Unless he has connections I'm not aware of, which is highly doubtful." Valek looked around the room. Only half of the lanterns had been extinguished. Setting the rock down, he finished the job just as the timid predawn light started to brighten the room.

He stopped as if he had a sudden thought and scowled at me. "What?"

"Magicians will come north to smuggle one of their own kind to safety," Valek said. He studied me.

Before I could protest, he asked, "Then why kill you? Unless you're a Soulfinder, they wouldn't want you dead." Valek yawned and gently fingered the bruise on his face. "I'm too tired to think straight. I'm going to bed." He walked to the stairs.

Soulfinder? I had no idea what that was, but more important concerns needed to be addressed.

"Valek."

He paused with a foot on the first step.

"My antidote."

"Of course." He continued up the steps.

While he was upstairs, I wondered how many times in the future I would have to ask for the antidote. The knowledge that it was keeping me alive poisoned my mind as surely as the Butterfly's Dust poisoned my body.

As the early morning light brightened, I thought of my bed with longing. Valek could sleep, but I had to taste the Commander's breakfast soon.

Valek came downstairs. Handing me the antidote, he said, "You might want to wear your hair down today."

"Why?" I ran my fingers through my hair. The ribbons I had braided were torn and knotted.

"To cover the marks on your neck."

Before going to the Commander's office, I hurried to the baths. I had just enough time to wash and change into a clean uniform before I had to appear at breakfast. The garrote had left a bright red ring around my neck that I couldn't cover no matter how I styled my hair.

On my way to the Commander's office, I saw Liza. She set her mouth in a firm frown and looked away when she passed. Oh well, I thought, another person I'd angered. I regretted having taken my ire out on her, but I wasn't about to apologize. After all, she had started the argument.

Most mornings the Commander ignored my arrival. I would taste his breakfast, and then sort through his box of Criollo, randomly selecting a piece to verify that no one had poisoned it during the night. Each morning my mouth watered as I anticipated the taste of the bittersweet dessert. Its nutty flavor coating my mouth was the one pleasure I could look forward to during my day. I had argued with Valek that I should test it every time the Commander wanted some, but the Commander hoarded his supply. He rationed out one piece of Criollo after every meal. And I had heard through Rand that the Commander had already requested more from Brazell, along with a copy of the recipe from his cook, Ving.

Each morning after placing the Commander's breakfast tray on his desk, I would pick up his daily schedule and leave without a word being uttered. But this morning, when I set the tray down, he told me to sit.

Perched on the edge of the hard, wooden chair facing his desk, I felt a feather of fear brush my stomach. I laced my fingers tight together to keep my face impassive.

"Valek has informed me that you had an incident last night. I'm concerned that another attempt on your life will jeopardize our exercise." The Commander's golden eyes regarded me as he sipped his tea. "You have presented Valek with a puzzle, and he has *assured* me that keeping you alive will aid in a speedy resolution. Convince me that you'll be able to play fugitive without getting yourself killed. According to Valek, you failed to recognize him even after he bumped into you."

My mouth opened, but I closed it as I considered his words. A hastily explained or illogical argument would not sway the Commander. Also, I had been given an easy out. Why should I risk my neck for his exercise? I wasn't a skilled spy; I hadn't been able to identify Valek even when I knew he was following me. But then again it was my neck the murderous assailants were after. If I didn't try to draw them out on my own terms, they'd pick the time and location. I weighed the argument in my head, feeling as though I was forever on a tightrope, unable to decide which way led to the perfect dismount. Walking back and forth until some outside force came along to push me one way or the other.

"I'm new to the hunt-and-chase game," I told the Commander. "For someone untrained, trying to spot a tail in a noisy, crowded festival is a difficult task. It's like asking a child to run when she has just learned how to walk. In the woods, alone and trying to avoid everyone, picking up a tail will be easier and within my abilities." I stopped. No response from the Commander, so I continued, "If we can lure this magician out, maybe we can discover why she wants to kill me."

The Commander sat as still as a frog that watched and waited for a fly to come closer.

I played my last card. "And Valek has *assured* me he will be following."

My use of the Commander's word was not lost on him.

"We will proceed as planned. I don't expect you to get far, so I doubt we'll see this magician." He said the word *magician* as if it left a foul taste in his mouth. "I do expect you to keep quiet about this entire affair. Consider it an order. You're dismissed."

"Yes, Sir." I left his office.

I spent the remainder of the day collecting and borrowing provisions for the exercise, which was scheduled to begin the next morning at dawn. I visited Dilana's workroom and the smithy. Just mentioning Valek's name produced remarkable results from the blacksmiths, who hurried to procure the items I said Valek needed.

Dilana would have given me anything I requested. She seemed disappointed that I only wanted to borrow a leather backpack.

"Keep it," she had said. "No one has claimed it. It's been underfoot since I started."

I kept her company as she mended uniforms, told me the latest gossip and fussed about how I needed to eat more.

My last stop was the kitchen. With the hope of finding Rand alone, I waited until after the staff had cleaned up dinner. He was standing at a counter, working on menus. Each week's menus had to be approved by the Commander before Rand could give them to Liza, who made sure the required food and ingredients were available.

"You look better than I feel," Rand said in a soft tone. He held his head like a full cup of water, moving slowly as if to avoid spilling over. "I don't have anything for you to taste today. I haven't had the energy."

"That's okay." I noted his white face and the dark smudges under his eyes. "I won't keep you. I just need to borrow some things."

Interested, Rand almost returned to his jovial self. "Like what?"

"Bread. And some of that glue you invented. Medic Mommy used it to seal a cut on my arm. It's wonderful stuff."

"The glue! One of my best recipes yet! Did she tell you how I discovered it? I was trying to make an edible adhesive for this mammoth, ten-layer wedding cake and—"

"Rand," I interrupted, "I would love to hear the story, and you must promise to tell me another time. But we're both short on sleep."

"Oh, yes. You're right." He pointed to a stack of loaves and said, "Take what you need."

While I collected bread, he rummaged around in a drawer, then handed me a jar of white glue.

"It's not permanent. The glue will stick for about a week then it loses its grip. Anything else?"

"Um. Yes." I hesitated, reluctant to make my last request, which was my main reason for wanting to be alone with Rand.

"What?"

"I need a knife."

His head jerked. I could see a spark behind his eyes as the memory of how I had killed Reyad flashed through his mind. I saw the gears in his head turning as he weighed our fledgling friendship against this unusual request.

I fully expected him to question me as to why I needed a knife. Instead he asked, "Which one?"

"The scariest-looking one you've got.

14

THE NEXT MORNING, I headed out the south gate just as the sun crested the Soul Mountains. Soon a glorious sweep of sunlight rushed over the valley, indicating the start of the Commander's exercise. My heart pulsed with excitement and fear. A strange combination of feelings, but they fueled my steps. I scarcely felt the weight of my backpack.

I had worried that the items contained in my knapsack could be considered cheating. After much thought, I decided that a prisoner intent on escaping from the dungeon would save some of her bread rations, smuggle a weapon from the guard room and steal the other items from the blacksmiths. And if I was stretching things a bit, then so what. No one had told me I must flee with nothing.

My determination to "escape" had increased since the plan had first been proposed. The money was merely a bonus at this point. I wanted to prove the Commander wrong. The Commander, who thought I wouldn't get far, who had been concerned *my death* would jeopardize *his* exercise.

Before leaving the castle complex, I had stopped for a moment to view the main building in the daylight. My first impression was that a child had built the palace with his toy blocks. The base of the castle was rectangular. It supported various upper levels of squares, triangles and cylinders built atop one another in a haphazard fashion. The only attempts at symmetry were the magnificent towers at each corner of the castle. Streaked with brilliantly colored glass windows, the four towers stretched toward the sky.

The castle's unusual geometric design intrigued me, and I would have liked to view it from other angles, but Valek had instructed me to leave the complex at dawn as I only had an hour's head start. Then, the soldiers and dogs in pursuit would try to discover which gate I had exited, tracking me from there. Valek had taken one of my uniform shirts in order to give the dogs my scent. I had asked him who would taste the Commander's food while I was gone, and he'd given me some vague reply about having others trained in the art of poisoning who were too valuable to be used on a regular basis. Unlike me.

My southern route was an obvious direction, but I didn't plan to maintain it for long. I hoped the soldiers would assume I was headed straight for the border. The castle complex was in Military District 6 and quite close to the southern lands, wedged between MD–7 to the west and MD–5 to the east. The dead King, who had built the complex, had preferred the milder weather.

Alternating between jogging and walking, it wasn't long before I entered Snake Forest, avoiding Castletown. While studying some of Valek's maps the previous night, I had noticed that the forest surrounded Castletown on three sides. The northern district of the town faced the castle. Snake Forest also spread out to the east and west like a thin belt of green.

At the official southern border, Commander Ambrose's soldiers had cleared a hundred-foot-wide swath from the Soul Mountains in the east all the way to the Sunset Ocean in the west. Since the takeover it was a crime for anyone, Ixian or Sitian, to cross this line.

I jogged through the forest, making a conspicuous trail. Breaking branches and stomping footprints in the dirt, I remained southbound until I reached a small stream. My hour head start was almost up. I knelt by the stream's bank and reached into the water. Pulling out a handful of mud, I let the water drain through my fingers. I hunched over the stream and smeared the wet sediment on my face and neck. Since I had pulled my hair into a bun, I rubbed mud on my ears and the back of my neck. I hoped the men would guess I had knelt here for a drink. After stamping footprints near the stream's bank to mislead my pursuers into thinking I had walked into the water, I traced my route back until I found a perfect tree.

About six feet from my path, a Velvatt's smooth trunk rose high into the air. The first sturdy branch off the main trunk stretched fifteen feet above my head. Trying not to disturb the ground surrounding my scent path, I removed my backpack and pulled out one of the items I had borrowed from the blacksmiths. It was a small metal grappling hook. I tied it to the end of a long thin rope coiled inside my bag.

With my head start gone, a sudden image of guards and dogs exploding from the castle flashed through my mind. Hastily I threw the hook up to the branch. It missed. I caught it on the way down. Frantic, I threw the hook again. Missed. I calmed my raging pulse and focused on the task. The hook snagged the branch. Confident the hook was secure, I tied the extra line around my waist so it wouldn't drag and put on my backpack. Grabbing the rope with both hands, I pulled my weight off the ground and wrapped my legs around the slack.

It had been a long time since I had climbed this way. All the way up the rope, my arm, shoulder and back muscles complained over my year-long inactivity. Once I reached the top, I straddled the branch and repacked the rope and hook in my backpack.

A strong breeze blew from the west. Wanting to stay downwind of the dogs, I spent the next half hour climbing east through the trees until I was well away from my original path. For once, my small size and acrobatic abilities proved a benefit.

When I came across a Cheketo tree, I found a secure nook near the trunk and unslung my backpack. The Cheketo's leaf was the biggest that grew in the Snake Forest. Its circular-shaped green leaf, spotted with brown, was perfect for my needs. I sat still for a minute, listening for sounds of pursuit. Birds chirped and insects buzzed; I heard the quick rustling of leaves as a deer moved. I detected the faint baying of dogs, but it might have been just my imagination. There was no sign of Valek. But knowing him, he had to be close behind.

Taking Rand's glue from my pack, I stripped leaves off the tree. When I had enough, I removed my shirt and glued the leaves onto it. Feeling self-conscious in just my sleeveless undershirt, I worked fast.

I covered the shirt, then my pants, boots and backpack with leaves. Finally, I glued a large leaf onto my hair and two smaller ones onto the backs of my hands, leaving my fingers free to move. Rand's warning that the glue only held for a week passed through my mind, and I smiled as I envisioned his reaction when he saw me walking around the castle with leaves attached to my head and hands.

I didn't have a mirror, but I hoped I had camouflaged my entire body in green and brown. I wasn't concerned with the small black patches that might show through; it was the bright red of my uniform shirt that would immediately give me away.

Too nervous to stay in one place for long, I continued to climb east as fast and quiet as I could. My eastern direction wandered. Since I was unwilling to let my scent touch the ground, I had to detour either north or south on occasion. My grappling hook and rope were employed many times as I used them to bring branches within reach, or to swing from tree to tree. My muscles protested the abuse, but I ignored them. Laughing to myself whenever I overcame a difficult hurdle, I enjoyed the pure freedom of traveling above the ground. I grinned as I sweated through the entire morning. Eventually I knew I would have to head south again because that was the only place a fugitive could find safety and asylum.

Sitia welcomed the refugees from Ixia. Their government had

had an open relationship with the King, trading exotic spices, fabrics and foods for metals, precious stones and coal. When the Commander ceased trade, Ixia lost mainly luxury items while Sitia's resources became limited. Worry that Sitia would try to conquer the north for needed resources had dissipated when the Sitian geologists discovered that their Emerald Mountains, a continuation of the northern Soul Mountains, were rich in ores and minerals. Now, it seemed, Sitia was content to keep a wary eye on the north.

Soon my climb through the trees intersected a well-used path in the forest. I saw deep wagon ruts in the hard-packed dirt. The road was probably a part of the main east-west trading route, which turned north for a few miles to detour around Lake Keyra before resuming its easterly direction. The lake was just over the border of MD–5.

Settling on a sturdy branch within sight of the path, I leaned back on the tree's trunk, rested and ate my lunch while deciding where to go next. After a while, the soothing noises from the forest almost lulled me to sleep.

"See anything?" A male voice beneath me disrupted the quiet.

Startled, I grabbed the branch to keep from falling. Caught, I froze in shock.

"No. All clear," another man's voice replied from a distance. His tone was rough with annoyance.

There had been no barking to alert me; it must be the other team. I had been so worried about the dogs that I had forgotten about the smaller team. Too cocky, I thought. I deserved to be caught early.

I waited for them to order me down, but they remained quiet. Looking below, I searched the forest but couldn't locate them. Maybe they hadn't seen me after all. After a bit of rustling, two men emerged from the dense underbrush. They, too, wore green and brown camouflage, although their snug overalls and face paint were more professional than my glued-together ensemble.

"Stupid idea, coming east. She's probably at the southern border by now," Rough Voice grumbled to his partner.

"That's what the dog boys figured, even though the hounds lost her scent," said the second man.

I smiled. I'd outsmarted the dogs. At least I had managed to accomplish that much.

"I don't know if I follow the logic of going east," Rough Voice said.

The other man sighed. "You're not supposed to follow the logic. The Captain ordered us east; we go east. He seems to think she'll head deeper into MD–5. Familiar territory for her."

"Well, what if she doesn't come back? Another stupid idea, using the food taster," Rough Voice complained. "She's a criminal."

"That's not our concern. That's Valek's problem. I'm sure if she got away he would take care of her."

I wondered if Valek was listening. We both knew he wouldn't need to hunt me down; all he had to do was wait the poison out. I found the conversation helpful, especially the fact that it wasn't common knowledge that I'd been poisoned.

"Let's go. We're supposed to rendezvous with the Captain at the lake. Oh, and try to keep the noise down. You sound like a panicked moose crashing through the woods," the smarter man chided.

"Oh yeah. Like you could hear me over your specially trained 'woodland-animal footsteps,'" Rough Voice countered. "It was like listening to two deer humping each other."

The men laughed and in a wink disappeared into the underbrush, one on each side of the path. I strained to hear them moving but couldn't tell if they were gone. I waited until I couldn't bear the inactivity. The men had decided my next move. The lake was to the east. Climbing through the trees, I headed south.

As I worked my way along, an odd, creepy feeling burrowed its way into my mind. Somehow I became convinced that the men I had seen on the path were following me, hunting me. An uncontrollable urge to move fast pushed on me like a strong hand on the back of my neck, propelling me forward. When I couldn't stand it any longer, I threw all precautions of keeping hidden and quiet aside. I dropped to the ground and bolted.

When I burst into a small clearing in the trees, I stopped. The overpowering feeling of panic had disappeared. My sides stitched with pain. Dropping my pack, I collapsed onto the ground, gasping for breath. I cursed myself for such panicky behavior.

"Nice outfit," a familiar voice said. Dread and fear gave me the energy to jump to my feet.

No one in sight. Yet. I ripped open my backpack and pulled the knife. My heart performed somersaults in my chest. I turned in slow circles as I scanned the forest, searching for the voice of death.

15

LAUGHTER SURROUNDED ME. "Your weapon won't do you any good. I could easily convince you that it was your heart you want to plunge that knife into instead of mine."

I spotted her across the clearing. Clad in a loose, green camouflage shirt cinched tight at the waist and identical colored pants, the southern magician lounged against a tree with her arms crossed in front of her, her posture casual.

Expecting the southern magician's goons to attack me from the forest, I kept the knife out in front of me, turning in circles.

"Relax," the magician said. "We're alone."

I stopped circling but retained a firm grip on my weapon. "Why should I trust you? Last time we met, you ordered me killed. Even supplied that handy little strap." The sudden realization that she hadn't needed her thugs at all leaped into my mind. I began reciting poison names in my head.

The magician laughed like someone amused by a small child. "That won't help you. The only reason reciting worked at the festival was because Valek was there."

She stepped closer. I waved the knife in a threatening gesture.

"Yelena, relax. I projected into your mind to guide you here. If I wanted you dead, I would have pushed you from the trees. Accidents are less trouble than murders in Ixia. A fact you're well aware of."

I ignored her jibe. "Why didn't I have an 'accident' at the festival? Or at another time?"

"I need to be close to you. It takes a lot of energy to kill someone; I'd rather use mundane methods if possible. The festival was the first time I could get close to you without Valek nearby, or so I thought." She shook her head in frustration.

"Why didn't you kill Valek with your magic at the festival?" I asked. "Then I would have been easy prey."

"Magic doesn't work on Valek. He's resistant to its effects."

Before I could ask for more information, she hurried on. "I don't have time to explain everything. Valek will be here soon so I'll make this brief. Yelena, I'm here to make you an offer."

I remembered my last offer, to be the food taster or to be executed. "What could you possibly offer me? I have a job, color-coordinated uniforms and a boss to die for. What more could I need?"

"Asylum in Sitia," she said, her tone tight. "So you can learn to control and use your power."

"Power?" The word squeaked out of my mouth before I could stop it. "What power?"

"Oh, come on! How could you not know? You've used it at least twice at the castle."

My mind whirled. She was talking about my survival instinct. That strange buzzing that possessed me whenever my life was in serious jeopardy. My body numbed with dread. I felt as if she had just told me I had a terminal disease.

"I was working undercover nearby when I was overcome by your screaming, raw power. Once I was able to pinpoint the source to Commander Ambrose's food taster, I knew a rescue effort to smuggle you south would be impossible. You're either with Valek, or he's been one step behind you. Even now, I'm taking an extraordinary risk. But it's too dangerous to have a wild magician in the north. It's amazing you lasted this long without being discovered. The only choice left was termination. A task that proved more difficult than I'd first imagined. But not impossible."

"And now I'm supposed to trust you? Do you think I'd meekly follow you to Sitia like a lamb to the slaughter?"

"Yelena, if you weren't playing fugitive, which brought you out of the castle and away from Valek, you'd be dead by now."

I wasn't sure if I believed her. What would she gain by helping me? Why go to all this effort if she had the power to kill me? Something else must be motivating her.

"You don't believe me." She grunted in frustration. "Okay, how about a little demonstration?" She tilted her head to the side and pressed her lips together.

A searing, hot pain whipped through my mind like lightning. Wrapping my arms and hands around my head, I tried in vain to block the onslaught. Then a fist-size force slammed into my forehead. I jolted backward and fell to the ground. Sprawled on my back, I felt the pain disappear as fast as it had arrived. Through vision blurred with tears, I squinted at the magician. She still stood near the edge of the clearing. She hadn't touched me, at least not physically. The weight of her mental connection felt like a wool cap encompassing my skull.

"What the hell was that?" I demanded. "What happened to the singing?" I was dazed by her attack, the air on my body feeling as if it had liquefied, and when I moved to a sitting position the dense air swirled and lapped at my skin.

"I sang at the festival because I was trying to be kind. This was an effort to convince you that if I wanted you dead, I wouldn't be wasting my time talking to you now. And I certainly wouldn't wait until you were in Sitia." Her head cocked as if she listened to an invisible person whispering in her ear.

"Valek has dropped all pretense of stealth. He's traveling fast. Two men pursue him, but the men believe they're chasing you." She paused and her mouth settled once again into a hard line as she concentrated. "I can slow the men down, but not Valek." She focused her faraway gaze on me. "Are you coming with me?"

I couldn't speak. The thought that her idea of kindness was singing someone to death had left me quite distracted. I stared at her in complete astonishment.

"No." I had to force the word out.

"What?" It wasn't the answer she'd expected. "You enjoy being the food taster?"

"No, I don't, but I'll die if I go with you."

"You'll die if you stay."

"I'll take my chances." I stood, brushed the dirt off my legs and retrieved my knife. The last thing I wanted to do was explain to the magician about the poison in my blood. Why give her another weapon to be used against me? But with her mental link to me, I only had to think about the Butterfly's Dust and she knew.

"There are antidotes," she said.

"Can you find one before morning?" I asked.

She shook her head. "No. We would need more time. Our healers would need to understand where the poison is hiding. It could be in your blood, or in your muscles or anywhere, and they would need to know how it kills in order to banish it."

When she saw my complete lack of understanding, the magician continued, "The source of our power—what you call magic—is like a blanket surrounding the world. Our minds tap into this source, pulling a slender thread down to enhance our magical abilities, to turn them on. Every person has the latent ability to read minds and influence the physical world without touching it, but they don't have the ability to connect with the power source."

She sighed, looking unhappy. "Yelena, we can't have your wild power flaring uncontrolled. Without knowing it, you're pulling power. Instead of a thread, you're grabbing whole sections and bunching the power blanket around you. As you grow older you will have amassed so much power that it will explode or flame out. This flameout will not only kill you, it will warp and damage the power source itself, ripping a hole in the blanket. We can't risk a flameout and soon you'll be untrainable. That is why we have no choice but to terminate you before you reach that point."

"How long do I have?" I asked.

"One year. Maybe a little more if you can control yourself. After that you'll be beyond our help. And we need you, Yelena. Powerful magicians are scarce in Sitia."

My mind raced over my options. Her display of power had convinced me she was more of a threat than I had ever imagined and that I would be a complete idiot to trust her at all. However, if I didn't go, she'd kill me where I stood.

So I delayed the inevitable. "Give me a year. A year to find a permanent antidote, to find a way to escape to Sitia. A year free from worrying that you're plotting my death."

She stared deep into my eyes. Her mental touch pressed harder in my mind as she searched for a sign that I might be deceiving her.

"All right. One year. My pledge to you." She paused.

"Go on," I said. "I know you want to end this meeting with some kind of threat. Maybe a dire warning? Feel free. I'm used to it. I wouldn't know how to deal with a conversation that didn't include one."

"You put on such a brave front. But I know if I took another step toward you, you'd wet your pants."

"With your blood." I brandished my knife. But I couldn't keep a straight face; the boast sounded ridiculous even to my own ears. I snickered. She laughed. The release of tension made me giddy, and soon I was laughing and crying.

The magician then grew sober. Cocking her head again, she listened to her invisible companion. "Valek is close. I must go."

"Tell me one more thing."

"What?"

"How did you know I'd be the fugitive? Magic?"

"No. I have sources of information that I'm unable to reveal."

I nodded my understanding. Asking for details had been worth a try.

"Be careful, Yelena," she said, vanishing into the forest.

I realized that I didn't even know her name.

"Irys," she whispered in my mind, and then her mental touch withdrew.

As I thought about everything she had told me, I realized I had many more questions to ask her, all more important than who had leaked information. Knowing she was gone, though, I suppressed the desire to call after her. Instead, I dropped to the ground.

With my body shaking, I replaced my knife in the backpack. I pulled out my water bottle and took a long drink, wishing the container was filled with something stronger. Something that would burn my throat on its way down. Something to focus on besides the disjointed and lost feeling that threatened to consume me.

I needed time to think before Valek and the two men caught up with me. Taking out the rope and grappling hook, I searched once again for a suitable tree and reentered the forest canopy. Moving south, I let the physical effort of climbing keep my body busy while I sorted through all the information the magician had given me.

When I reached another path in the forest, I found a comfortable position on a tree branch within sight of the trail. I secured myself to the trunk of the tree with my rope. The magician had promised me one year, but I didn't want to tempt her with an easy target. She could change her mind; after all, what did I know about magicians and their pledges?

She claimed I had power. Magical power that I had always thought of as my survival instinct. When I had been in those dire situations, I had felt possessed. As if someone else more capable of dealing with the crisis took temporary control over my body, rescued me from death and then left.

Could the strange buzzing sound that erupted from my throat and saved my life really be the same as Irys's power? If so, I must keep my magic a secret. And I had to gain some control of the power to keep it from flaming out. But how? Avoid life-threatening situations. I scoffed at the notion of evading trouble. Trouble seemed to find me regardless of my efforts. Orphaned. Tortured. Poisoned. Cursed with magic. The list grew longer by the day.

I didn't have the time to resolve these complex issues that circled without end in my mind. Focusing my thoughts on the present, I studied the trail below. Small saplings threatened to retake the narrow forest path; it must have been one of the abandoned roadways used to trade with Sitia.

I waited for Valek. He would demand an explanation about my encounter with the magician, and I was ready to give one.

My only warning of Valek's arrival was a gentle rustling of the branch above mine. I looked up to see him uncoiling from the upper branch like a snake. He dropped soundlessly beside me.

Green camouflage seemed to be the outfit of choice today. Valek's was skintight and came equipped with a hood to cover his hair and neck. Brown and green paint streaked his face, causing the bright blue of his eyes to stand out in stark contrast.

I looked down at my own ragtag outfit. Some of the leaves had frayed at the edges, and my uniform had sustained many tears from climbing through the trees. Next time I planned to flee through the woods, I'd persuade Dilana to sew me an outfit like Valek's.

"You're unbelievable," Valek said.

"Is that good or bad?"

"Good. I assumed you would give the soldiers a good chase, and you did. But I never expected this." Valek pointed at my leaf-covered shirt and swept his arms wide, indicating the trees. "And to top it all off, you encountered the magician and somehow managed to survive." Sarcasm tinged Valek's voice during his last comment.

His way of asking for an explanation, I supposed.

"I don't know what exactly happened. I found myself tearing through the woods until I reached a clearing, where she was waiting. The only thing she told me was that I had ruined her plans by killing Reyad, and then pain slammed into my skull." The memory of her attack was still fresh in my mind, so I allowed the full horror of it to show on my face. If Valek ever suspected what had really happened, I wouldn't live the year the magician had granted me. And mentioning Reyad's name supported one of Valek's theories about why the magician was after me.

I took a deep breath. "I started reciting poisons. I tried to push the pain away. Then the attack stopped, and she said you were getting too close. When I opened my eyes she had disappeared."

"Why didn't you wait for me in the clearing?"

"I didn't know where she had gone. I felt safer in the trees, knowing you'd be able to find me."

Valek considered my explanation. I covered my nervousness by sorting through my backpack.

After a long while, he grinned. "We certainly proved the Commander wrong. He thought you'd be caught by midmorning."

I smiled with relief. Taking advantage of his good mood, I asked, "Why does the Commander hate magicians so much?"

The pleased expression dropped from Valek's face. "He has many reasons. They were the King's colleagues. Aberrations of nature, who used their power for purely selfish and greedy reasons. They amassed wealth and jewels, curing the sick only if the dying's family could pay their exorbitant fee. The King's magicians played mind games with everyone, taking delight in causing havoc. The Commander wants nothing to do with them."

Curious, I pushed on. "What about using them for his purposes?"

"He thinks magicians are not to be trusted, but I'm of two minds about that," Valek said. He gazed out over the forest floor as he talked. "I understand the Commander's concern, killing all the King's magicians was a good strategy, but I think the younger generation born with power could be recruited for our intelligence network. We disagree on this issue, and despite my arguments the Commander has—" Valek stopped. He seemed reluctant to continue.

"Has what?"

"Ordered that those born with even the slightest amount of magical power be killed immediately."

I had known about the execution of the southern spies and the magicians from the King's era, but imagining babies being ripped from their mother's arms made me gasp in horror. "Those poor children."

"It's brutal, but not that brutal," Valek said. A sadness had softened his eyes. "The ability to connect with the power source doesn't occur until after puberty, which is around age sixteen. It usually takes another year for someone other than their family to notice and report them. Then, they either escape to Sitia, or I find them."

His words had the weight of a wooden beam pressing down on my shoulders. I found it difficult to breathe. Sixteen was when Brazell had recruited me. When my survival instinct had started to flare, defending against Brazell and Reyad's torture. Had they been trying to test me for magic? But why didn't they report me? Why hadn't Valek come?

I had no idea what Brazell wanted. And knowing now about my power only added yet another way I could die. If Valek discovered my magic, I was dead. If I didn't find a way to go to Sitia, I was dead. If someone poisoned the Commander's food,

I was dead. If Brazell built his factory and sought revenge for his son, I was dead. Dead, dead, dead and dead. Death by Butterfly's Dust was beginning to look attractive. It was the only scenario where I would get to choose when, where and how I died.

I would have sunk into a deep, brooding bout of self-pity, but Valek grabbed my arm and put a finger to his green lips.

The distant sounds of hoofbeats and men talking reached my ears. My first thought was that it was an illusion sent by the magician. But soon enough, I saw mules pulling wagons. The width of the wagons filled the entire path, saplings and bushes thwacked against the wheels. Two mules pulled one wagon, and one man dressed in a brown trader's uniform led the team. There were six wagons and six men who conversed among themselves as they traveled.

From my post in the tree, I could see that the first five wagons were loaded with burlap sacks that might have been filled with grain or flour. The last wagon held strange, oval-shaped yellow pods.

Snake Forest was just bustling with activity today, I thought in wonder. All we needed was the fire dancers to jump from the trees to entertain us all.

Valek and I sat still in our tree as the men passed below us. Their uniforms were soaked with sweat, and I noticed a few of them had rolled up their pants so they wouldn't trip. One man's belt was cinched tight, causing the extra material to bunch around his waist, while another's stomach threatened to rip through his buttons. These poor traders obviously didn't have a permanent residence. If they had, their seamstress would never have permitted them to walk around looking like that.

When they were out of sight and hearing range, Valek whispered, "Don't move, I'll be back." He dropped to the ground and followed the caravan.

I fidgeted on my branch, wondering if the other two men Irys had said were tracking Valek would find me before he returned. The sun was disappearing in the west, and cooler air was replacing the day's heat. Muscles stiff from inactivity throbbed as the last of my energy faded. The strenuous day of climbing caught up to me. For the first time the possibility of spending a night alone in the forest made me apprehensive; I had never imagined staying free this long.

At last, Valek returned and waved me down from the tree. I moved with care, fumbling with the rope around my waist as my abused muscles trembled with fatigue.

He carried a small sack, which he handed to me. Inside were five of the yellow pods that had been stacked in the last wagon. I took one out. Now that I could see it up close, I noticed that the elongated, oval pod was about eight inches in length, with close to ten furrows running from one end to the other. It was thick around the middle. With two hands wrapped around its center, my fingers just overlapped.

I was amazed by Valek's ability to steal them in the daylight from a moving wagon. "How did you get these?"

"Trade secret," Valek said with a grin. "Getting the pods was easy, but I had to wait for the men to water their mules to look in the burlap sacks."

When I slid the pod back in with the others, I saw that in the bottom of the sack was a pile of dark brown pebbles. Reaching deeper, I pulled a handful into the waning light. They looked like beans.

"What's this?" I asked.

"They're from the sacks," he explained. "I want you to take these back to Commander Ambrose. Tell him I don't know what they are or where they came from and I'm following the caravan to see where they're going."

"Are they doing something illegal?"

"I'm not sure. If these pods and beans are from Sitia, then yes. It's illegal to trade with the south. One thing I do know, those men aren't traders."

I was about to ask him how he knew this, when the answer clicked in my mind. "Their uniforms don't fit. Borrowed maybe? Or stolen?"

"Most likely stolen. If you're going to borrow a uniform, I would think you'd find one that fits." Valek was quiet for a moment, listening to the sounds of the forest. I could hear the droning of the insects grow louder as the sun set.

"Yelena, I want you to find those two men you saw this afternoon, and have them escort you back to the castle. I don't want you alone. If the magician plans on attacking you again, she'll have to deal with two more, and I doubt she'd have the energy. Don't tell anyone about your tree climbing, the magician or the caravan. But give a complete report about everything to the Commander."

"What about my antidote?"

"The Commander keeps a supply handy. He'll give it to you. And don't worry about your incentive. You've earned every penny. When I get back, I'll make sure you get it. Now, I need to keep moving or I'll spend the rest of the night catching up to the caravan."

"Valek, wait," I demanded. For the second time today someone wanted to disappear before explaining everything to my satisfaction, and I was growing weary of it.

He stopped.

"How do I find the others?" Without the sun, my sense of direction failed. I wasn't sure if I could find my way back to the clearing, much less to the castle on my own.

"Just follow this path." He pointed in the direction the wagons had come from. "I managed to shake them off my tail before I caught up with you. The soldiers were heading south-west; they're probably staking out this trail. Technically, that's the best strategy."

Valek jogged away along the path. I watched him go. He moved with the light grace and speed of a deer, his muscles rippling under his formfitting camouflage.

When he was out of sight, I crunched my feet on the loose stones of the trail, making noise. Twilight robbed the trees of color as darkness descended. Uneasiness settled over me. Every rustle caused my heart to jump, and I found myself peering over my shoulder, wishing Valek was here.

A shout pierced the air. Before I could react, a large shape rushed me, tackling me to the ground.

16

"GOT YOU!" SAID THE MAN sitting on top of me.

Even with my face pressed into the stones, and my mouth full of dirt, I recognized his rough voice from earlier in the day. He yanked my arms behind me. I felt cold metal bite into my wrists as I heard the snap and clink of manacles.

"Isn't that a bit much, Janco?" asked Janco's partner.

Janco moved off me, and I was hauled to my feet. In the semidarkness, I saw the man that held me was thin, with a goatee. He wore his dark hair buzzed in the typical military style. A thick scar ran from his right temple to his ear. The lower half of his right ear was missing.

"She was too damn hard to find. I don't want her getting away," Janco grumbled.

His companion was about the same height but twice as wide. Thick, sculpted muscles bulged through his camouflage uniform. Small, damp curls clung to his head, and from this distance his eyes held no color except the black of his pupils.

I wanted to flee. It was almost dark; I was manacled and alone with two strange men. Logically, I knew that these were the Commander's soldiers, and they were professionals, but that didn't stop my pulse from racing.

"You made us look bad," Janco said. "Every soldier out here is probably going to be reassigned. We'll all be cleaning out latrines 'cause of you."

"That's enough, Janco," Colorless Eyes said. "*We* won't be scrubbing floors. We found her. And take a look at that getup. No one expected her to go camo, that's why she was so hard to find. But, still, the Captain's gonna shit when he sees this!"

"And the Captain's back at the castle?" I asked, trying to prompt them in that direction.

"No. He's leading a line farther southwest. We'll have to report to him."

I sighed at the delay. I had hoped for a quick trip back. "How about you send Janco here to find the Captain, while we head to the castle?"

"Sorry, but we're not permitted to split up. We're required to travel in pairs, no exceptions."

"Um…" Janco started.

"Yelena," I supplied.

"Why are you so anxious to get back?" he asked.

"I'm afraid of the dark."

Colorless Eyes laughed. "Somehow I doubt that. Janco,

take the cuffs off her. She's not going to run away. That's not
the point of this exercise."

Janco hesitated.

I said, "You have my word, Janco. I won't run if you take
off the manacles."

He grumbled some more but unlocked the cuffs. I wiped
the dirt from my face. "Thanks."

He nodded, and then pointed to his partner. "He's Ardenus."

"Ari, for short." Ari extended his hand, giving me an honor.
If a soldier offered his hand, he was acknowledging me as an equal.

I shook it gravely, and then the three of us headed southwest to find their Captain.

The trip to the castle was almost comical. Almost. If my stiff
and sore muscles hadn't protested my every step, and if the
bone-deep ache of pure exhaustion hadn't pulled at my body
like a stone cloak, I would have been amused.

Janco and Ari's Captain fumed and blustered when we
caught up with him. "Well, well, well. Look at what our two
sweethearts finally found," Captain Parffet said. His bald head
was beaded with sweat that rolled down the sides of his face,
soaking his collar. He was old for a Captain, and I wondered
if his surly disposition was the reason for his lack of promotion.

"I'm *supposed* to have the best scouts in Commander
Ambrose's guard," Parffet shouted at Ari and Janco. "Maybe
you can enlighten us as to which procedure you followed that
took you over seventeen hours to find the bitch!" Parffet con-

tinued his verbal bashing. Even in the darkness I could see his face turning purple.

I tuned him out and studied his unit. A couple of faces smirked, agreeing with their Captain, some were resigned, as if used to his tantrums, and others wore bored and tired expressions. One man, who had shaved his entire head except for his bangs, stared with an uncomfortable intensity at me. When I made eye contact, he jerked his glance to the Captain.

"Nix, put the bitch in manacles," Parffet ordered, and the man with the bangs pulled metal cuffs off his belt. "I see our two prima donnas can't be bothered to follow this unit's standard procedures."

As Nix approached, I searched for a chance to slip away. My promise to Janco had only extended to a "hands free" trip back to the castle. Ari, sensing my frame of mind, placed a large hand on my shoulder, anchoring me to his side.

"We have her word, sir, that she won't run off," he said in my defense.

"Like that means anything." Parffet spat on the ground.

"She has given her word," Ari repeated. A low rumble in his voice reminded me of a huge dog growling a warning.

Parffet grudgingly allowed procedure to be modified, but savored his bad temper by harassing the rest of his soldiers into formation, initiating a fast march back to the castle.

I walked wedged between Ari and Janco like some prized trophy. Ari explained that the Captain didn't handle surprises well, and had been frustrated by my daylong romp in the forest.

"It doesn't help that we found you. He didn't promote us to his unit like the others. We were assigned by Valek," Janco said.

Parffet's mood turned blacker when the dog team overtook our procession. Chaos erupted as barking dogs and more guards tangled together. I experienced a moment of panic when the canines rushed me. As it turned out, they greeted me with wagging tails and licking tongues. Their pure joy was infectious. I smiled, and scratched their ears, stopping only when Parffet scowled and shouted for order.

The dogs wore no collars. The kennel master was part of the tracking team. The dogs reassembled on Porter's command, following his orders without fail. The commander of the dog team seemed disappointed that Porter's dogs hadn't found me first, but she took it with better grace than Ari's Captain had. She introduced herself as Captain Etta and walked beside me to ask questions about my "run." I liked her easy, respectful manner. Her mop of dark blond hair pushed the limits of military regulation.

I stuck to the truth as much as I could during our conversation. When it came to questions regarding where my scent had disappeared, I lied. I explained that I had walked northward in the water for a while before heading east.

Etta shook her head. "We were so focused on you heading south. Parffet was right to look east."

"My eventual destination was south, but I wanted to try and confuse the dogs before I turned."

"You succeeded. The Commander won't be pleased. Good thing Ari and Janco found you. Had you stayed out till morning, both teams would have been demoted."

The last two miles to the castle were a blur. Using every ounce of my dwindling energy to keep my feet moving forward, I concentrated all my strength on keeping up with the soldiers. When we stopped, it took me a moment to realize that we had entered the castle complex.

It was well past midnight. The noise of our arrival bounced and amplified off the silent stone walls. The dogs followed Porter to the kennels while the weary parade of soldiers trod up the steps toward the Commander's office. We finished our march among the empty desks of the throne room.

Lantern light blazed from the open door of the Commander's office. The two soldiers standing guard wore amused expressions, but remained quiet and still. Parffet and Etta shared a look of resignation before going in to report to the Commander. I found a chair and collapsed into it, accepting the risk that I might have difficulties regaining my feet.

Soon the Captains returned. Parffet's face was creased in a dark frown, but Etta's showed no emotion. They dismissed their units. I was summoning the energy to stand, when Etta came over and helped me to my feet.

"Thanks," I said.

"The Commander awaits your report."

I nodded. Etta left to rejoin her unit, and I headed toward the office. I hesitated in the doorway; I was used to the semi-darkness of the throne room, and the lantern light stung my eyes.

"Come in," Commander Ambrose ordered.

I stood before his desk. He sat immobile and impassive as always, his smooth, ethereal face barren of wrinkles. A stray thought plucked at my mind, and I wondered about his age. Gray streaks painted the Commander's short hair. His rank alone suggested an older man, but his slight build and youthful face made me guess his age was closer to forty. About seven years older than Valek, if my estimation of Valek's age was accurate.

"Report."

I described my actions for the day in detail, including my tree swinging and the magician. Giving the same version of my encounter with the southerner that I had told Valek, I concluded my report with the caravan and Valek's orders that I return. I waited for the Commander's questions.

"So Ari and Janco didn't capture you?" he asked.

"No. But they were the only ones who even came close. They passed right below a tree I hid in, and were skilled enough to track Valek for a while."

The Commander stilled for a moment. His golden eyes looked past me as he absorbed the information. "Where are the items Valek procured?"

I opened my backpack, and placed the pods and beans on his desk.

He picked up a yellow pod and rotated it in his hands before returning it. Grabbing a handful of beans, he hefted them, feeling their weight and texture. After sniffing one, he broke the bean in half. The inside was as unrevealing as the outside had been.

"They're not native to Ixia. They must be from Sitia. Yelena, take them with you and do some research. Find out what these are and where they're grown."

"Me?" Stunned, I had expected to dump them on the Commander and forget about them.

"Yes. Valek is constantly reminding me not to underestimate you, and once again you've proven yourself. General Brazell gave you a good education. I'd hate to see it go to waste."

I wanted to argue, but I was curtly dismissed. Sighing, I dragged my unwilling body to the baths. Painfully peeling off my leaf-covered clothes, I washed the mud from my face and neck before submerging into a steaming pool.

There, I luxuriated in the warmth, stretching my aching muscles under the hot water to loosen them. Hoping to dissolve some of the glue from my hair, I dipped my head back, pulled my bun apart and let the long black strands float on the surface. The gentle sounds of lapping lulled me.

Strong hands grabbed my shoulders. I jerked awake under the water. Liquid filled my mouth and nose. I pushed the hands away in a panic. They released their grip for a second. I began to sink. Instinctively, I clutched my unknown assailant's arms. Before I could curse my stupidity, I was yanked out of the bath and dumped onto the cold floor.

I sprang to my feet to meet the next assault. But there stood Margg with a disgusted expression anchored on her broad face. Water dripped from her hands and had soaked her sleeves. I shivered and pulled wet clumps of hair off my face.

"What the hell do you think you're doing?" I yelled.

"Saving your worthless life," she snarled.

"What?"

"Don't worry. I took no pleasure in it. Frankly, I would have rejoiced to see you drown. Justice finally served! But the Commander ordered me to find you and see to your needs." Margg grabbed a towel from the table and threw it at me. "You may have the Commander and Valek fooled into thinking you're smart. But how smart can you be to fall asleep in a deep pool of water?"

I tried to think of a rude retort, remembering Dilana's advice to be nasty right back. Nothing. My brain felt waterlogged with fatigue. The idea that Margg had just saved my life kept sloshing around in my head. It was such a foreign concept that I couldn't find a proper place to dock it.

Margg snorted, hatred oozing from her. "I followed my orders. Some might even agree that rescuing you was beyond the call of duty. So don't you forget it, rat."

She spun around to leave. Her skirts wrapped around her legs, and she stumbled through the door. So much for a dramatic exit, I thought as I toweled dry.

I felt no gratitude toward Margg for saving my life—assuming that was what she'd done. She might have pushed me under in spite, then "saved" me. And I didn't owe her a favor. She had left me in a puddle of my own vomit after I had taken My Love, had refused to clean out my room in Valek's suite, had written me a nasty message in the dust, and even worse, was probably leaking information about me to Brazell. If she had saved me from drowning, then, in my mind, it was a payback for some of those indiscretions, but not for all. As I saw it, she still owed me.

The hot soak helped restore some flexibility to my muscles.

I peeled the leaves from my hands. Although green still clung to parts of my hair, I thought with some artful braiding I might be able to hide it.

The walk back to Valek's suite seemed endless. In a zombie-like state of mind, I passed through countless hallways, intersections and doorways. My steps were fueled by the single-minded desire of getting to bed.

For the next few days I fell into a routine. I tasted the Commander's meals, went to the library for research and took a daily walk around the castle complex. My day as a fugitive had caused me to crave the outdoors, and if I couldn't swing through the trees, at least I could explore the grounds.

I used the map of the castle that I had copied in my journal to find the library. It was a multilevel suite of rooms, burgeoning with books. The smell of decay and dust floated in the air along with a sense of abandonment. I was saddened by the knowledge that this tremendous source of information was going to waste because the Commander discouraged his people from educating themselves beyond what was necessary for their jobs.

Within his military structure, a person was trained specifically for their position only. Learning just for the sake of learning was frowned on, and greeted with suspicion.

Once I had ascertained that the library was truly a forgotten place, I brought the pods and beans there instead of carrying the heavy books back to my room. I found a small nook tucked away in a corner. The nook had a wooden table which faced one of the large, egg-shaped windows that randomly perforated the back wall of the library. Sunlight streamed into the nook and, after clearing the table of dust, it became my work area.

Cutting one of the yellow pods in half, I discovered it was filled with a white mucilaginous pulp. A taste of the pulp revealed it to have a sweet and citrus flavor with a taint of sour, as if it was starting to rot. The white flesh contained seeds. I cleaned the pulp from the seeds and uncovered thirty-six of them. They resembled the beans from the caravan. My excitement diminished as I compared seed against bean in the sunlight. The pod seed was purple instead of brown, and when I bit into the seed, I spit it out as a strong bitter and astringent taste filled my mouth. Nothing close to the slightly tart and earthy taste of the brown beans.

Assuming that the pods were a fruit and the beans edible, I pulled out every botany book I could find in the library and piled them on my table. Then I went through the shelves again. This time, I grabbed any volume with information about poisons. A much smaller stack; Valek had probably taken the interesting ones back to his office. My third trip through the shelves was an effort to find books on magic. Nothing.

I paused by an empty shelf, an oddity in this tightly packed library, and wondered if it had contained manuals about magic. Considering how the Commander viewed magic, it was logical to destroy any pertinent information. On a whim, I explored the lower levels of the bookcase under the empty shelf. Thinking that a book from the empty shelf could have slid back behind the other books, I took out all the texts on the lower shelves.

My efforts were rewarded by the discovery of a slim volume entitled *Magical Power Sources*. I hugged the book to my chest as paranoia gripped me. Scanning the library, I made sure no one was there. With sweaty palms, I hid the book in my backpack. I planned to read it later, preferably in my room with the door locked.

Giddy with my illicit acquisition, I searched the various rooms of the library until I found a comfortable chair. Before dragging it back to my nook, I beat the dust from its purple velvet cushions. It was the most elegant seat I had seen in the castle, and I wondered who had used it before me. Had the dead King been a bibliophile? The considerable collection of books said as much. Either that or he had shown his librarian great favor.

I spent many hours in that chair reading through the botany books and discovering nothing. I planned to decipher the pod and bean puzzle while I researched information for myself. The tedious work was at least broken into small sessions by my tasting the Commander's meals and by my afternoon strolls around the castle.

It had been four days since the exercise, and that afternoon my walk had a purpose. I scouted for a place with a view of the east gate, but where I wouldn't be obvious to the flow of people passing through.

Valek still hadn't returned from his mission, and closing ceremonies had been performed the night before at the fire festival, ending the weeklong celebration. Rand, looking hungover, had informed me this morning that Brazell and his retinue would finally leave the castle, via the east gate, to go home. My desire to see Brazell's retreating back with my own eyes had driven me to seek the perfect position.

The barracks for the Commander's soldiers filled both the northeast and southwest corners of the castle complex. In the northeast barracks, the L-shaped building extended from the north gate to the east gate, and a large rectangular training area had been built next to the east leg of the building. There was a wooden fence around the yard and, when training was in progress, the fence attracted the castle's various residents to stop along it to watch the exercises. That afternoon I joined in with a group of observers, who not only had a clear view of the fighting drills, but the east gate as well.

Rand's information proved accurate. Soon I was rewarded by a parade of green-and-black–clad soldiers. I could see Brazell on his dappled mare, riding among his most trusted advisers, at the end of the procession. Brazell's retinue ignored the people around them.

As I watched Brazell's back, Reyad's ghost appeared next to me. He smiled as he waved goodbye to his father. A shudder vibrated down my spine. I glanced around. Did anyone else see him? The group of people that I had been standing with had dispersed. Had Reyad scared them off? But when I looked again, his ghost was gone.

A hand touched my arm. I flinched.

"Good riddance to that lot," Ari said, tilting his head toward the east gate. Seeing him for the first time in the sunlight, I noticed that Ari's eyes were such a pale blue that in the darkness his eyes had seemed to hold no color.

Ari stood with Janco on the other side of the fence. Both wore the sleeveless shirts and short pants that the soldiers liked to train in. Sweat-soaked and streaked with dirt, their faces and bodies sported new cuts and bruises.

"Bet you're as glad as we are to see them go," Janco said. Resting his wooden training sword on the fence, he rubbed the sweat off his face with the bottom of his shirt.

"Yes, I am," I said.

Looking toward the east gate, the three of us stood in companionable silence for a moment, watching Brazell's entourage disappear through the gate.

"We want to thank you, Yelena," Ari said.

"What for?"

"The Commander promoted us to Captains. He said you gave us a good report," Janco said.

Surprised and pleased that the Commander would heed my words, I smiled at them. I could see Ari and Janco shared a loyalty to one another, an obvious bond of friendship and trust. Three years ago, I had felt that kind of kinship with May and Carra at the orphanage, but Reyad had torn me away, and the empty space inside me still ached. Rand had given me friendship, but there was still a distance. I longed to connect with someone. Unfortunately, my life as the food taster made it impossible. Who would take the risk of connecting with me when my odds of living through the next year were little to none?

"We're scouting for the Commander's elite guard now," Janco said with pride in his voice.

"We owe you one. Anytime you need help, just let us know," Ari said.

His words gave me a bold idea. Brazell might be gone, but he was still a threat. I thought fast, searching for reasons why my plan wouldn't be to my benefit.

"I need help," I said.

Surprise flashed over their faces. Ari recovered first. "With what?" he asked warily.

"I need to learn how to defend myself. Can you teach me self-defense and how to use a weapon?" I held my breath. Was I asking too much? If they said no, I hadn't lost anything. At least I had tried.

Ari and Janco looked at each other. Eyebrows twitched, heads tilted, lips pursed and hands made small movements. I watched their silent conversation in amazement as they discussed my request.

"What kind of weapon?" Ari asked. Again that hesitation evident in his voice.

My mind raced. I needed something that was small enough to hide within my uniform. "A knife," I said, knowing I'd have to return Rand's to the kitchen.

More facial expressions were exchanged. I thought Ari might be agreeing, but Janco looked queasy, as if the idea didn't sit well with him.

Finally, I couldn't take it anymore. "Look," I said. "I'll understand if you refuse. I don't want to get you into trouble, and I know how Janco feels about me. I believe his exact words were: 'She's a criminal.' So, if the answer is no, that's fine with me."

They stared at me in astonishment.

"How did you—" Janco started to say, but Ari punched him on the arm.

"She overheard us in the forest, you dope. How close were you?"

"Fifteen feet."

"Damn." Ari shook his head, which caused his tight blond curls to bounce. "We're more worried about Valek. We'll train you if he doesn't object. Agreed?"

"Agreed."

Ari and I shook hands. When I turned to Janco, he seemed deep in thought.

"A switchblade!" he declared, grabbing my hand.

"What?" I asked.

"A switchblade would be better than a knife," Janco said.

"And where would I carry this…switchblade?"

"Strapped to your thigh. You cut a hole in your pants pocket. Then if you're attacked, you pull it out, hit the switch, and a nine-inch blade leaps to your disposal." Janco demonstrated the motion to me and mock stabbed Ari, who clutched his stomach dramatically and fell over.

Perfect, I thought. Thrilled by the idea of learning to defend myself, I asked, "When do we start?"

Janco scratched his goatee. "Since Valek isn't back we could

start with some basic self-defense moves, nothing objection-
able about that."

"Moves she could have learned by watching the soldiers
train," Ari said, agreeing with his partner.

They decided. "Right now," they said in unison.

17

STANDING NEXT TO THE two oversize soldiers, I felt like a plum wedged between a couple of canta-loupes. Misgivings crept into my mind. The notion that I could defend myself against someone of Ari's build seemed ri-diculous. If he wanted, he could pick me up and throw me over his shoulder, and there was nothing I could do about it.

"Okay. First, we'll start with some self-defense," Ari ex-plained. "No weapons until the basic moves are instinctive. You're better off fighting hand to hand than wielding a weapon you don't know how to use. A skilled opponent would simply disarm you. Then your troubles would be doubled. Not only would you be under attack, but you'd have to counter your own weapon."

Ari leaned his practice sword next to Janco's, scanning the training yard. Most of the soldiers were gone, but small clumps of men still worked.

"What are your strengths?" Ari asked.

"Strengths?"

"What are you good at?"

Janco, sensing my confusion, prompted, "Are you a fast runner? That's a handy skill."

"Oh." I finally understood. "I'm flexible. I used to be an acrobat."

"Perfect. Coordination and agility are excellent skills. And…" Ari grabbed me around the waist. He threw me high into the air.

My limbs flailed a moment before instinct kicked in. Still in midair, I tucked my chin, arms and legs close to my body, executed a somersault to align myself, and landed on my feet, wobbling to regain my balance.

Outraged, I turned on Ari. Before I could demand an explanation, he said, "Another advantage of having acrobatic training is the ability to stay on your feet. That maneuver of yours could mean the difference between life and death. Right, Janco?"

Janco rubbed the vacant spot where the lower half of his right ear used to be. "It helps. You know who else would make a great fighter?"

Ari's shoulders sagged, as if he knew what Janco was going to say next and resigned himself to it.

Intrigued, I asked, "Who?"

"A dancer. With the proper training, the fire dancers at the festival could take on anyone. With a blazing staff spinning around, I wouldn't go against one with *any* weapon."

"Except a pail of water," Ari countered.

He and Janco then launched into an intense argument, debating the technical aspects of a fight against a fiery staff wielded by an enraged dancer. Although fascinated by the discussion, I had to interrupt them. My time was limited. The Commander's dinner would soon be served.

With only occasional sarcastic comments about fire dancers, Ari and Janco spent the remainder of my first lesson teaching me to block punches, then kicks, until my forearms were numb.

Ari halted the exercise when another soldier approached. His and Janco's relaxed postures tightened. They shifted to defensive stances, as Nix, the guard from Captain Parffet's unit, came closer. The skin on Nix's bald head was sunburned, and his thin fringe of black hair lay damply on his forehead. An overpowering stench of body odor preceded him, gagging me. His lean muscles reminded me of a slender coil of rope, dangerous when pulled tight.

"What the hell do you think you're doing?" Nix demanded.

"That's—what the hell do you think you're doing, *sir?*" Janco corrected him. "We outrank you. And, I think a salute would be a nice touch."

Nix sneered. "You'll lose your promotion when your boss finds out you're associating with a criminal. Whose brainless idea was it to make her into a more effective killer? When another dead body shows up, you'll be accomplices."

Janco took a menacing step toward Nix, but Ari's meaty hand on his shoulder stopped him. With undertones of a threat laced into his voice, Ari said, "What we do with our free time is none of your business. Now, why don't you shuffle off to Parffet. I saw him heading toward the latrines. He'll need you to wipe his ass soon. It's the one skill you're most suited for."

Nix was outnumbered, but he couldn't resist a parting shot. "She has a history of killing her benefactor. I'd watch my necks if I were you."

Ari's and Janco's eyes stayed on Nix's back until he left the yard. Then they turned to me.

"That's a good start," Ari said, ending the lesson. "See you tomorrow at dawn."

"What about Nix?" I asked.

"No problem. We can take care of him." Ari shrugged it off, confident in his ability to deal with Nix. I envied Ari's self-assurance and physical power. I didn't think *I* could handle Nix, and I wondered if there was another reason, besides killing Reyad, that made Nix hate me.

"I taste the Commander's breakfast at dawn," I said.

"Then right after."

"What for?" I asked.

"The soldiers run laps around the compound to keep in shape," Janco answered.

"Join them," Ari said. "Do at least five circuits. More if you're able. We'll increase the amount until you've caught up to us."

"How many laps do you run?"

"Fifty."

I gulped. As I returned to the castle, I thought of the work and time I would need to devote to training. Learning self-defense would require the same commitment I had applied to my acrobatics. I couldn't go halfway. It had seemed like a good idea at the time. I had been giddy with fairy-tale visions of easily fighting off Brazell's guards. But the more I thought about it, the more I realized this wasn't something to do on a whim.

I wondered if I would be better off spending my time learning about poisons and magic. In the end, all the physical training in the world wouldn't save me from Irys's magical powers.

My feet dragged on the ground, and my body felt as if it were pulling a wagon full of stones. Why couldn't I just go for it? Why was I constantly considering each option, searching both sides of an argument for gaps in the logic? Like somersaulting on the trampoline, plenty of ups and downs but no forward motion. I longed for the days when a wrong decision wouldn't cost me my life.

By the time I reached the Commander's office, I had concluded that I had other enemies besides the magician, and being able to defend myself might save my life someday. Knowledge, whatever the form, could be as effective as a weapon.

Soon after I arrived, one of the tutors bustled into the office, dragging a young girl with him. At age twelve every child was assigned a profession based on their capabilities, and then they were sent to the appropriate tutor for four years to learn.

The tutor's red uniform had black diamonds stitched on the collar, making it the direct opposite of an adviser's black uniform. The girl wore the simple red jumper of a student. Her brown eyes were shiny with unshed tears. Her facial expressions alternated between terror and defiance as she battled to compose herself. I guessed she was about fifteen years old.

"What's the problem, Beevan?" the Commander asked, annoyance tainting his voice.

"This disobedient child is a constant disruption to my class."

"In what way?"

"Mia is a know-it-all. She refuses to solve mathematical problems in the traditional manner and has the gall to correct me in front of the entire class."

"Why are you here?"

"I want her disciplined. Whipped, preferably, and reassigned as a servant."

Beevan's request caused silent tears to spill down Mia's cheeks, although she maintained her composure, which was impressive for someone so young.

The Commander steepled his fingers, considering. I cringed for the girl, having her tutor bother the Commander for this dispute would not help her. Beevan must have gone over the training coordinator.

"I'll handle it," the Commander finally said. "You're dismissed."

Beevan wavered for a moment, opening and closing his mouth several times. His pinched expression revealed that this was not the response he had expected. Nodding stiffly, he left the office.

The Commander pushed his chair away from the desk and gestured to Mia to come around. Now eye level with her, he asked, "What's your side of the story?"

With a thin quavering voice, she answered, "I'm good with numbers, Sir." She hesitated as if expecting to be corrected for making a bold statement, but, when none came, she continued, "I was bored solving mathematical problems Tutor Beevan's way, so I invented new and faster ways. He's not good with numbers, Sir." Again she stopped, flinching as though she was anticipating a blow. "I made the mistake of pointing out his errors. I'm sorry, Sir. Please don't whip me, Sir. I'll never do it again, Sir. I'll follow Tutor Beevan's every command." Tears flowed down her bright pink cheeks.

"No, you won't," the Commander replied.

Terror gripped the girl's face.

"Relax, child. Yelena?"

Startled, I spilled some of his tea. I had been holding his tray. "Yes, Sir."

"Fetch Adviser Watts."

"Yes, Sir." I put the tray on the desk and hurried through the door. I had met Watts once. He was the Commander's accountant, who had given me the money I had earned playing fugitive. He was working at his desk, but immediately followed me back to the office.

"Watts, do you still need an assistant?" the Commander asked.

"Yes, Sir," Watts replied.

"Mia, you have one day to prove yourself. If you don't dazzle Adviser Watts with your mathematical skills, then you'll have to return to Beevan's class. If you do, then you can have the job. Agreed?"

"Yes, Sir. Thank you, Sir." Mia's pretty face was radiant as she trailed behind Watts.

I marveled at the Commander. Being compassionate, hearing Mia's side of the story, and giving her a chance, were the exact opposite of how I imagined the encounter would play out. Why would a man with such power take the time to go that extra step? He risked upsetting Beevan and the coordinator. Why would he bother to encourage a student?

His stack of reports reclaimed the Commander's attention, so I slipped out the door, heading toward the library to continue my research.

After a while, the sun began to set. I picked out a promising botany book to take with me as I was reluctant to have a lantern light betray my presence in the library.

The candlelight cast a dismal glow in the corridors. I watched my shadow glide along the walls as I headed for Valek's suite, wondering if I should move back to my old room in the servants' wing. Now that Brazell was gone, there was no logical reason for me to remain with Valek. But the thought of living in that small room, where I wouldn't have anyone to argue with or to discuss poisoning methods with, left a hollow feeling inside me. That same empty pang I'd been having on and off these last four days.

Only the cold darkness greeted me when I entered Valek's suite. My disappointment surprised me, and I realized I had been missing him. I shook my head at the foreign concept. Me? Miss Valek? No. I couldn't allow myself to think that way.

Instead, I focused on my survival. If I wanted to discover an antidote to Butterfly's Dust, paging through books on counteracting poisons while sitting in Valek's living room wouldn't be the smartest idea. Of course, the decision might not be mine to make. Once Valek found out Brazell had gone, he'd probably order me to move back anyway.

After I had lit the lanterns in Valek's suite, I relaxed on the couch with the botany book. Biology had never been a favorite subject of mine, and I soon found my mind wandering. My weak efforts to remain focused were lost to my daydreams.

A muffled slam brought my attention back to the present. It sounded like a book hitting the floor. I glanced down, but my volume remained in my lap, opened to a particularly boring passage about fruit trees. I scanned the living room to see if one of Valek's untidy piles of books had fallen over. Sighing at his mess, I couldn't tell if something had toppled or not.

A frightening thought crept into my mind. Maybe the noise had come from upstairs. Maybe it hadn't been a book but a person. Someone sneaking in to wait until I fell asleep to kill me. Unable to sit still, I grabbed a lantern and dashed into my room.

My backpack rested on the bureau. Rand hadn't asked for his knife yet, so I hadn't returned it. Pulling the blade from the pack, Ari's words about misusing a weapon flew through my mind. It was probably foolish to take the knife, but I felt more confident with it in my hand. Armed, I returned to the living room and considered my next move. Sleep would be impossible tonight until I investigated the upstairs rooms.

Blackness from above pressed down on my meager light as I ascended the staircase. Curving to the right, the stairs ended in a sitting room. Piles of boxes, books and furniture were scattered throughout the room in a haphazard fashion, casting odd-shaped shadows on the walls. I maneuvered with caution around the heaps. My blood slammed in my heart as I shone my lantern into dark corners, searching for an ambush.

A flash of light caused a yip to escape my lips. I spun, only to discover it was my own lantern reflecting in the tall thin windows that striped the far wall.

Three rooms were located to the right of the sitting chamber. A quick heart-pumping check of the box-filled rooms revealed they were empty of ambushers and identical to the three off the downstairs living area.

To the left of the upstairs sitting area was a long hallway. Doorways lined the right side of the corridor opposite a smooth stone wall. The hall ended in a set of locked double wooden doors. Carved into the ebony wood was an elaborate hunting scene. By the thin coating of white powder on the floor beneath the doors, I guessed this was the entrance to Valek's bedroom. The powder would show footprints, alerting Valek to an intruder. I breathed easier seeing the powder un-disturbed.

As I systematically checked the remaining rooms along the corridor, the growing realization that Valek was a true pack rat struck me. I had always imagined assassins as creatures of the dark, traveling light and never staying in one place for too long. Valek's suite resembled the house of an old married couple who had filled their rooms with all the things they had collected over the years.

Distracted by these thoughts, I opened the last doorway. It took me some time to properly register what I saw. Compared to the others, the room was barren. One long table lined the back wall, centered under a large, teardrop-shaped window. Gray rocks streaked with white—the same stones I had been tripping over in Valek's living room and office for the past month and a half—were arranged by size on the floor.

A thick layer of dust scrunched under my boots when I walked into the room. On the table, carving chisels, metal sanding files and a grinding wheel occupied the only dust-free spots. Small statues in various stages of creation were interspersed among the tools. To my delight, I realized that the gray rocks, when carved and polished, metamorphosed into a beautiful, lustrous black, and the white streaks transformed into brilliant silver.

Setting the lantern on the table, I picked up a finished butterfly with silver spots sparkling from its wings. It fit into the palm of my hand. The detail was so exquisite that it appeared the butterfly might beat its wings and lift into the air at any moment. I admired the other statues. The same devoted care had been applied to each. Lifelike animals, insects and flowers lined the table; apparently, nature provided the artist's favorite subjects.

Stunned, I realized Valek must be the artist. Here was a side of Valek I never imagined existed. I felt as though I had intruded upon his most personal secret. As if I had uncovered a wife and children living up here in happy seclusion, complete with the family dog.

I had noticed the figurines on Valek's desk and, at least once a day, I glanced at the snow cat in the Commander's office, attempting to understand why he had selected that particular statue for display. I now understood its significance. Valek had carved it for the Commander.

The shuffle of feet made me whirl around. A black shape rushed me. My knife was yanked from my grasp and pressed against my neck. Fear clenched my throat tight, suffocating me. The familiar feeling triggered a sudden flashback of soldiers disarming and dragging me off Reyad's dead body. But Valek's face showed mirth instead of wrath.

"Snooping?" Valek asked, stepping back.

With effort, I banished my fear and remembered to start breathing again. "I heard a noise. I came to…"

"Investigate." Valek finished my sentence. "Searching for an intruder is different from examining statues." He pointed with the knife to the butterfly clutched in my hand. "You were snooping."

"Yes."

"Good. Curiosity is a commendable trait. I wondered when you would explore up here. Find anything interesting?"

I held up the butterfly. "It's beautiful."

He shrugged. "Carving focuses my mind."

I placed the statue on the table, my hand lingering over it. I would have enjoyed studying the butterfly in the sunlight. Grabbing the lantern, I followed Valek from the room.

"I really did hear a noise," I said.

"I know. I knocked a book over to see what you would

do. I didn't expect a knife, though. Is it the one missing from the kitchen?"

"Did Rand report it?" I felt betrayed. Why hadn't he just asked for it back?

"No. It just makes sense to keep track of large kitchen knives, so when one goes missing you're not surprised when someone attacks you with it." Valek handed the knife back. "You should return it. Knives won't help you against the caliber of people after you."

Valek and I descended the stairs. I lifted the botany book from the couch.

"What does the Commander think of the pods?" Valek asked.

"He thinks they're from Sitia. He returned them to me so I could discover what they are. I've been doing research in the library." I showed Valek the book.

He took it from me and flipped through the pages. "Find anything?"

"Not yet."

"Your actions as our fugitive must have impressed the Commander. Normally, he would have assigned this sort of thing to one of his science advisers."

Valek's words made me uncomfortable. I wasn't convinced that I could discover the origin of the pods and beans. The idea of failing the Commander made me queasy. I changed the subject. "Where did the caravan go?"

Valek paused, undecided. Finally, he said, "Brazell's new factory." If Valek had been surprised by his discovery, it didn't show on his face.

It occurred to me that despite all the discussion about Brazell's permit, I didn't know what he was planning to make. "What's the product?"

"It's supposed to be a feed mill." Valek handed the book back to me. "And I don't know why he would need those pods and beans. Maybe they're a secret ingredient. Maybe they're added to the feed to enhance the cow's milk supply. Then every farmer would buy Brazell's feed instead of growing his own. Or something along that line. Or maybe not. I'm not an expert." Valek pulled at his hair. "I'll have to study his permit to see what I'm missing. Either way, I assigned some of my corps to stake out the route and infiltrate the factory. At this point I need more information."

"Brazell left the castle this afternoon."

"I passed his retinue on my way back. Good. One less thing to worry about."

Valek crossed to his desk and began sorting through his papers. I watched his back for a while, waiting. He didn't mention my moving out. I finally worked up the nerve to ask. "Should I return to my old room now that Brazell's gone?" I berated myself for my choice of words. I should have been firmer, but it was too late.

Valek stopped. I held my breath.

"No," he said. "You're still in danger. The magician hasn't been dealt with yet." His pen resumed its course over the paper.

Strong relief flushed through my body like a hot wave, alarming me. Why did I want to stay with him? Remaining was dangerous, illogical, and, by every argument I could muster, the worst situation for me. The book on magic was still hidden in my backpack, which went with me everywhere because I feared Valek would pull one of his stunts and surprise me.

Damn it, I thought, angry at myself. As if I didn't have enough to worry about. I shouldn't miss Valek; I should try harder to escape. I shouldn't figure out the bean puzzle; I should sabotage it. I shouldn't admire and respect him; I should vilify him. Shouldn't, should, shouldn't, should. So easy to say but so hard to believe.

"Exactly how do you deal with a magician?" I asked.

He turned around in his seat and looked at me. "I've told you before."

"But their powers…"

"Have no effect on me. When I get close, I can feel their power pressing and vibrating on my skin, and moving toward them is like walking through thick syrup. It takes effort, but I always win in the end. Always."

"How close?" Valek had been in the castle both times I had unknowingly used magic. Did Valek suspect?

"I have to be in the same room," Valek said.

Relief washed through me. He didn't know. At least, not yet. "Why didn't you kill the southern magician at the festival?" I asked.

"Yelena, I'm not invincible. Fighting four men while she threw every ounce of her power at me was exhausting. Chasing her down would have been a fruitless endeavor."

I thought about what he said. "Is being resistant to magic a form of magic?" I asked.

"No." Valek's face hardened.

"What about the knife?" I pointed to the long blade hanging on the wall. The crimson blood gleamed in the lantern light. In the three weeks I'd lived in Valek's suite, it hadn't dried.

Valek laughed. "That was the knife I used to kill the King. *He* was a magician. When his magic couldn't stop me from plunging that knife into his heart, he cursed me with his dying breath. It was rather melodramatic. He willed that I should be plagued with guilt over his murder and have his blood stain my hands forever. With my peculiar immunity to magic, the curse attached to the knife instead of me." Valek looked at the weapons wall thoughtfully. "It was a shame to lose my favorite blade, but it does make for a nice trophy."

18

MY LUNGS BLAZED. Flushed and sweat-soaked, I lagged behind the main group of soldiers, my throat burning with every gasp. It was my fourth lap around the castle complex. One more to go.

I had hovered by the northeast barracks right after tasting the Commander's breakfast. When a large clump of soldiers ran past, I spotted Ari, who waved me to join in. I worried that the other guards would resent my presence, but there were servants, stable boys and other castle workers mixed in with the soldiers.

The first two laps quickened my pulse and shortened my breath. Pain began in my feet during the third lap and traveled up my legs by the fourth. My surroundings blurred until all I saw was the small patch of ground right in front of me. When I limped to my finishing point, ending my agony, I found a thick row of hedges and threw up my breakfast of sweet cakes. Straightening, I saw a grinning Janco give me a thumbs-up as he jogged by. He didn't even have the decency to look winded, and his shirt was still dry.

As I wiped vomit off my lip, Ari paused beside me. "Training yard, two o'clock. See you then," he said.

"But…" I said to nobody as Ari jogged away. I could hardly stand, I couldn't imagine doing anything more strenuous.

In the training yard that afternoon, Ari and Janco leaned against the fence watching two men sparring with swords. The loud ring of metal striking metal echoed. The fighters had drawn the attention of every soldier. I realized with surprise that one of the men was Valek. I hadn't seen him since early that morning, and I had assumed he was resting after being up late the night before.

Valek was liquid in motion. As I watched him, one word came to my mind: beautiful. His movements had the speed and cadence of a complex dance performance. In comparison, his adversary resembled a newborn colt, lurching and jerking his arms and legs as if this were his first time on his feet. Valek's smooth lunges and graceful parries disarmed his opponent in no time.

Pointing with his sword, he sent his beaten foe to a small group of men, and motioned for another to attack.

"What's going on?" I asked.

"Valek's challenge," Janco said.

"What's that?"

"Valek has declared a challenge to anyone in Ixia. Beat him in a fight with the weapon of your choice, or hand to hand,

and you can be promoted to his second-in-command." Ari
gestured to Valek, now engaged in combat with a third man.
"It's become a sort of graduation from basic training for the
soldiers to fight Valek at least once, although you can try as
many times as you like. The Captains watch the matches and
recruit the more promising soldiers. And if you manage to
impress Valek with your skills, he may offer you a post in his
elite intelligence corps."

"How did you guys do?" I asked.

"Okay," Ari demurred.

"Okay!" Janco snorted. "Ari came close to beating him.
Valek was pleased. But Ari would rather be a scout than a spy."

"I want all or nothing," Ari said with a quiet intensity.

We continued to watch. Ari and Janco made technical
comments about the different fights, but I couldn't tear my eyes
from Valek. With the sunlight glinting off his sword, he dispatched two more men. He tapped them with the flat of his
weapon, just to let them know he had broken through their
defenses without shedding any blood. The next opponent approached with a knife.

"Bad choice," Ari said.

Valek put down his sword and unsheathed his blade. The
match was over in two moves.

"Valek excels in knife fighting," Janco commented.

The last challenger was a woman. Tall and agile, she wielded
a long wooden staff. Ari called it a bow. She held her own against
Valek, and their sparring lasted longer than any of the previous
six fights. With a loud crack, her bow snapped in two, ending

the match. As the crowd dispersed, Valek spoke with the woman.

"That's Maren," Ari said. "If she doesn't disappear into Valek's corps, you should ask her to teach you the bow. With your smaller size, it would extend your reach against a taller attacker."

"But you can't conceal a bow," I said.

"Not around the castle. But if you're hiking through the woods, you wouldn't look out of place holding a walking stick."

I looked at Maren and considered the possibilities. Would she agree to help me? Probably not. What would she stand to gain?

As if reading my thoughts, Ari said, "Maren's aggressive and encouraging. Every new female recruit gets her personal attention whether they want it or not. Since so many women fail due to the rigors of training, she tries to coach them through. We've more women in the guard now than ever because of her. We tried to get her to teach us—a bow would make a good weapon for a scout—but she has no interest in training men."

"But I'm not a new recruit, I'm the food taster. Why would she waste her time with me? I might be dead by tomorrow."

"Aren't we grumpy today," Janco said cheerfully. "Too much exercise this morning?"

"Shut up," I said. Unfazed, his grin only widened.

"All right, that's enough. Let's get started," Ari said.

I spent the rest of the afternoon learning to punch someone without breaking my hand and practicing the proper technique of kicking. The first two knuckles of both hands turned bright red as I punched into a training bag over and over. Mastering the front kick was a challenge since my stiff thigh muscles hindered my flexibility.

When Ari finally dismissed me, I aimed my battered body toward the castle.

"See you in the morning," Janco said with a gleeful sound in his voice.

I turned to tell him where to stick it and came face-to-face with Valek. I held my breath. He had been watching us. I felt self-conscious.

"Your punches are slow," he said. Taking my hand, he examined the bruises, which were starting to purple. "At least your technique is good. If you hold weights in your hands while you train, your punches will be much quicker without them."

"I can continue?" I asked in disbelief.

He still held on to my hand, and I couldn't summon the will-power to pull it back. The warmth of his touch coursed through my body, temporarily vanquishing my aches and pains.

With the memory of his stunning physical display fresh in my mind, I gazed at his strong face. His flashing and dangerous blue eyes had always taken my attention. I had learned to read his facial expressions as a survival tactic but I had never really looked at him in this way before. He was a study in contradiction. The man who carved delicate statues was also capable of disarming seven opponents without breaking a sweat. My interactions with Valek resembled a performance on the tightrope. One minute I was confident and balanced, and the next insecure and unstable.

"I think it's an excellent idea," he said. "How did you get the power twins to agree to teach you?"

"Power twins?"

"Combine Ari's strength with Janco's speed, and they would be unbeatable. But, so far, I haven't had to test my theory since they haven't tried to fight me together. No one said I couldn't have more than one second-in-command. You're not going to give me away, are you?"

"No."

Valek gave my hand a small squeeze, and then released his grip. "Good. They're probably the best instructors at the castle. How did you meet them?"

"They were the men who found me in the forest. The Commander promoted them, and I took advantage of their gratitude." My hand tingled where he had touched it.

"Opportunistic and underhanded, I love it." Valek laughed. He was in a good mood as he walked beside me to the castle. Probably a rush from beating so many opponents. Before we reached the east entrance, he stopped. "There's one problem."

My heartbeat increased to double time. "What?"

"You shouldn't train so visibly. Word spreads quickly. If Brazell finds out and makes a fuss, the Commander will order you to stop. And it'll make the Commander suspicious."

We entered the cool, dark air of the castle. It was a relief to be out of the hot sun.

"Why don't you make use of all those empty storerooms in the lower level of the castle? You can still run laps in the morning for exercise," Valek said.

Great, I thought sarcastically, jogging was the one aspect of training I would have been willing to give up. However,

Valek was right, working with Ari and Janco in the middle of the yard had already attracted negative attention. Mainly Nix, whose scowls and nasty glares burned on my skin.

Valek was quiet as we traveled through the castle. I was headed to the Commander's office to taste his dinner. He walked with me.

"Mentioning Brazell reminds me that I've been wanting to ask you about that Criollo that the Commander enjoys. Do you like the taste of it?"

I chose my words with care. "Yes, it's an excellent dessert."

"If you stopped eating it, how would you feel?"

"Well…" I hesitated, unsure where this conversation was leading. "Truthfully, I would be disappointed. I look forward to eating a piece every morning."

"Have you ever craved the Criollo?" Valek inquired.

I finally understood where his pointed questions were leading. "Like an addiction?"

He nodded.

"I don't think so, but…"

"But what?"

"I only eat it once a day. The Commander has a piece after every meal, including his evening snack. Why this sudden concern?" I asked.

"Just a feeling. It might be nothing." Valek was silent during the rest of the trip.

"Well, Valek, any new promotions?" the Commander asked as we entered his office.

"No. But Maren shows promise. Unfortunately she doesn't

want to be in my corps or even be my second. She just wants to beat me." Valek grinned, delighted by the challenge.

"And can she?" the Commander inquired. His eyebrows rose.

"With time and the proper training. She's deadly with her bow; it's just her tactics that need work."

"Then what do we do with her?"

"Promote her to General and retire some of those old windbags. We could use some fresh blood in the upper ranks."

"Valek, you never had a good grasp of military structure."

"Then promote her to First Lieutenant today, Captain tomorrow, Major the next day, Colonel the day after, and General the day after that."

"I'll take it under advisement." The Commander flashed me an annoyed glance. I was dawdling, and he had noticed.

"Anything else?" he asked Valek.

I finished tasting, placed the Commander's tray on the desk, and headed for the door.

Valek grabbed my arm. "I'd like to try an experiment. I want Yelena to taste the Criollo every time you do for a week, then the next week I'll taste it for you. I want to see if anything happens to her when she stops eating the dessert."

"No." The Commander raised a hand when Valek started to argue. "I recognize your concern, but I think it's misplaced."

"Humor me."

"We can try your experiment once Rand duplicates the recipe from General Brazell. Acceptable?"

"Yes, Sir."

"Good. I want you to join me in a meeting with General

Kitvivan. We're just starting the cooling season, and he's already worried about snow cats." The Commander's eyes found me. "Yelena, you're dismissed."

"Yes, Sir," I said.

After stopping at the baths to wash, I visited the kitchen to borrow a large sieve and bowl, which I carried to the library. The remaining four pods had turned brown and were starting to rot, so I opened them, scraped out the browning pulp and seeds into the colander, and placed it into the bowl. Its bottom and sides were suspended above the inside of the bowl by the metal handles. The strong odor from the seeds permeated the room. I set the bowl on the windowsill, and opened the window to air out the smell. My experiment wasn't based on any scientific research; I just wanted to see if the pulp would ferment. Maybe Brazell was using it to make some kind of alcoholic beverage.

My careful reading of the various botany books hadn't revealed anything useful so far. The poison books, while interesting, had made no mention of Butterfly's Dust. In four different volumes on poisons, I had discovered missing pages. Poking up from the binding were ragged edges where the paper had been ripped out. Valek had probably removed all pertinent information long ago in anticipation of the food tasters' keen interest in Butterfly's Dust.

Sighing, I piled the books at the end of my table. I knew Valek was attending the Commander's meeting, so I slid the book of magic out of my backpack. The silver lettering of the title glinted. My stomach knotted.

Opening the slim volume, I began to read a technical discussion of the source of a magician's power. Unable to understand all of the detailed descriptions, I only sensed that the
power source blanketed the entire world, making it accessible
from anywhere.

The magicians used this power in different ways, depending on their talents. Some could move objects, while others
could read and influence minds. Healing, lighting fires and
mental communication were also magical skills. Some could
only do one thing, but the stronger the magician, the more
the magician could do. A weaker magician could only read
someone's mind, while a more powerful one could not only
read but communicate and even control someone's mind. I
shuddered at the thought of Irys controlling my mind.

But the magicians had to be careful when drawing power.
By pulling on the source too hard or misusing it, a magician
could cause creases that would set off a ripple effect. This
effect, or warping, would concentrate power in certain areas
and leave other places bare. Fluctuating unpredictably, another
wave might reverse the amount of power available. In order to
tap the power, the magicians would have to seek areas of
power, but once they found a pocket, they wouldn't know how
long it would remain.

The book chronicled a time when a strong magician had
tapped into the source, pulling it toward him. Because he was
so powerful he was able to control the blanket without causing
an explosion. The other magicians were then uncovered.
Stripped of their power, they united and searched for him.

Once found, and after a battle that left many dead, they tapped into his stolen source, and killed him. Eventually, the blanket had smoothed out and returned to normal, but that had taken over two hundred years.

Fingering the raised lettering on the cover, I now understood why Irys had been so determined that I should either be trained or be killed. When my magic reached a flameout, it would cause major ripples in the blanket of power. I sank deep into my chair, disappointed that the book hadn't contained magic spells or lessons. I had been hoping for an answer. Something along the lines of: this is why you have the power, here's how you use it, and while we're at it, this is how to conjure up the antidote to Butterfly's Dust.

It had been wishful thinking, plain and simple, dangerous for me to indulge in. Hope, happiness and freedom were not in my future. They had never been, not even as an ignorant child in Brazell's orphanage. While hoping for a normal life, I had been raised as a laboratory rat for his experiments.

I slumped in my chair until the sun set, allowing self-pity to run its course. When the muscles in my legs began to throb with inactivity, I stood and physically shook off my gloom. If I couldn't find the antidote in the books, I would find it another way. Someone had to know something. There had been food tasters on Commander Ambrose's staff for fifteen years. If no one could help me, then I would try another way, perhaps stealing the antidote or following Valek to its source. Skills I lacked, but I was determined to learn.

* * *

The next morning, prepared with an empty stomach, I joined in the flow of jogging soldiers. Ari and Janco breezed past me. Janco flashed a jaunty wave and mischievous smile. Later, when I heard heavy steps pounding behind me, I assumed Janco was up to no good.

I moved aside to let him pass, but the runner stayed close on my heels. I glanced back in time to see Nix thrust his arms out. His hands connected with my back. I fell forward, crashing to the ground. As Nix ran over me, his boot slammed into my solar plexus, knocking the wind out of me.

Pain bloomed in my chest. I gasped for breath while curled in a fetal position on the ground. Once I regained my wind, I pushed myself to a sitting position. The flow of soldiers remained unabated, and I wondered if anyone had witnessed what that bastard had done.

If he was trying to discourage me, he was going about it the wrong way. Nix had just increased my resolve to learn self-defense so I didn't fall victim to mongrels like him. I stood up and waited for Nix's next circuit, but he never came back.

Ari stopped. "What happened?"

"Nothing." Nix, like Margg, was my problem. If I didn't deal with him, he would never leave me alone. A tingle of doubt touched my stomach. It had been that kind of thinking that had landed me in the dungeon, awaiting execution.

"Your face is covered with blood," Ari said.

I wiped the blood on my sleeve. "I fell."

Before he could question me further, I changed the subject

by giving him something else to think about. I repeated Valek's advice about concealing our training sessions; Ari agreed that it was prudent to go "underground." He offered to scout out a suitable location.

"You're Maren, right?" I asked between gasps for air. I had been running laps for a week, and this morning I had timed my pace to run beside Maren.

She shot me a quick, appraising glance. Her blond hair was pulled back in a ponytail. Wide muscular shoulders atop a thin waist made her figure appear disproportionate. She moved with athletic ease, and I had to scramble to keep up with her long, loping strides.

"And you're the Puker," Maren said.

It was an insult aimed with a purpose; her interest in my response was keen. If she had wanted to dismiss me, she would have made her comment and sprinted away, not bothering to watch for a reaction.

"I've been called worse."

"Why do you do it?" Maren asked.

"What?"

"Run till you're sick."

"Five circuits were assigned. I don't like to fail." I received another measuring look. With my words coming out as huffs, I knew I wouldn't be able to maintain a conversation for long. "I watched you fight Valek. I've heard you're the best with a bow. I want to learn to use one."

Her pace slowed. "Who told you that?"

"Ari and Janco."

Maren snorted as if she thought a con artist had duped me. "Friends of yours?"

"Yes."

Her mouth formed a small *o* as she made a mental connection. "They found you in the forest. It's rumored they were training you to fight but you quit. Are they foisting you off on me?"

"The problem with rumors—" I panted "—is the difficulty in sorting the truth from the lies."

"And the reason I'm willing to donate my time?"

I had anticipated this question. "Information."

"About what?"

"You want to beat Valek, right?"

Her gray eyes focused on me like two sword points pressing against my skin.

With the last of my breath, I wheezed out, "Come to the east entrance of the castle this afternoon at two and I'll tell you." Unable to keep up with her any longer, I slowed down. She pulled ahead. I lost sight of her in the press of soldiers.

Throughout the rest of the morning, I replayed the conversation in my mind, trying to guess her response as I tasted the Commander's meals. At two o'clock, I waited in the castle's east doorway, chewing on my lip. Ari and Janco had spread a rumor that my training had stopped. I'd taken a considerable risk by indicating to Maren that this might not be true. When I spotted a tall figure carrying two bows heading in my direction, my anxiety eased a little.

Maren paused when she entered the corridor. She spotted me leaning against the wall.

Before she could comment, I said, "Follow me." I led her to a deserted hallway where Janco and Ari waited.

"I guess gossip is not to be trusted," Maren said to Ari.

"No. But there are certain rumors we would like to keep as is." A thinly disguised threat laced Ari's words.

Maren ignored him. "Okay, Puker, what's your information? And it better be good or I'm walking."

Ari's face reddened and I could see that he bit back a remark. Janco, as always, grinned in anticipation.

"Well, as I see it, the four of us can help each other out. Ari, Janco and I want to learn how to fight with the bow. You want to beat Valek. Working together, we may be able to achieve our goals."

"How's my teaching you going to help in a match against Valek?" Maren asked.

"You're skilled with the bow, but your fighting tactics need work. Ari and Janco can help you with that."

"One week of training and the Puker thinks she's an expert," Maren said to Ari with an incredulous voice. He remained mute, but his face darkened.

"I'm not an expert, but Valek is."

She shot me a cold stare. "He said that? About me?"

I nodded.

"So I teach bow, and Ari and Jan teach tactics. What's your contribution?"

I gestured to the four of us. "This. And…" I hesitated,

unsure if my next statement would have any sway. "I could teach you some flips, and help you to gain greater flexibility and balance that might benefit you in a fight."

"Damn." Janco was impressed. "She's got you there. And four does make for a better training group than three."

Annoyed, Maren shifted her focus to Janco. He smiled sweetly at her.

"All right, I'll try it on a temporary basis. If it doesn't work, I'm walking." Before anyone could interject, she said, "Don't worry. I may listen to the rumor mill, but I don't participate in it."

Once we shook hands on the arrangement, my apprehension dissipated. We showed her where we had been meeting for the last week.

"Cozy," Maren said as she entered our training room.

Ari had found an abandoned storeroom on the lower level in the deserted southwest corner of the castle. Two windows near the ceiling let in enough light to work by.

We spent the remaining time practicing the rudiments of bow fighting.

"Not bad, Puker," Maren said at the end of the session. "I see some potential."

When she picked up her bows to leave, Ari placed a large hand on her shoulder. "Her name's Yelena. If you don't want to call her by her name, then don't come back tomorrow."

I could see my astonished expression mirrored on Maren's face, but she recovered quicker than I did. Nodding curtly, she shook off Ari's hand and walked away. I wondered if she would join us again.

She returned the next day, and showed up without fail for the next two months as we trained together throughout the cooling season. The air held a fresh crisp scent, and true to the season's name, each day grew cooler than the last. The bright flowers of the hot season wilted while the trees turned orange, russet and finally brown. The leaves dropped to the ground and were blown away by the frequent rainstorms.

My research on the pods had stalled, but Valek appeared unconcerned by my lack of progress. On occasion he observed us training, and he would comment and make suggestions.

Nix continued to plague me during my morning run. He threw rocks, he spat on me and tripped me. I had to change my routine to avoid him by running laps around the outer wall of the castle complex. My defensive abilities were still in the beginning stages, and not sufficient for a confrontation with Nix. At least, not yet. There were advantages to running outside the complex. The smooth grass was softer on my feet than the dirt path inside the complex, and by jogging before dawn, I encountered no one, which added to the deception that I had quit training.

At the end of the cooling season, the hours of daylight shortened, and our training sessions ended with the setting sun. In the semidarkness of twilight I headed to the baths, moving with care to accommodate my bruised ribs. Janco, that annoying jackrabbit, had gotten through my defenses with his speedy little jabs.

As I approached the entrance to the baths, a large shadow detached from the stone wall. Alarmed, I stepped back into a fighting stance. Fear, excitement and doubt raced through my body. Would I need to defend myself? Could I do it? Should I run?

Margg's ample shape coalesced out of the shadows, and I relaxed a bit.

"What do you want?" I asked. "Are you running another errand for your master like a good doggie?"

"Better than being a rat caught in a trap."

I brushed past her. Exchanging insults, while enjoyable, was a waste of my time.

"Would the rat like some cheese?" she asked.

I turned. "What?"

"Cheese. Money. Gold. I bet you're the kind of rat that would do anything for a piece of cheese."

19

"WHAT WOULD I HAVE TO DO to get a piece of cheese?" I asked. I knew it! Margg was the one leaking information about me, and now she wanted to use me. Finally, some evidence.

"I have a source that pays well for information. It's the perfect setup for a little rat," Margg said.

"What kind of information?"

"Anything you might overhear while you're scurrying around the Commander's office or Valek's apartment. My contact pays on a sliding scale; the juicier the news, the bigger the chunk of cheese."

"How does it work?" My mind raced. Right now it was her word against mine. I needed proof I could show Valek. To be able to finger both Margg and her source would be a sweet treat.

"You give me the information," she said, "and I pass it

along. I collect the money, and give it to you, minus a fifteen percent fee."

"And I'm supposed to believe that you'd stick to fifteen percent cut of a total I'd be unaware of?"

She shrugged. "It's either that or nothing. I'd think that a half-starved rat like you would pounce on any morsel, no matter how small." Margg began to walk away.

"What if we went to your source together?" I suggested. "Then you'd still receive your fee."

She stopped. Uncertainty creased her fleshy face. "I'll have to check." She disappeared down the hallway.

I lingered outside the baths for a while, considering the possibility of following Margg around for a couple of days, but dismissed the idea. If her contact didn't like my suggestion, I'd scamper to Margg with my tail between my legs, begging for another chance. She'd enjoy that! Then I'd follow her. Revealing her as a traitor to Valek would be a pleasure.

My conversation with Margg had used up my bath time, so I headed to the Commander's office. When I arrived, Sammy, Rand's kitchen boy, hovered outside the closed door holding a tray of food. I could hear a muffled angry voice inside.

"What's going on?" I asked Sammy.

"They're arguing," he said.

"Who?"

"The Commander and Valek."

I took the tray of cooling food from Sammy. No reason we both had to be there. "Get going. I'm sure Rand needs you."

Sammy smiled his relief and sprinted through the throne

room. I'd seen the kitchen during dinnertime. Servers and cooks swarmed like bees with Rand directing the chaos. Barking orders, he controlled his kitchen staff like the queen bee of the hive.

Knowing the Commander disliked cold food, I stood close to his door, waiting for a break in the conversation. From my new position I could hear Valek clearly.

"Whatever possessed you to change your successor?" Valek demanded.

The Commander's soft reply passed through the wooden door as an indecipherable murmur.

"In the fifteen years I've known you, you've *never* reversed a decision." Valek's tone became more reasonable. "This isn't a ploy to discover your successor. I just want to know why you changed your mind. Why now?"

The response wasn't to Valek's liking. With a sarcastic jab in his voice, he said, "Always, Sir."

Valek jerked the door open. I stumbled into the office.

He wore a glacial expression. Only his eyes showed his fury. They were pools of molten lava beneath an icy crust. "Yelena, where the hell have you been? The Commander's waiting for his dinner." Not expecting an answer, Valek strode briskly through the throne room. Advisers and soldiers melted from his path.

Valek's anger seemed extreme. Everyone in Ixia knew that one of the eight Generals had been chosen as the Commander's successor. In the typical paranoid custom of the Commander's ruling, the name of the selected General was kept secret. Each General held an envelope that contained a piece of a puzzle. When the Commander died, they would assemble the puzzle to reveal an encrypted message. A key would be required to decipher the note. A key only Valek held. The chosen General would then have the complete support of the military and the Commander's staff.

The theory behind the puzzle was that secrecy would prevent someone from staging a rebellion in support of the chosen heir, since the heir was unknown. The added risk that the inheritor might be even worse than the Commander was another deterrent. As far as I could see, a change in the chosen General probably wouldn't affect day-to-day life in Ixia. We didn't know who had been originally selected, so the switch would have no bearing until the Commander died.

I approached Commander Ambrose's desk. He read his reports, unaffected by Valek's rage. I performed a quick taste of his dinner; he thanked me for the food then ignored me.

On my way back to the baths, I wondered if the information I had just overheard would fetch a decent price from Margg's contact. I quenched my curiosity; I had no desire to commit treason for money. I just wanted to get out of my present situation alive. And knowing Valek, I had no doubt that he would discover any clandestine meetings with Margg. For that reason alone, I had to prove that, no matter what Margg believed, I was not a spy. Just the mental vision of Valek's burning eyes focused on me sent a hot bolt of fear through me.

A long soak in the bath eased my sore ribs. As it was still early in the evening, I thought it prudent to avoid Valek for a while. I stopped in the kitchen for a late dinner. After helping myself to the leftover roast meat and a hunk of bread, I carried my plate to where Rand worked. He had an array of bowls, pots and ingredients messily spread out on his table. Dark smudges rimmed his bloodshot eyes, and his brown hair stuck straight out where he had run his wet hands through it.

I found a stool and a clean corner on Rand's table and ate my dinner.

"Did the Commander send you?" Rand asked.

"No. Why?"

"I finally received the Criollo recipe from Ving two days ago. I thought the Commander might be wondering about it."

"He hasn't said anything to me."

Two large shipments of Criollo, sans the recipe, had arrived for the Commander since Brazell had left the castle. Each time, the Commander had responded with a "thank you" and another request for the formula. As the quantity received had been plentiful, the Commander had given Rand some Criollo to play with. Rand hadn't disappointed. He had melted it, mixed it into hot drinks, invented new desserts, chipped it and remolded it into flowers and other edible decorations for cakes and pies.

I watched Rand stir a mahogany-colored batter with tight agitated movements. "How's it going?" I asked.

"Horrible. I have repeatedly followed this recipe, and all I've gotten is this awful-tasting mud." Rand banged the spoon on the bowl's edge to knock off the pasty residue. "It won't even solidify." He handed me a sheet of once-white paper smeared with brown stains and flour. "Maybe you can see what I'm doing wrong."

I studied the list of ingredients. It looked like a normal recipe, but I wasn't a cooking expert. Tasting, on the other hand, was becoming my forte. I took a scoop of his batter and slid it onto my tongue. A sickeningly sweet flavor invaded my mouth. The texture was smooth and the batter coated my tongue like Criollo, but it lacked the nutty, slightly bitter taste that balanced the sweetness.

"Maybe the recipe's wrong," I said, handing the sheet back to Rand. "Put yourself in Ving's position. Commander Ambrose loves Criollo, and you hold the only copy of the recipe. Would you give it away? Or would you use it to manipulate a transfer?"

Rand plopped wearily onto a stool. "What do I do? If I can't make Criollo, the Commander will probably reassign me. It'll be too much for my ego to stand." He attempted a weak smile.

"Tell the Commander that the recipe's a fake. Blame Ving for your inability to duplicate the Criollo."

Sighing, Rand rubbed his face in his hands. "I can't handle this type of political pressure." He massaged his eyelids with the tips of his long fingers. "Right now, I'd kill for a cup of coffee, but I guess wine will have to do." He rummaged around in the cabinet and produced a bottle and two glasses.

"Coffee?"

"You're too young to remember, but before the takeover, we imported this absolutely wonderful drink from Sitia. When the Commander closed the border, we lost an endless list of luxury items. Of all those, I miss coffee the most."

"What about the black market?" I asked.

Rand laughed. "It's probably available. But there's nowhere in this castle that I could make it without being discovered."

"I'll most likely regret asking you this, but why not?"

"The smell. The coffee's rich and distinct aroma would give me away. The scent of brewing coffee can weave its way throughout the entire castle. I woke up to it every morning before the takeover." Rand sighed again. "My mother's job was to grind the coffee beans and fill the pots with water. It's very similar to brewing tea, but the taste is far superior."

I sat up straighter on my stool when I heard the word *beans.* "What color are coffee beans?"

"Brown. Why?"

"Just curious," I said in a calm tone, but excitement boiled within me. My mystery beans were brown, and Brazell was old enough to know about coffee. Maybe he missed the drink, and planned to manufacture it.

My efforts to ferment the pod's pulp had resulted in a thin chestnut-colored liquid that tasted rotten. The purple seeds inside the pulp had been sopping wet, and covered with flies. I had closed the window and dried the seeds on the windowsill. As they dried, the seeds turned to brown and looked and tasted like the beans from the caravan. Thrilled to link the pods with the beans, my excitement had faded when I hadn't been able to learn anything further.

"Does coffee taste sweet?" I asked.

"No. It's bitter. My mother used to add sugar and milk to half of her finished pots, but I liked it plain."

My beans were bitter. I couldn't sit still any longer; I had to find out if Valek remembered coffee. I felt uncomfortable asking Rand, unsure if Valek wanted him to know about the southern pods.

After bidding farewell to Rand, who stared morosely into the failed batter as he drank his wine, I rushed back to Valek's suite. The sound of slamming books greeted my entrance. Valek stormed around the living room, kicking piles of books over. Gray rock debris littered the floor and clung to impact craters on the walls. He clenched a stone in each fist.

I had wanted to discuss my coffee hypothesis with him, but decided to wait. Unfortunately, Valek spotted me staring. "What do you want?" he snarled.

"Nothing," I mumbled and fled to my room.

For three days, I endured Valek's temper. He vented his ill humor on me at every opportunity. Thrusting the antidote at me, speaking curtly, if at all, and glaring whenever I entered a room. Weary of avoiding him and hiding in my room, I decided to approach him. He sat at his desk, his back to me.

"I may have discovered what those beans are." It was a weak opening. What I really wanted to say was, "What the hell's the matter with you?" But i thought a soft approach more prudent.

He swiveled to face me. The energy of his anger had dissipated, replaced by a bone-chilling cold. "Really?" His voice lacked conviction. The fire in his eyes had extinguished.

I stepped back. His indifference was more frightening than his anger. "I…" I swallowed, my mouth dry. "I was talking to Rand, and he mentioned missing coffee. Do you remember coffee? A southern drink."

"No."

"I think our beans might be coffee. If you don't know what coffee is, perhaps I should show them to Rand. If that's all right with you?" I faltered. My suggestion had sounded like a child pleading for a sweet.

"Go ahead; share your ideas with Rand. Your buddy, your best friend. You're just like him." Icy sarcasm spiked Valek's words.

I was stunned. "What?"

"Do as you like. I don't care." Valek turned his back on me.

I stumbled to my room, and then locked the door with shaky fingers. Leaning against the wall, I replayed the last week in my mind to see if there had been some clue to Valek's withdrawal. I could remember nothing that stood out. We had barely said a word to each other, and I had believed his anger had been directed toward the Commander—until now.

Maybe he had discovered my magic book. Perhaps he suspected I had some magical power. Fear replaced my confusion. Lying on my bed that night, I stared at the door. With every nerve tingling, I waited for Valek's attack. I knew I was overreacting, but I was unable to stop. I couldn't erase the way he had looked at me as if I was already dead.

Dawn arrived, and I moved through my day like a zombie. Valek ignored me. Even Janco's ever-present good humor couldn't snap me out of my funk.

I waited a few days before bringing the beans along to show Rand. He was in better spirits. A big smile graced his face, and he greeted me with an offer of a cinnamon swirl.

"I'm not hungry," I said.

"You haven't eaten in days. What's the matter?" Rand asked.

I dodged his question by asking about the Criollo.

"Your plan worked. I informed the Commander that Ving's recipe was wrong. He said he'd take care of it. Then he inquired about the kitchen staff: were they working well? Did I need more help? I just stared at him because I felt like I was in the wrong room. I'm usually greeted with suspicion and dismissed with a threat."

"That doesn't sound like a good relationship."

Rand stacked a few bowls and straightened a row of spoons. His smile faded. "My interaction with the Commander and Valek could be considered rocky at best. Being rather young and rebellious right after the takeover, I attempted every trick of sabotage possible. I served the Commander sour milk, stale bread, rotten vegetables and even raw meat. At that point, I was just looking to be a nuisance." He picked up a spoon and tapped it against his knee. "It became a battle of wills. The Commander was determined that I cook for him, and I was determined to either be arrested or be reassigned."

Thump, thump, thump went the spoon, and Rand continued his story, his voice husky. "Then Valek made my mother the food taster—that was before they implemented that damn Code of Behavior —I couldn't bear to have her taste the garbage I served the Commander." Old sorrows pulled at Rand's features. He twirled the spoon in circles between his fingers.

Words failed me. Dread crept up my spine as I contemplated the fate of Rand's mother.

"After the inevitable happened, I tried to run away, but they caught me just shy of the southern border." Rand rubbed his left knee. "They shattered my kneecap, hobbling me like some damn horse. Threatened to do my other leg if I ran again. And here I am." He snorted, sweeping all the spoons off the table. They clattered on the stone floor. "Shows you how much I've changed. The Commander's nice to me and I'm happy. I used to dream of poisoning the bastard, of taking that final step in our battle. But I have this weakness of caring for the food taster. When Oscove died, I promised myself never to care again." Rand pulled out a bottle of wine. "Only I failed. Again." He retreated to his rooms.

I hunched over the table, regretting that my comment had caused Rand pain. My pockets bulged uncomfortably with the beans. I shifted in my seat. Liza would have good cause when she blamed this mood swing on me. Valek's actions with Rand's mother seemed harsh from Rand's perspective, but when I thought about it from Valek's point of view, it made sense. His job was to protect the Commander.

I lived the next two days in a fog. Events blurred together. Tasting, training, tasting, training. Ari's and Janco's curses and attempts to rouse me remained unsuccessful. The news that I could start knife defense failed to produce any enthusiasm. My body felt as wooden as the bow I held.

When Margg materialized after one of my training sessions to inform me that a meeting with her contact had been scheduled for the following evening, it was with great difficulty that I summoned the strength to rally.

I thought out each possible scenario, and each combination of events kept leading me to one conclusion. Who would believe me if I reported the meeting? No one. I needed a witness who could also act as a protector. Ari's name sprang to mind. But I didn't want any suspicion to fall on him if something went wrong. It was also possible that Margg's contact had a boss, or a whole network of informers, and I could be getting in over my head. Dance as I might, there was but one course of action, and it led to but one person: Valek.

I dreaded the encounter. My interaction with him had dwindled to the silent awkward dispensing of my antidote every morning. But after tasting the Commander's dinner, I sought Valek out, my stomach performing flips. His office was locked, so I tried his suite. He wasn't in the living room, but I heard a faint sound from upstairs. A thin slash of light glowed under the door to Valek's carving studio. A metallic grinding noise raised goose bumps on my flesh.

I faltered at the entrance. This was probably the worst time to disturb him, but I was to meet Margg's contact the next day. I had no time to waste. Gathering courage, I knocked and opened the door without waiting for an answer.

Valek's lantern flickered. He stopped grinding. The wheel spun in silence, reflecting pinpricks of light that whirled along the walls and ceiling.

He asked, "What is it?"

"I've had an offer. Someone wants to pay me for information about the Commander."

He spun around. His face was half hidden in shadows, but it was as rigid as the stone he held. "Why tell me?"

"I thought you might want to follow along. This might be the one who has been leaking information about me."

He stared at me.

I wished then that I held a heavy rock, because I had the sudden desire to bash it on his head. "Espionage is illegal. You might want to make an arrest, or maybe even feed this leak some misinformation. You know, spy stuff. Remember? Or have you become bored with that, too?" Anger fueled my words.

I took a breath to launch into an attack, but it slid unvoiced past my clenched teeth. There was a slight softening in Valek's face. Renewed interest emanated from him, as if he had been holding every muscle taut and had just relaxed.

"Who?" he asked finally. "And when?"

"Margg approached me, and she mentioned a contact. We're meeting tomorrow night." I studied his expression. Was he surprised or hurt by Margg's treachery? I couldn't tell. Reading Valek's true mood was like trying to decipher a foreign language.

"All right, proceed as planned. I'll tail you to the rendezvous, and see who we're dealing with. We'll start by feeding this contact some accurate information to make you look reliable. Perhaps the Commander's change of successor would work. It's harmless information that will be made public anyway. Then we'll go from there."

We outlined the details. Even though I was placing my life

in danger, I felt cheerful. I had my old Valek back. But for how long? I wondered as wariness crept back in.

When we were through, I turned to go.

"Yelena."

I halted in the doorway, looking back over my shoulder.

"You once said I wasn't ready to believe your reason for killing Reyad. I'll believe you now."

"But I'm not ready to tell you," I said and left the room.

20

DAMN VALEK! DAMN, DAMN, damn him! Gave me the cold shoulder for four days and then expected me to trust him? I'd admitted to murder. They'd arrested the right person. That was all he should care about.

Walking down the stairs in the darkness, I headed toward my room. I have to get out of this place, I thought with sudden intensity. The overwhelming desire to take off and damn the antidote was strong. Run away, run away, run away sang in my mind. A familiar tune. I had heard it before when I was with Reyad. Memories I had thought were tightly locked away now threatened to push free, seeping through the cracks. Damn Valek! It was his fault I couldn't suppress my memories any longer.

In my room, I locked the door. When I turned around, I spied Reyad's ghost lounging on my bed. The wound in his neck hung open, and blood stained his nightshirt black. In contrast, his blond hair was combed in the latest style, his mustache groomed to perfection, and his light blue eyes glowed.

"Get out," I said. He was, I reminded myself, an intangible ghost and not, absolutely not, to be feared.

"What kind of greeting is that for an old friend?" Reyad asked. He lifted a book on poisons off my nightstand, and flipped through the pages.

I stared at him in shock. He spoke in my mind. He held a book. A ghost, a ghost, I kept repeating. Reyad was unaffected. He laughed.

"You're dead," I said. "Aren't you supposed to be burning in eternal damnation?"

Reyad wasn't banished so easily. "Teacher's pet," he said, waving the book in the air. "If only you had worked this hard for me, everything would have been different."

"I like the way it turned out."

"Poisoned, pursued and living with a psychopath. Not what I would consider the good life. Death has its perks." He sniffed. "I get to watch your miserable existence. You should have chosen the noose, Yelena. It would have saved you some time."

"Get out," I said again, trying to ignore the touch of hysteria in my voice and the trickle of sweat down my back.

"You do know you'll never get to Sitia alive? You're a failure. Always were. Always will be. Face it. Accept it." Reyad rose from the bed. "You failed all our efforts to mold you. Do you remember? Remember when Daddy finally gave up on you? When he let me have you?"

I remembered. It had been the week of the fire festival, and Reyad had been so preoccupied with General Tesso's visiting retinue, especially Tesso's daughter, Kanna, that he hadn't bothered to check on me. Since I'd been meekly obeying his every command to gain some trust, he was smug in the assumption that he'd cowed me into submission. As a result, it was more than a month since he'd locked me into my tiny room that was next to his suite.

But the festival had once again tempted me into disobeying Reyad's instructions to stay away. The beatings and humiliations of the year before were insufficient to deter me this year. In fact, I felt a stubborn pride in refusing to be intimidated by him. I was terrified of getting caught, knew deep down in a small corner of my mind that I would get caught, but I threw all caution to fate. The fire festival was a part of me. The only time I tasted true freedom. Even though it was for but a few moments, it was worth the consequences.

My defiance added an edge to my acrobatic routines, making me bold and reckless. I sailed through the first five rounds with aplomb, dismounts steady, flips tight, energy level unlimited. I advanced to the final round of competition, which was scheduled for the last day of the festival.

I scrambled to put the finishing touches on my costume for the competition, while Reyad guided Kanna and a group of friends on a hunting party in the countryside.

I had scrounged around the manor for the preceding two weeks to acquire the necessary supplies for my attire. Now I stitched scarlet silk feathers onto a black leotard, and then outlined them with silver sequins. Wings tied to a harness completed the outfit, but I folded them small and flat so they wouldn't impede my motion. Braiding my hair into one long rope, I wound it tightly around my head and secured two flaming red feathers in the back. Pleased with the results, I arrived early at the acrobatics tent to practice.

When the competition started, the tent bulged with people. The crowd's cheers soon dimmed to a dull roar in my ears as I performed my routines. The only sounds reaching me were the thump of my hands and feet on the trampoline, the creaking of the tightrope as I launched myself in midair to execute a two-and-a-half twist and the crack of the slender rope when I landed on it without falling.

The floor routine was my last event. I stood on the balls of my feet at the edge of the mat, breathing deeply. The heavy earthy smell of sweat and the dry scratch of chalk dust filled my lungs. This was my place. This was where I belonged. The air vibrated like a thunderstorm poised to blow in. Energized as lightning, I started my first tumbling run.

I flew that night. Spinning and diving through the air, my feet hardly touched the ground. My spirit soared. I felt like a bird performing aerial tricks for sheer delight. At the end of my last run, I grabbed my wings with both hands. Pulling them open, I raised them over my head as I somersaulted and landed on my feet. The bright scarlet fabric of the wings billowed out behind me. The crowd's thunderous cheers vibrated deep in my chest. My soul floated with crimson wings on the updraft of the audience's jubilant praise.

I won the competition. Pure uncomplicated joy consumed me, and I grinned for the first time in two years. Face muscles aching from smiling, I stood on the platform to receive the prize from the Master of Ceremonies. He settled a bloodred amulet, shaped like flames and engraved with the year and event, on my chest. It was the greatest moment of my entire life—followed by the worst, as I spotted Reyad and Kanna watching me from the crowd. Kanna was beaming, but Reyad's expression was hard and unforgiving as suppressed rage leaked from his twitching lips.

I lingered inside the changing room until everyone had gone. There were two exits to the tent, but Reyad had positioned his guards at both. Knowing Reyad would take my amulet and destroy it, I buried it deep under the earthen floor of the room.

As I expected, Reyad grabbed me as soon as I stepped from the tent. He dragged me back to the manor. General Brazell was consulted. He agreed that I would never be "one of his group." Too independent, too stubborn and too willful, Brazell said, and gave me over to his son. No more experiments. I had failed. That night, Reyad just managed to control his temper until we were alone in his room, but once the door was closed and locked, he vented his full anger with his fists and feet.

"I wanted to kill you for disobeying me," Reyad's ghost said as he glided across my room. "I planned to savor it over a very long period of time, but you beat me to it. You must have had that knife tucked under my mattress for quite a while." He paused, creasing his brow in thought.

I had stolen and hidden a knife under Reyad's bed a year before, after he had beaten me for practicing. Why his bed? I had no real strategy, just a terrible foreboding that when I needed it, I would be in Reyad's room and not in my small room next door.

Dreaming of murder was easy; committing it was another story. Even though I'd endured much pain that year, I hadn't crossed the threshold of sanity. Until that night.

"Did something set you off?" the ghost asked. "Or were you procrastinating, like now? Learning to fight!" He chuckled. "Imagine you fighting off an attacker. You wouldn't last against a direct assault. I should know." He floated before me, forcing the memories out.

I flinched from him and from that night's recollection. "Go away," I said to the specter. Picking up the book on poisons, I stretched out on my bed, determined to ignore him. He faded slightly as I read, but brightened whenever I glanced his way.

"Was it my journal that set you off?" Reyad asked when my eyes lingered too long.

"No." The word sprang from my mouth, surprising me. I had convinced myself that his journal had been the final straw after two years of torment.

The painful memories flooded with a force that shook me and left me trembling.

After I had regained consciousness from the beating, I'd found myself sprawled naked on Reyad's bed. Flourishing his journal before me, he ordered me to read it, taking pleasure in watching the growing horror on my face.

His journal had listed every single grievance he had against me for the two years I'd been with him. Every time I disobeyed or annoyed him, he noted it, and then followed with a specific description of how he would punish me. Now that Brazell no longer needed me for his experiments, Reyad had no boundaries. His sadistic inclinations and overwhelming depth of imagination were written in full detail. As I struggled to breathe, my first thought was to find the knife and kill myself, but the blade was on the other side of the bed near the headboard.

"We'll start with the punishment on page one tonight." Reyad purred with anticipation as he crossed to his "toy" chest, pulling from it chains and other implements of torture.

I flipped back to the beginning with numb fingers. Page one recorded that I had failed to call him *sir* the first time we met. And for lacking the proper deference, I would assume a submissive position on my hands and knees, and then be whipped. He would demand that I call him *sir*. With each lash, I would respond with the words, "More, *sir*, please." During the following rape, I would address him as *sir*, and beg him to continue my punishment.

His journal slipped from my paralyzed hands. I flung myself over the bed, intent on finding the knife, but Reyad, thinking I was trying to escape, caught me. My struggles were useless, as he forced me to my knees. With my face pressed into the rough stone floor, Reyad chained my hands behind my neck.

The anticipation was more frightening than the actual event. In a sick way, it was a comfort, because I knew what to expect and when he would stop. I played my part, understanding that if

I denied him his intended moves, I would only enrage him further.

When the horror finally ceased, blood covered my back and coated the insides of my legs. I curled into a ball on the edge of Reyad's bed. My mind dead. My body throbbing. His fingers were inside me. Where he would always be, he breathed into my ear as he lay beside me.

This time the knife was within my reach. My thoughts lingered on suicide.

Then Reyad said, "I guess I'll have to start a new journal." I did not respond.

"We'll be training a new girl now that you've failed." He sat up, and dug his fingers deeper into me. "Up on your knees. Time for page two."

"No!" I screamed. "You won't!" Fumbling for a frantic second, I pulled the knife out and sliced at his throat. A surface cut only, but he fell back on the bed in surprise. I leaped onto his chest, slashing deeper. The blade scraped bone. Blood sprayed. A warm feeling of satisfaction settled over me when I realized I could no longer determine whose blood pooled between my thighs.

"So that's what set you off? The fact that I was going to rape you again?" Reyad's ghost asked.

"No. It was the thought of you torturing another girl from the orphanage."

"Oh, yes." He snorted. "Your friends."

"My sisters," I corrected. "I killed you for them, but I should have done it for me." Anger surged through my body.

I cornered him. My fists struck out even though I knew in a tiny part of my mind that I couldn't hurt him. His smug expression never changed, but I punched again and again until the first rays of dawn touched Reyad's ghost. He vanished from sight.

Sobbing, I sank to the floor. After a while, I became aware of my surroundings. My fists were bloodied from hitting the rough stone wall. I was exhausted and drained of all emotions. And I was late for breakfast. Damn Valek!

"Pay attention," Ari said. He jabbed me in the stomach with a wooden knife. "You're dead. That's the fourth time today. What's the matter?"

"Lack of sleep," I said. "Sorry."

Ari gestured me to the bench along the wall. We sat down and watched Maren and Janco, engaged in a friendly bow match on the far side of the storeroom. Janco's speed had overpowered Maren's skill, and she was on the retreat, backing into a corner.

"She's tall and thin, but she's not going to win," Janco sang. His words aimed to infuriate her—a tactic that had worked before. Too often, Maren's anger caused her to make critical mistakes. But this time, she remained calm. She planted the end of her bow between his feet, which trapped his weapon close to his body. Then she flipped over his head, landed behind him, and grabbed him around the neck until he conceded.

My bleak mood improved a notch watching Maren use

something I had taught her. The indignant expression on Janco's face was priceless. He insisted on a rematch. They launched into another rowdy duel. Ari and I remained on the bench. I think Ari sensed that I had no energy to continue our lesson.

"Something's wrong," he said in a quiet voice. "What is it?"

"I—" I stopped, unsure of my answer. Should I tell him about Valek's cold shoulder and change of heart? Or about my night-long conversation with the ghost of the man I'd murdered? No. Instead I asked him, "Do you think this is a waste of time?" Reyad's words about procrastination had held a ring of truth. Perhaps the time I spent training was merely a subconscious ploy to avoid solving my real problems.

"If I thought this was a waste of time, I wouldn't be here." A trace of anger colored Ari's voice. "You need this, Yelena."

"Why? I might die before I even have a chance to use it."

"As I see it, you're already good at running and hiding. It took you a week to get up the nerve to talk to Maren. And if it was up to you, she'd still be calling you Puker. You need to learn to stand and fight for what you want." Ari fidgeted with the wooden knife, spinning it around his hand.

"You hover on the edges, ready to take off if something goes wrong. But when you can knock the bow from Janco's hands, and sweep my feet out from under me, you'll be empowered." He paused, and then said, "If you feel you need to spend your time on something else, then do it...in *addition* to your training. Then the next time someone calls you Puker, you'll have the confidence to tell her to go to hell."

I was amazed at Ari's assessment of me. I couldn't even say if I agreed or disagreed with him, but I did know he was right about my compulsion to do something else. He didn't know what it was, but I did: find the antidote to Butterfly's Dust.

"Is that your idea of encouragement?" I asked in a shaky voice.

"Yes. Now quit looking for an excuse to stop training, and trust me. What else do you need?"

The quiet intensity of Ari's voice caused a chill to ripple up my spine. Did he know what I was planning, or was he guessing? My intentions had always been to get the antidote and run to Sitia. Run away, run away, run away. Ari had been right about that. But running south would require me to be in top physical condition, and to have the ability to defend myself from guards. However, I had been evading one important detail: Valek.

He would follow me to Sitia, and crossing the border wouldn't make me safe from him. Even Irys's magic couldn't protect me. He would consider my recapture or my death a personal responsibility. And that was what I'd been so afraid to face. What I'd been dancing around. I'd been concentrating on training so I wouldn't have to deal with the dilemma I feared I wasn't smart enough to solve. I had to enhance my strategy, to include not only obtaining the antidote, but dealing with Valek without killing him. I doubted Ari had the solution.

"You might beat Valek with these blows." Janco puffed while blocking Maren's bow. "He'll laugh himself silly at how pathetically weak they are, giving you the perfect opening."

Maren remained silent, but increased the pace of her attack. Janco backed off.

Janco's words stirred in my mind. An odd little long-shot plan began to take shape. "Ari, can you teach me how to pick locks?"

He considered my words in silence. Finally, he said, "Janco could."

"Janco?"

Ari smiled. "He seems harmless and happy-go-lucky, but as a boy he got into all kinds of mischief until he was trapped in a tight spot. Then he was given the choice of either joining the military or going to jail. Now he's a Captain. His biggest advantage is that no one thinks he is serious, and that's exactly what he wants."

"I'll try and remember that the next time he's cracking jokes and my ribs." I watched Maren beat Janco a second time.

"Best three out of five, my lady can not deny," Janco called tirelessly.

Maren shrugged. "If your ego can handle it," she replied, swiping at his feet with her bow. He jumped, avoiding her attack with an athletic grace, and lunged. The rhythmic crack of wood striking wood filled our practice room.

Ari stood, assumed a defensive stance, and somehow I found the energy to face him.

After the workout, the four of us were resting on the bench when Valek arrived. Maren shot to her feet, as if she thought being found sitting idle was a crime, but the rest of us kept our relaxed positions. I found it fascinating to watch the small changes in Maren's behavior whenever Valek was around. Her rough edge softened, she smiled more and tried to engage him in conversation or a match. Most of the time he would review fighting tactics with her, or conduct a practice, and she would preen like an alley cat attracting the biggest tom. But this time he wanted to talk to me. Alone. The others left the room. Maren shot me a dark look with the force of one of her bow strikes. I would pay for this tomorrow, I thought.

Valek paced. With an uneasy feeling, I hoped that he wasn't searching for a rock to throw.

"What's wrong?" I asked him. "Is it about tonight?" Excitement over exposing Margg soured to nervousness when I thought of the risk I'd be taking. The idea that this might be another waste of time surfaced. Damn Reyad's ghost! He was making me doubt everything. The leak impacted my life. Someone had tipped off those goons at the fire festival, and Irys had known I was in the forest. Margg needed to be plugged.

"No. We're all set for tonight," Valek said. "This is about the Commander." He paused.

"What about him?"

"Has he been meeting with anyone strange this week?"

"Strange?"

"Someone you don't know or an adviser from another Military District?"

"Not that I've seen. Why?"

Valek paused again. I could see his mental wheels turning as he considered whether or not to trust me. "Commander Ambrose has agreed to admit a Sitian delegation."

"That's bad?" I asked, confused.

"He hates southerners! They've requested a meeting with him every year since the takeover. And for the last fifteen years, the Commander has replied with a single word: no. Now they're due to arrive in a week." Valek's pacing increased. "Ever since you became the food taster and that Criollo showed up, the Commander has been acting different. I couldn't put my finger on it before, it was just a nagging feeling, but now I have two particular incidents."

"The change in his successor and now the southern delegation?"

"Exactly."

I had no response. My experience with the Commander had been the complete opposite of what I had expected from a military dictator. He considered other opinions, was firm, decisive and fair. His power was obvious; every command was instantaneously obeyed. He lived the spartan life that he endorsed. There was no fear in his advisers and high-ranking officers, just an unflappable loyalty and immense respect. The only horror story since the takeover that I'd heard was about Rand's mother. Of course, the assassinations before were infamous.

Valek stopped and took a deep breath. "I've misdirected some Criollo to our suite. I want you to eat a piece whenever he does. But you're not to tell anyone, not even the Commander. That's an order."

"Yes, sir," I replied automatically, but my mind reeled over his calling the suite "ours." Did I hear that right? I wondered.

"Keep your meeting with Margg tonight. I'll be there."

"Should I tell Margg's contact about the southern delegation?"

"No. Use the change of the Commander's successor. It's
already floating around as a rumor, so you'll just confirm it."
Valek strode from the room.

In case someone would discover our training room, I hid the
practice weapons, removed all visible traces of our presence and
locked the door. On my way to the baths, my thoughts dwelled
on the meeting tonight. Distracted, I walked by an open
doorway. An oddity. In this section of the castle, most of the doors
led to storerooms and were kept locked.

Movement blurred to my left. Hands grabbed my arm and
yanked me inside. The door slammed shut. Complete darkness
descended. I was flung face-first against a stone wall. The air
in my lungs whooshed out from the impact. I turned. My back
to the wall, I gasped for breath.

"Stay put," a male voice growled.

I aimed a front kick toward the voice but met air. Laughter
taunted. A candle was uncovered. The weak yellow glow reflected off a long silver blade. Terrified, I traced the knife to
the hand, then along the arm, and up to the face. Nix.

21

"WHY?" NIX PLACED THE candle among the cobwebs lacing the tabletop. "Why am I always the smartest one?" He stepped closer.

I kicked again, but he blocked it with ease.

"Why haven't my attempts to discourage you worked?" In the flicker of the candlelight he moved. The edge of his knife pressed against my throat. "Maybe I need to be more obvious?"

The smells of boiled cabbage and body odor penetrated my nose. Keeping my body still, I asked in the most neutral and un-frightened voice I could manage, "What's your problem?"

"My problem is that no one sees you as a threat. But I'm smarter than Ari, Janco and Maren. I'm even smarter than Valek. Aren't I?" When I failed to respond, Nix added pressure to the knife. "Aren't I?"

A thin line of pain burned across my neck. "Yes," I replied.

In the air behind Nix, Reyad's ghost coalesced out of the dust motes, sporting a smug smile.

"My boss wants you to stop training. I'm not allowed to kill you. Pity." Nix stroked my face with his free hand. "I'm here to warn you off."

"Parffet? Why would he care?" As I tried to distract him, my mind frantically shuffled through my brief sessions with Ari on knife defense. Damn, I thought, why hadn't I paid more attention?

"He doesn't care. The only thing dull-witted Parffet cares about is getting promoted. But General Brazell has a keen interest in your new hobby." Nix thrust his free hand between my legs, and leaned his body against mine.

For a terrified second, I froze. Panic erased all techniques of self-defense from my mind. A soft buzzing began to grow inside my head, but I stifled it, pushed it away, and it transformed into a simple musical scale of notes. Calm flowed. The necessary defense moves appeared before my eyes.

I moaned and rocked my hips, widening my stance.

Nix smiled with delight. "You're just the whore I thought you'd be. Now, remember, you're to be punished." His upper thigh replaced his hand. He began to tug at my belt.

I rubbed my knee between his legs then rammed it straight up into his groin. Grunting, Nix doubled over. I grabbed his blade with both hands to prevent it from biting farther into my throat. Ari's practical voice, "Better to cut your hands than your neck," echoed in my head even as I winced at the sharp pain. Focusing on the knife, I pushed the weapon from me. Nix stumbled back.

"Bitch!" He snarled and pulled his arm back to swing the knife.

As the blade swept toward me, I stepped in close to his body, so when I turned, my right shoulder brushed his chest. Using the edges of my opened hands, I struck his upper and lower arm. The combined force of my strike and his swing made Nix's arm go limp. The weapon clattered to the floor.

Grabbing his arm, I twisted it until the heel of his hand pointed toward the ceiling. Then I pivoted, placing my right shoulder under his elbow. With all my might, I yanked his hand down. I heard a loud crack followed by a scream as Nix's arm broke. Spinning around to face him, I punched him twice in the nose. Blood gushed out. While he was off balance, I kicked his kneecap, breaking it. Nix crumpled to the ground.

I danced around him, kicking him in the ribs. My blood hummed and sizzled. His weak attempts to block me only fueled my frenzy. In that state of mind, I might have killed him.

Reyad's ghost cheered me on. "That's it, Yelena," he urged. "Kill another man, and it's the noose for sure."

Somehow, his words reached the rational part of my mind, and I stopped, breathing hard. Nix was still. I knelt beside him and felt for a pulse. A strong throb met my fingertips. The relief that coursed through me vanished when Nix clutched my elbow.

I yelped and punched him in the face. His grip relaxed, and I pulled my arm free. Snatching the knife from the floor, I took Janco's often-repeated advice for self-defense: "Hit and git." I ran. But this time fear didn't follow me. I ran with imaginary scarlet wings flowing behind me.

Moving fast to ward off the shakes that threatened to over-power me, I reached the baths. They were empty at this time of day, so I hid Nix's knife under one of the towel tables. I checked the extent of my wounds in the mirror. The cut on my neck had stopped bleeding. But two deep gashes on my palms looked serious enough to require the medic's attention. There was also a wild, unrecognizable shine to my eyes, as if I had turned feral. I bared my teeth and thought, *Now who's the rat?* Pondering my next move, I wavered. The Commander expected me to taste his dinner, but I couldn't bleed all over his food. My initial surge of energy from the fight with Nix was waning. A wave of dizziness swelled. I headed toward the infirmary, hoping to reach it before I passed out.

Medic Mommy gave me a quick appraisal. She pointed to an examining table. I perched on the edge and held my hands out for inspection.

"How..." she started.

"Broken glass," I said.

She nodded, lips pressed tight in thought. "I'll get my med-kit."

I stretched out on the bed when she returned with her metal tray full of instruments. A jar of Rand's glue seemed out of place among the medical supplies, like a child's toy surrounded by adult paraphernalia. My hands had started to throb, and I dreaded the medic's ministrations. I turned my head in time to see Valek burst into the infirmary. Just what I needed, I thought, sighing. This had turned out to be one hell of a bad day.

"What happened?" Valek demanded.

I glanced at the medic.

She took my right hand and began to clean my wound. "Broken glass leaves jagged lacerations. These clean slices are obviously from a knife. I'm required to report it."

The medic had reported me to Valek and he wasn't going to leave without an answer. With resignation I focused on him, hoping to distract myself from the pain in my hands. "I was attacked."

"By who?" His tone sharp.

I cut my eyes at the medic, and Valek understood.

"Could you excuse us for a minute?" he asked her.

She pursed her lips as if considering his request. Her authority overruled Valek's for all medical situations.

"Five minutes," she ordered, and walked to her desk on the far side of the infirmary.

"Who?" Valek repeated.

"Nix, a guard in Parffet's unit. Said he worked for Brazell and warned me to stop training."

"I'll kill him."

The intensity of Valek's voice shocked and alarmed me. "No, you won't," I said, trying to sound firm. "You'll use him. He's a link to Brazell."

His hard blue eyes found mine and held my gaze, probing deep. "Where did he attack you?"

"A storeroom about four or five doors up from our training room."

"He's probably long gone by now. I'll send someone to the barracks."

"He won't be there."

"Why not?" Valek gave me a look that reminded me of the Commander. His eyebrows were raised in an effort to suppress his emotions, inviting me to continue.

"If he's not in the storeroom, he won't have gotten far. You might want to send a couple of men."

"I see." Valek paused. "So your training has been progressing to your satisfaction?"

"Better than expected."

Valek left the infirmary. Medic Mommy, the stoolie, returned to my side. Next time, I thought bitterly, I'll heal myself and avoid being betrayed by the medic. I still had a jar of Rand's glue in my backpack. How hard could it be to seal a couple of cuts?

I chewed on my lower lip while she finished cleaning and sealing my cuts. Wrapping bandages tightly around my hands, she gave me instructions that would allow them to heal: no immersion in water for a day, no lifting or writing for a week. And that meant no training for a while, I thought.

Valek's men entered. They dumped Nix onto another examining table. The medic shot me a quizzical expression, then she bustled over to Nix's groaning form, giving me the perfect opportunity to leave.

I hurried to the Commander's office, but Valek had beaten me there. He closed the door behind him as he joined me in the throne room.

"I've taken care of dinner," he said, guiding me back through the maze of desks. It was early evening, and only a handful of advisers were working.

"Find Margg and cancel tonight's meeting, then go back to our suite and get some rest," he said.

"Cancel? What for? It would look suspicious. I'll wear gloves to cover the bandages. It's cold enough at night; nobody will notice." When he didn't reply, I added, "I'm fine."

He smiled. "You should take a look at yourself in a mirror." He hesitated, his face creasing in indecision. "All right. We'll proceed as planned."

We stopped at the door to Valek's office. "I have some work to finish. Rest and don't worry. I'll be close by tonight." He inserted his key.

"Valek?"

"Yes."

"What will happen to Nix?"

"We'll patch him up, threaten him with years in the dungeon if he doesn't cooperate, and when he's done helping us, I'll reassign him to MD–1. Good enough? Or should I kill him?"

Military District 1 was the coldest, bleakest district in Ixia. The possibility of Nix falling prey to a snow cat brought a wicked grin to my face. "No. Reassignment's good. If I had wanted him dead, I would have done it myself."

Valek straightened his spine, snapping me a look. A combination of surprise, amusement and wariness over my comment flashed across his face before he reined in his emotions and was once again my stone-faced Valek.

I smiled my best Janco impression and headed down the hall.

Resting would have to wait since I had a number of errands to run before the evening's meeting. First, I needed a pair of gloves and a cloak. As the cooling season dwindled toward the cold season, the nights had turned sharp and brisk, coating everything in a blanket of ice so that the blades of grass sparkled like diamonds when touched by the morning sun.

Thanking fate that Dilana was still in her sewing room, I chatted with her about the latest gossip before I made my request.

"My goodness," she said, sounding like a worried matron. "You don't have any clothes for the cold!" She bustled about her stacks of uniforms. Her soft, honey-colored ringlets bounced with each movement. "Why didn't you come to me sooner?" she admonished.

I laughed. "I haven't needed them till now. Dilana, do you mother everyone in the castle?"

She stopped piling clothes to look at me. "No, dear, just the ones that need it."

"Thanks," I said in a tone of affectionate sarcasm.

By the time she was through outfitting me for the cold season, I was inundated with a heap of clothing. With all of the flannel undergarments, wool socks and heavy boots, I probably could survive on the pack ice for weeks. I stashed the pile into a corner of the room and asked Dilana to have someone deliver them to Valek's suite.

"Still there?" she asked with a grin.

"For now. But I think when things settle down, I'll be back in my old room." When, I thought sourly. It was more like *if.*

I selected a heavy black cloak from the stack, tucked black

wool gloves into its deep pockets, and then draped it over my arm. The cloak had two hand-size red diamonds stitched on the left breast and an oversize hood whose function was more to keep the rain off my face than to keep my head warm.

"I think you'll be there a long time," Dilana said.

"Why?"

"I believe Valek's sweet on you. I've never seen him take such an interest in a food taster before. He usually trains them and leaves them alone. If there was any potential for trouble, he would assign one of his sneaks to spy on the taster, but he wouldn't bother with him personally, let alone live with one!" Her face had the avid glow of a gossip at full steam.

"You're crazy. Deluded."

"In fact, he's never taken an interest in a woman before. I was beginning to suspect he might prefer one of his male sneaks, but now..." She paused dramatically. "Now, we have the lovely, intelligent Yelena to get Valek's cold heart pumping."

"You really should get out of your sewing room more. You need fresh air and a dose of reality," I said, knowing better than to believe a word Dilana said, but unable to control the silly little grin on my face.

Her sweet, melodious laughter followed me into the hallway. "You know I'm right," she called.

The only reason Valek was interested in me, I thought as I walked through the dim corridors, was because I was a puzzle for him to solve. Once he thought he had all the answers about the southern magician and Brazell, I'd be sent back to my room in the servants' wing. I couldn't let myself believe

anything else. It was one thing for me to have a harmless in-
fatuation that wouldn't have any influence on my plans. It
wouldn't. Absolutely not. To think he felt the same toward me
would be disastrous.

So I tried to convince myself that Dilana, although a sweet-
heart, was a victim of her own overactive imagination and was
mistaken. I tried very hard. I tried all the way to the kitchen. I
tried when I saw Rand lurching around his ovens, reminding
myself that Valek was ruthless, murdering dozens of people. The
King's blood still adorned Valek's knife. Valek was deadly, moody
and exasperating. But for some reason, I couldn't get that silly grin
to go away no matter how hard I tried.

Draping my cloak over a stool, I helped myself to a late
dinner. Rand finished spinning his pigs and pulled up a stool
beside me. My mouth watered at the smell of roasting pork.

"What's the occasion?" I asked. Pork roast was a rare meal,
requiring an entire day to cook and served only at special times.

"Generals coming to visit this week. All my special dishes
have been requested. I've also been ordered to prepare a feast
for next week. A feast! We haven't had one of those since…"
He shook his head, pursing his lips. "Actually, we've never had
one with the Commander in charge." Rand sighed. "I won't
have any time to experiment."

"Would you have time to look at these?" Pulling a handful
of the mystery beans out of my pocket, I handed them to
Rand. I had been waiting for the perfect opportunity to show
them to him. "I found them in an old storeroom, and I thought
maybe they were your coffee beans."

He immediately ducked his head and took a deep sniff of the beans. "No, unfortunately not. I don't know what these are. Coffee beans are smooth and have a rounder shape. These are oval. See? And bumpy." Rand spread them out on the table and picked one up. He bit into it. Chewing, he cringed at the bitter taste. "I've never seen or tasted anything like this. Where did you find them?"

"Somewhere on the castle's lower level." Oh well, I thought, it had been worth a try. My disappointment pressed on my shoulders. I had hoped to solve this puzzle for Commander Ambrose, but it looked as though I had hit another dead end.

Rand must have sensed my frustration. "Important?" he inquired.

I nodded.

"Tell you what," he said. "Leave these here and after the feast I'll work on them for you."

"Work?"

"I'll try grinding, cooking and boiling the beans. Ingredients can change their flavor and texture when you add heat, and these might turn into something I recognize. All right?"

"I don't want to inconvenience you."

"Nonsense. I like a challenge. Besides, after the feast, it'll be back to my daily routine anyhow, and this will give me a project to look forward to." He funneled the beans into a jar, and placed it high on a shelf full of other strange edibles similarly encased in their own glass jars.

We discussed menu options for the feast until Rand needed to turn his pigs again. A quarter turn every hour, he said, reminding me that my time to meet Margg was fast approaching. A small pang of nervousness touched my stomach as I bade Rand good-night.

I stopped by the baths, intending to retrieve Nix's knife, but there were too many people there. Maybe being unarmed would be for the best, I told myself as I tried to calm the butterflies in my stomach. Maybe they would search me. If they found a weapon, I might be in more trouble.

Margg wore her usual expression of distaste when I met her just past the south gate of the castle complex. We exchanged insults by way of greeting and continued the walk into Castletown in silence. I hoped Valek was close behind, but I knew better than to glance over my shoulder and make Margg wary.

Stars decorated the night sky, and the full face of the moon shone brightly, casting shadows. The road to town was grooved with ruts from wagon wheels and worn smooth by the passage of many boots. I took a deep breath of the cool night air and felt a sense of renewal as the heavy scent of earth and dried leaves cleansed my lungs.

At the outskirts of town, I saw neat rows of four-story wooden buildings. I was struck by their symmetry. I had grown so accustomed to the wild, asymmetrical style of the castle, with its windows of every geometric shape, that the ordinary plainness of the town seemed bizarre. Even the placement of businesses among the residences had been planned in a logical manner.

The few townspeople that I spotted on the street walked

with a purpose. Nobody hung about, or talked, or looked as if they were out for a casual stroll. Nobody, except the town's guards.

Soldiers who had once played a major part in the takeover had been reassigned as policemen for the towns throughout the Territory of Ixia. Enforcing curfew and the dress code, they dealt justice in accordance with the Code of Behavior by checking papers, arranging transfers and making arrests. Every visitor to each town was required to report to the main station to complete the proper paperwork before seeking lodging.

Our meeting had been carefully scheduled to give us time to return to the castle before our presence on the street would be viewed with suspicion. The pairs of soldiers stationed on the streets followed us with their gazes. I felt my skin prickle under their scrutiny, and I had myself half convinced that they would swoop down on us at any moment.

In the middle of a street free from guards, Margg came to a stop at a house indistinguishable from its neighbors. She knocked twice on the door. After a pause, the door swung inward and a tall, red-haired woman in an innkeeper's uniform poked her head out. Glancing at Margg, she nodded in recognition. She had a sharp, sloping nose, which guided the movements of her head as she pointed her face at me. Her dark eyes rested upon me with an intensity that made me want to fidget. A bead of sweat trickled down my spine. Finally, she pulled her nose away to look down the street. Sniffing for a trap, I guessed. Apparently satisfied, she opened the door wider and let us in. Still no one spoke as we proceeded up three flights of steps.

The top floor of the house was ablaze with light, and I squinted in the harsh brightness. A profusion of candles ringed the room on multiple levels, heating the air with the smoky scent of apples. I glanced at the window. With the amount of light in the room, I was sure it would spill out into the street, but black curtains covered the glass and pooled on the floor.

Bookshelves, a desk and a scattering of comfortable armchairs led me to believe that the room was used as a study. The woman who had let us in sat behind the desk. Odd metal statues that resembled lanterns with rings around the top graced each side. Other strange and gleaming objects had been artfully arranged on shelves and tabletops. Some even hung from the ceiling. These spun in the air stirred by our passage.

The sharp-nosed woman didn't offer us a seat, so Margg and I stood before her desk. Most of her ruby hair was confined in a bun, but small, curly wisps had sprung free.

"The food taster," she said with a satisfied curl to her lip. "I knew it was only a matter of time before I had you in my employ."

"Who are you?" My bluntness informed her that I wouldn't tolerate games.

"You can call me Captain Star."

I looked at her innkeeper's uniform.

"I'm not part of Ambrose's military. I have my own. Has Margg explained how I work?"

"Yes."

"Good. This will be a simple exchange. This isn't a social call; I don't want gossip or hearsay. And don't inquire about my business or about me. All you need to know is my name. Agreed?"

"Agreed." Since I wanted to gain her trust, I wasn't about to cause any trouble, at least not yet.

"Good. What do you got?" With her nose leading the way, she leaned forward in her chair.

"The Commander has changed his successor," I said.

Star's body stilled as she absorbed this tidbit. I glanced at Margg, who looked shocked and annoyed that I had such interesting news.

"How do you know?" Star asked.

"I overheard the Commander and Valek talking."

"Ah, yes. Valek." Star tilted her nose at me. "Why are you living in his apartment?"

"None of your business," I said with a firm tone.

"So why should I trust you?"

"Because Valek would kill me if he knew I was here. You know it as well as I do. How much is my information worth?"

Star opened a black velvet purse and pulled out one gold coin. She tossed the coin to me like a master would throw a bone to a dog. I snatched it from the air, suppressing a wince. The cuts on my hands started to throb.

"Your fifteen percent." She sent one silver and one copper coin flying at Margg, who knew Star's ways, and caught them easily. "Anything else?" Star asked me.

"Not at this time."

"When you have something for me, tell Margg. She'll arrange another meeting."

Dismissed, I followed the silent Margg out of the house and down the street. Just as she guided me into a dark alley, Valek appeared out of the shadows. Before I could wonder why, he pulled me through a doorway and into a small room.

I was surprised and confused by his sudden arrival; I had thought he would wait a while before arresting Margg. She had followed me into the room, and stood with a sneering grin on her round face. It was the closest expression to pleasure that I had ever seen from her, and the opposite of what I had anticipated when she was caught as the leak. I tilted my head at Valek, hoping to prompt an explanation.

"I was right, Valek. She sold the Commander out for a gold coin. Check her pocket," Margg urged.

"Actually, Yelena came to me before the meeting. She believed she was going to expose *you*," Valek said to Margg.

Her gloating grin disappeared. "Why didn't you tell me?" she demanded.

"No time."

"Margg's not the leak?" I asked, still confused.

"No. Margg works for me. We've been feeding Star some rather unique information and hoping to find out who her other clients are. Star's been pestering Margg to get you involved, and I thought it would be a good opportunity to test your loyalty."

A complete understanding of Valek's ill temper snapped into my mind. He had expected me to betray him and the Commander. How could he have believed that? I wondered. Didn't he know me at all? Anger, disappointment and relief warred in my heart. I was unable to propel any words past my throat.

"I had hoped to send this rat back to the dungeon where

she belongs," Margg complained to Valek. "Now she'll still be scurrying around. Still a threat." Annoyed, she poked my arm with a meaty finger.

I moved. In a heartbeat I twisted her arm behind her back. She yelped as I raised her hand up high, forcing her to bend forward.

"I am *not* a rat," I said through clenched teeth. "I've proved my loyalty. You *will* get off my back. No more nasty messages in the dust. No more prying into my things. Or the next time, I'll break your arm." I shoved her hard as I released my grip.

She stumbled and landed on the ground in a heap. Pink-faced, she lurched to her feet. As she opened her mouth to protest, Valek stopped her with a glance.

"Well said, Yelena. Margg, you're dismissed," Valek said.

Margg's mouth snapped closed as she spun on her heel and left the room.

"She's not friendly," I said.

"No. That is precisely why I like her." He studied the door for a moment, then said, "Yelena, I'm going to show you something you're not going to like, but I think it's important that you know."

"Oh yeah? Like I enjoyed your test of faith?" Sarcasm rendered my voice sharp.

"I warned you that I tested the food taster from time to time."

Before I could reply, he stopped me. "Be quiet and stay close behind me." We went back out into the alley. Keeping in the shadows, we walked back to Star's house, where Valek guided me into a dark entrance within sight of Star's door.

"The person who has been leaking information to Star is due to arrive soon," Valek whispered close to my ear. His lips lightly rubbed my cheek. Shivers rippled down my spine at his touch, distracting me from what he had said.

The impact of Valek's words didn't hit me until I saw a lone figure with an uneven gait walking down the street.

22

I RECOGNIZED THAT STRIDE. My heart melted as I watched Rand limp to Star's house, knocking twice.

She admitted Rand into her home without a moment's hesitation. The faint thump of the closing door echoed hollowly in my chest.

"Another test?" I asked Valek with desperate urgency. "Is he working for you?" But I knew the answer deep in my soul, even before I saw the sad shake of his head. I felt empty, as if every emotion had been wrenched out of me. It was just too much. After Reyad's ghost, Nix's attack and Valek's test, I was mentally unable to handle another blow. I just stared at Valek with no thoughts, no feelings and no desires.

Valek motioned for me to follow him. I complied. We circled around to the back of Star's house. Entering the building to the left, we padded up three stories. The interior was dark and empty except for the top floor. One of Valek's men sat cross-legged with his back resting against the wall shared with Star's study. He wrote in a notebook, using a single candle as illumination.

Rand's voice could be heard clearly. Using hand signals, Valek communicated with the man. He gave the notebook to Valek and disappeared down the steps. Valek sat in the man's spot, and then tapped the floor next to him.

I crouched beside him, facing the wall. I had no desire to hear Rand's deceit, but I didn't have the willpower to leave. Valek pointed to an array of small holes in the wood. I peered through. All I could see was the back of a piece of furniture. I guessed that the holes were for listening purposes only. Squatting on the floor, I rested my forehead against the wall and closed my eyes as I eavesdropped on Rand's conversation.

"Generals are coming to town this week. That's nothing new, but the Commander ordered a feast, so something's up. Something significant. But I haven't been able to figure out what," Rand said.

"Let me know as soon as possible," Star replied. Then she paused. "Maybe Yelena knows what's going on."

My heart lurched when I heard my name. Run away, run away, run away, my mind screamed, but I only pressed my forehead harder on the wall.

"I doubt it. She was surprised when I mentioned the feast, so I didn't ask her. She might know more later this week. I'll try again."

"Don't bother. I'll ask her myself." The sleek tone of Star's voice implied that she had concealed this revelation until the time when exposing it would cause maximum damage.

"Yelena?" Rand sputtered. "Working for you? Impossible. That's not her style."

"Are you suggesting she's working for Valek?" Alarm tightened her voice.

Equally upset, I glanced at Valek. He shook his head, waving his hand in a "don't worry" gesture.

"No. She wouldn't." Rand had recovered. "I'm just surprised, but I shouldn't be. She could use the money, and who am I to think any less of her for it?"

"Well, you shouldn't be thinking of her at all. As I see it, she's disposable. The only concern I'll have when she dies is, who's going to replace her and how quickly can I bribe him?"

"Star, once again you've shown me in the most repulsive way that the sooner I pay off my debt to you the better. How much credit do I get for tonight's information?"

"Two silvers. I'll mark it in my book, but it won't make much difference."

"What do you mean?"

"Haven't you figured it out by now? You'll never pay off your debt. As soon as you get close, you always gamble yourself right down another hole. You're too weak, Rand. Too swayed by your own emotions. Easily addicted, and lacking in willpower."

"Oh, that's right. You *claim* to be a magician. Have you read my mind, Captain? 'Captain Star'—what a laugh! If you really had magic, Valek would have taken care of you long ago. I know you're not as smart as you claim." The heavy uneven tread of footsteps resounded through the wall as Rand started to walk away.

I was astounded. I had never heard Rand speak with such harsh sarcasm before, and more than that, if Star was a magician, I could be in serious danger. My mind spun, but it was all too complex to contemplate at this time.

"I don't need to read your mind," Star called after him. "All I have to do is review your history, Rand. It's all there."

Silence settled. The only noise coming from Star's study was the crinkle of papers being turned. Valek stood, pulling me up with him. His man had returned. Handing him the notebook, Valek descended the steps.

I followed Valek through the dark streets of Castletown. We kept to the shadows, avoiding the patrolmen. Once we had escaped the city's limits, Valek relaxed and walked beside me on the main road to the castle.

"I'm sorry," Valek said. "I know Rand was your friend."

His use of the past tense jabbed like a knife's point between my ribs.

"How long have you known?" I asked.

"I've suspected for the last three months, but only procured the hard evidence this month."

"What tipped you off?"

"Rand and his staff helped me with that poison test I gave you. He stayed while I laced the food with poison. I left that goblet of peach juice on my desk to keep it clean. It *was* a fair test. Blackberry poison was in that cup, but I didn't put it there." Valek paused, letting the information sink in.

"An interesting property of blackberries is that only when they're prepared in a special solution of grain alcohol and yeast and cooked with extreme care to the proper temperature are they poisonous. Most cooks, and certainly not their assistants, don't possess the skills or the knowledge to achieve that result." Valek sounded as if he admired Rand's ability to brew the poison.

The full understanding that Rand had tried to poison me almost knocked me off my feet. I stumbled as a surge of nausea boiled in my stomach. Dashing to the side of the road, I vomited into the bushes. Only when my body had ceased its convulsions did I realize Valek was supporting me. One of his arms was wrapped around my waist, while a cold hand pressed against my forehead.

"Thanks," I said, wiping my chin clean with some leaves. With trembling legs, I let Valek lead me to the castle. If he hadn't continued to support me, I would have curled up on the ground and called it a night.

"There's more. Do you want to hear it?" Valek asked.

"No." The truth, but as we drew closer to the outer wall of the castle complex, I made an ugly connection. "Did Rand set me up at the fire festival?"

"In a way."

"That's not an answer."

"The goons that nabbed you waited for you near the baking tent, so I suspected that Rand had told Star you would be there. But then he wouldn't let you out of his sight. It was as if he was protecting you. Remember how upset he was when he couldn't find you. How relieved he was when he spotted you alive and whole?"

"I thought he was drunk," I said.

"I suspect Rand is an unwilling participant. At the time of the poison test, he hardly knew you, but as your friendship grew, I imagine he finds himself in a difficult situation. He doesn't want to hurt you, but he needs to pay off his gambling debt. Star has an extensive organization, with plenty more thugs to replace the ones I took care of, thugs who would be willing to break a few bones for their boss. Does that make you feel any better?"

"No." My reaction to Rand's betrayal seemed extreme even to me, but I couldn't switch it off. It wasn't the first time someone had played false with me and it wasn't going to be the last. Brazell had deceived me. I had loved him like a father, and been loyal to him. In the end, it took almost a year of enduring his experiments before my feelings dwindled to the point where I could see him as he really was. But I had always known my young devotion to him was one-sided. Since he had never given me any reason to think he cared for me, his actions had been easier to stomach.

Rand's friendship, on the other hand, appeared genuine. I had begun to feel as if I had finally made a decent-size hole in the stone barricade I had built around myself. Big enough for me to slip through and enjoy our time together. Now the wall was crumbling. I felt stones pelting me and burying me deep beneath the rubble. How could I trust anyone again?

"Anything else you want to tell me?" I asked Valek as we

stopped a few feet short of the castle's south entrance. "Did Ari and Janco set me up for Nix's attack? Do you have another test of loyalty for me up your sleeve? Maybe the next time, I'll actually fail. A prospect that seems appealing!" I pushed away Valek's supporting arm. "When you warned me that you would test me from time to time, I thought you meant spiking my food. But it seems there is more than one way to poison a person's heart, and it doesn't even require a meal."

"Everyone makes choices in life. Some bad, some good. It's called living, and if you want to bow out, then go right ahead. But don't do it halfway. Don't linger in whiner's limbo," Valek said, his voice gruff. "I don't know what horrors you faced prior to your arrival in our dungeon. If I had to guess, I would think they were worse than what you have discovered tonight. Perhaps that will put things into perspective."

He strode into the castle. I leaned against the cold wall, resting my head on the unyielding surface. Maybe if I stayed here long enough, my heart would turn to stone. Then betrayals, tests of loyalties and poisons would have no effect on me. But the cold eventually drove me inside.

"Apply a force on the wrench. Not too much. You need a firm yet gentle touch," Janco said.

With healing hands still sore, I clumsily placed the tension wrench into the keyhole and applied pressure.

"Now use your diamond pick to lift the pin that's trapped by the tension, lift it until it breaks," he instructed.

"Breaks?" I asked.

"Reaches alignment. When you put a key into a lock, the metal ridges push the pins up so you can turn the cylinder and open the lock. The pins hold the cylinder in place. You'll need to do one pin at a time, and continue the pressure."

I slid the pick into the lock past the wrench. I maneuvered the pick, lifting each of the five pins. I could feel a tiny vibration in my finger joints as each pin broke with a subtle yet distinct click. When they were all aligned, the cylinder turned and the door unlocked.

"Good job! Damn, Yelena, you're a fast learner." Janco paused, his brow creased in concern. "You're not going to use this to do something stupid, right? And get us into trouble?"

"Define stupid," I said. When Janco's eyes widened, I added, "Don't worry. I'm the only one who would get into trouble."

He relaxed, and I practiced on another lock. We were in the lower level of the castle where no one would surprise us. It had been four days since the night I had learned about Rand. Valek's orders had been to act as if nothing had happened. He wanted to discover the full extent of Star's organization before exposing them. Valek was a true predator, I thought sourly, eyeing his prey before pouncing for the kill.

I knew I wasn't ready to play the friend to Rand, so I had been avoiding him, which wasn't hard to do. The castle crawled with Generals and their retinues, making every worker in the complex busy, including Rand.

Brazell was another reason I was glad to be out of sight. His black-and-green soldiers had infected the castle, and keeping away from them was becoming difficult. Although, I didn't mind hiding in Valek's suite. He had stolen a box of Criollo, and I was contented to munch a piece each time I tasted the Commander's food.

Ari, Janco and I had postponed our training sessions for the duration of the Generals' visit, but I had managed to rope Janco into teaching me to pick locks. Giving him the gold coin from Star had provided an added incentive. Valek had said I could keep it since working undercover wasn't part of the food taster's job. But the heavy weight of it in my pocket had been a constant reminder of Rand's treachery, so I decided to put it to good use.

"This last lock has ten pins. If you can open this one, you'll be able to handle all the pin-tumbler locks or key locks in the castle. Except the dungeon bolts. They're complicated, and it's not like we can practice on them." Janco's forehead furrowed. "You're not going to need that skill, are you?"

"I sincerely hope not."

"Good."

After several failed attempts, I managed to pop the lock open.

"Now you need to practice. The quicker you can spring a lock the better," Janco instructed. "I would let you borrow my picks, but I never know exactly when I might need them." He winked, a mischievous glint sparkling in his eyes. "So…" He pulled another set from his pocket. "I used that coin you gave me to buy a set for you." He handed me a black cloth case.

"That money was for you."

"Oh, there's plenty left. Even after I bought you this." He flourished an ebony-colored wooden rod as long as my hand.

It was decorated with a bright silver button, and silver symbols were engraved on the side.

"What's that?" I asked.

"Push the button," he said with glee.

I pressed down with my thumb, and started when a long gleaming blade shot out. It was a switchblade.

Amazed, I stared at my gifts. "Thank you, Janco. But why did you buy these for me?"

"Guilt, I suppose."

"Guilt?" Not the answer I had expected.

"I called you a criminal. I was once a criminal, but I've gone past it, and no one has held it against me. Besides, I have a terrible feeling you may need them. General Brazell's soldiers have been swaggering around the barracks, bragging about who is going to 'take out' Reyad's killer. They're quite imaginative, and I had to hold Ari back from challenging the lot a couple of times. Ten against one isn't good odds, even for Ari and me."

"I'll stay away from them," I said.

"Good. I'd better get moving. I've drawn the night shift. But, first, I'll escort you to your room."

"That's not necessary."

"Ari would kill me if I didn't."

We walked together toward Valek's suite. When we reached the corner before the main doors, Janco stopped just out of sight of the guards.

"Almost forgot," he said, reaching into his uniform pocket. He pulled out a sheath for the switchblade. "It goes around your right thigh. Remember to make a nice big hole in your pants pocket, so when you pull the weapon it won't get caught in the fabric."

He was about to leave when I stopped him. "Janco, what are these symbols?" I pointed to the silver markings on the handle of the knife.

Janco smiled. "They're the old battle symbols used by the King when he sent out messages and orders during war times. It didn't matter if the enemy intercepted them, because they were unintelligible to anyone who didn't know how to decipher them. Some of the soldiers still use them. They work well in military exercises."

"What do they say?"

His grin widened. "Too easy, Yelena. I'm sure you'll figure it out…eventually." Always the prankster, Janco laughed with delight.

"Come here," I said, "so I can punch you."

"I'd love to oblige you, my dear." Janco dodged beyond my reach. "But I'm late."

23

AFTER HIDING JANCO'S GIFTS deep in my uniform pocket, I went into Valek's suite. He was working at his desk, but he looked up as soon as I entered the room, giving me the impression that he had been waiting for me.

"Where have you been?" he asked.

"With Janco," I said. But I was wary. As long as I arrived at the scheduled times during the day, Valek didn't ask about what I did with my free time.

"Doing what?" Valek demanded, standing with his hands on his hips.

The comical image of a jealous husband popped into my mind. I stifled a smile. "Discussing fighting tactics."

"Oh." Valek relaxed his stance, but moved his arms awkwardly as if he felt he had overreacted and was trying to cover it up. "Well, that's all right. But from now on, I need to know where you are at all times, and I suggest you stay in the castle and keep a low profile for a while. General Brazell's guards have set a bounty on your head."

"A bounty?" Fear pulsed through my chest.

"It could be a rumor or just drunken soldiers' talk. But until they leave, I want you protected." Valek's tone was firm, but then he added, "I don't want to train another taster."

"I'll be careful."

"No. You'll be paranoid. You'll move in a crowd, keep to well-lit areas and you'll make certain to have an escort with you whenever you're walking down empty hallways late at night. Understood?"

"Yes, sir."

"Good. The Generals' brandy meeting is scheduled for tomorrow evening. Each General will bring a bottle of his finest brandy to share as they discuss Ixian business late into the night. You will be needed to taste the Commander's drinks." Valek lifted a box of eight bottles from the floor. They clinked musically as he set the carton on the table.

Pulling out a small drinking glass, he said, "I want you to sample each brandy once tonight and at least twice tomorrow, so you know how each tastes clean of poisons." He handed me the glass. "Each bottle is labeled according to the type of brandy, and which General brings it."

I grabbed a decanter at random. It was General Dinno's cherry brandy made in MD–8. Pouring a mouthful, I took a sip and rolled the liquid around my tongue, attempting to commit the taste to memory before swallowing. The strong alcohol burned down my throat, leaving behind a small fire in my chest. My face flushed with the heat.

"I suggest you use the 'slurp and spit' method so you don't get drunk," Valek said.

"Good point." I found another glass for spitting, and then worked my way through the remainder of the bottles.

On the day of the meeting, I tasted each brandy twice more in Valek's suite, and then tested myself with a third round. Only when I could pinpoint by taste alone which cordial belonged to which General was I satisfied.

That night, I waited for Valek to escort me to the war room. He came downstairs decked out in full dress uniform. Red braids draped his shoulders; medals were lined up six deep over his left breast. He oozed dignity, a man of stature. I would have been impressed, except for the uncomfortable and peevish look he wore. A petulant child forced to wear his best clothes. I covered my mouth, but was unable to block my laughter.

"Enough. I have to wear this damn thing once a year and, as far as I'm concerned, it's one time too many." Valek tugged at his collar. "Ready?"

I joined him at the door. The uniform enhanced his athletic body, and my thoughts drifted to how magnificent he would look with his uniform puddled around his feet.

"You look stunning," I blurted. Mortified, I blushed as a rush of heat spread through my body. I must have swallowed more brandy than I'd realized.

"Really?" Valek glanced down at his uniform. Then he set

his shoulders back and stopped yanking at his collar. His cross expression changed to a thoughtful smile.

"Yes. You do," I said.

We arrived in the Commander's war room just as the Generals assembled. The long, slender, stained-glass windows glowed with the weak light of the setting sun. Servants scurried around the circular chamber, lighting lanterns and arranging platters of food and drink. All military personnel were attired in their dress uniforms. Medals and buttons sparkled. I knew only three Generals by sight; the rest I deduced by the color of the diamonds on their otherwise black uniforms. Scrutinizing their faces, I memorized their different features in case Valek tested me later.

Brazell glared when I made eye contact. Adviser Mogkan stood next to him, and I shivered as Mogkan's eyes slid over me with cunning appraisal. When Brazell and Reyad had performed their experiments on me, Mogkan had always hovered nearby. His presence, sensed but unseen, had given me violent nightmares. Brazell's usual advisers were missing; I wondered why he had brought Mogkan instead.

The Commander sat at the tip of the egg-shaped conference table. His uniform was simple and elegant with real diamonds stitched onto his collar. The Generals, flanked by their advisers, seated themselves around the rest of the table. Valek's chair was to the Commander's right, and my stool was placed behind them, against the only stone wall in the room. I knew the meeting would last all night, and I was glad I would be able to rest my back. Another advantage to my position was that I wasn't in direct sight of Brazell. Although I could avoid seeing the poisonous looks he might flash my way, I couldn't hide from Mogkan's pointed stares.

The Commander pounded a wooden gavel on the table. Silence fell. "Before we launch into the scheduled topics," the Commander said, indicating the detailed agenda which had been distributed earlier, "I have an important announcement. I have appointed a new successor."

A murmur rippled through the war room as the Commander walked around the table and handed a sealed envelope to each General. Inside the envelopes were eight pieces to an encoded puzzle that would reveal the new successor's name when deciphered by Valek's key.

Tension permeated the room. I felt it pressing against me like an overfilled water-skin about to burst. A maelstrom of expressions, surprise, anger, concern and contemplation crossed the Generals' faces. General Rasmussen of MD–7 whispered into his adviser's ear, the General's cheeks turning as red as his hair and mustache. I leaned forward in my seat and saw Brazell struggle to keep his face neutral as delight tweaked at his features.

Instead of erupting, the tension simmered, and leaked away as the Commander ignored it by beginning the meeting. Items related to MD–1 were the first order of business, to be followed by each district in order. As a bottle of General Kitvivan's special white brandy slid around the table, the Generals discussed snow cats and mining rights.

"Come on, Kit. Enough about the cats. Just feed them up on the pack ice like we do, and they won't bother you,"

General Chenzo of MD–2 said in exasperation, running a meaty hand through his moon-white hair. His full mane stood out starkly against his tanned skin.

"Feed them so they'll get healthy and fat and start breeding like rabbits? We'll go broke supplying the meat," Kitvivan shot back.

My interest in the proceedings waxed and waned depending on the subject. After a while I began to feel light-headed and warm as the brandy influenced my body, since protocol dictated that I swallow when tasting for the Commander.

The Generals voted on various topics, but the Commander held the final vote. Mostly he ruled in favor of the majority. No one ventured a complaint when he didn't.

Commander Ambrose had lived in MD–3, scratching out a meager existence with his family in the foothills of the Soul Mountains. Nestled between the mountains and the ice pack, his home was atop a vast diamond mine. When the rich find had been discovered, the King had claimed the diamonds, and "allowed" the Commander's family to live there and work in the mines. He lost many family members to cave-ins, and to the damp and dirty environment.

As a young man seething at the injustices of the monarchy, Ambrose educated himself and began preaching about reform. His intelligence, bluntness and pervasiveness gained him many loyal supporters.

My mind focused back on the meeting when the Generals reached issues regarding MD–5. General Brazell caused a considerable stir. Instead of sliding around his best brandy, he sent a silver tray containing what looked like small brown stones. Valek handed one to me. It was a round drop of Brazell's Criollo.

Before protests about ignoring tradition could escalate, Brazell rose and invited everyone to take a bite. After a brief moment of silence, exclamations of delight filled the war room. The Criollo was filled with strawberry brandy. I gave the Commander the all-clear sign so I could savor the rest of my morsel. The combination of the sweet, nutty taste of the Criollo mixed with the smooth texture of the brandy was divine. Rand would be upset that he hadn't thought of mixing the two, I supposed, then regretted feeling sorry for Rand as I envisioned his deceitful face.

After the praise died down, Brazell made the announcement that the construction of his new factory was complete. Then he went on to more mundane matters of how much wool had been sheared and the expected output of the cotton plantations.

Military District 5 produced and dyed all the thread for Ixia, and then sent it to General Franis's MD–3 to be woven into fabric. Franis nodded his head in concern as he wrote down the figures Brazell quoted. He was the youngest of the Generals, and had the habit of tracing the purple diamonds on his uniform with a finger whenever he was concentrating.

I dozed on my stool as fuzzy thoughts gathered like storm clouds in my mind. Strange dreams about brandy, border patrols and permits swirled like snowflakes. Then the images turned bright and sharp as a picture of a young woman dressed in white hunting furs snapped into my mind.

She held a bloody spear high in the air in celebration. A dead snow cat lay at her feet. She slammed the tip of her weapon into the pack ice and drew a knife. Cutting a slash in the cat's fur, she used a cup to collect the blood that spilled out.

She exalted as she drank, scarlet rivulets spilling down her chin. I heard her thoughts clearly in my mind. "No one has managed this feat," she thought. "No one but I!" she shouted over the snow. Her exhilaration filled my heart. "Proof that I am a strong cunning hunter. Proof that my manhood was taken from me. Proof that I am a man. Men will not rule me any longer," she cried. "Become the snow cat to live with snow cats, become a man to live with men."

The hunter turned her face. At first, I took her to be the Commander's sister. They shared the same thin delicate features and black hair. She wore power and confidence like a cloak. Peering at my dreaming self, her gold almond-shaped eyes drove through me like a lightning strike. Sudden recognition that she *was* the Commander jerked me awake. My heart pounded and my head thumped and I realized I was staring directly into Mogkan's searing gaze. He smiled with satisfaction.

The Commander's reason for hating magicians was as clear to me as glass. He was a she, but with the utter conviction that she should have been born a man. That cruel fate had chosen to burden him with a mutation that he had to overcome. And the Commander feared that a magician might pull this secret from his mind. Pure foolishness, I thought, shaking my head to dismiss the whole crazy notion. Just because I had dreamed about a woman didn't mean that the Commander was one. It was absolute nonsense. Or was it?

Rubbing my eyes, I glanced around to see if anyone else had noticed that I had fallen asleep. The Commander stared off into the distance, and Valek sat stiff and alert, scanning the room, seeking something or someone. General Tesso had the floor.

Valek pulled his gaze back to the Commander, and bumped his arm in alarm. "What's going on?" he whispered urgently. "Where were you?"

"Just remembering a time long ago," the Commander said in a wistful voice. "More enjoyable than listening to General Tesso's excruciatingly detailed report on the corn harvest in MD–4."

I studied the Commander's features, trying to superimpose the woman from my dream. They matched, but that meant nothing. Dreams twisted reality and it was easy to envision the Commander killing a snow cat.

The rest of the meeting continued without incident, and I dozed on my stool from time to time, untroubled by strange dreams. When the Commander pounded his gavel, I was awake in an instant.

"Last item, gentlemen," the Commander announced. "A Sitian delegation has requested a meeting."

The room erupted with voices. Arguments sprang to life as if the Generals were picking up an old debate right where they had left off. They discussed trade treaties, and quarreled about attacking Sitia. Instead of trading for goods, why not take them? they argued. They wanted to expand their districts and gain more men and resources, ceasing all worries about Sitia attempting to attack Ixia.

The Commander sat in silence and let the flow of advice wash over him. The Generals settled enough to proclaim their beliefs about allowing the Sitians to come. The four northern Generals (Kitvivan, Chenzo, Franis and Dinno) didn't want to meet with the delegation, while the four southern Generals (Tesso, Rasmussen, Hazal and Brazell) favored a summit with the Sitians.

The Commander shook his head. "I acknowledge your opinions about Sitia, but the southerners would rather trade with us than attack us. We have more men and metal. A fact they are well aware of. To attack Sitia we would expend many lives and large sums of money. And for what? Their luxury items aren't worth the cost. I'm content with Ixia. We have cured the land of the King's disease. Perhaps my successor will want more. You'll have to wait until then."

A murmur rippled through the Generals. Brazell nodded in agreement, with his thin lips anchored in a predator's smile.

"I have already agreed to meet with the southern contingent," the Commander continued. "They're due to arrive in four days. You have until then to express your specific concerns to me before departing for your home districts. Meeting adjourned." The bang from the Commander's gavel echoed throughout the dead silent room.

The Commander rose and with his bodyguards and Valek close behind, he prepared to leave. Valek gestured for me to join them. I lurched to my feet. The full effect of the brandy I had consumed washed over me. Giddy, I followed the others from the room. An explosion of sound slipped through the door just before it closed behind us.

"That should stir things up a bit," the Commander said with a wan smile.

"I would advise against vacationing in MD-8 this year," Valek said sarcastically. "The way Dinno reacted to your announcement about the southern delegation I would expect him to pepper your beach house with sand spiders." Valek shivered. "A horribly painful way to die."

My skin crawled too, thinking of the lethal spiders the size of small dogs. Our procession continued in silence for a while as we headed back to the Commander's suite. My gait was unsteady. The stone walls blurred past me, as if they were moving and I was the one standing still.

Outside the Commander's suite, Valek said, "I'd watch out for Rasmussen too. He didn't take the news of the change in your successor well."

The Commander opened his door. I stole a quick glance inside his suite. The same plain utilitarian style that decorated his office and the rest of the castle was present. What had I expected? Maybe a splash of color, or something a bit more feminine? I gave my head a little shake to banish such absurd thoughts. The motion made my head spin, and I had to put a hand to the wall to keep myself from stumbling.

"I watch out for everyone, Valek. You know that," the Commander said before shutting the door behind him.

Upon entering our suite, Valek stripped off his uniform jacket and threw it on the couch. He pointed to a chair and said, "Sit. We need to talk."

I plopped into the chair and dangled a leg over the

armrest, watching Valek pace the room in his sleeveless undershirt and formfitting black pants. Imagining my hands helping to ease the tension in the long ropy muscles of his arms almost started a giggling fit. Brandy flowed through my blood, quickening my pulse.

"Two things were very wrong tonight," Valek said.

"Oh, come on. I just dozed for a minute," I said in my defense.

Valek shot me a quizzical look. "No, no. You did fine. I meant about the meeting; the Generals." He continued to pace. "First, Brazell seemed unusually happy about the change in successor and the Sitian delegation. He's always wanted a trade treaty, but he typically exercises a more cautious approach. And second, there was a magician in the room."

"What?" My breath locked. Had I been discovered?

"Magic. Very subtle, from a trained professional. I only felt it once, a brief touch, but I couldn't pinpoint the source. But the magician had to be in the room, or I wouldn't have felt it."

"When?"

"During Tesso's long-winded dissertation about corn." Valek's posture had relaxed a little, as if the act of talking out a problem helped him deal with it. "About the same time your snoring could be heard halfway across the room."

"Ha," I said rather loud. "You were so stiff at that meeting I thought rigor mortis had set in."

Valek snorted with amusement. "I doubt you could have looked any better sitting in that uncomfortable dress uniform all night. I imagine Dilana sprayed on extra starch with malicious glee."

Then he grew serious again. "Do you know Adviser Mogkan? He eyed you most of the evening."

"I know of him. He was Reyad's primary adviser. They also hunted together."

"What's he like?" Valek asked.

"Same kind of vermin as Reyad and Nix," I said. The words poured off my lips. I slapped both hands over my mouth, but it was too late.

Valek studied me for a moment. Then he said, "There were a number of new advisers at the meeting. I guess I'll have to check them out one by one. It seems we have a new southern spy with magic abilities." He sighed. "It never ends." He dropped onto the edge of the couch as weariness settled on him like a coating of dust.

"If it did, you'd be out of a job." Before I could stop myself, I squeezed behind Valek and started to massage his shoulders. The alcohol had taken complete command of my movements, and the tiny sober section of my brain could do nothing but yell useless admonishments.

24

VALEK STIFFENED UNDER my touch. Was he expecting me to strangle him? I wondered. As my hands kneaded his muscles, he relaxed.

"What would you do," I asked him, "if suddenly the world was perfect and you had no one to spy on?"

"I'd be bored," Valek said with amusement.

"Come on, seriously. A change in profession." I dug my thumbs into the muscle at the base of his neck. "A fire dancer?" A rush of warmth radiated as brandy pumped through my blood.

"No. An arms teacher?" Valek suggested.

"No. It's a perfect world. No weapons allowed." I moved my hands down his back. "How about a scholar? You've read all these books lying around, haven't you? Or are they just to make it difficult for someone to sneak in?"

"Books serve me in so many ways. But I doubt your perfect society would need a scholar on murder."

My hands paused for a second. "No. Definitely not."

"A sculptor? I could carve extravagant statues. We could re-decorate the castle and liven things up. How about you?" he asked as I pressed my fingertips into the small of his back. "What would you do?"

"Acrobatics." The word flowed without conscious thought. I had thought I left acrobatics behind with my fire amulet, but it seemed my excursion through the trees had reawakened my desire.

"An acrobat! Well, that explains a lot."

Aroused by my contact with Valek's sculpted body, I slid my hands around to his stomach. Reyad be damned. The brandy had relaxed me past fear. I started to unfasten Valek's pants.

He grabbed my wrists, stopping me. "Yelena, you're drunk." His voice was hoarse.

Valek released my hands and stood. I sat, watching him with surprise as he swooped down to lift me from the couch. Wordless, he carried me to my room and laid me on the bed.

"Get some sleep, Yelena," Valek said softly as he left the room.

My world spun as I stared into the darkness. Placing a hand on the cold stone wall next to my bed helped to steady my thoughts. Now I knew. Valek had no interest in me other than my job as the food taster. I had allowed myself to get caught up in Dilana's gossip and Maren's jealousy. The ache of rejection throbbing in my soul was my own fault.

Why hadn't I learned by now? People turned into monsters. At least the people in my experience. First Brazell, then Rand, although Reyad had stayed consistent. What about Valek? Would he transform into one or had he already? Like Star said, I shouldn't be thinking of him at all, not as a companion, and not to fill the dead place in my heart.

As if I could. I laughed. A drunken sound, tattered and ragged, the music of my thoughts. Look around you, Yelena, I chided myself. The poisoned food taster who converses with ghosts. I should be thankful that I breathed, that I existed. I shouldn't long for more than freedom in Sitia. Then I could fill the emptiness. Dismissing all sentimental, weak thoughts, I focused on the business of staying alive.

Escaping to Sitia would break no bonds with Valek. Once I obtained the antidote to Butterfly's Dust I could set my plans into motion. Determined, I reviewed lock-picking techniques in my mind until I fell into a deep alcohol-induced sleep.

I woke an hour before dawn with a pounding head. My mouth felt like an abandoned spiderweb. I imagined dust blowing from my lips with each exhaled breath. Moving with extreme care, I inched out of bed. Wrapping my blanket around my shoulders, I went to get a drink. Valek liked cold water and always kept a pitcher outside on the balcony.

The crisp night air blew away the lingering fuzziness of sleep. The castle's stone walls glowed, eerily reflecting the moonlight. I located the metal pitcher. A thin film of ice had formed on the top. Breaking it with a finger, I poured the water into my mouth, gulping.

When I tipped my head back for a second drink, I noticed a black spider-shaped object clinging to the castle wall above my head. With growing alarm, I realized the shape was descending toward me. It wasn't a spider but a person.

I searched for a hiding spot, but stopped when I realized that the intruder had probably already seen me. Locking myself in the suite and waking Valek seemed a better plan. But before I could enter the pitch-black living room, I hesitated. Inside, the intruder's dark clothes would be hard to see. A locked door no longer gave me a sense of security since my lock-picking lessons with Janco.

Cursing myself for leaving my switchblade inside, I moved to the far end of the balcony, clutching the water pitcher in my hand.

The wall climber jumped the remaining distance to the balcony floor. The effortless movement triggered recognition.

"Valek?" I whispered.

A bright flash of white teeth, then Valek removed a pair of dark glasses. The rest of his face was hidden behind a hood that covered his head and was tucked into a skintight body leotard.

"What are you doing?" I asked.

"Reconnaissance. The Generals tend to stay up late after the Commander leaves the brandy meeting. So I had to wait until everyone had gone to bed." Valek went into the suite. He removed his hood. Lighting the lantern on his desk, he pulled a paper from his pocket.

"I hate a mystery. I would have let the identity of the Commander's successor remain a secret, as I have for fifteen years, but tonight's opportunity was too tempting. With eight drunken Generals sleeping it off, I could have danced on their beds without waking them. Not one among them has any imagination. I watched all the Generals put their envelopes from the Commander right into their briefcases." Valek motioned for me to join him at the desk. "Here, help me decipher this."

He handed me a stiff piece of paper. A jumble of words and numbers were scrawled on it. He had copied the eight different pieces of the encrypted message by stealing into each General's room. I wondered why he was confiding in me. Too curious to question, I pulled up a chair to help him.

"How did you break the wax seal?" I asked.

"Rookie trick. All you need is a sharp knife and a tiny flame. Now read me the first set of letters." He wrote it down then reordered the letters until he had created the word *siege*. Opening a book, he flipped through the pages. Symbols like the ones on my switchblade's handle peppered the document. The page Valek stopped on was decorated with a large blue symbol that resembled a star in the middle of three circles.

"What's that?" I asked.

"The old battle symbol for *siege*. The dead King used these markings to communicate with his Captains during times of war. They were originally created hundreds of years ago by a great strategist. Read me the next set. They should be numbers."

I told him the numbers. He began to count the lines of text.

It occurred to me that I could borrow this book and figure out Janco's message on my switchblade. Eventually, my ass. Won't Janco be surprised.

When Valek reached that number, he wrote a letter down

on a clean page. After he had finished deciphering the message, Valek sat as still as a held breath. Unable to wait any longer I asked, "Who is it?"

"Guess," he said.

I looked at him. I was tired and hungover.

"I'll give you a hint. Who was the happiest about the change? Whose name keeps popping up during the most bizarre situations?"

Terror swept over my body like a cloak. If something happened to the Commander, Brazell would be in command. I would probably be his first order of business, and wouldn't live long enough to see any changes he might implement in Ixia.

Valek understood the look on my face. He nodded. "Right. Brazell."

For two days the Commander met with each General in turn. My brief and periodic interruptions to taste the Commander's food created uncomfortable moments of silence. The tension around the castle was palpable as the Generals' retinues snarled and fought with everyone.

On the third day, when I arrived to taste the Commander's breakfast, I found him absorbed in conversation with Brazell and Adviser Mogkan. The Commander's eyes were glazed, his voice a monotone.

"Get out of here!" Brazell barked.

Mogkan pushed me into the throne room. "Wait here until we summon you," he ordered.

I hesitated outside the door, uncertain if I should heed this unusual request. If it had come from Valek or the Commander I wouldn't have doubted, but being expected to follow Mogkan's orders rankled. My worries grew as I imagined Brazell attempting an assassination. I was about to search for Valek, when he burst into the throne room, his expression hard as he hurried toward the Commander's office.

"What are you doing out here?" Valek demanded. "Haven't you tasted his breakfast yet?"

"I was ordered to wait. He's with Brazell and Mogkan."

Sudden fear crossed Valek's face. He pushed past me into the office. I followed. Mogkan was standing behind the Commander with his fingertips pressing into the Commander's temples. When Valek appeared, Mogkan stepped away. He said smoothly, "You can definitely feel, Sir, that this is an excellent way to ease a headache."

Animation returned to the Commander's face. "Thank you, Mogkan," he said. Glaring at Valek's intrusion, he demanded, "What's so important?"

"Disturbing news, Sir." Valek stared daggers at Brazell and Mogkan. "I would like to discuss it in private."

The Commander rescheduled their meeting for later that day, then dismissed them.

"Yelena, taste the Commander's breakfast now."

"Yes, Sir."

Valek watched me taste the food. An intense expression lined his face, making me nervous. Did he think the food was tainted? I rechecked the cooling tea and lukewarm omelet, but detected no foreign substances. I placed the tray on the Commander's desk.

"Yelena, if I have to eat cold food again, I'll have you whipped. Understand?" The Commander's voice lacked passion, but the threat was genuine.

"Yes, Sir," I replied, knowing an excuse was useless.

"You're dismissed."

I fled from the office, barely noticing the bustling activity in the throne room. Walking past the entrance, I paused. "Hungry," said a flat voice in my head. My stomach growled; I was ravenous. I headed toward the kitchen.

When I rounded a corner, Adviser Mogkan stood there, blocking my path. He linked his arm through mine and guided me to an isolated section of the castle. Going with him seemed natural. I wanted to pull away. I wanted to be afraid, terrified even, but I couldn't produce the emotions. My hunger had dissipated. I felt content.

Mogkan steered me down a deserted corridor. A dead end, I thought, still unable to conjure a reaction. His silky gray eyes stared at me for a moment before he unhooked his arm from mine. His fingers traced the line of black diamonds down my uniform sleeve.

"My Yelena," he said possessively.

Fear blazed up my arm and exploded in my chest the second physical contact with Mogkan was broken. My emotional ennui had dissolved, but I couldn't move. The muscles in my body wouldn't obey my mind's frantic commands to fight.

A magician! Mogkan had power. He had used it during the brandy meeting, tipping Valek off. But further contemplation on this revelation was cut short when Mogkan stepped closer.

"Had I guessed you would cause such trouble I never would have brought you to Brazell's orphanage." He smiled at my confusion. "Didn't Reyad tell you that I found you?"

"No." My voice was husky.

"You were lost in the jungle, only six years old. Such a beautiful, bright child. Such a delight. I rescued you from the claws of a tree leopard because I knew you had potential. But you were too stubborn, too independent. The harder we tried, the more you resisted." Mogkan cupped his hand under my chin, forcing me to meet his gaze. "Even now, when I'm locked into you, you're still fighting me. I can command your body." He raised his left arm, and my own left arm mirrored his movement. "But if I tried to control both your mind and body, you would eventually thwart me." He shook his head in disbelief, as if the whole concept amazed him.

"Fortunately, subtle pressure is all that's required." He pulled his hand away, and then made a pinching gesture with his fingers and thumb.

My throat closed. I was unable to breathe. Powerless to defend myself, I sank to the ground. My mind's screaming went unvoiced. Logic grabbed the panic and wrestled it to the ground. Mogkan was using magic. Maybe I could block it before I passed out. I tried reciting poisons in my mind.

"Such strength," Mogkan said in admiration. "But it won't save you this time." He bent down and kissed me tenderly, almost fatherly, on the forehead.

Peace flowed through me. I stopped resisting. My vision blurred. I felt Mogkan take my hand, holding it in his own.

25

RECLINING AGAINST THE WALL, I clung to Mogkan's hand as the world faded around me. I felt an unwelcome jolt, then the tight blockage in my throat released. Gasping for breath, I came to my senses and realized I was lying prone on the floor. Next to me sat Valek atop Mogkan's chest. Valek's hands were wrapped around Mogkan's neck, but his eyes were on me.

Mogkan smiled when Valek stood and yanked him to his feet. "I hope you're aware of the penalty for being a magician in Ixia," Valek said. "If not, I'd be delighted to enlighten you."

Mogkan smoothed out his uniform and adjusted his long dark braid of hair. "Some would say your ability to resist magic makes *you* a magician, Valek."

"The Commander thinks otherwise. You're under arrest."

"Then you're in for a big surprise. I suggest you discuss these false accusations with the Commander before you do anything drastic," Mogkan said.

"How about I kill you right now?" Valek stepped closer to him.

A hot, searing pain stabbed my abdomen. I yelped and rolled into a tight ball. The agony was relentless. Valek took another step. I screamed as fire blazed up my back and circled my head.

"Any closer, and she'll be a corpse," Mogkan said, a cunning sleekness in his voice.

Through eyes tearing with anguish, I saw Valek shift his weight to the balls of his feet, but he remained in place.

"Well, now. That's interesting. The old Valek really wouldn't have cared if I killed his food taster. Yelena, my child, I just realized how incredibly useful you are."

The intense pain was unbearable. I would have gladly died to escape from it. Before I passed out, my last glimpse was of Mogkan's back as he walked away unharmed.

I woke to blackness. Something heavy pressed against my forehead. Alarmed, I tried to sit up.

"It's all right," Valek said, pushing me down.

I touched my head and pulled off a damp cloth. Blinking in the light, I looked around at the familiar furniture of my own room. Valek stood next to me, a cup in his hand.

"Drink this."

I took a sip and cringed at the medicinal flavor. Valek insisted I finish it. When the cup was empty, he placed it on the night table.

"Rest," he ordered, then turned to leave.

"Valek," I said, stopping him. "Why didn't you kill Mogkan?"

He considered for a moment, tilting his head. "A tactical maneuver. Mogkan would have killed you before I could finish him. You're the key to too many puzzles. I need you." He strode to the door but paused at the threshold. His grip on the doorknob was hard enough to whiten his knuckles. "I've reported Mogkan to the Commander, but he was…" Valek's hand twisted on the knob, and I heard the metal crack. "Unconcerned, so I'll be guarding the Commander until Brazell and Mogkan leave. I've reassigned Ari and Janco as your personal bodyguards. Don't leave this suite without them. And stop eating Criollo. I'll taste the Commander's Criollo. I want to see if anything happens to you." Valek pulled the door shut, leaving me alone with my swirling thoughts.

True to his word and much to the Commander's annoyance, Valek didn't leave the Commander's side. Ari and Janco enjoyed a change in routine, but I made them work hard. Whenever I wasn't tasting the Commander's meals, I had Ari drill me with knife defense and Janco give me more lessons on picking locks.

The Generals' departure was scheduled for the next day, which meant it was time to do some of my own reconnaissance. It was early evening and I knew Valek would still be with the Commander until late. I told Ari and Janco that I was going to bed early, and bade them good-night at the threshold to Valek's suite. After waiting an hour, I slipped back into the hallway.

The corridors of the castle were not as deserted as I had

hoped, but Valek's office was located off the main through-way. I approached his door, scanning the hallway for activity. Seeing no one, I inserted my picks into the first of the three keyholes, but my nerves made popping the lock impossible. I took a couple of deep breaths and tried again.

I had two locks sprung when I heard voices approaching. Standing, I pulled the picks out of the keyhole and knocked on the door just as two men came into view.

"He's with the Commander," said the guard on the left.

"Thanks," I replied and started to walk in the opposite direction with my heart beating like a hummingbird's wings. I glanced behind me until they were gone, then raced back to Valek's office. The third lock proved to be the most difficult. I was covered with sweat by the time I popped it. I hurried into the room, locking the door behind me.

My first task was to open the small wooden cabinet that held my antidote. Perhaps Valek had locked the recipe in there. I lit a dim lantern to peer inside. Glass bottles of various shapes and sizes gleamed in the light. Most of the bottles were marked Poison. A growing sense of urgency consumed me as I searched. All I uncovered was a large bottle containing the antidote. I poured only a few doses into the flask I had hidden in my pocket, knowing that Valek would notice if I took too much.

After relocking the cabinet, I began a systematic search of Valek's files, starting with the desk drawers. Even though his office was strewn with books and maps, his personal dossiers were well organized. I found files on Margg and the Commander and was tempted to read them, but I stayed focused on finding any folder bearing my name or a reference to Butterfly's Dust. Valek had written many interesting comments about my tasting abilities in my personnel file, but there was no mention of the poison or the antidote.

When I finished with the desk, I moved to the conference table. Books on poisons were interspersed with files and other espionage documents. I sorted through the piles. My time was running out. I had to be back in Valek's suite before he escorted the Commander to his apartment.

I suppressed my disappointment as I finished with the table. There was still half of his office left to search.

I was halfway across the quiet room when I heard the distinct sound of a key being inserted into the lock. One click, then the key was withdrawn. I snuffed out the lantern as the second lock clicked open. Diving behind the conference table, I hoped the boxes piled underneath would hide me from view. Please, I prayed to the forces of fate, let it be Margg and not Valek. A third click made my heart squeeze.

The door opened and closed. A light tread of footsteps crossed the room. Someone sat at the desk. I didn't risk peeking, but I knew it was Valek. Had the Commander retired early? I reviewed my meager options: be discovered or wait Valek out. I eased into a more comfortable position.

A few minutes later, someone knocked on the door.

"Come," said Valek.

"Your, ah…package has arrived, sir," said a male voice.

"Bring him in." Valek scraped his chair on the stone floor.

I heard the rustle of chains and a shuffling step. "You're dismissed," Valek said. The door clicked shut. A familiar rancid smell of the dungeon reached my nose.

"Well, Tentil. Are you aware that you're next in line for the noose?" Valek asked.

My heart went out to the doomed prisoner. I knew exactly how he felt.

"Yes, sir," a voice whispered.

Pages crackled. "You're here because you killed your three-year-old son with a plow, claiming it was an accident. Is that correct?" Valek asked.

"Yes, sir. My wife had just died. I was unable to afford a nanny. I didn't know he had climbed under." The man's voice was pinched with pain.

"Tentil, there are no excuses in Ixia."

"Yes, sir. I know, sir. I want to die, sir. The guilt is too hard to bear."

"Then dying wouldn't be adequate punishment, would it?" Valek didn't wait for a response. "Living would be a harsher sentence. In fact, I know of a profitable farmstead in MD–4 that has tragically lost both the farmer and his wife, leaving behind three sons under the age of six. Tentil will hang tomorrow, or so everyone shall believe, but you will be escorted to MD–4 to take over the operation of a corn plantation and the job of raising those three boys. I suggest your first order of business should be to hire a nanny. Understand?"

"But..."

"The Code of Behavior has been excellent at ridding Ixia

of undesirables, but it is somewhat lacking in basic human compassion. Despite my arguments, the Commander fails to grasp this point, so I occasionally take matters into my own hands. Keep your mouth shut, and you will live. One of my associates will check on you from time to time."

I huddled behind the boxes, frozen in disbelief. Hearing Valek use the word *compassion* was as incomprehensible to me as the thought of Margg apologizing for her rude behavior.

There was another knock on the door.

"Come," Valek said. "Perfect timing as always, Wing. Did you bring the documents?"

I heard a rustle of papers. "Your new identity," Valek said. "I believe our business is concluded. Wing will escort you to MD–4." Chains clanked to the floor. "You're dismissed."

"Yes, sir," Tentil said. His voice cracked. He was probably overwhelmed. I knew how I would feel if Valek offered me a free life.

After the men left, a painful quiet descended. I feared the sound of my breath would give me away. Valek's chair scraped. Two faint thumps were followed by a loud yawn.

"So, Yelena, did you find our conversation interesting?"

I held still, hoping he was guessing. But his next statement confirmed my dismay.

"I know you're behind the table."

I stood. There was no anger in his voice. He lounged in his chair with his feet resting on the desktop.

"How did you…" I began.

"You favor lavender-scented soap, and I wouldn't be alive

today if I couldn't determine when someone had picked my locks. Assassins love to ambush, leaving dead bodies behind mysteriously locked doors. Fun stuff." Valek yawned again.

"You're not angry?"

"No, relieved actually. I wondered when you would search my office for the recipe to the antidote."

Sudden fury welled in my throat. "Relieved? That I might try to escape? That I rifled through your papers? You're that confident that I won't succeed?"

Valek cocked his head to one side, considering. "I'm relieved that you're following the standard steps of escaping, and *not* inventing a unique plan. If I know what you're doing, then I can anticipate your next move. If not, I might miss something. Learning how to pick locks naturally leads to this." Valek gestured around the room. "But, since the formula has not been written down and only I know it, I'm confident you won't find it."

I balled my hands into tight fists to keep them from wrapping around Mr. I-Know-Everything's superior neck. "Okay, so there's no chance for escape. How about this? You gave Tentil a new life, why not me?"

"How do you know I haven't already?" Valek put his feet on the floor and leaned forward. "Why do you think you were in the dungeon for almost a year? Was it only luck that *you* happened to be the next in line when Oscove died? Perhaps I was merely acting at our first meeting when I seemed so surprised that you were a woman."

It was too much to bear. "What do you want, Valek?" I

demanded. "Do you want me to give up trying? Be content with this poisoned life?"

"Do you really want to know?" Valek's voice intensified. He stood and walked over to me.

"Yes."

"I want you...not as an unwilling servant, but as a loyal staff member. You're intelligent, quick-thinking and becoming a decent fighter. I want you to be as dedicated as I am at keeping the Commander safe. Yes, it's a dangerous job, but, on the other hand, one miscalculated somersault on the tightrope could break your neck. That's what I want. Will you be able to give it to me?" Valek's eyes seared deep into mine, searching for an answer. "Besides, where would you go? You belong here."

I was tempted to concede. But I knew that if I wasn't poisoned or murdered by Brazell, the wild magic in my blood would eventually explode, taking me with it. The only physical mark I would leave on this world would be a ripple in the power source. Without the antidote, I was lost anyway.

"I don't know," I said. "There's too much..."

"That you haven't told me?"

I nodded, unable to speak. Telling him about my magical abilities, I thought, would only get me killed faster.

"Trusting is hard. Knowing who to trust, even harder," Valek said.

"And my track record has been rather horrendous. A weakness of mine."

"No, a strength. Look at Ari and Janco. They appointed themselves your protectors long before I assigned them. All because you stood up for them to the Commander, when their own Captain wouldn't. Think about what you have right now before you give me an answer. You have gained the Commander's and Maren's respect, and Ari's and Janco's loyalty."

"What have I earned from you, Valek? Loyalty? Respect? Trust?"

"You have my attention. But give me what I want, and you can have everything."

The next morning, the Generals prepared to leave. It took four hours for eight retinues to assemble. Four hours of noise and confusion. When everyone had finally passed through the outer gates, it seemed that the castle breathed a sigh of relief. In the wake of this sudden release of tension, servants and guards milled about. They grouped together in small clumps, taking a break before cleaning the eight guest suites. It was during this lull in activity that the Commander informed the rest of the castle staff that the Sitian delegation was scheduled to arrive the next day. His words struck like lightning. A flash of stunned silence was followed by a frenzy of activity as servants dashed off to make the proper preparations.

Although happy to see the backs of Mogkan and Brazell, I wandered listlessly about the castle. I hadn't given Valek his answer. To live, I had to go south, but without the antidote, I wouldn't survive. Dread filled my heart as the reality of my inevitable fate filled my mind.

The next day, my presence was required at the special greeting ceremony for the arriving southern delegation. Apprehension about seeing the Sitians unsettled my stomach. I felt as if someone were saying, "Yelena, take a good look at what you can't have."

Since the throne room had been converted into an office, the only place in the castle suitable for state affairs was the Commander's war room. Once again, Valek stood stiffly in his dress uniform on the Commander's right side, while I waited behind them.

My apprehension turned to awe as I felt the waves of nervous energy pulsing from the high-ranking officials and advisers selected to be a part of the ceremony. When the delegation was announced and invited to enter, I moved to get a better view.

The Sitians floated into the room. Their long, brightly colored, exotic robes draped to the floor, covering their feet. Wearing animal masks trimmed with bright plumes of feathers and fur, they stopped before the Commander and fanned out into a V-shape.

Their leader, wearing a hawk's face, spoke in formal tones. "We bring you greetings and salutations from your southern neighbors. We hope this meeting will bring our two lands closer together. To show our commitment to this endeavor, we have come prepared to reveal ourselves to you." The speaker and the four companions removed their masks in one rehearsed movement.

I blinked several times in astonishment, hoping that during the seconds of darkness everything would be set right. Unfortunately, my world had just mutated from bad to wretched.

Valek glanced at me with a resigned look as if he, too, couldn't believe this new turn of events.

The Sitian leader was Irys. A master-level magician stood a mere three feet before Commander Ambrose.

26

"Ixia welcomes you to our land, and hopes to make a fresh start," the Commander announced to the southern delegation.

As I waited behind the Commander, I wondered what would happen to the Sitians once Valek informed the Commander that Irys was a magician. Contemplating the mischief she might create before leaving the castle, I tried to envision a best-case scenario. I failed, realizing this was probably only the beginning of the end.

Valek watched thoughtfully as the southerners and the Commander exchanged more formal statements. I guessed from Valek's demeanor that Irys had not used her magic. After the official greeting ceremony concluded, the delegation was guided to their quarters to rest from their journey and to await the evening's feast. Protocol decreed that pleasantries and entertainment preceded hard-core negotiations.

Everyone, except the Commander and Valek, filed out of the war room. I started to leave, but Valek grabbed my arm.

"Okay, Valek, let's hear it. Some dire warning I presume?" the Commander asked, sighing.

"The Sitian leader is a master magician," Valek said, a hint of annoyance in his voice. He probably wasn't used to being sighed at.

"That's to be expected. How else could they know we're sincere about creating a trade treaty? We could have ambushed them instead. It's a logical move." Unconcerned, the Commander turned toward the door.

"She doesn't trouble you?" Valek asked. "She's tried to kill Yelena."

The Commander looked at me for the first time since we had entered the war room. "It would be unwise to kill my food taster. Such an act could be misinterpreted as an assassination attempt and halt negotiations. Yelena is safe…for now." He shrugged off any more thought of my future safety and left the war room.

Valek grimaced. "Damn."

"Now what?" I asked.

He kicked at one of the conference chairs. "I anticipated a magician with the southern delegation, but not *her.*"

He shook his head, as if to clear the frustration that gripped his voice. "I'll leave the power twins assigned to you while she's here. Although, if she's determined to get you, there's nothing they or I can do. I lucked out with Mogkan. I was just around the corner when I felt his power surge. Let's hope she behaves while she's a guest in our land."

Valek pushed the chair against the table with a loud bang. "At least I know where all the magicians are. Mogkan was the one I felt during the Generals' brandy meeting. And the southern master is now in the castle. Unless any more decide to show up, we should be safe."

"What about Captain Star?" I asked.

"Star's a charlatan. Her claims of being a magician are just a tactic for scaring her informers so they don't double-cross her." Valek sighed.

"Generals, Sitians and feasts increase my workload. Which reminds me, you need to stay for the entire feast tonight. A tiresome chore, but at least the food should be good. I've heard Rand wanted to use the Criollo for a new dessert, but the Commander refused his request. Another puzzle, since Brazell has been sending the stuff by the wagonload, and has promised to ship the dessert to all the other Generals. They were clamoring after it like it was gold."

I saw a flash in Valek's eye. "Any unusual symptoms, feelings or appetites since you stopped eating the Criollo?"

It had been three days since I had eaten a piece, and I couldn't recall any actual physical symptoms that might be linked to it. Eating it had lifted my spirits and given me a boost of energy. I longed for its sweet taste especially now that my chances for freedom had dwindled.

"A mild craving," I told Valek. "But nothing like an addiction. I find myself thinking about it from time to time, wishing for a piece."

Valek frowned. "It might be too soon. The Criollo could still be in your bloodstream. You'll inform me if something happens?"

"Yes."

"Good. I'll see you tonight."

Poor Valek, I thought, stuffed into his dress uniform three times in as many days. Elaborate decorations had been hung in the dining room for the feast. Crimson and black drapes hung along the walls, and red and gold streamers twisted and dipped from the ceiling. The room was ablaze with light. An elevated platform had been constructed to support a head table where the southern delegation, the Commander and Valek all wore their finest clothes. High-ranking officers and upper-level advisers were seated at round tables circling the room, leaving the middle empty. In the corner a twelve-piece band played sedate music, which was a surprise since the Commander frowned on music, considering it a waste of time.

I sat behind Commander Ambrose so he could pass his plate to me. As predicted, the food was marvelous. Rand had outdone himself.

My dark uniform blended in with the black drapes along the wall, and since I doubted anyone beyond the dais noticed I was there, I watched the others as I waited between courses. Ari and Janco sat next to each other at a table by the door. Attending their first formal function as Captains, they were clearly uncomfortable. Knowing them, I was sure they would rather be drinking beer with their comrades back in the barracks.

Irys and her retinue were seated to the Commander's left. Their formal robes had swirls of color and glittered in the firelight. Irys wore a diamond pendant shaped like a flower, which sparkled on her chest. She ignored my presence, which was fine with me.

After the servants cleared the meal from the tables, they extinguished half of the lanterns. The band quickened their tempo until a pulsating rhythm vibrated the glassware on the tabletops. Costumed dancers burst into the room, holding blazing staffs high above their heads. Fire dancers! They performed an intricate and complex routine. Watching them whirl and spin to the beat left me gasping for breath. I understood now why their festival tent had been so packed with enthusiastic fans.

At one point, Valek leaned back in his chair and said to me, "I don't think I would have made it past the audition, Yelena. I probably would have set my hair on fire by this point."

"What's a singed head for the sake of art?" I teased. He laughed. The mood of the room was energetic and elated. I hoped the Commander wouldn't wait fifteen more years before having another feast.

The dancers finished their second encore and exited the room. Irys rose to offer a toast. The Sitians had brought their finest cognac. Irys poured a glass for the Commander, Valek and herself. She didn't seem offended when the Commander's goblet passed to me.

I swirled the amber liquid and inhaled the sharp odor. Taking a small sip, I rolled the cognac around my tongue, then spat it onto the floor. Gagging and retching with the effort, I tried to expel every last bit of it from my mouth. Valek stared in alarm.

I choked out, "My Love."

Valek knocked over the other two glasses, spilling their contents on the table. As my body reacted to the poison, I watched Valek turn into a black ink spot, and the walls run with blood.

I floated on a crimson sea, colors dancing and whirling around my head. The sound of broken glass raining on stones created an odd melody in my mind. I drifted on a raft made of curly white hair, carried along by a strong current. Irys's soothing voice spoke amidst the tempest of colors, "You'll be fine, just hold on to your life raft. You can ride out this storm."

I awoke in my room. A dim lantern had been lit, and Janco sat in a chair, reading a book. This was much nicer than the last time I had tasted My Love. A soft bed was preferable to lying in a pool of my own vomit. Although this habit of waking in my room without knowing how I got here had to stop.

"Why, Janco, I didn't know you could read," I teased. My voice was hoarse, my throat sore and a dull ache resided deep in my head.

"I'm a man of many unknown talents." Janco smiled. "Welcome back."

"How long have I been out?"

"Two days."

"What happened?"

"After you turned into a madwoman?" Janco asked. "Or why you turned into one?"

I grimaced. "After."

"It's amazing how fast Valek can move," Janco said with admiration. "He pushed you out of sight onto the floor while corking the tainted bottle and using some sleight of hand to swap it for another. He apologized to everyone about being clumsy, and proceeded to pour three new glasses so that southern witch could make her phony toast. The whole incident was smoothed over so quick that only the people on the dais knew what really happened."

Janco scratched at his goatee. "Well, they and Ari. He had his eye on you all night, so when you went down, we were on our way. We slipped behind the head table during the toast and he carried you here. He'd still be here, but I forced him at knifepoint to get some sleep."

Ah, that explained my curly-haired raft. I sat up. The ache in my head intensified. A water pitcher rested on my night table. I poured a glass, draining it dry.

"Valek said you'd be thirsty. He's been here a couple of times, but he's been busy with the southerners. I can't believe that witch had the audacity to try to poison the Commander."

"She didn't. Remember? She poured three glasses from the same bottle. Someone else must have," I said. But the culprit eluded me as the effort of concentrating made my head pound.

"Unless she was going for a murder-suicide. A quick death instead of waiting in our dungeon to be hanged."

"Possible," I said, but I thought it unlikely.

"Valek must agree with you. The treaty discussions are proceeding as if nothing happened." Janco yawned. "Well, now that you're coherent again, I'll get some sleep. It's another four hours until dawn." Janco pushed me back down on the bed. "Get some rest. We'll be back in the morning."

He studied me, indecision creasing his face. "Ari said you screamed and raved a lot while he took care of you. In fact, he said that if Reyad was alive today, he'd gut the bastard without a moment's hesitation. I just thought you might want to know." Janco gave me a brotherly kiss on the forehead and left.

Oh great, I groaned. What else did Ari know? How would I be able to face him in the morning? Well, I thought, nothing I could do about it now. I tried to go back to sleep, but my empty stomach kept growling. All I could think of was food. I examined my hunger, trying to deduce if it was a mental command from Irys like Mogkan had done to me before, but I couldn't come up with a good reason why she would summon me.

Once I had decided to risk the trip, I strapped on my switchblade and made my way on wobbly legs to the kitchen, where I hoped to sneak in and grab some bread before Rand woke up to start his dough.

Slicing off a chunk of cheese to eat along with my loaf, I was about to leave, when Rand's door opened.

"Yelena," he said in surprise.

"Morning, Rand. Just stealing some food."

"I haven't seen you in weeks," he grumped. "Where've you been?" He moved toward the ovens. Opening the first black metal door, he stoked the embers of the fire and added more coal.

"I've been busy. You know. The Generals. The delegation. The feast. Which, by the way, was magnificent, Rand. You're a genius."

He perked up after I appealed to his ego. I resigned myself to the fact that, if I wanted him to think we were still friends, I would have to talk to him. I placed my breakfast on a table and pulled up a stool.

Rand limped toward me. "Someone said you were sick?"

"Yeah. Stomach bug. Haven't eaten in two days, but I'm better now." I gestured to the bread.

"Hold off, I'll make you some sweet cakes."

I watched him mix the batter, making sure he didn't slip in a poisonous ingredient. But after the cakes were under my nose, I dug into them with mindless abandon. The familiar scene of Rand making bread while I sat close by dissolved the awkwardness between us. We were soon chatting and laughing.

It wasn't until his questions turned pointed and specific that I realized Rand was pumping me for information about the Commander and Valek. I clenched my fork, stabbing it hard into my sweet cakes.

"Hear anything about this southern treaty?" Rand asked.

"No." My tone was harsh, and he looked at me with curiosity. "Sorry, I'm tired. I better get back to bed."

"Before you go, you might as well take these beans along." Rand pulled down the glass jar. "I've sautéed, ground, even boiled them, but they still taste unrecognizably terrible." He poured them into a bag, and went to check on his baking fires.

Watching him stir the glowing coals gave me an idea. "Maybe they're not to eat," I said. "Maybe they're a source of fuel." The southern pods had been delivered to Brazell's new factory. Perhaps he was using them to heat his ovens.

"Worth a try," Rand said.

I threw the beans into the hearth fire. We waited for a while, but there were no sudden flames or increase in temperature. While Rand switched his bread pans, I stared into the embers, thinking that as far as the mystery of the beans was concerned, I was out of options.

When Rand started again with his questions, I turned my eyes away from the oven's fire. Pressure knotted in my throat. "I'd better get going or Valek will be wondering where I am."

"Yes, by all means go. I noticed you and Valek have become close. Tell him, for me, not to kill anybody, will you?" Sarcasm rendered Rand's voice sharp.

I lost control and slammed the oven door shut. It echoed in the quiet kitchen. "At least Valek has the decency to inform me when he's poisoning me," I blurted out, but wished I could pull the words from the air and stuff them back into my mouth. Blaming my fatigue, my anger, or Rand for my outburst wouldn't erase what I had just said.

His facial expressions contorted and vacillated from surprise to guilt to anger. "Did Star tell you?" he demanded.

"Ah…" I was at a loss. If I said yes, he would find out from Star that I was lying, and if I said no, he would insist on knowing my source. Either way, he'd figure it out. I had just revealed Valek's entire undercover operation.

Fortunately, Rand didn't wait for me to answer before launching into a tirade. "I should have known she would tell you. She loves to play nasty head games. When you came along, I didn't want to know you. All I wanted was the heap of gold credit that Star offered to apply to my debt if I spiked Valek's test." Rand pounded the table. "Then my damn morals and your damn niceness complicated things. Selling information about you, then having to protect you without looking like I was protecting you made my life hell."

"Sorry for the inconvenience," I said. "I guess I should be grateful, poisonings and kidnappings aside." Sarcasm sharpened my voice.

Rand rubbed his hands over his face. His anger had dissipated. "I'm sorry, Yelena. I was backed into a corner and I couldn't get out without hurting someone."

I softened. "Why did Star want me poisoned?"

"General Brazell commissioned her. *That* shouldn't be a surprise."

"No." I thought for a moment, and then asked, "Rand, is there anyone who can help you get out of this mess? Maybe Valek?"

"Absolutely not! Why do you have such an elevated opinion of him? He's a murderer. You should hate him just for giving you Butterfly's Dust. I would."

"Who told you?" I demanded. "Who else knows? I thought only the Commander and Valek knew."

"Your predecessor, Oscove, told me why he never tried to run, and no, I haven't sold that information to anyone. I do have limits." He tugged at his apron. "Oscove's hatred of Valek rivaled my own, and I understood that, but your relationship with Valek…" Rand's furrowed brows spiked up toward his forehead.

"You're in love with him," he cried.

"That's preposterous," I shouted.

We gaped at each other, too stunned to say anything more.

Then a sweet, nutty aroma reached my nose. Rand, too, sniffed the air. I followed the scent to the oven where I had tossed the mystery beans into the fire. Opening the door, I was greeted by a strong puff of heavenly scent. Criollo.

27

"WHERE DID YOU FIND those beans?" Rand asked. "They're the missing ingredient to the Criollo recipe. I didn't think of roasting them to change the flavor."

"A storeroom downstairs," I lied. I wasn't about to tell him that Valek and I had intercepted them on the way to Brazell's new factory. Which, I now realized, was probably not producing feed but manufacturing Criollo.

"Which storeroom?" Rand asked, a hint of desperation in his voice.

"I don't remember."

"Try harder. If I can duplicate Ving's recipe for Criollo, then maybe I won't be transferred."

"Transferred? Where?"

"You mean Valek hasn't gloated over it by now? He's wanted to get rid of me since the takeover. I'm being sent to Brazell's manor house, and Ving will come here. He won't last a week!" Rand spat the words out with bitter force.

"When?"

"Don't know. I haven't gotten my transfer papers yet. So there's some hope to stop it. *If* you can find me those beans."

He thinks we're still friends, I realized in amazement. Even after admitting to poisoning me and accusing me of loving his enemy, he believes I'll do it for him. I had no response. I stalled. "I'll try," I said, then made a hasty exit.

The first flicker of dawn was cresting the Soul Mountains as I arrived at Valek's suite unseen. The tall windows in the living area faced east, and in the weak gray light I saw Valek's profile as he sat on the couch, waiting for me.

"Back so soon?" he asked. "Too bad. I was just about to organize a search for your dead body. What happened when you knocked on the southerner magician's door to sacrifice yourself? Did they kick you out, thinking you too half-witted to waste their time on?"

I plopped on a chair to wait out Valek's sarcastic lecture. No excuse I could offer would satisfy him. He was right, going out alone had been a foolish thing to do, but logic and an empty stomach were like oil and water, they didn't mix.

When he was quiet, I asked, "Are you done?"

"What? No rebuttal?"

I shook my head.

"Then I'm finished."

"Good," I said. "Since you're already in a bad mood, I might as well tell you what happened while I was in the kitchen. Actually two things: one bad, one good. Which would you like to hear first?"

"The bad," Valek answered. "That allows me the hope that the good will balance things out."

I braced myself and admitted to revealing his undercover operation. Valek's face hardened.

"It's your fault. I was defending you!" I blurted.

He paused. "In protecting my honor, you exposed months of work. I should be flattered?"

"You should," I said. I wasn't about to feel guilty. If he hadn't tested my loyalty with Star and then used me to further his investigation, he wouldn't be in this situation.

His shoulders drooped as he leaned back on the couch, kneading his temples. "I hadn't planned on making arrests till later this month. Better implement my cleanup plan before Rand has a chance to alert Star." Valek rubbed his eyes. "Still, this might be a benefit. I think Star's becoming suspicious. She hasn't been conducting any illicit business in her office. If I bring her in now, I might discover who hired her to poison the Sitian's bottle."

"Star? How?"

"She has a southern assassin in her employ. He would be the only one with the skill and the opportunity. I'm sure the poisoning wasn't a result of Star's personal political views. Her organization would do anything for anybody for the right price. I must find out who would risk so much to compromise the delegation."

He stood up, energized. "What's the good news?"

"The mystery beans are an ingredient in making Criollo."

"Then why did Brazell lie on his permit application? There's no law against manufacturing a dessert," Valek said, matching my leap of logic about the true nature of Brazell's factory.

"Perhaps because the beans are imported from Sitia," I theorized. "That would be illegal; at least until the trade treaty is finalized. Maybe Brazell's been using other southern ingredients or equipment as well."

"Possible. Which is why he was so eager to have a treaty. You'll have to take a good look around when you visit the factory."

"What?"

"The Commander has scheduled a trip to MD–5 when the southerners leave. And where the Commander goes, you go."

"What about you? You're going too, aren't you?" The panic welling in my throat made my voice squeak.

"No. I've been *ordered* to stay here."

"One, and two, and three, four, five. Keep fighting like this and you will die," Janco sang.

I was pinned against the wall. My bow clattered to the floor as Janco's staff tapped my temple, emphasizing his point.

"What's wrong? You're rarely *this* easy to beat." Janco leaned on his bow.

"Too distracted," I said. It was only a day ago that Valek had informed me of the Commander's plans.

"Then what are we doing here?" Ari asked. He and Maren had watched the match.

Still uncomfortable about what he might have heard when I was delusional, I had a hard time meeting Ari's gaze. "Next round, I'll try harder," I said as Janco and I caught our breath. Reviewing our fight, I asked Janco, "Why do you rhyme when you fight?"

"It helps keep my rhythm."

"Don't the other soldiers give you a hard time about it?"

"Not when I beat them."

We started another match. I made an effort to concentrate, but was beaten again.

"Now you're trying too hard. I can see you planning each offensive move," Janco said. "You're giving yourself away, and I'm there for the block before you even strike."

Ari added, "We drill for a reason. Offensive and defensive moves must be instinctive. Let your mind relax, but stay alert. Block out all distractions. Stay focused on your opponent, but not too focused."

"That's a contradiction," I cried in frustration.

"It works," was all Ari said.

I took a couple of deep breaths and cleared the distressing thoughts of my upcoming trip to Brazell's district from my mind. Rubbing my hands along the bow, I concentrated instead on the smooth solidness of the weapon. I hefted it in my grip, trying to make a connection, creating an extension of my thoughts through the bow.

A light vibration tingled through my fingertips as I traced the wood grain. My consciousness flowed through the bow, twisting and turning along the grain, and back along my arm. I possessed the bow and my body at the same time.

I moved into the third round with a sense of heightened

awareness. Intuitively, I knew what Janco was planning. A spilt second before he moved I had my bow up to block. Instead of scrambling to defend myself, I had more time to counter as well as block. I pushed Janco back. A beat of music pulsed in my mind, and I allowed it to guide my attack.

I won the match.

"Amazing," Janco shouted. "Did you follow Ari's advice?"

"To the letter."

"Can you do it again?" Ari asked.

"Don't know."

"Try me." Ari snatched his bow and assumed a fighting stance.

I rubbed my fingers along the bow's wooden grain, setting my mind back into its previous mental zone. It was easier the second time.

Ari was a bigger opponent than Janco. What he lacked in speed, he made up for in strength. I had to modify my defense by dodging his strikes or he would have knocked me off my feet. Using my smaller size to duck under one of his blows, I swept my bow behind his ankles and yanked. He dropped like a sack of cornmeal. I had won again.

"Unbelievable," Janco said.

"My turn," Maren challenged.

Again, I tuned in to that mental zone. Maren's attacks were panther-quick. She favored the fake jab to the face, which usually lured my guard up and away from protecting my torso, leaving it exposed for a body strike. This time, I was one step ahead of her, ignoring the fake and blocking the blow.

A clever opponent, she applied tactics instead of speed or

strength. She charged me. And I knew she planned to move to my side when I stepped up to engage her. Instead of moving up, I spun and tripped her with my bow. Pouncing on her prone form, I pressed my staff against her neck until she conceded the match.

"Damn!" she said. "When a student starts beating her teacher, it means she doesn't need her anymore. I'm walking." Maren strode from the room.

Ari, Janco and I looked at each other.

"She's kidding, right?" I asked.

"Blow to her ego. She'll get over it," Ari said. "Unless you start beating her every time you fight."

"Unlikely," I said.

"Very," huffed Janco, who was probably nursing his own bruised ego.

"That's enough fighting," Ari said. "Yelena, why don't you do some katas to cool down, and we'll quit for the day."

A kata was a fixed routine of different defensive and offensive blocks and strikes. Each kata had a name, and they grew more complex with each skill level. I started with a simple defensive bow kata.

As I moved I watched Ari and Janco become absorbed in conversation. I smiled, thinking that they bickered like an old married couple, and then concentrated on my kata. I practiced finding my mental fighting zone, sliding into and out of it while I performed the appropriate kata moves. Panting, I finished the routine, and noticed Irys watching me from the doorway with great interest.

She was wearing her hawk mistress uniform. Her hair had been tied back in accordance to Ixia's military regulations. She had probably walked through the castle unchallenged.

I glanced toward my "bodyguards." They were engrossed in their conversation, ignoring Irys and me. Uneasiness rolled in my stomach. I inched closer to my companions as she came into the room.

"Won't Valek sense your magic?" I asked her, gesturing to Ari and Janco.

"He's on the other side of the castle," she said as she stepped nearer. "But I did feel someone pulling power before we arrived. Two brief surges. So there is or was another magician in the castle."

"Wouldn't you know?" I asked in alarm.

"Unfortunately no."

"But you do know who it is? Right?"

She shook her head. "There are several magicians that have disappeared. They're either dead or hiding. And some keep to themselves and we never know about them. It could be anyone. I can only identify a magician if I have established a link with him or her, as I have linked with you." Irys examined the weapons lined against the wall.

"What's wrong with the Commander?" she asked. "His thoughts are practically dripping out of his head. He's so open, I could go in and extract any information I wanted if it weren't against our moral code of ethics."

I couldn't answer her. "What are you doing here?" I asked instead.

Irys smiled. She gestured to the bow in my hands. "What were you doing with that weapon?"

Seeing no reason to lie, I explained about my training.

"How did you do today?" she asked.

"I beat all three opponents for the first time."

"Interesting." Irys seemed pleased.

I glanced over at Ari and Janco, who were still involved in their conversation. "Why are you here?" I asked again. "You promised me a year." Then I had a sudden horrific thought. "Am I closer to flameout?"

"There's still time. You've stabilized for now, but how close are you to coming to Sitia?"

"The antidote is beyond my reach. Unless you can steal the information from Valek's mind?"

She frowned. "Impossible. But my healers say if you can filch enough antidote to last a month, there's a possibility we can remove the poison from your body. Come with us when we leave. I have an adviser just your size. She'll wear your uniform and lure Valek and his men away while you take her place. With a mask on, no one would know." Irys spoke with assurance. She was either unconcerned or unaware of the risks.

Hope bloomed in my chest. My heart raced. I had to calm myself with a cold reminder that Irys had said there was a possibility of removing the poison. In other words, no guarantees. The escape plan appeared straightforward, but I searched for loopholes anyway. I knew better than to fully trust her.

Deciding, I said, "Adviser Mogkan was here last week. Is he one of your spies?"

"Mogkan, Mogkan." She turned the name over her tongue.

"Tall with gray eyes and wears his long black hair in a single braid." I formed a picture of him in my mind. "Valek said he has power."

"Kangom! How unoriginal! He dropped from sight ten years ago. There was a big scandal about his alleged involvement with some kidnapping ring. Oh." Irys inhaled sharply and studied my face. Giving her head a tight shake, she asked with keen interest, "So where has he been hiding?"

"MD–5. Is he wanted?"

"Only if he becomes a danger to Sitia. But that explains why we've been picking up occasional flares of magic from that direction." She cocked her head as if straining to hear some faint music. "There is a faint flow of magic to the castle. It could be from Kangom…Mogkan, although it's highly unlikely. He doesn't have that kind of strength. It's probably just a tiny ripple in the power source, like a loop of thread hanging down. It happens from time to time. But I did feel someone pulling power recently." She paused, staring at me with her direct emerald gaze. "Are you coming with me?"

Mogkan's magic might not concern her, but it concerned me. There seemed to be a link between Mogkan's magic and the Commander's unusual behavior, but I couldn't quite grasp the reason why.

Undecided, I rolled it around my mind, much as I moved food in my mouth, tasting for danger. Running away had always been an automatic defensive move, and going south offered my best chance for survival. Months ago, I would have jumped at the offer, but now I felt as if I would be abandoning ship too soon, that there was a remedy yet to be discovered.

"No," I said. "Not yet."

"Are you crazy?"

"Probably, but I need to finish something first, then I'll keep my promise and come to Sitia."

"If you're still alive."

"Maybe you can help me. Is there some way I can shield my mind from magical influence?"

Irys cocked her head. "You're worried about Kangom?"

"Very."

"I think so. You're strong enough to handle it." She handed me the bow. "Do one of your katas, eyes closed, and clear your mind."

I started a blocking bow kata.

"Imagine one brick. Place the brick on the ground, and then make a row of them. Using imaginary mortar, build another row. Keep building until you have a wall as high as your head."

I did as she instructed, and heard a distinct tone as each brick was laid. A wall formed in my mind.

"Stop," she ordered. "Open your eyes."

My wall disappeared.

"Now block me!"

Loud music vibrated in my head, overwhelming me.

"Imagine your wall," Irys shouted.

My brick defense flashed complete in my mind. The music stopped midnote.

"Very good. I suggest you finish your business and escape south. With that kind of strength, if you don't achieve complete control of your magic, someone else might grab it and use it, leaving you a mindless slave." Annoyance quirked her face as she spun on her heel and left the training room.

The moment the door clicked into place, Ari and Janco ended their conversation and blinked as if they had just woken from a deep sleep.

"Done already? How many katas?" Ari asked.

I laughed and put my bow away. "Come on, I'm hungry."

When the Sitian delegation left three days later, I had a sudden panic attack. What the hell was I doing? My one perfect opportunity for escape had slipped away to the south, while I remained behind, preparing to leave for Brazell's manor. Irys had been right; I was crazy. My breath hitched every time I thought of the trip. The Commander's retinue was scheduled to depart in the morning.

I rushed around the castle, packing my own special provisions for the journey. Dilana's sorrowful face greeted me when I stopped by her room for some traveling clothes. Rand's paperwork had been finalized, she said. He was coming with us.

"I requested a transfer, but I doubt it'll be approved," Dilana said as she searched through her piles of clothing. "If only the lout had married me, then we wouldn't be in this predicament."

"There's still time to submit the application. If it's approved, you can travel to MD–5 for the wedding."

"He doesn't want to let anyone know how much he cares for me. He's worried that my safety might be used as leverage against him." She shook her head, refusing to be cheered even when I told her that the new trade treaty with Sitia would allow silk to be imported.

The southern treaty was a simple exchange of goods. Specific items were listed. Only merchants with the proper permits and licenses would be able to buy and sell these items at a fixed price. All caravans would be subject to inspection when crossing the Ixian border at the approved locations. Rand's cup of coffee was only a few months away, but I doubted he would brew some for me since I hadn't spoken to him since our argument in the kitchen. I couldn't get him more beans, and I couldn't explain why.

The morning of our departure was gray and overcast, hinting at snow. The cold season was beginning, which usually indicated the end of travel, not the onset of it. The snows would most likely keep the Commander's retinue at Brazell's until the thawing season. I shuddered at the thought.

Valek stopped me before I left our suite. "This is a very dangerous trip for you. Maintain a low profile and keep your eyes open. Question thoughts in your mind; they might not be your own." He handed me a silver flask. "The Commander has your daily dose of antidote, but if he *forgets* to give it to you, here's a backup supply. Tell no one that you have it, and keep it hidden."

For the first time, Valek trusted me. The metal flask felt warm in my hands. "Thanks."

A feather of fear brushed my stomach as I packed the flask into my backpack. Another danger I hadn't recognized. What else had I missed?

"Wait, Yelena, there's one more thing." Valek's manner and tone were strangely stiff and formal. "I want you to have this." He extended his hand. On his palm sat the beautiful butterfly he had carved. Silver spots on the wings glinted in the sunlight, and a silver chain hung from a small hole drilled into its body.

Valek looped the necklace around my neck. "When I carved this statue, I was thinking about you. Delicate in appearance, but with a strength unnoticed at first glance." His eyes met mine.

My chest felt tight. Valek acted as if he would never see me again. His fear for my safety seemed genuine. But was he worried about *me* or his precious food taster?

28

COMMANDER AMBROSE'S TRAVELING
entourage consisted of nearly fifty soldiers from his elite guard.
Some led the way, others walked beside the Commander and
his advisers atop their horses. Guards also bracketed the small
group of servants, who preceded the horses. The remaining
soldiers followed behind. Ari and Janco scouted the Commander's planned route and were hours ahead of the procession.

We advanced at a brisk pace in the crisp morning air. The
vivid colors of the hot season had long since drained from the
forest, leaving behind a barren, gray-hued simplicity. I had
tucked Valek's butterfly underneath my shirt, and found myself
fingering the lump it made on my chest as we traveled. Valek's
gift had caused my emotions to roil. Just when I believed I had
figured him out, he surprised me.

Carrying a pack, I also held a walking staff that was a thinly
disguised bow. A few of the guards cast suspicious glances my

way, but I ignored them. Rand refused to meet my gaze. He stared straight ahead in stony silence. It wasn't long before he lagged behind; his leg prevented him from maintaining the pace.

After a stop for lunch, we continued until an hour before sunset. Major Granten, the official leader of the expedition, wanted to set up camp in the daylight. Spacious tents were raised for the Commander and his advisers, and smaller two-man tents were erected for the servants. I found I would share space with a woman named Bria, who ran errands and served the Commander's advisers.

I settled into the tent while Bria warmed herself by the fire. Lighting a small lantern, I pulled out the book on war symbols that I had borrowed from Valek. After we had deciphered the name of the new successor, I hadn't had a spare moment to interpret Janco's message on my switchblade. There were six silver markings etched into the wooden handle. I began with the top and worked my way to the bottom. My smile grew wider with each translation. Janco could be so annoying, but underneath he could be so sweet.

When Bria entered the tent smelling of wood smoke, I shoved the book into my pack.

Disturbing dreams made for a restless night. I awoke tired in the gray fuzz of dawn. With the amount of time the procession took to eat and reassemble, plus the shorter hours of daylight, I estimated the excursion to Brazell's manor house would take about five days.

On the second night of the trip, I found a note in my tent.

A request for a rendezvous. The next evening while the soldiers set up camp, I was to follow a small, northbound trail that intersected the main road just past our campsite. The message was signed Janco, in a lavish hand. I examined the signature in the fading light, trying to remember if I'd ever seen Janco's writing.

Genuine note or a trap? Should I go or should I stay in camp where it would be safe? I worried the question in my mind throughout the night and all through the third day on the road. What would Valek do in this particular situation? The answer helped me to form a plan.

When the signal to stop for the night sounded, I waited until everyone was occupied before leaving the clearing. Once out of sight, I swept off my cloak and turned it inside out. Before departing the castle I had procured gray cloth from Dilana, which I had then sewn into the inside lining of my cloak just in case I needed to hide in the winter landscape. I hoped the improvised ashen camouflage would be adequate in concealing my presence when I neared the meeting site.

I strapped my bow to my back, sheathed my switchblade on my right leg, then grabbed my rope and grappling hook from my backpack. I found the northern trail. Rather than walk down the narrow path, though, I sought a suitable tree and tossed my hook up into its branches. My first concern was the potential noise of my passage through the treetops, but I soon discovered that trees without leaves only creaked under my weight as I followed the trail.

Maneuvering close to the meeting site, I spotted a tall dark-haired man waiting at the prearranged location. He seemed restless and agitated. Too thin for Janco, I thought. Then the man turned in my direction. Rand.

What was he doing here? I circled the clearing. Discovering no threat lurking in the bushes, I climbed down to the path, leaving my rope hanging from the branch. I tucked my backpack behind the tree's trunk.

"Damn," Rand cursed. "I thought you weren't going to show." His haggard face had dark smudges under his eyes.

"And I thought Janco was supposed to be here."

"I wanted to explain, but there's no time, Yelena." Rand's haunted eyes bored into mine. "It's a trap! Run!"

"How many? Where?" I demanded, pulling the bow from my back. I scanned the woods.

"Star and two goons. Close. Leading you here was supposed to pay off my debt." Tears streaked Rand's face.

I spun on him. "Well, you did a good job. I see you're actually following through on this assignment." I spat the words at him.

"No," he cried. "I can't do it. Run, damn you, run."

Just as I moved to go, Rand's eyes widened with fright.

"No!" He shoved me aside. Something whistled past my ear as I fell to the ground. Rand dropped beside me, an arrow in his chest. Blood welled, soaking his white uniform shirt.

"Run," he whispered. "Run."

"No, Rand," I said, brushing the dirt from his face. "I'm tired of running."

"Forgive me, please." He clutched my hand as his eyes beseeched me through tears of pain.

"You're forgiven."

He sighed once, then stopped breathing. The shine in his brown eyes dulled. I pulled his hood over his head.

"Get up," a man's voice ordered.

I looked into the dangerous end of a loaded crossbow. Leaning on my bow, I rose. With my weight balanced on the balls of my feet, I rubbed my hands along the wooden staff, finding my zone of concentration.

"The area is secured, Captain," the man called out to the woods. "Don't move," he said to me, leveling his weapon at my chest.

Footsteps approached. The man took his eyes off me to look for his companions. I moved.

My first bow strike landed across his forearms. The crossbow sailed from his hands, firing into the woods. My second strike went to the back of his knees. I knocked his feet out from under him. Lying flat on his back, he blinked at me with a stunned expression.

Before he could draw breath, I slammed the point of my bow straight down onto his neck, crushing his windpipe.

A quick glance over my shoulder revealed Star and another man rushing into the clearing. Star shouted and pointed. Her goon drew his sword. I raced down the trail, his heavy footsteps thundering after me. When I reached my rope, I tossed my bow into the woods before scrambling up into the tree. The man's blade stabbed at my legs. Cloth ripped as his sword cut through my pants. The brush of cool steel on my thigh spurred me on.

He cursed as I leaped to the next tree. Moving fast, I swung through the treetops. When the sound of his crashing through the underbrush was far enough behind me, I found a good place to hide. Wrapping myself in my cloak, I hunkered down on a low branch and waited.

Star's thug barreled though the woods. Not far from my perch, he stopped to listen, searching the treetops. My heart raced. I muffled my heavy breathing with my cloak. Sword raised, he hunted for me.

When he was below me, I threw off my cloak and launched myself, hitting his back with my feet. We fell hard. I rolled away and stood before he could recover, then kicked his sword from his hand. He was faster than I had anticipated. He grabbed my ankle, yanking me down.

Next thing I knew, his weight pressed on top of me and his hands were wrapped around my neck. Banging my head on the hard ground, he muttered, "That's for giving me trouble." Then he pressed his thumbs deep into my throat.

Dazed and choking, I plucked at his arms before I remembered my switchblade. I fumbled in my pockets as my vision blurred, turning to snow. The smooth feel of wood greeted my fingertips. I grasped the handle, pulled it out and triggered the button.

The snick of the blade caused fear to flicker in his eyes. For a moment he stared straight into my essence. Then I plunged the knife into his stomach. With a low growl, he increased the pressure on my neck. Blood, hot and sticky, ran down my arms, soaking my shirt. Through dizziness and pain, I jerked the weapon out and tried again. This time, I pointed the tip of the blade up toward his heart. The man hunched forward, driving the knife in farther, and finally collapsed.

The dead man's weight impeded my starved lungs. Summoning my last bit of strength, I rolled his body off of me.

Dazed, I wiped my switchblade clean in the dirt, found my bow and went in search of Star.

Two men. I had just killed two men. A killing machine, I hadn't even hesitated. Fear and rage settled deep in my chest, forming a layer of ice around my heart.

Star hadn't gone far. She waited in the clearing. Her red hair blazed against the dark gray background of the forest dusk. Night would soon be on us.

She made a small noise of surprise when I stepped clear of the trees. Peering through the gloom, she studied the blood on my shirt. The wet material clung to my skin. When she saw I was unharmed, her sharp nose jerked her head around, searching for her goon.

"He's dead," I said.

The color drained from her face. "We can work this out." A pleading note entered her voice.

"No, we can't. If I let you walk away, you'll only return with more men. If I take you to the Commander, I'd have to answer for killing your thugs. I'm out of options." I stepped toward her, my body frozen with dread. The others I had killed in self-defense during the heat of battle; this would be difficult—this would be premeditated.

"Yelena, stop!" someone called from behind me. I spun.

One of the Commander's soldiers stood with a sword in his hand. As he moved closer, I judged the distance between us.

He must have recognized my battle stance because he stopped and sheathed his sword. Pulling the wool cap off his head, he let his black curls spring free.

"I thought you had orders to stay at the castle," I said to Valek. "Won't you be court-martialed?"

"And I thought your killing days were over," he replied as he examined the prone form of Star's thug. His crushed windpipe had suffocated him. "Tell you what. If you don't tell, I won't. That way we can both avoid the noose. Deal?"

I jerked my head at Star. "What about her?"

"There's an arrest warrant out for her. Did you even consider taking her to the Commander?"

"No."

"Why not?" Valek didn't try to hide his disbelief. "Killing isn't the only solution to a problem. Or has that been your formula?"

"*My* formula! Excuse me, Mr. Assassin, while I laugh as I remember my history lessons on how to deal with a tyrannical monarch by killing him and his family."

Valek flashed me a dangerous look.

I was on the edge. Changing tactics, I said, "My actions were based on what I thought you would do if you were ambushed."

He considered my words in silence for an uncomfortable length of time.

Star seemed horrified by our discussion. She glanced around as if planning her escape.

"You really don't know me at all," Valek said.

"Think about it, Valek, if I took her to the Commander and explained the details, what would happen to me?"

The sad knowledge in his face said it all. I would be arrested for killing Star's men, the food taster's job would pass on to the next prisoner awaiting execution and I would spend my last few days in a dank dungeon.

"Well, then, it was fortunate for both of you that I arrived," Valek said. He whistled a strange birdcall just as Star made her escape.

She dashed down the trail. I moved to follow, but Valek told me to wait. Two gray forms materialized from the dark forest on either side of the road. They grabbed Star. She yelped in surprise and anger.

"Take her back to the castle," Valek ordered. "I'll deal with her when I get back. Oh, and send a cleanup crew. I don't want anyone stumbling onto this mess."

They began to pull Star away.

"Wait," she said. "I have information. If you release me, I'll tell you who plotted to ruin the Sitian treaty."

"Don't worry." Valek's blue eyes held an icy glare. "You'll tell me." He was about to walk past her, when he paused. "However, if you want to reveal your patron now, then we can skip a painful interrogation later."

Star's nose twitched as she considered his offer. Even in this situation, she was still the shrewd businesswoman.

"Lying would only worsen your predicament," Valek warned.

"Kangom," she said through clenched teeth. "He wore a basic soldier's uniform with MD–8 colors."

"General Dinno," Valek said without surprise.

"Describe Kangom," I ordered, knowing that Kangom was another name for Adviser Mogkan, but unable to tell Valek how I had come by this information.

"Tall. Long black hair in a soldier's braid. An arrogant bastard. I almost kicked him out, but he showed me a pile of gold I couldn't refuse," Star said.

"Anything else?" Valek asked.

Star shook her head. Valek snapped his fingers. As the camouflaged men escorted Star back toward the castle, I said, "Could it be Mogkan?"

"Mogkan?" Valek looked at me as if I had sprouted antennae. "No. Brazell was far too happy about the delegation. Why would he jeopardize the treaty? That doesn't make sense. Dinno on the other hand was furious with the Commander. He probably sent one of his men to hire Star."

I tried to fathom the reason why Mogkan would endanger the treaty negotiations when trade with Sitia was to Brazell's benefit. Unable to deduce a logical answer, I wondered how I could convince Valek that Mogkan had hired Star.

I began to shiver. Blood soaked my uniform shirt and stained my hands. I wiped the blood on my ripped pants. Retracing my steps, I found my cloak, but before I could swing it over my shoulders, Valek said, "You better leave your clothes here. There would be quite a fuss if you showed up for dinner soaked with blood."

I retrieved my pack from behind the tree. Valek turned his back while I changed into a clean uniform. I wondered if he had any more sneaks in the woods as I wrapped my cloak around me.

We set out for the camp.

"By the way, nice work," Valek said as we passed the second dead body. "I saw the fight. I wasn't close enough to help. You held your own. Who gave you the knife?"

"I bought it with Star's money." A stretch of the truth, but I wasn't about to get Janco into trouble.

Valek snorted. "Fitting."

When we arrived, Valek melted into a group of soldiers while I rushed to the Commander's tent to taste his dinner. The entire Star episode had taken only an hour and a half, but my battered body felt as if I'd been gone for days.

As I sat by the campfire that night, my muscles trembled in reaction to the fight. Grief for Rand surprised me as melancholy thoughts filled my mind. The flames of the fire wiggled accusing red fingers at me. What do you think you're doing? they asked. Three men are dead because of you. How are you going to help anyone? Pure conceit, the flames admonished. Go south. Let Valek worry about the Commander and what Brazell's up to, you silly girl. The fire pulsed, making shooing motions at me.

I pulled my gaze away, blinking into the darkness. Was it my imagination or was someone trying to influence me? Summoning the mental image of my protective brick wall cooled some of the doubts, but not all of them.

Rand's disappearance wasn't noticed until the next morning. Thinking he had run away, Major Granten sent out a small search party, while the others continued deeper into Brazell's district.

The rest of the journey was uneventful except for the disturbing fact that the closer we drew to Brazell's manor house, the blanker the look grew on the Commander's face. He had ceased to give orders or to take an interest in the events surrounding him. The intelligent, piercing glint that had made his gaze lethal faded with each step, leaving only a vacant, dull expression in its place.

In contrast to the Commander, I was beginning to feel rather warm. My hands left slick prints on my bow as we neared Brazell's. I scanned the woods for an ambush as dread hovered behind me like a pair of hands waiting to wrap around my neck. The ground felt soft and sucked at my boots so that each step required an extra effort. Big mistake, big mistake, coming to Brazell's, I thought as my mind whirled on the edge of panic. To calm myself I imagined my brick wall, and focused my thoughts on survival.

An hour away from Brazell's, the rich aroma of Criollo hung heavy in the air. As a precaution, I slipped into the forest off the main trail and stashed my backpack in the crook of a tree, hiding my bow nearby. Taking only my picks from the bag, I pulled my hair into a bun, using the thin metal tools to hold it in place.

At the outer buildings of Brazell's manor our pace slowed. A collective sigh of relief rippled through the soldiers. They had safely delivered the Commander. Now they could rest in the barracks until it was time to return home.

I experienced the opposite of the soldiers' ease despite my

mental protection. I found it difficult to breathe as I followed the Commander and his advisers to Brazell's office. I heard the liquid slamming in my heart, and felt light-headed.

When we entered, Brazell rose from behind his desk, a large smile adorning his square face. Mogkan hovered behind Brazell's right shoulder. With my mental shield in place, I remained near the door, hoping to be inconspicuous. As Brazell recited a formal greeting, I surveyed his office. Lavish in its decoration, the room had a heavy, brooding feel. Black walnut wood framed hunting scenes, and crimson and purple velvet draped the windows. Brazell's oversize ebony desk seemed a barrier between his high-backed leather chair and the two overstuffed, velvet seats facing it.

"Gentlemen, you must be tired from your trip," Brazell said to the Commander's advisers as a tall woman entered the office. "My housekeeper will guide you to your rooms."

She motioned for them to follow her. As the advisers exited the room, I tried to slip out with them, but Mogkan grabbed my arm.

"Not yet," he said. "We have special plans for you."

Alarmed, I glanced at the Commander, sitting in one of the chairs. The abundant purple fabric of the cushion exaggerated his pale face and slight build. No expression touched his features; he stared into the distance. A puppet waiting for his master to pull the strings.

"Now what?" Brazell asked Mogkan.

"We put on a show for a few days. Take him to see the factory as planned." Mogkan gestured toward the Commander.

"Keep his advisers happy. Once everyone's hooked, then we don't have to pretend."

"And her?" Satisfaction bent the edges of Brazell's mouth.

I kept the picture of the brick wall in my mind.

"Yelena," Mogkan said, "you've learned a new trick. Red brick, how mundane. But…"

I heard a faint scraping noise like stone grinding on stone.

"Weak spots. Here and here." Mogkan pointed a finger in the air. "And I do believe this brick is loose."

Mortar crumbled. Small holes appeared in my mental wall.

"When I have a moment, I'll smash your defenses into dust," Mogkan promised.

"Why waste your time?" Brazell asked, drawing his sword. "Dead. Now." He advanced with murderous intent blazing in his eyes. I flinched back a step.

"Stop," Mogkan ordered. "We need her to keep Valek in line."

"But we have the Commander," Brazell whined like a child.

"Too obvious. There are seven other Generals to consider. If we kill the Commander while he's here they would be suspicious. You'd never become his successor. Valek knows this, so any threat to the Commander won't work." Mogkan turned his calculating eyes on me. "But who cares about a food taster? No one except Valek. And if she dies here, the Generals will agree that it was justified."

Mogkan leaned over the Commander, whispering in his ear. The Commander opened his briefcase, withdrew a flask and handed it to Mogkan. My antidote.

"Starting now, you'll come to me for your medicine," Mogkan said, smiling.

Before I could react, someone knocked on the door. Two soldiers entered the office without waiting for permission.

"Your escorts are here, Yelena. They'll take good care of you." Mogkan turned to the guards. "She doesn't need a tour. Our infamous Yelena has come home."

29

I SCANNED THE TWO MUSCULAR guards. Swords, short knives and manacles hung from their belts. They were well armed, and wore grim expressions of recognition. I was outmatched. I touched the familiar lump of the switchblade strapped to my thigh, but decided to wait until the odds were more in my favor.

The guards gestured for me to accompany them. I shot a final beseeching look at the Commander, but nothing so far had roused him from his oblivious stupor.

I felt a small surge of hope when the guards led me to a tiny, barren room in the guest wing instead of the underground cells in which Brazell housed his prisoners. Having spent a week in those dank, rat-infested chambers after I killed Reyad, I loathed the thought of ever going back.

After the door was locked behind me, I took comfort from removing the picks from my hair. The lock was a basic pin-

and-tumbler type, which would be easy to open. Before springing it, I slipped a small pick with a mirror on the end under the door. With the mirror, I spied a pair of boots standing on either side. Those overachieving guards had stationed themselves outside my room.

I went to the window. The guest wing was on the second floor. My view included the main courtyard. I could jump to the ground if I was desperate, but for now I would wait.

The next day, I was permitted out of my room only to taste the Commander's meals. After breakfast, Mogkan waved a small vial of antidote in front of my face.

"If you want this, you must answer a question," he said.

I steadied my nerves. With a calm voice, I replied, "You're bluffing. If you wanted me dead, I wouldn't be standing here now."

"I assure you, it's only a temporary condition." Anger burned in his eyes. "I'm merely offering you a choice. Death by Butterfly's Dust is a long, ugly and excruciating experience, while, say, slitting your throat is quick—a moment of pain."

"What's the question?"

"Where's Valek?"

"I don't know," I said truthfully. I hadn't seen Valek since the fight in the woods. Mogkan considered my answer. Taking advantage of his distracted state, I plucked the vial from his hand and drained it in a single gulp.

Mogkan's face reddened with fury. He seized my shoulders then shoved me toward the guards. "Take her back to her room," he ordered.

Once there, I wondered what mischief Valek was creating. I doubted he was sitting idle. Mogkan's questions on Valek's whereabouts confirmed my suspicions. Restless, I paced the small chamber, longing for a workout with Ari and Janco.

During my brief visits with the Commander over the next few days, I began to recognize that my presence was part of Mogkan's show. In order to keep the Commander's advisers from becoming suspicious, Brazell pretended the Commander was still giving orders. At one point, Brazell leaned close to the Commander as if they were having a private conversation, then proclaimed that, per Commander Ambrose's request, a factory tour would be scheduled for the next day.

I was allowed to join the group going to the plant. This surprised me almost as much as the fact that none of the Commander's advisers made a protest or comment about Brazell manufacturing Criollo instead of the livestock feed he had reported on his permit. They munched on bars of Criollo, content to nod and agree with Brazell that the factory was a marvelous invention.

As we walked through the building, sweltering heat pulsed from the gigantic roasters that were continuously fed with Sitian beans. Workers, streaked with sweat and black dust, shoveled coal into the massive fires under the ovens. Once roasted, the beans were conveyored to a large area where other workers cracked their shells with mallets, extracting a dark brown nib. Steel rollers crushed the nibs into a paste. The paste was spooned into a five-foot-wide metal container to which sugar, milk and butter were added. Using steel pitchforks, workers stirred these ingredients until the mixture became a smooth, thick liquid, which was then poured into square and rectangular-shaped molds.

A veritable shop of delightful smells and flavors, the place was, however, a joyless environment. The dour employees, uniforms soiled with Criollo and sweat, grunted and strained under the physical exertion. During the tour, I searched the various work areas for poisonous or addictive ingredients that might be slipped into the mix but found none.

When the group returned to Brazell's manor house, I watched the animated expressions on the advisers' faces leak away, leaving behind the same blank look that had taken over the Commander's face. Which meant that there must be a link between eating Criollo and succumbing to Mogkan's magic. Mogkan's show would end as soon as he had gained control of the advisers' minds, and when that happened my accommodations would change for the worse.

That night, under cover of darkness, I dropped my cloak out the window of my room and banged on the door, calling to the guards.

When the door opened, I declared, "I need a bath." Without waiting for a response, I strode with purpose down the hallway. The guards followed.

At the baths, one guard stopped me in the hallway while his companion looked around inside. Only when he was sure I would be alone did he nod and step back.

As I went through the entrance, I said in an authoritative voice, "I don't need an audience. Wait here, I won't be long."

To my delight they remained outside. I scurried to the far wall where, hidden from view, there was another entrance. The guards might work in the manor house, but I'd grown up here. With a child's curiosity and free time, I had been able to explore almost every corner of the house. Only Brazell's private suite, office and Reyad's wing had been off-limits. Unfortunately once I turned sixteen, Reyad's wing became my daily nightmare. Pushing away the thought, I concentrated on the present.

I pulled the handle of the door and encountered my first unwanted surprise. It was locked. No problem, I thought, reaching for my picks. The mechanism popped with ease, the door swung open, and I discovered a second nasty shock. One of the guards waited in the hallway.

He smirked. I rushed him. Using my momentum, I shoved him off balance and punched him in the groin. A dirty Valek move, but I didn't care as I raced down the corridor, leaving the guard far behind.

Slipping out the south entrance, I retrieved my cloak, and then headed west to find my pack and bow. Bright moonlight illuminated my path, and I could see where I was going; however, my true path was less evident. I knew I couldn't help the Commander from a locked room, but I was unsure what I could do from the outside. I needed to talk to Valek. Deciding it would be too risky to go to the barracks, I took to the treetops. Only Valek knew this trick. Once he learned of my escape, he would track me.

When I reached the open area reserved for the annual fire

festival's visit to MD–5, I stopped for the night. Shivering in my cloak, I huddled against a tree trunk, blowing clouds of steam from my mouth. Once, I heard the baying of dogs and distant shouts, but no one came close to my makeshift bed in the tree. Sleep eluded me; I was too cold and nervous. Instead, I envisioned the bright fabric of the festival tents in the clearing, hoping to warm myself by remembering the hot energy of the festival nights.

I imagined the big tops in their proper places. Dancers, singers and acrobats lined up in the middle of the clearing. Food stands huddled in and around the big tents, scenting the air with mouthwatering treats. I went to the festival every hot season when I had lived under Brazell's roof. It had been the high-light of my existence. Although my memories of those last two years, when I had been Reyad's laboratory rat, were dreadful.

Unable to resist, I climbed down from the tree and walked through my imaginary festival. I stopped where the acrobatics tent had stood, wondering if I could still perform the tumbling routine that had won me first place and the fire amulet. Without thought, I tossed off my cloak and started a warm-up. In the back of my mind, I knew I should be hiding, that it was stupid to be this exposed to discovery, but the desire to relive my one moment of true joy was too strong to deny.

Soon all thoughts of Brazell, Reyad and Mogkan were banished as I spun and soared through the air. My mind settled into the mental zone of pure concentration I used when I fought. I relished the release, brief as it might be, from my days of tension and threat.

As I performed my routine, I discovered that I could push my heightened awareness beyond my body to encompass the trees, even sense the animals in the forest. An owl, perched high on a branch, tracked the movements of a field mouse. A family of possums slipped without sound through the underbrush. A woman, crouched behind a stone, watched me.

Stealing into Irys's mind was as easy as slipping on a pair of gloves. Her thoughts flowed into my mind like silk. I reminded her of her younger sister, Lily, and she longed to be back home with her family, not sneaking around in cold, horrid Ixia. The situation in the north was getting dangerous; she would be safer in Sitia. But for how long? she wondered. As a master-level magician, she couldn't allow the abuse of power that she had felt emanating from this area to continue. Kangom, who called himself Mogkan, was producing Theobroma at alarming quantities. He had also rigged a way to intensify his power.

Irys's thoughts returned to me, and I felt a tug on our mental connection.

Yelena, what are you doing in my mind?

I'm not sure how I got here.

Haven't you figured it out by now? You're focusing your magic when you fight. That's why you instinctively anticipate your opponent's moves. I felt you at the castle when you were fighting your friends. Now that you have learned to harness your power, you have taken the next logical step by expanding it beyond the immediate area.

My surprise broke our link. I stopped, panting in the cold night air as Irys emerged from the woods.

"Does that mean I'm not going to flame out?" I asked.

"You've stabilized, but you won't get any stronger unless you receive the proper training. You don't want to waste your potential. Come south now; your pursuers are miles away."

"The Commander…"

"Is ensorcelled. Nothing you can do; his mind is probably gone. Mogkan has been feeding him Theobroma. I've smelled it since I arrived."

"Theobroma? Do you mean Criollo? The brown-colored sweet that Brazell's manufacturing."

"That sounds right. It opens a mind to magical influence. It relaxes the mental defenses, allowing easy access to someone's mind. We use it as a training tool in controlled situations where a fledgling magician is close to the subject. The Commander has a strong personality, very resistant to magical suggestion. Theobroma breaks down that barrier, which helps when a student is learning, but using it on the Commander to gain control of his mind is the same as rape." Irys pulled her cloak tight around her shoulders. "Even with Theobroma, a magician shouldn't be able to reach the Commander's mind from this distance, but Mogkan has. He has found a way to boost his power."

Irys rubbed her arms with her hands, trying to warm up. "I'm guessing Mogkan's visit to the castle was to lock himself into the Commander's mind so he could lead him out here."

"What can we do to break the lock?" I asked.

"Kill Mogkan. But it'll be difficult. He's very powerful."

"Isn't there another way?" I recalled my conversation in the

woods with Valek about murder as a solution. *My* formula, he
had said, and it still annoyed me. He'd probably never been in
the lose–lose situation I was always finding myself in.

"Block Mogkan's power supply. That might work. He'll still
have his magic, but it won't be enhanced."

"What would his extra power look like? How do we find it?"

"My guess would be that he's either recruited a number of
magicians to pool their power, or he's devised a way to concentrate the power source without warping it." She paused,
considering. "Diamonds."

"Diamonds?" A cold knot of anxiety churned in my
stomach. There was so much I didn't know about magic.

"Yes. Very expensive, but they will gather and store power
like a hot coal holds heat. He might be using diamonds to
enhance his magic. He would need a man–size circle of
diamonds, and that's not easily hidden. If we could find this
circle I might be able to use it to block his power or, at least,
redirect it long enough for you to awaken the Commander."

"What if the source is a group of magicians? How would I
recognize them?"

"Unfortunately, Ixia doesn't have a uniform for magicians,"
Irys said, her voice sharp with sarcasm. "Instead of searching for
them, look for an empty room with a wagon-wheel design
painted on the floor. To link magical power, each magician must
be perfectly aligned along the edge of a circle."

"I can search the manor, but I need help," I said. "I need
Valek."

"You need a miracle," Irys replied with a wry twist to her lips.

"Can you direct Valek here?"

"He's already on his way. You two have forged a strong connection, although I don't know if it's of magical origin." Irys pursed her lips. "I'd better go before Valek arrives. When and if you discover the source of Mogkan's extra power, chant my name in your mind. I'll hear your call because we, too, have created a bond. Our mental link grows stronger each time we communicate. I'll try to help you with the Commander. But no promises. I'm after Mogkan." She disappeared into the forest.

While I waited for Valek, I paced on the packed dirt and tried to think of a way to find Mogkan's power source. Irys's words about needing a miracle were, indeed, an understatement.

To distract myself, I focused on my surroundings. The tread of many feet had rubbed out the grass and trampled the earth until it was worn smooth and shiny. I remembered digging my heels into this same hard dirt the last time I was here, when Reyad dragged me to the manor house to punish me for disobeying him and winning the amulet. I had pressed that prize so tight against my skin it had left a mark. Then I had hidden it to keep it out of Reyad's cruel hands.

Two years had passed since I had buried my amulet. Someone had probably discovered it by now. For an exercise, I tried using my new magical skill. Directing my awareness downward, I circled the clearing. I made many circuits and was growing bored, when suddenly, the soles of my feet felt hot. When I continued they cooled. I moved here and there until, once more, heat stabbed my feet.

Taking my grappling hook from my pack, I dug at the

spot. My efforts revealed some fabric. I tossed my hook aside and clawed at the ground with my fingernails, uncovering my lost amulet.

It was dull and covered with dirt. The ribbon that held it was torn and stained. Pressing the flame-shaped amulet against my chest, I felt warmth emanating from it. I put it down to fill the hole, humming a tune. Cleaning the palm-size medal on my pants, I strung it onto the necklace chain with Valek's butter-fly.

"Not the best hiding place. Wouldn't you agree?" Valek asked.

I jumped. How long had he been standing behind me?

"They're searching for you. Why did you run?" he asked.

I briefed Valek on the Commander, Mogkan, the factory and the advisers, hoping he would draw the same conclusions I had.

"So Mogkan is using Criollo to take control of their minds, but where's he getting the power?" Valek asked.

"I don't know. We need to search the manor."

"You mean, *I* need to?"

"No, *we*. I grew up there. I know every inch." The first place I wanted to look was in Reyad's laboratory wing. "When do we start?"

"Now. We have four hours till dawn. What are we looking for?"

When I explained that we were seeking either a circle of diamonds or a painted wheel, Valek's thin eyebrows puckered as if he wanted to question me about how I had come by this information. He held his peace and headed back toward the barracks.

I hid outside while Valek changed into his black skintight sneak suit. He brought me a dark-colored shirt to wear over my bright red uniform shirt, and carried an unlit bull's-eye lantern. My cloak would be too cumbersome for creeping through the halls, so I hid it in the bushes.

We found a back door near the servants' quarters. Valek lit the lantern. Pushing the slide almost closed, he allowed only a thin ray of light to escape. Inside the manor, I took the lead.

Reyad's suite was in the east wing on the ground floor, opposite the laboratory. The entire wing had been his, and there were a number of doors that he'd kept locked while I had been the resident laboratory rat.

Old horrors haunted me as we searched. My skin felt tight and hot. I recognized the faint acidic aroma of fear that mixed with the dust stirred by our footsteps. It was my smell. I had worn it like a perfume whenever Reyad dragged me to his test.

The thick air pressed down on me, filling my mouth with the taste of ashes and blood. I had bitten my hand without conscious thought. It was an old habit, a way to stifle my cries.

Exploring the laboratory room, the thin lantern's beam spotlighted instruments hanging from the walls and piled on the tables. Each revelation sent a cold numbing pulse through my body, and I shrank away from the large shadows of equipment unrevealed, unwilling to even brush against them. The room resembled a torture chamber rather than a place for experiments.

Feeling like an animal pierced in the metal jaws of a trap, I wanted to scream and bolt from the room. Why had I brought Valek here? Brazell's advisers were housed on the second floor. Mogkan's diamond device, if there was such a thing, was probably hidden near his room, not down here.

Valek hadn't said a word since lighting the lantern. In the hallway outside Reyad's bedroom, a physical force prevented me from entering. My muscles trembled. An icy sweat soaked my uniform. I waited at the door while Valek went in. I could see the dark malevolent shape of Reyad's sadistic "toy" chest lurking in a corner of the room. If I burned that chest to cinders, I wondered, would my nightmares cease?

"Not if I can help it," Reyad's ghost said, materializing beside me in the hallway.

I jerked back, hitting the wall. A yelp escaped my lips before I could shove my hand into my mouth.

"I thought you were gone for good," I whispered.

"Never, Yelena. I will always be with you. My blood has soaked into your soul. You have no chance of cleansing me away."

"I have no soul," I said under my breath.

Reyad laughed. "Your soul is drenched black with the blood of your victims, my dear, that is why you can't see it. When you die, that heavy blood-filled essence will sink to the bottom of the earth where you will burn in eternity for your crimes."

"From the voice of experience," I whispered with a rage that made my voice hiss.

Valek came out of Reyad's room. With a face pale as bone, he stared at me with a horrified expression so long that I wondered if he had been struck dumb. Finally, closing the

door, Valek walked past the ghost without seeing him, then
stopped at the next locked room, pausing a moment with his
head bowed to press a hand to his forehead.

"*There's* someone who really needs to be haunted," Reyad
said, stabbing a ghostly white finger at Valek. "It's a shame he
doesn't let his demons bother him, because I know a certain
dead King that would love to plague him." Reyad looked at
me. "Only the weak invite their demons to live with them.
Isn't that right?"

I refused to answer Reyad as I followed Valek. We continued
our search but it was obvious that, other than the laboratory, the
wing had been abandoned. There were three doors left.

While Valek picked the two locks, Reyad chatted on. "My
father will soon send you to me, Yelena. I'm looking forward
to spending eternity with you." He leered and wiggled his
fingers at me.

But I was no longer interested in the ghost. The contents
of the room before me riveted my attention. Inside, dozens of
women and a few men flinched from the yellow beam of
Valek's lantern. Greasy hair obscured their dirt-streaked faces.
Rags clung to their emaciated bodies. None of them spoke or
cried out. To my increasing horror, I realized they were
chained to the floor. In circles. One outer circle and two inner
rings with lines painted between them.

When Valek and I stepped into the room, the foul stench of
unwashed bodies and excrement wafted through the air.
Gagging, I covered my mouth. Valek moved among them,
asking questions. Who are you? Why are you here? His queries

were met with silence. Their vacant eyes followed his passage. They remained where they were chained, staring.

I began to recognize some of the grubby faces. They had lived in the orphanage with me. They were the older girls and boys who had "graduated" and were supposed to be employed throughout the district. The sight of one girl, her ginger hair dull and matted, finally made me cry out in pain.

Carra's soft brown eyes held no sign of intelligence as I stroked her shoulder and whispered her name. The free-spirited girl I had cared for in the orphanage had become a mindless, empty shell of a woman.

"My students," Reyad said. His chest puffed out in pride as he floated in the middle of the room. "The ones who *didn't* fail."

"What now?" I asked Valek with a shaky voice.

"You're arrested and thrown in the dungeon," Mogkan answered from the entrance.

Valek and I spun in unison. Mogkan loomed in the doorway, his arms folded across his chest. Valek charged him; fury blazed in his eyes. Mogkan stepped back into the hallway. I saw Valek stop just past the doorway and raise his hands in the air. Damn, I thought, racing to help him.

Mogkan stood like a coward behind eight guards. The tips of their swords were aimed mere inches from Valek's chest.

30

AS SWORD POINTS PRICKED my back, I watched Valek, expecting him to spring into action during the whole miserable trip to Brazell's holding cells. I waited for him to blur into motion as they stripped and searched us, enduring the humiliation of being prodded and poked by rough hands as they confiscated my backpack, switchblade and necklace. Losing my clothing didn't upset me as much as losing Valek's butterfly and my amulet.

I prepared for a sudden jailbreak when we were led down into the prison, and was still waiting as we were shoved into adjoining cells.

I held my breath as the heavy metal lock clanged shut on our underground chambers. The soldiers tossed our clothing in through the bars. Then they left, abandoning us to blackness. I fumbled with my uniform, trying to button my shirt in the dark.

Here I was again. A nightmare turned real as we went

through the guardroom, down one flight of steps, and into Brazell's small dungeon, which only contained eight cells, four on each side of a short corridor. Valek and I were in the two cells closest and to the left of the steps. A familiarly loud, rancid stench permeated the prison. The thick, silty air so overpowered my senses that it took me a while to realize we were the only occupants.

Unable to bear the sudden quiet, I asked, "Valek?"

"What?"

"Why didn't you fight the guards? I would have helped you."

"Eight men had drawn swords pointed at my chest. Any sudden movement and I would have been skewered. I'm flattered that you think I could win against those odds. Four armed opponents, maybe, but eight is definitely too many."

I could hear the amusement in Valek's voice.

"Then we pick the locks and make our escape?" My confidence was based on the fact that Valek was a master assassin and trained fighter, a man who wouldn't stay confined for long.

"That would be ideal, provided we had something to pick them with," Valek replied, dashing my hopes.

I searched my cell with my hands. Finding nothing but filthy straw, rat droppings and unrecognizable muck, I sank to the floor with my back against the one stone wall I shared with Valek.

After a long moment, Valek asked, "Was that your fate? If you hadn't killed Reyad, were you slated to be chained to the floor, mindless?"

The image of those captives burned in my mind. My flesh

crawled. For the first time, I was content to have failed Reyad's tests.

As I thought more about them, I remembered a comment Irys had made regarding a magician's ability to steal magic from others. Finally, the significance of the women and men sitting in circles hit me. Mogkan's extra power came from those chained captives. Brazell, Reyad and Mogkan must have screened the children of the orphanage for magical potential. Then, while experimenting on them, Mogkan had wiped their minds clean, leaving them mindless vessels from which to draw more power.

"I think Brazell and Reyad were determined to reduce me to that mental state. But I endured." I explained my theory about the captives to Valek.

"Tell me what happened to you," Valek said, his voice tight.

I paused. Then my tale flowed from my lips, in bits and pieces at first, but the words soon gushed with the same speed as the tears streaking down my face. I didn't spare him any details. I didn't gloss over the unpleasant parts. Telling Valek everything about my two years as a laboratory rat, Reyad's tortures and torments, the cruel games, the humiliations, the beatings, the longing to be good for Reyad, and, finally, the rape that led to murder, I purged myself of the black stain of Reyad. I felt light-headed with the release.

Valek remained silent throughout my disclosure, neither commenting nor questioning. Finally, with ice crystallizing in his voice he said, "Brazell and Mogkan will be destroyed."

Promise or a threat, I couldn't tell, but with all of Valek's force behind it, it was more than idle talk.

As if they had heard their names, Brazell and Mogkan stepped through the main door of the dungeon. Four guards holding lanterns escorted them. They stopped at our cells.

"It's good to see you back where you belong," Brazell said to me. "My desire to feel your blood on my hands has tempted me, but Mogkan has kindly informed me of your fate, should you not receive your antidote." Brazell paused, and smiled with pure satisfaction. "Seeing my son's killer writhing in excruciating pain will be better justice. I'll visit later to hear your screams. And if you beg me, I might put you out of your misery, just so I can breathe in the hot scent of your blood."

Brazell's gaze bored into Valek's cell. "Disobeying a direct order is a capital offense. Commander Ambrose has signed your death warrant. Your hanging is scheduled for noon tomorrow." Brazell cocked his head, appraising Valek like a thoroughbred. "I think I shall have your head stuffed and mounted. You'll make an effective decoration in my office when I become Commander."

Laughing, Brazell and Mogkan left the dungeon. The darkness that flowed in after them felt even heavier than before. It pressed against my chest, giving me a tight, panicky feeling around my ribs. I paced my cell. My emotions swung from sheer terror to overwhelming despondency. I kicked at the bars, threw straw into the air and pounded on the walls.

"Yelena," Valek finally said, "settle down. Get some sleep; you'll need your strength for tonight."

"Oh yeah, everyone needs to be well rested to die," I said,

but regretted my harshness when I remembered that Valek, too, faced death. "I'll try."

I lay on the foul straw, knowing it was futile to try and rest. How could anyone sleep her last hours away?

Apparently, I could.

I woke with a cry. My nightmare about rats melded with reality as I felt a warm, furry mass resting on my legs. Leaping to my feet, I kicked the rodent. It crashed into the wall and skittered away.

"Nice nap?" Valek asked.

"I've had better. My sleeping companion snored."

Valek grunted in amusement.

"How long was I out?"

"It's hard to tell without the sun. I'm guessing it's close to sunset."

I had received my last dose of antidote yesterday morning. That gave me until tomorrow morning to live, but the symptoms of the poison would take hold sometime tonight.

"Valek, I have a confess…" My throat closed. My stomach muscles contracted with such severity that I felt as if someone were trying to rip them from my body.

"What's the matter?"

"Stomach cramp from hell," I said, still gasping even though the pain had subsided. "Is this the start?"

"Yes. They begin slowly, but soon the convulsions will be continuous."

Another wave of agony hit, and I crumpled to the floor. When it passed, I crawled to my straw bed, waiting for the next assault. Unable to endure the anticipation in silence, I said, "Valek, talk to me. Tell me something to distract me."

"Like what?"

"I don't care. Anything."

"Here's something you can take some comfort from—there's no poison called Butterfly's Dust."

"What?" I wanted to scream at him, but a doubling-over, vomit-inducing convulsion hit, causing my abdominal muscles to feel as if they were being shredded with a knife.

When I was sensible again, Valek explained, "You're going to want to die, wish you were already dead, but in the end you'll be quite alive."

"Why tell me now?"

"The mind controls the body. If you believed that you were going to die, then you might have died from that conviction alone."

"Why wait until now to tell me?" I demanded, furious. He could have relieved my anguish.

"A tactical decision."

I bit back a nasty reply. I tried to see his logic; to put myself in his place. My training sessions with Ari and Janco had included strategy and tactics. Janco had compared sparring to a card game. "Keep your best moves close to your chest and only use them when you've nothing left," he had said.

An opportunity to escape might have presented itself during the day. In that case Valek wouldn't have to show his last card and tell me about the poison.

"What about the cramps?" I asked just as another one seized

my body. I rolled into a tight ball hoping to relieve some of the pain, but to no avail.

"Withdrawal symptoms."

"From what?"

"Your so-called antidote," Valek said. "It's an interesting concoction. I use it to make someone sick. As the potion wears off, it produces stomach cramps worthy of a day in bed. It's perfect for putting someone temporarily out of commission without killing him. If you continue to drink it, then the symptoms are forestalled until you stop."

Of all the books I had studied, I didn't recall reading about a tonic like that. "What's the name?"

"White Fright."

The knowledge that I wasn't going to die erased the frightened panic and helped me to endure the pain. I viewed each contraction as a step that must be taken in order for me to be free of the substance.

"What about Butterfly's Dust?" I asked.

"Doesn't exist. I made it up. It sounded good. I needed some threat to keep the food tasters from running away without using guards or locked doors."

An unwelcome thought popped into my head. "Does the Commander know it's a ruse?" If he did, Mogkan would also know.

"No. He believes you've been poisoned."

During the night, it was hard for me to remember that I had not been poisoned. Torturous cramps refused to release me. I crawled around the cell, retching and screaming.

I was vaguely aware, at one point, of Brazell and Mogkan gloating over me. I didn't care that they watched. I didn't care that they laughed. All I cared about was finding a position that would alleviate the pain.

Finally, I fell into an exhausted sleep.

I woke lying on the muck-covered floor of the cell. My right arm stretched through the bars. I marveled more over the fact that I clutched Valek's hand than the fact that I was alive.

"Yelena, are you all right?" The concern in Valek's voice was evident.

"I think so," I replied with a rasp. My throat burned with thirst.

A clank rang out as someone unlocked the prison door.

"Play dead," Valek whispered, releasing my hand. "Try to get them close to my cell," he instructed as two guards came into the dungeon. I yanked my Valek-warmed hand into the cell, and poked my ice-cold left hand out just as the men descended the stairs.

"Damn! The stench down here's worse than the latrine after a brew party," said the guard holding the lantern.

"You think she's dead?" the second guard asked.

With my face to the wall, I closed my eyes and held my breath as the yellow light swept my body.

The guard touched my hand. "Cold as snow-cat piss. Let's drag her out before she starts to rot. You think it smells bad now..." The snap of the lock was followed by a squeak of metal as the cell door opened.

I concentrated on being a dead weight while the guard

dragged me out by my feet. When the light moved away from me, I risked a peek. The guard with the lantern walked ahead to light the way, leaving my upper body in darkness. As we passed Valek's cell, I seized the bars with both hands.

"Ugh. Hold up, she's stuck."

"On what?" the lantern guard asked.

"I don't know. Come back here with that bloody light."

I released my grip, hooking my arm inside the cell.

"Back off," the lantern guard warned Valek.

His meaty hand tugged at my elbow. Then he grunted softly. I opened my eyes in time to see the lantern's light extinguish as it toppled to the ground.

"What the hell?" the other man exclaimed. He was still holding my feet. He backed away from Valek's bars.

I bent my legs, pulling my body close to his boots. He yelped with surprise when I grabbed his ankles. He tripped and fell back.

The sickening crunch of bone striking stone wasn't what I expected. His body went limp. I stood on shaky legs.

Hearing a thud and the jingle of keys, I turned back in time to see Valek lighting the lantern. The other guard was propped against the bars, his head cocked at an unnatural angle.

In the weak glow, I gazed at the prone form at my feet. The soldier's head had struck the edge of the bottom step. A black liquid began to pool around my boots. I had just killed another man. I began to tremble. A fourth man had died because of me. Had the robbing of my soul reduced me to a heartless killer? Did Valek feel any remorse or guilt when he took a life? I watched him through a veil of blood.

Efficient as always, Valek stripped the dead guards of their weapons.

"Wait here," he instructed. Unlocking the main door of the prison, he sprang through the entrance to the guardroom.

Shouts, grunts and the sound of flesh striking flesh reached my ears as I waited on the stairway. No remorse, no guilt, Valek did what he had to for his side to win.

When Valek motioned me to join him, I saw that blood had splattered on his face, chest and arms. Three guards, either unconscious or dead, were strewn about the room.

My backpack sat on a table, its contents scattered about. I stuffed everything back in while Valek tried to open the remaining locked door between freedom and us. Although meager, I wanted my possessions, including my butterfly and amulet, back. Once I wrapped the chain around my neck, I felt strangely optimistic.

"Damn," Valek said.

"What?"

"The Captain has the only key to this door. He will open it when it's time to change the guards."

"Try these." I handed Valek my picks.

He grinned.

While he worked on the lock, I found a pitcher of water and a wash barrel. The fear of being caught couldn't override the desire to rinse off my face and hands. But that was not enough. The need to rid myself of the stench of vomit and blood overpowered me. Soon, I was dumping buckets of water over my head until I was soaked through. I drained half the water pitcher before I thought to offer some to Valek. He stopped to drink, then continued to pick the lock.

Finally, it popped open. Valek peered out into the hallway. "Perfect. No guards." He pulled the door wide. "Let's go."

Taking my hand and a lantern, Valek turned away from our only escape, and led me back down into the prison, pausing to leave the door to the cells wide open as well.

"Are you insane?" I whispered as he dragged me toward the last cell. "Freedom's that way." I pointed.

He ignored me as he unlocked the door. "Trust me. This is the perfect hiding spot. The mess we left will soon be discovered, the open doors proof we've fled." Valek pushed me ahead of him into the cell. "Search parties will be sent out. When all the soldiers have left the manor, we'll make our move. Until then, we lay low."

Valek made a makeshift bed of straw in the far corner of the cell. After extinguishing and hiding the lantern, he yanked me down. I curled on my side with my back to him, shivering in my wet clothes. Valek pulled some straw on top of us and wrapped an arm around me. He drew me close. I stiffened at the contact, but his body heat warmed me, and I soon relaxed into his grip.

At first, every tiny noise made my heart race. But I shouldn't have worried; the commotion that ensued when our escape was discovered was deafening.

Angry and accusing voices shouted. Search parties were organized and dispatched. It was agreed that we had an hour head start, but Brazell and Mogkan argued on which direction we had taken.

"Valek's probably retreating west to well-known territory," Brazell stated with authority.

"South *is* the logical choice," Mogkan insisted. "We have the Commander; there's nothing they can do. They're running for their lives, not toward some strategic position. I'll take a horse and scan the forest with my magic."

Valek harrumphed in my ear, and whispered, "They actually think I would abandon the Commander. They have no concept of loyalty."

When the prison had been quiet and empty for a few hours, I grew bored and anxious to be gone. The door to the cells had remained wide open, allowing a faint light to illuminate our surroundings.

"Can we go now?" I asked.

"Not yet. I believe it's still daylight. We'll wait until dark."

To help pass the time, I asked Valek how he had become involved with the Commander. I thought it an unintrusive question, but he grew so quiet that I regretted asking it.

After a long pause, he spoke. "My family lived in Icefaren Province before it was renamed MD–1. A particularly harsh winter collapsed the building that housed my father's leather business, ruining all of his equipment. He needed to replace his equipment to stay in business, but the soldiers who came to our house to collect the tax money wouldn't listen to reason." Valek's arm tightened around me.

A minute stretched longer before he continued. "I was just a skinny little kid at the time, but I had three older brothers. They were about Ari's size and had his strength. When my father told the soldiers that if he paid the full tax amount he wouldn't have enough money left to feed his family—" Valek paused for several heartbeats "—they killed my brothers. They laughed and said, 'Problem solved. Now you have three less mouths to feed.'" The muscles on Valek's arm trembled with tension.

"Naturally, I wanted revenge, but not on the soldiers. They were only messengers. I wanted the King. The man who had allowed his soldiers to murder my brothers in his name. So I learned how to fight, and I studied the assassin's art until I was unbeatable. I traveled around, using my new skills to earn money. The royal upper class was so corrupt they paid me to kill each other.

"Then I was commissioned to kill a young man named Ambrose, whose speeches called for rebellion and made the royals nervous. He'd become popular, gathering large crowds. People started to resist the King's doctrines. Then Ambrose disappeared, hiding his growing army and employing covert operations against the monarchy.

"My payment to find and kill Ambrose was significant. I ambushed him, expecting to have my knife in his heart before he could draw breath to cry out. But he blocked the blow, and I found myself fighting for my life, and losing.

"Instead of killing me, though, Ambrose carved a C on my chest with my own knife. The same weapon, by the way, that I later used to kill the King. Then Ambrose declared himself my Commander, and announced that I now worked for him and no one else. I agreed, and I promised him that if he got me close enough to kill the King, I would be loyal to him forever.

"My first assignment was to kill the person who had paid me to assassinate Ambrose. Throughout these years, I've watched him achieve his goals with a single-minded determination and without excess violence and pain. He hasn't been corrupted by power or greed. He's consistent and loyal to his people. And there's been no one in this world that I care for more. Until now."

I held my breath. It had been a simple, innocent question. I hadn't expected such an intimate response.

"Yelena, you've driven me crazy. You've caused me considerable trouble and I've contemplated ending your life twice since I've known you." Valek's warm breath in my ear sent a shiver down my spine.

"But you've slipped under my skin, invaded my blood and seized my heart."

"That sounds more like a poison than a person," was all I could say. His confession had both shocked and thrilled me.

"Exactly," Valek replied. "You have poisoned me." He rolled me over to face him. Before I could make another sound, he kissed me.

Long suppressed desire flared to life as I wrapped my arms around his neck, returning his kiss with equal passion.

My response was a delightful surprise. I had feared, after Reyad's abuse, my body would clench tight in horror and revulsion. But the intertwining of our bodies linked our minds and spirits together.

The distant sound of music vibrated in the air. Pulsing, the magical harmony soon rose to a crescendo and encompassed us like a warm blanket. The prison cell and filthy straw dropped away from our awareness. Whiteness draped in snowy silk surrounded us. On this plane we were equals, partners. Our souls bonded. His pleasure was my ecstasy. My blood pumped in his heart.

Utter bliss came in short snatches, although, Valek and I were happy to try again. We had merged, our minds had become one. I drew in his essence, feasting on the feel of his body in mine, exhilarating in the caress of his skin against mine. He filled the hollow emptiness inside my heart with joy and light. Even though we lay in the grubby straw and faced an uncertain future, a deep hum of contentment vibrated throughout my body.

31

REALITY AND THE RANK ODOR of a decomposing animal intruded. Darkness had descended.

"Let's go," Valek said, pulling me to my feet.

"Where?" I asked, adjusting my uniform.

"The Commander's room, so we can take him back to the castle with us." Valek brushed the straw from his hair and clothes.

"Won't work."

"Why not?" Valek demanded.

"As soon as you touch him, Mogkan will know." I explained about Mogkan's link with the Commander and how he had established that connection using Criollo.

"How do we break the bond?" Valek asked.

It was time to tell him about my magic. I felt light-headed, as if I stood on the edge of the world. Taking a deep breath, I related the encounters and conversations I'd had with Irys, and how she might be able to help us.

Valek stood still for a full minute, while my heart thumped madly in my chest.

"Do you trust her?" he asked.

"Yes."

"Is there anything else you haven't told me?"

My head spun. So much had happened and we still needed to stop a powerful magician. Death was a real possibility. I wanted Valek to know how I felt.

"I love you."

Valek wrapped me in his arms. "My love has been yours since the fire festival. If those goons had killed you, I knew then that I would never be the same. I didn't want or expect this. But I couldn't resist you."

I molded my body to him, wanting to share his skin.

He took my hand. "Let's go."

We raided the guardroom for uniforms before slipping into the hallway. Wearing Brazell's colors of black and green, we hoped to avoid discovery as we stole through the manor.

Valek needed his bag of tricks, so we headed toward the barracks. While I retrieved my cloak, Valek slid inside the empty wooden building. The soldiers had gone to search for us.

I paced in the shadows of the building, chanting Irys's name in my mind. We needed a plan of attack. We had to move tonight.

Shouts and curses emanated from the barracks. Running inside, I found Ari and Janco with their swords drawn and pointed at Valek.

"Stop," I said.

Spotting me, Ari and Janco sheathed their weapons, smiling.

"We thought Valek had escaped without you," Ari said, giving me a bear hug.

"Aren't you supposed to be with a search party?" Valek asked as he pulled his black bag from under a bunk. He had changed into an ebony coverall with numerous pockets.

"We're too sick," Janco said, his best smirk in place.

"What?" I asked.

"The charges against you were obviously fabricated, so we refused to take part in the hunt," Janco said.

"That's insubordination." Valek extracted a long knife and some darts from his bag.

"That was the point. What's a fellow have to do around here in order to get arrested and thrown in the dungeon?" Janco asked.

I stared at Janco in amazement. They had been willing to risk a court martial in order to help me. He had meant what he had inscribed on my switchblade.

"Which direction did the search parties go?" Valek asked. He placed weapons in various pockets and strapped his sword and knife onto his belt.

"Mainly south and east, although a few small groups were sent west and north," Ari replied.

"Dogs?"

"Yes."

"And the manor?"

"Minimal coverage."

"Good. You're with us," Valek ordered them both.

They snapped to attention. "Yes, sir."

"Prep for covert ops, but keep the swords. You're going to need them." Valek finished dressing as Ari and Janco got ready.

"Wait," I said. "I don't want them getting into trouble." My heart started to skitter around in my chest and a nauseous wave threatened to send bile up my throat as fear of what we were planning to do overcame me.

Valek squeezed my shoulder. "We need their help."

"You're going to need more than that." Irys's voice came out of the darkness. Three men simultaneously drew their swords. When she stepped into the weak lantern light, Valek relaxed, but Ari and Janco brandished their weapons.

"At ease," Valek ordered.

Seeing their reluctance, I said, "She's a friend. She's here to help." I looked at her. "We discovered Mogkan's extra power source."

"What is it?"

I told her about the mindless captives and how they had been chained in circles, and then explained my theory that Mogkan had wiped their minds to seize their power. Horror and revulsion touched her face. Despite her rough exterior, her concern went deep. She managed to regain her no-nonsense frown, but Ari and Janco looked a little green, as if they were going to be sick.

"What's this all about?" Ari asked.

"I'll explain it later. Right now—" I stopped short. A complete plan of attack snapped into my mind, but it included Ari and Janco. I had been hoping to keep them safe, but Valek was right. We needed their help.

"I want you to protect Irys with everything you have. It's very important," I told my friends.

"Yes, sir," Ari and Janco said together.

Stunned, I stared at them. They had addressed me as *sir*, meaning they would follow my orders, even if it led to their death.

Valek's eyes drilled into mine. "You have a strategy?"

"Yes."

"Tell us."

Why, I thought as Valek and I crept through the silent empty halls of the manor, had I opened my mouth? *My* plan. What did I know? Valek, Ari and Janco had years of experience doing this nerve-racking, stomach-turning work, but everyone risked their necks following *my* plan.

In the dark corridor, I swallowed my fear and reviewed the strategy. At the Commander's door, we waited to give the others time to move into position. My short breaths seemed to echo off the walls, and I felt as if I was either going to scream or pass out.

After a few moments, Valek picked the lock and we slipped inside. He secured the door. Lighting a lantern, he moved toward the oversize four-poster bed. The Commander was stretched out on top of the bedding, fully clothed. His vacant eyes were open, staring at the ceiling. He made no acknowledgment of our presence.

I sat beside him and took his hand in mine. Following Irys's brief instructions, I imagined my brick wall, then expanded it until I had built a dome of brick that encompassed us both.

Valek pressed against the wall next to the door, waiting for Mogkan. His expression had hardened into his battle face. He was stone cold on the exterior, but I knew that a lethal, molten fury resided within.

It wasn't long before a key turned in the lock. Silence. Then the door burst open. Four armed guards rushed in. Valek had one down before the man could react. The ringing of swords filled the room.

Mogkan slinked into the chamber after his men had Valek fully engaged. Avoiding the fighting, he moved toward me. A condescending smile touched his lips.

"A brick igloo. How nice. Come on, Yelena, give me some credit. A stone fortress or a steel wall would have been more of a challenge."

I felt a solid blow strike my mental defenses. Brick crumbled. Patching holes as he hammered on my shield, I prayed with desperation that Ari, Janco and Irys had made it to the room where Mogkan kept the prisoners chained. Irys had explained that she needed to be there with them in order to block Mogkan's extra power. Even if she succeeded, I would still have to deal with Mogkan's own magic.

Halting his attack for a second, Mogkan jerked his head to the side, staring off into the distance. "Nice trick," he said. "Friends of yours? They're in Reyad's hallway, but unless they can fight their way through ten men, they won't make it to my children."

My heart sank. Mogkan resumed his onslaught with renewed determination. One guard out of four remained in battle with Valek. Hurry, I thought. My defenses weakened with each blow. I threw every ounce of strength into my wall, but it collapsed into a cloud of dust.

Mogkan's power gripped me like a giant's fist around my rib cage. I yelped in pain and dropped the Commander's hand. I stood on weak legs beside the bed just as Valek yanked his sword from the last guard's dead body.

"Stop or she dies," Mogkan ordered.

Valek froze. Three more guards hustled into the room, Brazell on their heels. They surrounded Valek. Taking his sword, they forced him to his knees with his hands on his head.

"Go ahead, General. Kill her," Mogkan said, stepping back to let Brazell pass. "I should have let you slit her throat the first day she arrived."

"Why listen to Mogkan?" I asked Brazell. "He's not to be trusted." Pain crawled along my spine as Mogkan turned his burning eyes upon me.

"What do you mean?" Brazell demanded. He gripped his sword as he glanced from me to Mogkan.

Mogkan laughed. "She's only trying to delay the inevitable."

"Like when you tried to delay the Sitian treaty negotiations by poisoning the cognac? Or were you aiming to stop the delegation altogether?" I asked him.

Mogkan's shock revealed his guilt. Although surprise touched Valek's face, he remained silent. His body tensed, ready to spring into action.

"That doesn't make sense," Brazell said.

"Mogkan wants to avoid contact with the southerners. They

would know about—" My throat closed. I clawed at my neck, unable to breathe.

Brazell turned on Mogkan. His square face creased with anger. "What have you been up to?"

"We don't need a treaty with Sitia. We were getting our supplies without any problems. But you wouldn't listen to me. You had to be greedy. After establishing a trade treaty it would only be a matter of time before we'd have southerners crossing the border, sniffing around, finding us." Mogkan showed no fear of Brazell, only anger that he had to explain his actions. "Now, do you want to kill her or should I?"

Spots spun in my eyes as my vision blurred. Before Brazell could answer, Mogkan staggered. His hold on me slipped slightly, releasing my airway. I gasped for air.

"My children!" Mogkan roared. "Even without them, I still have more power than you!"

Like a fish on a hook, I was yanked off my feet and hurled against the wall. My head banged on the stone. Pinned in midair, Mogkan's power pelted me. Each blow felt like a boulder crashing into me. This is it, I thought. Reyad was right; becoming the food taster had just delayed the inevitable.

Out of the corner of my eye, I saw Valek fighting his guards as he tried to reach Mogkan. Too late for me. With a final surge of strength, I mentally reached out. I hit an impenetrable barrier as I felt my consciousness drain. Blackness filled my world.

Then Irys's voice was there in my mind, soothing. "Here," she said, "let me help you." Pure power flowed into me. I reconstructed my mental shield and deflected Mogkan's on-slaught, pushing him back. He crashed into the opposite wall with a satisfying thud.

Confusion reigned in the Commander's chambers. Inex-perienced with magic as I was, I couldn't restrain Mogkan. He bolted from the room. With a knife in his hand, Valek fought three guards with swords. As I rushed to help Valek, Brazell grabbed my arm and spun me around to face him.

He raised his sword. Murder blazed in his eyes. I jumped back to avoid the first swing of his sword and bumped against the Commander's bed. I leaped onto the bed to avoid Brazell's next swing. I glanced down. The Commander's gaze was still fixed on the ceiling. Brazell's third swing severed one of the bedposts.

As I dived from the end of the bed to avoid another blow, I seized the post from the floor.

Now I was armed. The post wasn't balanced properly for a bow, but it was thick. Better than nothing.

Brazell was a powerful opponent. Each swing of his sword hacked chunks out of my weapon.

At first, he scoffed at my attempts to fight him. "What do you think you're doing? You're a skinny nothing. I'll gut you in two moves."

When I found my mental zone of power, he stopped wasting his breath. Even sensing his next attack, I still scram-bled to stay one step ahead of him. My wooden post was no match for his sword.

Reyad's ghost materialized in the room. He cheered his

father on, trying to distract me. His tactics worked. My back hit the wall. Brazell's sword split my post in half.

"You're dead." With gleeful satisfaction, Brazell pulled his sword back to slash at my neck. But I still held a part of the wood. As his sword swung close, I deflected the weapon downward with my broken post. The tip cut across my waist. The sound of ripping fabric accompanied a line of fire across my stomach. Blood soaked the ripped ends of my uniform shirt.

Then Brazell made his first error. Thinking I was finished, he relaxed his guard. But I was still on my feet. I raised my weapon. With desperate strength, I struck him across the temple. We crumpled to the floor together.

I gazed at the ceiling, trying to regain my breath. Valek hovered over me. I shooed him away. "Find Mogkan." He disappeared from my view.

Once strength returned to my limbs, I examined my wound. Running a finger along the gash, I thought all I needed was some of Rand's glue.

Reyad's ghost floated over me, sneering. I couldn't bear lying on the ground with him in the room. Cursing and bleeding, I stood.

"You." I stabbed a bloody finger at him. "Go away."

"Make me," he challenged.

How could I fight a ghost? I moved into a defensive stance. He scoffed. No, not a physical fight, a mental one.

I thought about what I had accomplished in the year and a half since I had slit Reyad's throat. Overcoming my fears to make friends. Confronting my enemies. Finding love. How I felt about myself. Who I was. I looked into the gilded floor-length mirror of the Commander's room. My hair was wild. My shirt soaked with blood. My face streaked with dirt. Almost the same reflection when I first became the food taster. But this time there was something different. The shadows of doubt were gone.

I peered deeper and found my soul. A little tattered and with some holes, but there all the same. It had always been there, I realized with a shock. If Reyad and Mogkan had truly driven it from me, I would be chained to a floor right now and not standing over Brazell's unconscious form.

I was in control. This new person in the mirror was free. Free of all poisons. I glanced at Brazell. He was still breathing, but I was in charge of him and of myself. In command. No longer a victim. No longer the rat caught in the metal jaws of a trap.

"Be gone," I ordered Reyad's ghost. His shocked expression gave me great joy as he vanished.

But joy was like a butterfly alighting on a hand; a brief rest before flying away.

"Janco's hurt." Irys's alarmed voice resounded in my skull. "We need a medic. Come now."

Using manacles from a dead guard's belt, I handcuffed Brazell to the heavy bed. Then I bolted from the room. I raced through the corridors. He can't die, I thought. Not Janco. I wouldn't be able to bear his death. Horrible scenarios played in my mind. I was so preoccupied that I rushed right toward Valek and Mogkan without even recognizing them.

They dueled with swords. The reason the scene had taken a while to clarify in my mind was because Mogkan had the upper hand. Valek's pale face was haggard. He swung his sword as if it was a dead weight. His natural grace had fled, and what remained were sporadic, jerky movements. Mogkan, on the other hand, was quick and competent, technically accurate, but lacking style.

My disbelief and concern grew as I watched the match. What was wrong with Valek? Was it Mogkan's magic? No, Valek was immune to it, I thought. Then realization dawned. Valek had said being close to a magician felt like wading in thick syrup. And Valek had fought seven guards in the Commander's room after spending the last two days in the dungeon without food or sleep. Exhaustion had finally caught up to him.

Mogkan's grin widened when he spotted me hovering nearby. He executed a lightning-quick feint, and then lunged. Valek's sword clattered to the floor as a crimson slash snaked up his arm.

"What an incredible day!" Mogkan exclaimed. "I get to kill the famous Valek and the infamous Yelena at the same time."

I triggered my switchblade. Mogkan laughed. He sent me a magical command to drop my weapon.

Just as my hand released the blade, I heard Irys's voice in my head. "Yelena, what's wrong? Did you find the medic?"

"I need help!" I cried in my mind. Power swelled inside me, pushing to break free. I aimed a finger of power toward Mogkan. His sword dropped from his hand. Terror gripped his face as the magic swaddled him like a baby, then tightened like a noose. He was paralyzed, rooted to the floor.

"You rat-spawned daughter of a demon!" Mogkan cursed. "You're a blight on this earth. An incarnation of hell. You're just like the rest of them. The Zaltana bloodline should be burned out, erased, exterminated…"

Mogkan raged on, but I ceased to listen. Valek picked up my switchblade. Mogkan's curses grew louder and more frantic as Valek approached him. A blur of movement, a shriek of pain, then Mogkan was finally silent. His body sank into a heap on the ground.

Valek handed me the bloody knife. With an exhausted bow, he said, "My love, for you."

32

I GASPED, REMEMBERING. "Janco!"
Grabbing Valek's arm, I dragged him with me, explaining
between huffs of breath. Still wearing Brazell's colors, although
torn and bloodstained, we roused the medic, who, with peevish
annoyance, fussed about protocol and proper authority until
Valek drew his knife.

My stomach heaved when we entered Reyad's wing. The
hallway leading to the captives' room was gruesome. Soldiers
littered the floor, pieces of arms and legs were scattered about
as if someone had hacked their way through them. The walls
were splattered with blood and pools of scarlet dotted the
floor.

The medic wanted to stop at the first man, but Valek yanked
him to his feet. Stepping carefully around the bodies, we
reached the doorway. Just inside, I saw Janco lying on his side
with his head in Ari's lap. He was unconscious, which was a

good thing since a sword had skewered his stomach, the bloody tip poking from his back. Ari's gore-splashed face held a grim expression. A crimson-coated ax, the weapon responsible for the carnage in the hallway, rested next to him. Irys sat cross-legged in the center of the circle of emaciated people. Her brow glistened with sweat. Her expression was distant. The chained women and men viewed the scene with dispassionate eyes.

The trip to the infirmary was a chaotic nightmare. Everything blurred together like a whirlwind until I found myself lying in a bed next to Janco, holding his hand. The medic did his best, but if the sword had pierced any vital organs or if there was internal bleeding, Janco wouldn't survive. Twice during the night Ari and I despaired that we would lose him.

My own wound had been cleaned and sealed with Rand's glue, but I hardly noticed or cared about the throbbing pain. I aimed all my energy and strength toward Janco, willing him to live.

Late the next day, I woke from a light doze.

"Sleeping on the job?" Janco whispered with a weak smile on his ashen face.

I breathed a sigh of relief. Surely if he was strong enough to insult me, then he was on his way to recovery.

Unfortunately, Irys couldn't say the same about the Commander. Four days after Mogkan's death, he still hadn't regained his spirit. His advisers had rebounded from their brief ensor-cellment, and they had commandeered Brazell's manor while

waiting for the Commander to return. They assumed temporary control of the Military District. Messengers were sent
north to General Tesso of MD–4 and west to General Hazal
of MD–6, requesting their immediate presence. The Generals
would have the authority to determine what the next step
would be in case the Commander failed to revive.

Just as confusing was the fact that none of Brazell, Mogkan
and Reyad's victims woke to Irys's probing. She had tried to
enter their minds, to break through to where their self-aware-
ness was hiding. Irys reported that their minds were like abandoned houses, fully furnished, with embers still smoking in the
fireplace, but no one home.

Irys and I resigned ourselves to the knowledge that the
victims would live out their days unaware of their new comfortable surroundings in Brazell's guest wing. I mourned over
the loss of my friend Carra. Irys had sought out the rooms used
by the orphans, and reported that May was still there, alive and
well. I planned to visit with May as soon as Janco regained some
of his strength.

"It's obvious that the children in Brazell's orphanage were
kidnapped from Sitia," Irys explained, visiting me in the infirmary at Janco's bedside.

"Mogkan's ring of child thieves spaced their abductions far
enough apart to avoid detection. Magic is usually stronger in
women, and that explains why there are more girls. The kid-
nappers targeted bloodlines where magic was present, although
they took a gamble with children that young. There's no way
to be sure the power will develop. Mogkan and Brazell must

have planned this for a long time." Irys raked her fingers through her long brown hair. "Finding your family shouldn't be too difficult."

I blinked at her in shock. "You're joking. Right?"

"Why would I joke?" She was unaware of the emotional tailspin she'd caused me.

She was right, joking wasn't her style, so I thought for a moment. "Before he died, Mogkan said something about the Zaltana bloodline."

"Zaltana!" Wiping away her usual serious expression, Irys laughed. It was like the sun coming out after weeks of rain. "I think they did lose a girl. My goodness, you're in for a real surprise if you're part of the Zaltana clan. That would explain why you alone didn't cave in under Mogkan's spell."

Questions hovered on my lips. I wanted to know more about this family, but I didn't want to get my hopes up. There was the possibility that I wasn't a Zaltana. I guess I would find out when I reached Sitia. Irys wanted to start my magical training right away.

Uneasiness hovered in my chest whenever I thought of leaving Ixia. I changed the subject. "How's the Commander?"

Irys confessed her frustration. "He's different from the children. There's nothing in their minds, but he's retreated to a white place. If I can only find where he is, then I might be able to bring him back."

I considered this for a while, and thought back to a time in the war room when I had fallen asleep. "May I try?"

"Why not?"

I made sure Janco was comfortable and had everything he

desired. Irys accompanied me to the Commander's room. The bodies had been removed and someone had attempted to clean up. I perched on the edge of the Commander's bed and took his cold hand in mine. Following Irys's instructions, I closed my eyes, sending my mental awareness toward him.

My feet crunched on ice. A cold wind stabbed my face and filled my lungs with tiny daggers. Dazzling white surrounded me. Diamond dust or snowflakes, it was hard to tell. I walked for a while and was immediately confused by the sparkling blizzard. Stumbling through the storm, I fought to remain calm and to remind myself that I was not lost. Whenever I took a step forward, the icy wind drove me back.

I was about to admit defeat, when I remembered why I had thought I could find the Commander. Focusing on the scene of a young woman exalting over a slain snow cat caused the wind to stop and the blizzard to clear. I stood next to Ambrose.

She was dressed in heavy white hunting furs that resembled the skin of the cat.

"Come back," I said.

"I can't," she said, pointing into the distance.

Thin black bars surrounded us on all sides. A birdcage was my first impression, but upon closer scrutiny I could see that the bars were soldiers armed with swords.

"Every time I tried to leave, they pushed me back." Fury flamed in her face before dying into weary.

"But you're the Commander."

"Not here. Here I am just Ambrosia trapped inside my mistake of a body. The soldiers know about my curse."

I searched my mind for a reply. The guards didn't belong to Mogkan, they belonged to her. My eyes were drawn to the snow cat's carcass. "How did you kill the cat?"

Her face came alive as she recounted how she had bathed in snow-cat scent and spent weeks cloaked in snow-cat furs, pretending to be one of the animals until they allowed her to be part of their pack. In the end it was only a matter of time and the perfect opportunity to make the kill.

"Proof that I was really a man. That I had won the right to be a man."

"Then perhaps you need to wear your prize," I suggested. "Skins will not help you against that lot." I jerked my head at the ring of guards.

Comprehension widened the woman's golden eyes. She gazed at the slain cat, then morphed into the Commander. Her shoulder-length hair shortened into his buzz cut, fine lines of age growing on her face as he emerged. The white furs dropped to the ground as his wrinkle-free uniform material-ized. He stepped away from the skins, kicking them dismis-sively.

"You shouldn't do that," I said. "She's a part of you. You might need her again."

"And do I need you, Yelena? Can I trust you to keep my mutation a secret?" the Commander asked with a fierce in-tensity.

"I came here to bring you back. Isn't that answer enough?"

"Valek swore me a blood oath of loyalty when I carved my initial on his chest. Would you do the same?"

"Does Valek know about Ambrosia?" I asked.

"No. You haven't answered my question."

I showed the Commander Valek's butterfly. "I wear this against my chest. I've pledged my loyalty to Valek, who is faithful to you."

The Commander reached for the butterfly. I stood still as he removed it from my necklace. He took a knife from the skins and sliced it across his right palm. Holding the pendant in his bloody hand, he extended the knife toward me. I held out my right hand, wincing as the knife bit into it. Our blood mixed as I shook his hand with the butterfly wedged between our palms. When he released his grip, Valek's gift was in my hand. I returned it to its proper place over my heart.

"How do we get back?" he asked.

"You're the Commander."

His eyes rested on the dead cat. Looking around at the ring of soldiers, he drew his sword. "We fight," he said.

I pulled the spear from the cat's side, and wiped the blood on the snow. Feeling the weight of the weapon in my grip, I swung it around in a few practice moves. It was lighter than a bow, and a bit off balance by the metal tip. But it would work.

We charged the men. The circle of guards tightened immediately around us. Back to back, the Commander and I fought.

The men were skilled, but the Commander was a master swordsman. He had bested Valek and killed a snow cat. It was like fighting with five more defenders by my side.

When I sunk the spear's tip into one guard's heart, he exploded into a shower of snow crystals that floated away with the wind.

Time slowed as I hacked at one man after another, until

finally time snapped to the present. I whirled around searching for an opponent only to discover that we had dispatched all the men. Snow swirled around us.

"Nice work," the Commander said. "You helped me rediscover my true self, killing off my demons." He took my hand and pressed it to his lips.

The wintry scene melted, and I found myself back on the bed, looking into the Commander's powerful eyes.

That night, Valek and I briefed the Commander on all that had happened since the Generals' brandy meeting. Valek had Brazell interrogated, and discovered that Brazell and Mogkan had been planning a coup for the past ten years.

"Brazell told me that Mogkan showed up at his manor with a group of children," Valek said. "He was looking for a place to hide and he struck a deal with Brazell to help Brazell become the next Commander. Once Mogkan achieved enough power to reach your mind from MD–5, they started feeding you Criollo, Sir."

"What about the factory?" the Commander asked.

"We have halted production," Valek said.

"Good. Salvage what equipment you can, then burn the factory and any Criollo to the ground."

"Yes, Sir."

"Anything else?"

"One more interesting item. Brazell said that once he and Mogkan had control of Ixia, they planned to take over Sitia."

The next day the Commander held court with Valek standing at his right side. Brazell was brought before him to face charges. As expected, Brazell was stripped of his rank and sentenced to spend the rest of his life in the Commander's dungeon.

Permitted a few last words, Brazell shouted, "You fools. Your Commander's a deceiver. You've been lied to for years! The Commander's really a woman dressed as a man!"

Silence blanketed the room, but the Commander's neutral expression never faltered. Soon laughter echoed off the stone walls. Brazell was hauled away amid cheers and jeers. Who would believe the ravings of a madman? Obviously, no one.

I thought about their jeers. They laughed not because the idea of a woman in power was so ridiculous, but because Commander Ambrose had a powerful presence. His frank and abrupt dealings were so honest and forthright that the thought of him deceiving anyone was laughable. And due to his beliefs and convictions about himself, even though I knew the truth, I could not think of him in any other way.

Later in the day, I went to visit the orphanage. I found May in the dormitory. This time, happy memories followed me as I walked through the rooms used by the orphans. When she saw me, May bounced off the bed and wrapped herself around me.

"Yelena, I thought I would never see you again," she gushed.

I squeezed her tight. When she pulled back, I smiled to see her crooked skirt and messy ponytail. As I braided her hair, May chattered about what had happened since I had left. Her excitement faded when she talked about Carra. And it was then that I could see how much she had grown.

When I finished her hair, she said, "We're going with you

to Sitia!" May spun in a circle, unable to remain still. She waved toward a suitcase on the floor.

"What?"

"That lady from the south told us that she would take us home. To find our families!"

A brief pang clenched my heart. Family had a different meaning to me. Valek, Ari and Janco felt like my family, and even Maren seemed like a grumpy older sister.

"That's wonderful," I said to May, trying to match her enthusiasm.

May stopped her dance for a moment. "There are so few of us left," she said in a sedate voice.

"Valek will make sure Carra and the others are taken good care of."

"Valek! He's *so* handsome." May laughed, and was so delightful I couldn't resist hugging her again.

Janco, on the other hand, greeted me with a gloomy face when I stopped to say goodbye. Irys, anxious to head south, wanted to be on the road in the morning.

Ari had taken over my role of nurse, and was sitting next to Janco.

"Whatever happened to 'Sieges weathered, fight together, friends forever'?" I asked him, quoting his message on my switchblade.

Janco's eyes lit up. "You little fox. Figured it out already, have you?"

I smirked.

"As soon as Janco's better, we're coming south," Ari said.

"And what would you do there?" I asked.

"Work on our tans," Janco said, smiling. "I could use a vacation."

"Protect you," Ari said.

"I don't need protection in the south," I said. "And I seem to remember that not long ago, I bested two of my instructors."

"She's cocky already." Janco sighed. "We can't go with her now, she'll be swaggering and boasting and generally obnoxious. It's bad enough I have to deal with that from Ari, I could never handle two."

"Besides," I said, "you'll be bored."

Ari grumped and crossed his massive arms, looking sour. "First sign of trouble, you send us a message and we'll be there. You got that?" Ari asked.

"Yes, sir," I said. "Don't worry about me, Ari. I'll be fine. And, I'll be back."

"You'd better," Janco said. "I want a rematch."

But I had spoken too soon about returning. Valek, Irys and I had discussed my future, but the Commander seemed to have other plans. Commander Ambrose called for a formal meeting that evening. With just Valek, Ari and Irys in attendance in Brazell's old office, the Commander agreed to honor the trade treaty, even though it had been enacted under Mogkan's influence. Then he told me my fate.

"Yelena," he began in a formal tone, "you have saved my life and, for that, I thank you. But you have magical abilities that are not tolerated in Ixia. I have no choice but to sign an order for your execution."

Valek placed a warning hand on Ari's shoulder to prevent him from charging the Commander. Ari stayed still, but his outrage was evident in his face. When the Commander held a paper out to Valek, coldness crept along my skin, leaving behind a numb feeling of dread.

Valek didn't move. "Sir, I've always believed that having a magician work for us would be beneficial and could have prevented this particular situation," Valek said. "We can trust her."

"A valid point." The Commander drew back his arm, resting it on the desk. "Even though we trust her, even though she saved my life, I must follow the Code of Behavior. To do otherwise would be a sign of weakness, something I can't afford right now, especially after this business with Mogkan. Plus, the Generals and my advisers will not trust her."

Once again the Commander extended the execution order to Valek. In my frantic mind I heard Irys telling me to flee. She would attempt to slow Valek down. No, I told her. I would see this to the end. I would not run away.

"I won't take it," Valek said in a flat voice. He betrayed no emotion.

"You would disobey a direct order?" the Commander asked.

"No. If I don't take the order, then I won't have to disobey it."

"And if I make it a verbal order?"

"I will obey. But it will be my very last task for you." Valek pulled a knife off his belt.

The ring of steel sounded as Ari unsheathed his sword. "You'll have to get through me first," he said, stepping in front of me. Ari had a better than average chance of beating Valek, but I knew he wouldn't win. And I didn't want him to try.

"No, Ari," I said. I pushed his sword arm down, and stood next to Valek. Our eyes met. I understood that Valek's loyalty to the Commander was without question. His blue eyes held a fierce determination and I knew in my soul that Valek would take his own life after he had taken mine.

The Commander gazed at us with a quiet consideration. I felt time freeze under his scrutiny.

"I've signed the order, per the Code," the Commander finally said. "I will assign someone else to carry it out. It may take a few days for me to find a suitable person." He looked at me and Irys. A hint that we needed to get on the road as soon as possible. "This order is valid in Ixia only. You're all dismissed."

The office emptied in a hurry. I was giddy with relief as Ari swept me into one of his bear hugs and whooped with joy. But then my heart seized with pain as I realized that I would be parted from Valek so soon after we had joined. After Irys and Ari left to organize the "escape," Valek pulled me aside. We kissed with passion and a desperate urgency.

After we drew apart to catch our breaths, I said, "Come with me." It wasn't a plea or a question. It was an invitation.

Valek's blue eyes closed with pain. "I can't."

I turned away, feeling like one of Valek's black statues, but he drew me back.

"Yelena, you need to learn, you need to find your family, you need to spread your wings and see how far you can fly. You don't need me right now, but the Commander needs me."

I clung to Valek. He was right, I didn't need him, but I wanted him to be with me forever.

We left that night. Irys led our ragtag group. Eight girls and two boys from Brazell's orphanage followed Irys through the forest toward the southern border. I took the rearguard position to make sure everyone stayed together, and to make sure no one tailed our group.

We hiked for a few hours until we found a suitable clearing to camp for the night. More than adequate provisions for our journey had been provided by Ari. I smiled, remembering his lecture to me about staying out of trouble. Just like an overprotective brother, he wasn't content until I promised to send him a message if I needed help. I would miss him and Janco dearly.

We set up six small tents in a circle. Irys amazed the children as she set fire to the kindling with a magical flourish. After everyone had gone to sleep, I sat by the fire, stirring the dying embers. Unwilling to join May in our tent, I gazed at the single flame that erupted when I poked at the fire. It danced by itself for an audience of one. I wondered for the hundredth time why Valek hadn't come to say goodbye, fingering my pendant.

I sensed movement. Jumping up, I drew my bow. A shadow detached from a tree. Irys had created a magical barrier around our tents. According to her, the barrier would deflect a person's vision, so all he would see was an empty clearing. The shadow stopped at the edge, unaffected by the magic, and smiled at me. Valek.

He held out a hand. I grasped his cold fingers with both

hands as he led me away from the tents and deeper into the forest.

"Why didn't you come before we left?" I asked him when we stopped at the base of a tree. The roots of the massive oak had broken through the ground, creating small protective hollows.

"I was busy making sure the Commander would have a hard time locating someone to carry out his orders." Valek grinned with vicious delight. "It's amazing how much work there is cleaning up after Brazell."

I thought about what that cleanup would entail. "Who is tasting the Commander's food?" I asked.

"For now, I am. But I believe Captain Star would make an excellent candidate. Since she knows who all the assassins are, I think her help will be invaluable."

It was my turn to smile. Star would do well if she passed the training. If.

"Enough talk," Valek said, guiding me down between the roots. "I need to give you a proper send-off."

My last night in Ixia was spent with Valek beneath the tree. The hours till dawn flew by. The rising sun intruded, waking me from a contented doze in Valek's arms, forcing me to face the day that I had to leave him.

Sensing my mood, Valek said, "An execution order hasn't kept us apart before. There are ways to get around it. We *will* be together."

"Is that an order?"

"No, a promise."

★ ★ ★ ★ ★

READ ON FOR AN EXTRACT FROM THE LATEST CHRONICLES OF IXIA NOVEL

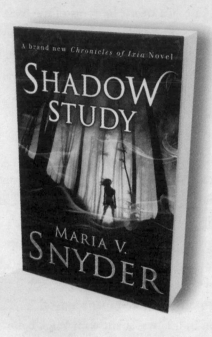

'A compelling new fantasy series'
—Rhianna Pratchett, *SFX* on *Poison Study*

1

YELENA

Ugh, mud, Kiki said as she splashed through another puddle. The wet muck clung to her copper coat and dripped from her long tail. It packed into her hooves and coated the hair of her fetlocks with each step.

Through our mental connection I sensed her tired discomfort. *Stop?* I asked. *Rest?*

No. Images of fresh hay, a clean stall and being groomed formed in Kiki's mind. *Home, soon.*

Surprised, I glanced around the forest. Melting piles of snow mixed with black clumps of dead leaves—signs that the cold season was losing its grip. Rain tapped steadily on the bare branches. The light faded, turning the already gray woods leaden. For the past few hours, I'd been huddling under my sopping-wet cloak, trying to keep warm. With my thoughts fixed on my rendezvous with Valek, I'd failed to keep track of our location.

I scanned the area with my magic, projecting my awareness out to seek life. A few brave rabbits foraged in the soggy underbrush and a couple of deer stood frozen, listening to the squishy plodding of Kiki's passage. No souls haunted these woods. No humans within miles.

That wasn't a surprise. This remote area in the northeastern Featherstone lands had been chosen for that very reason. After Owen Moon ambushed us about four years ago, Valek and I had decided to move to a less well-known location near the Ixian border.

I leaned forward in the saddle. We were getting close and my wet cloak no longer pressed so hard on my shoulders. At this pace, we'd reach our cozy cottage within the hour. Valek's involvement with our friend Opal's rescue from the Bloodrose Clan and the aftermath had kept him busy for months. Finally we would have a few precious days all to ourselves before he reported back to the Commander. He should already be there waiting for me. Visions of sharing a hot bath, snuggling by a roaring fire and relaxing on the couch once again distracted me.

Kiki snorted in amusement and broke into a gallop. Behind the clouds the sun set, robbing the forest of all color. I trusted Kiki to find the path in the semidarkness as I kept a light magical connection to the wildlife nearby.

In midstride, Kiki jigged to the right. Movement flashed to the left along with the unmistakable twang of a bow. Kiki twisted under me. I grabbed for her mane, but a force slammed into my chest and knocked me from the saddle.

Hitting the ground hard, I felt all the air in my lungs whoosh out as pain erupted. Fire burned with each of my desperate gasps. Without thought, I projected again, searching for the… person who had attacked me. Despite the agony, I pushed as far as I could. No one.

Kiki, smells? I asked. She stood over me, protecting me.

Pine. Wet. Mud.

See magician?

No.

Not good. The person had to be protected by a magical

null shield. It was the only way to hide from me. Null shields blocked magic. At least it also prevented the magician from attacking me with his or her magic since it blocked magic from both sides of the shield. But it wouldn't stop another arrow. And perhaps the next one wouldn't miss.

I glanced at the shaft. The arrow had struck two inches above and one inch to the left of my heart, lodging just below my clavicle. Fear banished the pain for a moment. I needed to move. Now.

Rolling on my side, I paused as an icy sensation spread across my chest. The tip had been poisoned! I plopped back in the mud. Closing my eyes, I concentrated on expelling the cold liquid. It flowed from the wound, mixing with the blood already soaked into my shirt.

Instead of disappearing, the poison remained as if being refilled as fast as I ejected it. With pain clouding my thoughts, the reason eluded me.

Kiki, however, figured it out. She clamped her teeth on the arrow's shaft. I had a second to realize what she planned before she yanked the arrow from my chest.

I cried as intense pain exploded, blood gushed and metal scraped bone all at once. Stunned, I lay on the ground as black and white spots swirled in my vision. On the verge of losing consciousness, I focused on the hollow barbed tip of the arrow coated with my blood, reminding me of the danger. I remained a target. And I wasn't about to make it easy for my attacker to get another shot.

Fix hole, Kiki said.

I debated. If I healed myself now, then I'd be too weak to defend myself. Not like I was in fighting condition. Although I still had access to my magic, it was useless against arrows and, as long as the assassin hid behind the null shield, I couldn't touch him or her with my magic, either.

Kiki raised her head. Her ears cocked. *We go. Find Ghost.*

I groaned. How could I forget that Valek was nearby? *Smart girl.*

With the arrow still clutched in her teeth, Kiki knelt next to me. Grabbing her mane, I pulled myself into the saddle. Pain shot up my arms and vibrated through my rib cage when she stood. She turned her head and I took the arrow. It might give us a clue about the assassin's identity.

I crouched low over Kiki's back as she raced home. Keeping alert for another twang, I aimed my awareness on the surrounding wildlife. If the animals sensed an intruder, I'd pick up on their fear. A sound theory, except I'd been in contact with the deer when the arrow struck. I'd be impressed by the assassin's skills if I wasn't in so much pain.

It didn't take long for us to reach our small stable. The main doors had been left open. A warm yellow glow beckoned. Kiki trotted inside. The lanterns had been lit and Onyx, Valek's horse, nickered a greeting from his stall. Kiki stopped next to a pile of straw bales. Relieved to be safe, I slid onto them then lay down.